Walker Street

Walker Street

Irene Roberts

PIATKUS

Copyright © 1997 by Irene Roberts

First published in Great Britain in 1997 by
Judy Piatkus (Publishers) Ltd of
5 Windmill Street, London W1

**The moral right of the author
has been asserted**

*A catalogue record for this book is available
from the British Library*

ISBN 0-7499-0374-0

Set in 11/12pt Times by
RefineCatch Limited, Bungay, Suffolk
Printed and bound in Great Britain by
Bookcraft (Bath) Ltd

Chapter One

It was Friday, 6 of September 1940. Night lay uneasily over the city. A sullen moon shone dimly on soot-begrimed warehouses and glittered in quivering pinpoints on the river. A row of wretched houses held blank faces towards a giant storehouse wall. This was Walker Street – pathetic buildings filled to over-crowding with human flotsam and jetsam. Some families were poor and honest. Others, the quick-witted and the outrageous, had already found ways to make a bob or two out of the war.

The wind whisked debris along the kerb; it rustled in an angry, helpless way. The Air Minister had given warning that the Battle of Britain had left the enemy's heavy-bomber force mainly inactive. And Goering had said bluntly that the night raids of July and August had merely been armed reconnaissances. Now everyone knew that matters were coming to a head, and they were ready. In the meantime life went on in the same old way.

In the Duck and Drake two sailors were calling the barman all the names they could think of, and demanding more beer. For all it was closing time a group of Dockies were squaring up for a fight. A tarted-up woman was arguing with a weedy man she called Frank. He was looking as if he wished he had left her years ago.

'Time gentlemen, please!' the call wafted above the clouds of tobacco fumes. Unwillingly, people began to shuffle through the doors, small groups of them talking and laughing. An old lag snarled that all he wanted out of life was Hitler's balls for breakfast. The sailors jauntily whistled as two young floozies pushed by.

The girls looked at each other and giggled. They were heavily made-up and their mascara had smudged all round their eyes. They wore tight skirts, high-heeled court shoes and painted-on stockings which were works of art in themselves. Their Lana Turner hair-dos, one red with henna, the other jet black, were fastened with colourful grips decorated with silver stars.

1

Ogling the pointy breasts and slowly retreating feminine back-sides, the matelots swaggered after them, sure of having it away. In their haste they forgot to shut the door. Instantly, there were furious yells.

'Mind the bleeding black-out!'

'Stupid gits!'

'Got your brains in them tarts' drawers, 'ave yer?'

The pub doors were hastily closed.

'I told you to sod off!' the weedy man, Frank, yelled as the woman with over-bleached hair tried to grab his arm. 'You're a pissing menace and you get on me bloody nerves.'

'Frank,' she whined. 'I didn't mean ter mess you about. I only went and said . . .'

'A bleeding mouthful, that's what you said. Shove off!'

She was turning nasty. 'You try and put me down, Frank Neilson, and my Biff will have your guts for garters.'

'Your bloody brother can go and hang hisself, d'yer hear? I ain't scared of him nor any of his Black Market cut-throats. Now sod off!' And he lurched away, swearing and cussing.

In number 32, Walker Street Hannah York, who was not yet eighteen and who had joined the Women's Land Army at seventeen and a half, waited. Her heart was beating against her sides in a frightening way. It always did where her stepfather was concerned. She heard the outer door slam; the house shuddered under the onslaught. She sat where she was, in the easy chair by the hearth, while Frank negotiated the small passageway. She said nothing when he appeared, clinging to the doorpost, glaring at her in a hateful way.

'You're alone. That means you've sent Val packing again,' she said quietly. 'I know that you have tried to get shot of her for years, and that you don't even like her. That Biff is too scary to defy, but—'

'Why don't you shut your trap, Han – eh?' Frank was looking wicked, his lips turned down. 'You don't know what you're talking about.'

'I know that two wrongs don't make a right.'

'Sod off!'

'I mean it,' she retorted, exasperated. 'You should be careful there. Biff Marner's an evil man, and his friend Ram Rawlins carries a knife! You shouldn't upset Val because—'

'You can't upset that nympho.' His tone held contempt. 'She always comes back.'

'Frank, listen to me! Biff Marner has already warned you about cold-shouldering Val. I was here that night when he came sliding in here like the snake he is, spitting and snarling. Saying that he couldn't

2

understand why his sister wanted you. Daring you to say no. So you had better look out!'

'For Chrissake shut up, Han. You don't understand.' He began to smirk. 'She thinks I'm a sort of Errol Flynn – in more ways than one.'

'Now you're just being common and uncouth.'

'Why don't you grow up? Accept that the woman wants me. Gawd help me, I can't get rid of her.'

'Shall I make you a cup of coffee?' she asked, changing the subject. She managed to keep her voice calm, thanks to her memories of Miss Pitt, who was now abroad with soldiers doing Christian work. It always helped, thinking of her.

Frank's lips curved in a snarl. 'Coffee? Who the hell wants that muck?'

'It was just a thought, that's all.'

'Coffee?' Frank was working himself up into a frenzy. 'Madam Marm-Stink offers me mud to drink and I'm s'posed to be happy?' He swung round and entered the room. Two steps to the table – a moment to steady himself, and then he picked up the tin tray already set with crockery and hurled it to the ground. 'That's for your coffee. Go to hell!'

Hannah slowly stood up. Her face was white, but small though she was, she stood her ground. With studied care she ran her hand through her dark curls; her hazel-coloured eyes held gold sparks of courage, and of utter contempt.

'Not hell, Frank,' she said firmly, 'I'm off to bed. Good night.'

'Oh no, you don't! Sit down and shut up.'

'Good night, Frank.'

For all he was drunk he moved quickly. He reached her and his grip on her arm was vicious. He staggered and would have fallen, but Hannah instinctively held on to him. His eyes were bloodshot, the red glittering against the dark iris in a vindictive way.

She felt sickened, but was unafraid. Never once, in all her life, had Frank really hit Hannah. Rant and rave, cuss and blind, and threaten all sorts of terrible things, yes. But he had never actually harmed her. She must, she thought wearily, at least give him credit for that.

'You'll do as you're told,' he grated. 'Understand? You might be a bloody Land Girl now, but when you come 'ome to this 'ouse, it's my way or nothing. Understand?'

'Your way?' she flared. 'Your drunken way? Do you know why I came home – do you? To pack my belongings for once and for all. One day I'll be going to a new hostel and I'll make sure I've left nothing, nothing to let you know where I am. No papers nor letters, nothing!'

'You stupid mare . . .'

3

'No. Wise! Or at least old enough and ugly enough to put a stop to things. Your Val will never again be able to go to my new hostel and ask about my wages, pathetic though they are. Got a flea in her ear from Mrs Lawrence our supervisor, didn't she?'

'You're talking out of the back of your neck, you silly moo.'

'Really? Made a change for Val to get her comeuppance, didn't it?' Her voice grew bitter. 'People from outside this area don't know about her big brother, do they? So they're not scared about what he'll do if anyone really upsets her. That's how she's always got away with her treatment of me, isn't it? Not that you care. You've closed your eyes to everything from the word go.'

'Shut up!'

Hannah had started now and couldn't have stopped the flow if she'd tried.

'Val's always tried to get at me. Lashing out, kicking, pinching me black and blue. Then from the moment I was fourteen and able to stick up for myself, she's found another way. She's deliberately gone to wherever I've worked just to embarrass me. Yes, the shoe shop, the menswear, even the market, just to try to make trouble, or to get my money. But mostly to make me leave home! She's always hated me because you've made looking after me your excuse for not marrying her. Well, I promise you, I'll soon be gone for good and all.'

'You'll be back,' he sneered. 'Like Val, you'll always be back!'

'I'm not Val and I never could be,' she replied emphatically. 'And for what it's worth, you're heading for real trouble there. I've stuck by you as best I could simply because when Mum died you never put me in an orphanage.' She glared and lifted her chin high, adding bitterly, 'Though God knows, I might have been better off. But one of these bright fine days, no more Walker Street – all right? I've found a new way of life in the country, and I'll never miss this little lot, I can tell you.'

'You'll do as you're told,' he threatened. 'Understand?'

'Will you,' she snapped furiously, 'or will you not leave go of me?'

His grip tightened, and his bony fingers were bruising her arm. Her eyes became twin brilliants with angry tears. She forgot Miss Pitt's teaching, and her own carefully nurtured ladylike façade, and became the child of Walker Street that she was.

'That's it!' she shouted. 'You hateful, wicked old swine! You've always been a shit, at least since you lost my mum, your horse, and your job all those years ago. You took to drink which sends you mad, and you'll never change. I'm *glad* I'm going! You can stew in your own juice from now on.' She twisted her arm away. 'I swear, you'll never lay hands on me again. I hate you, you skinny, rotten, boozy old sod.'

4

He let her go then and staggered to a chair in the corner of the room. Hannah, out of long years of habit, took a fresh cup and saucer from the dresser and poured some thick black coffee.

There had been a time when she had felt sorry for him. But listening to his maudlin whining over and over again had made pity pall. He must have been nice once, she thought, else her mother never would have married him. Sadly, she had died soon afterwards. Frank, so old Ma Carpenter said, went in on himself from that day. But he clung to his job for dear life.

At that time he had been employed by Hitchman's Dairy, happily delivering milk with the aid of the firm's horse, Firelord. Frank had loved that animal, and had worked with him from the day he'd left school. Sadly, in spite of loving care, Firelord eventually became ill and old. Frank went into work one early morning to find that his friend had gone. To the knackers. Frank went mad. He beat up the foreman and threatened to kill old man Hitchman stone dead. He got the sack for his pains, and from that day his whole character had changed.

Now Hannah stood over Frank and in spite of his mouthing, made him drink. He seemed quieter though he was still watching her, his eyes mean. When she turned to leave, he was on his feet at once, teetering, and threatening that she had better stay, better do as she was told if she knew what was good for her. That he might be a rotten skinny sod, but he knew enough to keep her in hand. She might act like a snot, but she'd always need a roof over her head.

Thoroughly incensed, he warmed to his theme.

'And as for Val and her bleeding brother, I've got them by the short and curlies, make no mistake. I've got evidence, oh yes! I could go to the cops tomorrow and spin a yarn that would stuff up Biff Marner and all his muckers for good. And I bloody well will too, if any of yer even try any funny business.'

There was a shocked exclamation from the passage behind them.

'Oo Frank, you don't mean that!' Val Marner whined. 'You couldn't, you wouldn't, not to me or Biff. Gawd, Franky . . .' her eyes were bulging with horror. 'You'd never grass on my Biffy, would you? I never heard you say that before and I didn't now, did I?'

''Ave yer got cloth bloody ears?' he snarled, beyond caring. 'An' anyway, what are you doing here? I told yer to shove off. You wear a bloke out and you make me sick.'

'You're only mouthing on just because I said I'd take on anyone,' she screeched. Her wide-open scarlet mouth looked like a clown's. 'I'd even do it with Ram Rawlins if it'd get me a gold ring.' Val's bleached hair was falling like rats' tails over her face. She stepped nearer, eyes

5

hot. 'You can't make this snotty cow-face your excuse no longer. She's been keeping herself since she was fourteen. Now she ain't even living at 'ome!'

He looked ready for apoplexy. 'She ain't no cow-face,' he shouted. 'And she's got guts, I'll say that for 'er. I thought I told you to shut your trap and piss off?'

'All I said was that it's about time we got married.' She was sobbing now. 'I was just trying to egg you on. I wanted you to get jealous about Ram.'

'You've already given him his oats, knowing you.' Frank was well in his stride now. 'You've had as many blokes as I've had hot dinners. Bugger off!'

She stepped nearer, daring him. 'Make me.'

Frank raised his fist. Val screamed, long varnished talons out, ready to kill, feet raised to kick. Struggling, they both fell to the floor. Knowing how it would all end, Hannah stepped over their interlocked figures, shut her ears to their mutually filthy insults, and made her way out of the house.

The night was quiet: It was All Clear. Most people were content to carry on at such times as best they could, she mused. War was war. You had to get on with things, no matter what. Nothing was sure, not even the price of sausages. Hannah smiled wryly at such an inconsequential thought. It was amazing how relatively unimportant matters like prices and rationing got right up women's noses even in dangerous times. But there was always the Londoner's humour to help bear the brunt.

'Sausages up to sevenpence a pound!' Only that morning the cry had gone round. 'What a bloody liberty! They think we're millionaires!'

'My ol' Bert would like a million hairs. He's going bald,' one woman quipped. 'And he reckons I'm a sight too careful at the best of times. Cheek! A penny ain't much, but it all adds up, don't it?'

'Too bloody true!' old Ma Carpenter agreed. 'And what about having to make the sugar ration do for cooking as well as for cups of tea?'

There was a further incensed outcry at this, and then the return of general remarks.

'I'd like to stuff old Hitler's jackboots right up his arse.'

'Wiv a pound of the Co-op's best pork an' beef!'

A chorus of laughter greeted this, and the mood was good-humoured by the time they arrived at the counter and found that the butcher allowed them just two sausages per book.

Hannah grinned at the memory, but the moment passed and she was back in the present, continuing to move slowly along Walker

Street. Conscious that any minute now the air-raid warning might go, her mouth went dry at the thought, and her limbs began to tremble.

Until the recent incident at the farm, the war for her had been little more than the shadowy image of activity in the skies above the Kentish fields – the vibrating hum of engines and the rattle of machine-guns, sometimes high and faint, but sometimes loud and clear. Bombs fell, but none near enough to her to be bothersome.

On the whole, Land Girls took their hands from the plough for long enough to put on their steel helmets, then carried on, intent on continuing with their war effort. Tractor drivers worked in pairs, facing opposite ways across the field, as their engines drowned the noise of planes. So it was reasoned, if they were to be machine-gunned, they wanted fair warning. No one could ask for more.

Out of the blue, Hannah's workplace took the full brunt of an attack. The farmhouse was destroyed, the farmer's wife killed. The farmer himself went to pieces. He had adored his wife and they had been married for many years. Hannah, who had been hoeing at the time, was both shocked and heartbroken. The rosy-cheeked old lady had been like a gran to her. Officials agreed that Hannah should be sent home on leave and then on to a hostel in Colchester.

Out of habit she had left her new address with Frank, before slipping into the hubbub of a fully inhabited hostel. The girls, a good-hearted bunch mostly from Plaistow, worked hard, and being stationed in a barrack town, when off-duty had the time of their lives.

Back in Sevenoaks and all the surrounding area, the bombardment continued. The enemy bombers hammered at aerodromes. Cows were slaughtered in the nearby meadows, and the craters multiplied. People in Tunbridge Wells habitually left their shelters to watch the combats taking place overhead, where Spitfires buzzed round like so many gnats. Jettisoned bombs, or deliberate attacks, wrecked villages and battered towns. All of this Hannah knew only too well. But the death of the farmer's wife, and the brutal destruction of the old farmer's happiness, had hit home.

Hannah had come face to face with the fact that life could be gutted as instantly as a candle flame. Also she realised that the world was huge and round, and amounted to a damned sight more than Walker Street. Despite her love of the country, Hannah remained a Londoner at heart – and proud of it. London was a wonderful city with its history, and buildings, and home of the King. It was only horrible Walker Street that got her down.

After a week or so at Colchester she decided that she must and would disappear from the landscape of her stepfather's life. She had played her cards deliberately and well. She had been sent away from

7

Lexton Hostel in Colchester as a punishment. That being the case, neither Frank nor Val, nor anyone else would find her there ever again. Her new address she kept safely to herself. She would be moving on the following Monday.

Pondering all this, Hannah passed by Walker Alley, a gloomy narrow space always stinking of urine. She could hear the scuffling and giggling of a couple in the shadows. A sailor and his partner were well away, the girl pressed against the wall, the man thrashing into her as though his life depended on it. But that was the general rule. Live for today, for tomorrow you die . . .

Frank and Val would be enjoying fireworks by now, Hannah thought and felt heartsick. With luck it would all be over and done with by the time she got back.

Finally, because a group of drunken louts approached her and scared her half to death, Hannah went back to number 32.

She stood in the kitchen, shocked. Everything was still, apart from the hissing of the gas-light. Frank and Val had not gone to bed. The kitchen looked as though a bomb-blast had sped through it and thrown everything about. The table was upended and a chair had been broken. Pieces of smashed crockery seemed to be everywhere. But Hannah's horrified gaze was on Val. The woman was crouching before Frank like a beaten cur. Then she began making harsh sobbing noises deep in her throat. Clearly Frank had smacked her face. His finger-marks showed. He had, at last, gone too far. There was going to be hell to pay.

Hannah turned to run, but Frank, braces hanging loose, hands and chin scratched to ribbons, was too quick for her. In spite of her struggling, she was forced, arguing and breathless, up the stairs and into her small back bedroom. She heard the outer bolt pushed into place. Frank had never raised a hand to her. However, he regularly locked her in the bedroom from the time she had been old enough to walk. She never knew why.

She would have to wait for him to open the door, she thought numbly.

This would not be until the next day, when he had sobered up. But, she comforted herself, it would be for the last time.

Shortly afterwards she heard the front door slam. Val would be off to find her bully brother, nicknamed Biff Bash'em from schooldays. There was no doubt that Biff and his cronies would come looking for Frank. It was also quite on the cards that they would come looking for her too. They would knock out her teeth, and break her nose in a calculated tit-for-tat because that was their way. They would probably kill her stepfather. No one messed with the Marners. No one at all!

8

Hannah began to shake. She knelt down by her battered old suit-case, which was packed with all of her personal things. Her skirts, one black, one brown. Her shirt-blouses, one white, one cream, the third pale blue. There were her two pairs of shoes, one black and one brown, and three sets of underclothes. The rest of her scant wardrobe consisted mainly of WLA uniform, including khaki-coloured passion kil-ler knickers and long thick brown service socks. There was also her birth certificate, ration book, and her gas-mask, plus her medical card, which showed up-to-date payments to the HSA, her identification card, and an insurance policy. Everything . . . Once she walked out of 32 Walker Street with her suitcase there would be no trace of her left at all. She could and would disappear for ever. She couldn't wait!

Her heart jumped into her throat as the air-raid warning growled into life and rose up to scream high before looping down, up again, and down in long, slow sweeping sounds. She could hear people mak-ing for the shelters. In the distance guns barked, there were crumps and thumps of distantly landing bombs. Ack-ack guns began to yak, hard and sharp and fast. She thought she heard the front door bang shut again, but couldn't be sure.

'Please God,' Hannah prayed. 'Please God!'

All night Hannah crouched there in the small, damp room. The cheap alarm clock on the mantelpiece ticked the minutes away, and finally, at three-thirty a.m. the All Clear shrieked out its strident one-note theme.

Grey daylight began to filter through the misty window that had been criss-crossed with sticky tape. Now Hannah was praying that Frank would come up, as he usually did first thing, to unbolt her door. It did not happen.

The day dragged on and Hannah remained a prisoner in her room. When the clock stopped, the silence of the house was unbearable. She rewound it furiously, accepting that Frank had gone out, and had probably forgotten her. Finally, in desperation, she began pounding on the wall, hoping that old man Grimes next door might hear, that his dog Meg would bark. But what if he did hear her and guess that she was locked in again? He wouldn't do anything, she thought furiously, Neither would the Oakses on the other side.

People in Walker Street were used to domestic violence; they never interfered. Especially so if Val or anyone to do with the Marners were involved. That would be more than their life was worth. What's more, it was common knowledge that Frank was hand in glove with Biff, so from where they stood, the three wise monkey syndrome was the order of the day.

Saturday dragged on and slowly matured into late afternoon. There

9

had been planes about, and some gun noise, but nothing too terrifying. Hannah, containing herself as best she could, waited. At 6 p.m. old Ma Carpenter, Frank's aunt, would be along having shut up the pawn shop in Sedgewick Street. Ma Carpenter had helped Hannah out often before. Fierce old Ma who could – and had when he was a boy – often cuffed Frank soundly round the ears. Ma was the only woman on God's earth that had Frank running scared . . .

Chapter Two

The Civil Defence Officer at his tower post looked at his watch. It was ten past five on a lovely summery evening, the sky a clear sheet of blue. But suddenly, he saw a great range of black specks breaking out to the north – huge waves of hostile planes, in numbers never before seen over the city. They were moving upriver from the east. As they progressed, there came the heavy thumps of distant bomb explosions, and then column after column of black smoke, growing up like trees, merging into a curtain, spreading into a great rolling cloud. This then was the business.

Within seconds, messages flew back and forth from Headquarters to all branches concerned. The Fire Fighters were on the ready. Ambulance, ARP, anyone and everyone in the Civil Defence, all had a job to do.

The Luftwaffe came in waves, bombers and fighters. The world seemed to have gone mad. Woolwich Arsenal was hit and the immense gasworks at Beckton, the docks at Millwall, as well as those at Limehouse, Rotherhithe, and also those by Tower Bridge. The Surrey Docks copped it, as did the West Ham Power Station.

German planes swept on across the City to Westminster and also bombed a crescent in Kensington. This was new. Daylight bombing!

German pilots could see what they were doing and they did it savagely and well. They searched for and found legitimate marks. Sadly, some bombs went wide and dockland houses and tenements suffered.

Hannah screamed and ducked as the window of her room shattered, held only by the sticky tape. She watched, hypnotised, as a large crack ran across her ceiling. Great lumps of plaster fell, one piece hitting her on her head. She saw a galaxy of shooting stars, then a wave of blackness and knew no more.

Outside, the docks blazed along all their miles, on both banks of the Thames. Wondering watchers looking downriver from the central bridges saw the sun's own light grow pale beside the crimson glare that hung and flickered above the eastern boroughs. By six o'clock the day raiders had gone.

Dazed, not sure of anything any more, seeming to have no strength in her legs, Hannah lay still on the brown lino that covered the floor. Two hours went by, then the air-raid warning revved up and flared into life again. Wailing Winnie, or Moaning Minnie it was called. Now it cried out the news that it was the night bombers' turn.

In spite of the barrage balloons and aerial dog-fights, enemy planes set out to stoke up already giant riverside fires with more high explosive, and thousands upon thousands of incendiary bombs.

Around 4 am the Luftwaffe made sure that Walker Street took its share. The Duck and Drake was flattened. Number 32 had its front caved in.

Hannah never heard it coming. There was just the sudden sensation that the world jumped, taking her stomach with it. It was a terrible feeling as her breath thumped out of her body. She felt caught in timelessness, and unreality; then came the urgent need to fight and survive.

Coughing and gasping because the air was thick with plaster dust, too dazed and shocked to think straight except to search for and grab her case, Hannah tentatively stepped to the door that had been blown off its hinges. Biting her lip, conscious of the punishing pain in her temples, she scrambled down the pile of rubble that had once been the stairs.

Outside, there were rescuers already digging frantically in smouldering ruins. A baby cried thinly in the night. A wild-eyed screaming woman ran by, the same one who had so recently been carrying on about the price of sausages.

'It's Bert.' She was wringing her hands, eyes huge in the sooty surround of her face. 'My Bert. Please, get 'im out. You've gotta get 'im out, but. . . he's caught by his legs and bleeding unmerciful!'

'All right, missus.' Two air-raid wardens turned with her as one and went pounding back, yelling as they ran, 'We'll get him, mate. Calm down.'

Ambulance sirens and fire-engine bells added to the frenzy all around. Everything seemed to be on fire. An ARP warden rushed up, to where Hannah stood unsteadily on a fallen mound of bricks and mortar.

'Need any help, miss? Let me take—'

She shook her head, tears of shock making white rivers against the grime of her face. 'I'm all right. Fine, thanks,' she was babbling. Was that high, stupid voice really coming from her? 'I think I heard a moaning sound next door,' her quavery voice continued, 'but I can't see anything because he seems to be buried out of sight. I feel a bit

12

sick, but. . . Yes, I've got everything. You're very kind. . . I must get away. I've got to get back to base . . .'

Her hand tightened over her suitcase. She was holding on to it as if her life depended on it. Her gas-mask was slung over her shoulders, yet she had no recollection of putting it on. Her uniform was grey with plaster dust, her face black, but she was still in one piece and wanting to run. Run for ever – away from the hell of what was left of Walker Street.

She wanted to fly like the wind, but her legs felt like jelly. She was willing herself to press on, to keep going, but deep inside she was crying for old man Grimes next door. She had heard him, but couldn't see. It looked as though the whole house had fallen on top of him, and what of Meg, his faithful old dog? She was probably, as ever, close to his side.

'Oi!' the ARP man yelled as other rescue crews ran up to join him, 'You won't be going nowhere tonight, miss. They've hit three of the main-line terminals. You might as well allow me my way. Like sending you to hospital for a check-up.'

'Not necessary,' she mouthed, and shook her head.

'Well, at least make for the Tube,' he shouted above the clanging of a fire-engine bell. 'You'll be safe down there.'

'Thanks!' she called and stumbled along. It was light as day. An exploded gas main had set flames licking along the top of the ware-house wall. The fire went higher, sparks glinting in the smoke like sequins on a black veil.

She heard the next bomb whistling down. It was close, too close. She ducked in the heap of rubble flanking Walker Alley. There was a God-awful crash as the explosion happened several streets away. Even so, the blast flattened her, and more masonry fell. A chimney pot clattered down, shedding dull red shards in the road to mingle with shrapnel fallen from guns. Somewhere, someone was screaming high and wild.

Suddenly there was a break in the death-dealing from directly above. Feeling paralysed from the waist down, Hannah stayed where she was. She was panting and badly needing to cry. She thought she could still hear Mr Grimes moaning, like the soundtrack from a Bela Lugosi film. Then the high-pitched screaming stopped abruptly, the swift cessation worse than any sound. Hannah wanted to clench her hands over her ears. She could not. She was clinging to her lifeline, the battered old suitcase that had given faithful service throughout the years. She was gripping the handle so hard, her fingernails were biting into her skin. The suitcase itself mattered as much as the contents, It had been used in happier times, like when Frank had taken her to Kent, picking hops, and Val had been nowhere in sight.

13

What on God's earth had made her think of hop-picking? Strangely her desire for tears had gone; instead she wanted to throw back her head and laugh! Laugh and cry and scream and run – back to the green fields and nature's good open air.

She thought she heard a movement to her right, and glanced into the rubble-filled end of Walker Alley. The flames running along the top of the warehouse wall flared even higher, lighting up the scene.

Fresh horror filled Hannah. There were three men in the alley, looking like grotesque shadows, and they were dragging something along. Hannah's throat went dry. Dear God in heaven – it was Frank! She would recognise that old jacket anywhere.

There was nothing she could do except watch as Biff Marner, Ram Rawlins, and a man called Fatty Blythe dumped the huddled body of Frank on to a pile of broken glass. Then they began to bury him, throwing bricks and wood and chunks of plaster on top of him. They worked hurriedly, ignoring the fact that guns and bombs were starting up again.

'No!' Hannah croaked, suddenly spurred into action. 'No – no – no!' She began stumbling towards them, frantic, half out of her mind. Not even Frank deserved this. As she neared them she saw her stepfather's uncovered face. He was dead. In that one horror-stricken glance she knew that Biff had had his revenge, and that Frank had been beaten to death!

They were looking over their shoulders at her now, startled, Biff and Fatty – and the huge, terrible Ram who was bald, and whose face looked like the corpse of Pharoah Rameses. Ram, the thickhead who did all of Biff's dirty work, and always had done ever since they were at school together.

Ram was mouthing threats and lumbering towards her, death in his eyes. She had seen too much.

A mobile ack-ack gun chasing down the street, saved her. As the three men ducked out of sight, Hannah fled. She reached a crowded shelter at last, and heaving and panting, all but fell into the arms of a sympathetic lady running an all-night canteen.

'Cuppa tea, luv?' the woman asked brightly. 'Looks like you've been through it.'

'Yes, please – and, yes, it's been pretty bad,' Hannah gasped and slid gratefully down, her back against the wall. She tried to laugh, a pathetic sound, adding, 'In fact, it's been a bit of a swine all round.'

'Never mind, dearie.' A mug of tea, hot and sweet, was handed to her. 'Drink up and cheer up. You're a long time dead.'

Like Frank, she thought wildly, as in all probability was the man next door. When you died they said you went to either heaven or hell.

14

No, it wasn't true! You didn't have to die to go to hell – all you had to do was be born and live here in Walker Street.

'Hang on, luv,' the canteen lady said, concerned. 'You've gorn as white as a sheet. Just you hang on like a good 'un. All right?'

'Thank – thank you,' Hannah whispered. 'Sorry.'

Hannah drank the scalding brew and felt as though the world had gone askew. Frank was dead. Biff Marner had finished him off for what he had done to Val. And the most petrifying truth was they could get away with it all. Officially Frank could have been a casualty of the war and no questions asked – but she had seen! She could bear witness. So wouldn't they now need to shut her up for good?

A little while later a group of people began to sing. Their voices rang out accompanied by an old man playing a mouth organ. A group of youngsters began flicking cigarette cards, and babies slept. More voices joined in. Smiles began to crack faces. Chins lifted and bodies rocked in time.

'*Roll out the barrel. We'll have a barrel of fun. Roll out the barrel, we've got the blues on the run . . .*'

By daylight Hannah's confidence had grown. She could get away with it once she had left the locality. Fate had played her a decent hand, since she had already planned an escape – from Frank. Poor old Frank. He was a brute, an animal, but surely he hadn't deserved to finish up like that! 'Really?' a little voice in her head asked the same old question. 'Maybe he treated my own mum like he did Val? She couldn't have stood a chance. She was little and nice, Ma Carpenter said, so she probably forgave him even if he did. But I'll never know. I'll never know anything now.'

Tears spurted as she found herself wishing that she had had a family. That she still had a mum to hang on to, to talk to, to love!

She took in a deep breath and pulled herself together. It was important to forget what she had seen and get on with her new life. She must act as though she was a person to whom nothing had happened. Nothing awful, that was. After all, having a house fall down round your ears happened during a war. It was nothing really. Not against having witnessed what Biff Marner did.

Whatever follows this little lot, she thought wildly, I must be the sort of person Miss Pitt told me to be. Brave and splendid and always wearing a smile. I must hold on to the thought that at the end of things it all evens out, just as she promised. That life usually boils down to having had more laughter than tears . . .

She wanted to laugh – had to! She forced her lips to curve upwards, angrily brushing her cheeks free of treacherous tears. The people around her recognised shock and understood. Everyone was helpful.

15

She was given water, a cloth, and a brush. She worked like the devil to become clean and tidy, and spruce up her uniform.

The All Clear sounded before dawn, but Hannah stayed where she was, falling asleep like the rest. When she awoke, having made enquiries, and told folk where she was heading, Hannah was introduced to an ambulance man who was going off-duty.

Although drawn and tired, looking all but dead on his feet, he had time for her. He gave her a lift to a bus depot before returning to his own base. The bus in its turn took her and a crowd of others to a station on a secondary line.

The station walls were braced with sandbags. There were posters up about careless talk costing lives, digging for victory, and drawings of good old Potato Pete up to his tricks – all meant to kid hungry children to fill up on spuds.

There were masses of people milling about on the platform. It was chilly, but friendly, nearly everyone having a story to tell. The overall mood was that the war effort would progress, bombs or no bombs. It would take more than the Jerries to get Londoners down.

Hannah looked about her, still feeling very trembly. The other people were mainly workers, by the looks of things, the women wearing turbans fashioned from headscarves to cover their hair, and the men mostly wearing cloth caps. All seemed utterly determined to get to their jobs somehow, and so help the war effort. Soldiers and airmen abounded. There were also matelots here and there, ready to jeer and make war with their old enemies the Royal Marines. Even they would club together to outwit the generally detested Military Police.

Amidst all these people, Hannah felt incredibly afraid and alone. Then her mouth went dry. She strained her eyes. Was that, could that be, Ram's bald head she saw over there? Was it in fact Ram hovering near the ticket office, tall and distinctive and evil? Had he actually been able to follow her?

Suddenly, like a companionable beacon, Hannah saw a lone Land Army girl. She was standing there waiting, serene and calm, unmindful of the masses. She was of medium height, her hair the colour of copperbeech-leaves. She looked crisp and businesslike, and she had a nice face.

Putting on the act of a lifetime, Hannah smiled widely as she hurriedly approached the girl.

'Stone me, one of our mob at last!' she laughed in a light-hearted way. 'Thank goodness! I was feeling outnumbered until I spotted you. Have you had to go all round the houses to get here, like me? Did you get caught in the raid? Where are you making for? My hostel's new to me and . . .'

Chapter Three

The carriage was thick with tobacco smoke, the upholstery was worn, but it was homely and crowded and it felt safe.

'There's supposed to be another one of us,' Hannah said brightly, forcing herself to keep up her air of not having a care in the world. It was getting easier with every second that passed. Relief had flooded through her from the minute the train moved out of the station. She heard herself adding, 'I bet she's said sod it and done a bunk back home.'

'She's probably on this train somewhere,' Virginia (Ginnie) Betts replied. She looked round at the various servicemen crowding the carriage. 'And like us, she's packed in like a sardine. It's something of a miracle that you and me met up.'

'No, it isn't. It's just that I'm a pushy bitch,' Hannah admitted, hazel eyes now sparkling, short brown curls bobbing against the brim of her Land Army hat. 'And brave with it. I don't think there's many who would tangle with you, not with that red hair of yours and them blue eyes. Are you engaged or anything?'

'Nosy devil, aren't you?' Ginnie asked, and thought the small, spritely young girl next to her was very likable, and rather vulnerable for all her bright-eyed, cock-bantam air. 'But to answer your question – no, I am not.'

'Go on!' Hannah teased desperately, determined to play her part until the bitter end. 'I felt sure there'd be a Sergeant in the background somewhere.' She paused, then went on: 'I don't half think it's strange. These days, girls ain't got chaps with names! They say, "I'm going out with a petty officer"! Or "My chap's a Corporal." Else it's pilot, marine, matelot, things like that. Yet you never hear them say "My fishermonger", do you?'

Two soldiers sitting opposite guffawed. And the sailor next to Ginnie nudged her in the ribs and winked. She ignored him and, lowering her voice so as not to be overheard, admitted, 'Well, there was a fellow named Aiden in my life – a soldier in the Essex Regiment. He has always acted as if he likes me a lot,' she gave the matelot a quick glance and continued, 'but I have no time for men. At least, not right now. Have you someone special?'

'I don't think there's anyone who would want me,' Hannah replied airily, having also lowered her voice. 'Not for keeps anyway. I took a tumble once. Fell hook, line and sinker I did. I believed all his old toffee and thought he was the next thing to God. It turned out that he only wanted a few dirty weekends.' She grinned ruefully. 'I told him nothing doing, and got the sack for my pains.'

Ginnie gave her companion a searching look, but kept her intuition to herself. It was telling her that Hannah York, who she learned was not yet eighteen, was scared stiff about something. Really afraid, but would die before admitting the fact. It had screamed it, the way she had burst up to join her on the station platform. Almost as though she had been running away from something or someone. . . She'd grabbed hold of her arm and almost fallen in her anxiety.

Hannah went on, 'I wonder what our number three's like?'

'We'll find out soon enough. Don't worry.'

'I'm not,' Hannah replied, confidence rapidly returning now they had left Walker Street far behind. 'Hawksley – sounds grim though, eh? Bet it's like a prison. Still, it can't be worse than being in London right now. The WLA's a bit of an escape really.' She leaned towards Ginnie in a conspiratorial way. 'I thought of being a Lumber Jill at first, but the idea of sawing down lovely trees seemed wicked some-how, specially in this day and age. I decided I'd like fieldwork best, and so here I am, a right old Londoner being a Land Army girl.'

Hannah looked at the girl next to her. Having someone wearing the same uniform as you, being in the same gang as it were, was like being part of a family. Of belonging! It was comforting. And Ginnie seemed – dependable. Yes, that was it. Obviously the quietly independent type. She was striking-looking, and fools, spivs and drones wouldn't last two minutes with her. More to the point, Hannah thought, Ginnie was the sort you were glad to have on your side.

Unbidden, the nightmare vision of the three men and Frank's corpse flew into her mind. Beads of sweat glistened on her forehead. Her mind began to feel as if it was expanding. She wanted to scream and yell and run hell for leather. As she had, back there at Walker Alley. Now she was here. And for once in a million years, luck had been on her side. Ginnie was bound for the same place. They had exchanged names and were already friends. And she, Hannah York, was on a train taking her away from that hell-hole to a village named

18

Lindell and a hostel called Hawksley, where, please God, she would be safe.

Ginnie was looking at her in a straight, no-nonsense sort of way. Hannah forced herself to laugh and ask, 'Have you got a big family? My mother died years ago. I can only barely remember her. I know she was little, and nice.'

'And your father?'

'Don't know nothing about him,' Hannah chuckled, not seeming to mind at all. 'I did hear that he worked on a Thames barge, till he drowned. When I was little, I made up yarns about him. About him being a proper sailor, I mean. I imagined him as a captain, all bluff and hearty, being pally with his crew, and them all calling him "Skipper", all matey like. But my dad could have been a right old sod for all I know. That's why I've come to think I'm best off without him, and without Frank, who was my stepfather, or anyone.'

'Sometimes we are better off rowing our own boats,' Ginnie agreed.

'I've managed very well.' Hannah's tone held a hint of defiance. 'Yes, even from the time I got the boot from the menswear shop.' Her eyes began to twinkle again. 'Here, talk about laugh! They told me to take this old man's inside-leg measurements. You ought to have seen his face when I walked up to him. Bold as brass I was, waving the tape-measure! Then Mr Reynolds took over.' Her voice faltered momentarily, then pulling herself together she went on, 'That was the manager, Mr Reynolds, the rotten swine. He gave me the bullet for telling him to sod off when he tried it on. I worked in the market after that. The moment I was old enough, I joined this mob.'

'So this is your first place?'

'No. I went to Kent, but the farm was bombed to hell and back. Then they sent me to Colchester, but that didn't last five minutes. I lipped Miss Lawrence, refused point blank to toe the line, so was transferred, and here I am. Why did you join?'

'I'm twenty-two, and I didn't want to go into a munitions factory, or any of the women's forces. My brother Luke's in the Navy and is just about spitting pips because I never chose the WRNS. No, I decided on this because I like the look and smell of all the fresh fruit and vegetables my father sells.'

Hannah's cherubic face lit up. 'I lived fairly near a market. Our street was one of the scruffiest – real slummy. Still, there's not much left of it now.' She grinned unashamed. 'So you can tell I'm not posh or anything. Has your dad got a veggy stall?'

'No.' Ginnie's tone was almost apologetic. 'A shop in Ilford, Essex. I have marvellous parents, and Luke whom I not only adore, but like very much. And there are lots of quite decent relatives near to hand.'

She smiled. 'I don't know how I'd handle things if I were alone like you. Yet you seem such a cheerful soul.'

'That's because of this nice old girl, Miss Pitt. She was my Sunday School teacher.' Hannah winked. 'I went when I was a kid and heard they were going to have a day out – a picnic at Southend! Joined like a shot, I did. I made a point of turning up for lots of things when the word got round about treats in store. You know, like bun-fights in church halls, or outings. Always left afterwards, of course. But it was different when I met Miss Pitt. She was nice and she seemed to take to me. She had the same taste as well. She just lapped up rock-eel and chips.'

'You mean that as well as eating fish and chips,' Ginnie raised her brows, 'Sunday school actually made you *happy*?'

'That bit was a bore,' Hannah admitted. 'Went on and on it did, all about turning the other cheek and that. Blow me! If you turned the other cheek down Walker Street they'd have your guts for garters. No, it was Miss Pitt who told me – on the day she found me blubbing because I'd had a fair old bashing from Val, Fred's woman – that I had to cheer up. She told me that in the end everything evened out.'

'She believed that? Even in this day and age?'

'That most of all. Oh, there was a lot of other guff. About faith and things that carried her through when she lost her fiancé in the Great War. But I liked what she said about trying to laugh back at Fate. I've tried to do that ever since . . . I said tried! Though to be honest, I don't really find this lark all that funny now I'm actually on the train – I mean Hawksley.'

'You're an old hand at surviving, at least that's what you say,' Ginnie commented. 'So what's scary about a name?'

'It's not the name,' Hannah replied, trying to push the picture of Biff, Fatty Blythe and Ram Rawlins out of her mind. 'It's just that there'll only be the three of us there, so Miss Lawrence said. It won't be like the crowded hostel at Colchester. Lots of larks there, seeing as how the city's crammed with barracks.'

'Exciting stuff, eh?'

'Oh yes!' Hannah, determined to hide her fear, rushed on. 'One morning Miss Lawrence, the old girl what run the hostel, went and found soldiers had blown up lots of French letters. You know, blew them up like you do balloons. They tied them on to her prized golden privet hedge. You should have seen her face! It was a scream. We was all on the carpet a minute later. I mean, fancy blaming us! It was all them Tommies. But she carried on and on about us having given the hostel a bad name. Us! I had to back-answer, had to. Anyway I was already in her black books, so I thought I might as well be hanged for a sheep as a lamb!'

'Then you really wanted to leave?'

'No! Yes! But in a way I'm sorry. There was always something going on. This place isn't going to be like that. I was told so very nastily by Miss Lawrence. It's going to be just the three of us out in the wilds.' She laughed breathlessly, trying to hide her fresh upsurge of panic. 'I mean to say, they reckon there's safety in numbers, don't they? And we don't know what we're going to come up against. Still, I'll always try to remember what Miss Pitt said.'

'Your Miss Pitt sounds a bit like my father,' Ginnie confided. 'He has the same ideas. Not about laughing so much, but he has always told me to put on a brave face. To keep a stiff upper lip, all that sort of thing.'

'Then with you and me standing shoulder to shoulder, grinning like mad,' Hannah replied, 'the enemy don't stand a chance.'

They looked at each other and beamed. After only a short space of time they were feeling like old friends.

Shortly after that the air-raid warning wailed high and mournful, then dipped, only to rise again, sweeping up and down in great arcs of sound.

'Gawd!' Hannah said. 'Talk about sitting ducks. I hear as how the Krauts just love following trains.'

The wheels beneath them continued to clickety-clack over the railway track. The sailor next to Ginnie folded his arms and went to sleep. The rest of the men in the compartment ruefully grinned at each other, shrugged and waited. The train came to a halt some five minutes later. Although there were distant thumps and the barking of ack-acks echoing over open spaces, nothing happened near to hand.

The train stood there, puffing and panting and spilling steam. An Air Force officer left the carriage and jumped down on to the track. He made his way up to the engine driver. Other servicemen did likewise. Much later the news filtered through. Something rotten bad had happened on the lines ahead. Everything was blocked. Patience must be the name of the game. People could leave and try to reach their destinations by some other means if they wanted to, but it was not to be recommended. Not at this stage anyway. Much better to hang on and see what happened. They would get there in the end.

'I'm in no hurry,' Hannah said. 'Are you?'

'Not really,' Ginnie replied. 'Let's talk and really get to know each other. After all, it looks like we'll be living in each other's pockets until the end of the war . . .'

21

Chapter Four

It was unnaturally dark when the train finally slid into the station that Raven Gray needed. Raven, so named because her hair had reminded her mother of birds' wings, stood on the platform, her slim figure encased in the brown and green uniform of the Women's Land Army. She wore her wide-brimmed, cowboy-style hat tilted at the back of her head. She was dark-haired, oval-faced and stood tall. She seemed strangely remote.

She looked around her. The station was a shrouded place, inky, misty and damp. Not for the first time she wondered if she had done the right thing. She could have stayed at the flat for a while, not perhaps jumped out of the frying pan. But she could stand her memories of the recent past no longer.

She and Francis had decided long ago on what would be the best thing for her to do, once she was alone. Nursing was out, Raven said, even though it was a very worthwhile thing to do. She admitted that she could never go through the heartache of it all again, and Francis had understood.

'Then why not work in the fields, darling?' he had asked her in his grave, gentle way. 'Spend your days with growing things and in God's good open air.'

Now here she was, come to this remote place in Essex and already she was alone. The few passengers who had alighted had all hurried away on business of their own. The porter seemed a rather unfriendly man.

'No transportation of any kind, miss,' he told her sourly. 'Sorry – you'll have to walk. Where are you off to – same place as the others?'

'Hawksley in the village of Lindell. The others?'

'They don't know it yet,' he shrugged, 'since I haven't got round to telling them, but they're stranded just like you.'

Hannah rushed out of the waiting room, calling over her shoulder,

'Here she is, Ginnie!' Then, laughing up at Raven, 'Blow me, you're even taller than her! I was beginning to think you'd buzzed off.' She turned back to the empty-faced porter. 'Where do we go from here, skipper?'

'When you leave this station,' he said stiffly, 'you'll have to use your own two feet, miss. Face to the right and go straight ahead. Follow your nose till you come to a turning leading to your left. Go that way and you'll be smack on to the village. Have you got a torch?'

'No, we haven't,' Ginnie said as she joined them. 'We never expected it to be dark.'

Raven smiled, crestfallen. 'I'm sorry. I just didn't think.'

'Well, miss,' he replied, 'no one expected that hold-up – least of all the poor devils living near the line. Killed one of 'em outright, I hear. And no one expected it to get as black as pitch, this time of night neither.'

'The sky looks menacing,' Raven agreed. 'Not welcoming at all.'

'We're in for foul weather all right. It's going to storm.'

'Shit!' Hannah swore. 'Oh bloody hell! I hate thunder and lightning.'

'Hang on a tick,' the porter said, continuing to address Raven and suddenly becoming human. He disappeared into the office and came back with a torch. 'It's not all that marvellous, but it'll help. All right?'

'Thank you,' Raven replied. 'I'll return it as soon as I can.'

'Never mind that. Now you'd best get started. It's going to bucket down and you'll all get drenched if you don't hurry up.'

Hannah gulped. Suddenly, very desperately, she did not want to leave the station, small and gloomy though it was. It held life and it held shelter. It also held a sense of security in a macabre kind of way. The tall, lovely Raven seemed to feel the same. She stood there, looking unapproachable.

Hannah and Ginnie stared at their number three, eyes questioning as they waited. Then Hannah shrugged and determinedly picked up her suitcase. Ginnie grabbed her luggage, hesitated, then turned round alongside Hannah and they were already on the way, torch or no torch.

Feeling frozen, Raven watched them. They had clearly struck up a friendship and wanted no truck with her. Her grief rose again, threatening to make her cry. She picked up her holdall, took in a deep breath and left the station. She found herself walking along a seemingly endless lane. It was like a very gloomy black tunnel, shrouded by overhanging trees.

'Excuse me,' she said loudly enough for the others to hear. 'Since you're going first, please take the torch.'

Hannah hesitated. Ginnie turned at once and walked back to join her. Hannah followed close on her heels.

'Not a good start, eh?' Ginnie said easily. 'I understood that we were to be met. I'm Virginia Betts, by the way. Ginnie for short. And this is Hannah. Hannah York.'

'Hello – I'm Raven Gray. And – and would you mind not walking so fast? I mean—' she smiled apologetically. 'I am one of you.'

'Corks!' Hannah laughed. 'That's all right then. I thought you was going to be one of the stuck-up sort. You don't half talk posh.'

'Pardon?'

'A snot. I mean, that's how you sound.'

'I'm sorry,' Raven replied quietly and wondered why she so badly needed to apologise, 'but I am one of you. I'm no snob and – and . . .,' She was remembering Francis's words, how open he had been, so went on: 'And to be honest, I feel out on a limb and I badly need friends.'

'Then you've got 'em,' Hannah instantly replied. 'All for one and one for all, eh?'

'That's nice,' Ginnie agreed. 'Once we get inside Hawksley, where I hope it's going to be warm, we can let our hair down and really get to know each other.'

'That's right!' Hannah replied, adding wistfully, 'I couldn't half do with a cuppa and I'm starving. In fact, I can't remember when I had my last meal. Come on, you hang on to the torch, Raven. Stone me! What a funny name!'

Hannah's voice held chirpy friendliness, and Ginnie merely reached out and gently squeezed Raven's arm. They began to move along the lane again. Raven was staring at the dancing circle of torchlight, feeling that she was in an empty world.

As time went by Hannah found herself as confused as the others. There had been no right turning. Lightning flashed in the far distance and it began to rain. A wind soughed into life, gusting the drops, turning them into cold pellets against her cheeks. It grew darker than before. There was an awful kind of waiting feeling in the air. It was stormy and she was scared. It seemed she was fated to live in fear, her mouth permanently dry. This was a time of nightmares. Awful dreams that held a dead man, Black Marketeers who were nothing less than murdering gangsters, and the wicked-looking Ram. It did not help when the pathway fizzled away into a track, then to nothing. They were lost.

Now she was stumbling through what must be a copse. Trees above and around her were weaving and dancing in the teeming rain. Without warning, a far nearer zig-zag of lightning razored the sky. Hannah

24

yelled, 'Shit!' at the top of her voice. Then Ginnie stumbled and nearly fell.

The torchlight made a small gold circle on the rough bark of a conifer, a living thing that seemed alien somehow – as were the writhing shapes of shrubs buffeted by the wind. Hannah could smell damp earth; she waited for the thunder, counting the seconds. Each second was a mile. She counted to ten and heard a distant rumble. Good! The storm was ten miles away. What a blessing. It could be nasty if it was directly overhead – trees were great lightning conductors.

In daylight, she told herself firmly, I would find all this to be very lovely, and not frightening at all. She thought of a poem she had learned at school, about forests. That was why she couldn't make herself join the Women's Timber Corpse. The poem had spoken of tall, magnificent, living and breathing things that lived longer than man. But on this night, the wood was intimidating. Dark bushes were hunchbacks waiting to pounce; trees were devils with snakes in their hair.

'If this is the sodding country,' Hannah bawled to the others, 'you can bloody well keep it!'

'We're lost, of course!' Ginnie said. 'Damn!'

'Hang on!' Hannah looked to a gap at her left just as fresh lightning lit the sky. 'There's a break in the trees – look over there. Come on!' She began to run, her light luggage banging against her leg. Ginnie, struggling with her over-large suitcase, went after her.

Raven began to follow as fast as she could, and as she did so, she was saying goodbye to happiness for ever. Forgetting the other girls, she was screaming silently in her mind . . . for her mother, her father, and for Francis – all of whom she had so adored, and who were now part of an airy existence somewhere billions of miles away, up there among the stars. And she was down here, in the rain and the dark, afraid of the future without them. It was unbearable. She felt empty, a shell, just a thing existing in the rain.

She was following Hannah's whippet-like outline and the longer, leaner figure of Ginnie. They reached a large building and ran round until they came to a door, which was half-open. They all stopped, chests heaving, wet and bedraggled, covered in mud.

Through the din of the storm, music could be heard. It came in waves – delicate, like the scent of roses. It gusted away until it became a mere whisper in the cold air, then it was banished, shut off into nothingness. And all there was left once more was the sad song of the rain.

Hannah stood with the others by the cracked door that hung askew on a broken hinge and peered into the damp darkness of the hall. Her

25

breath was coming in hard little gasps. Water squelched inside her brown Land Army shoes. Her hair clung wetly to her face. Since the others, uncertain, hung back, she knocked on the door with her knuckles. No one came. The place looked empty but she knew that it was not. There had been the music.

She tried again, then half-angrily she stepped inside the house that crouched against the darkness like an exhausted animal waiting to die. Holding their breath, the others followed her.

'Is there anyone at home?' Hannah called. There was no reply but the music began again. She took a few more tentative steps, forgetting Raven and Ginnie, who stayed where they were.

A thin sliver of light coming from under a door at the far end of the hall was now discernible. In spite of her brave air, Hannah shivered. This house was larger than she had at first thought, she could sense it. It was also a bit creepy – sad, too. Perhaps the poignancy of the music helped the illusion, but the moist coldness and emptiness about her were real enough.

Hannah walked towards the light that ran like a strand of yellow silk from under the door. She knocked, then because the music continued without pause, she turned the handle and walked into the room. It was very large and edged with shadows. Candlelight wavered and sent pools of radiance outward, but this radiance served only to accentuate the darkness. It was from a patch of darkness that the music came. She walked towards the music and in the dimness saw first the piano and then the man. She stepped forward. The others remained behind.

'Who the hell are you?' The man said rudely. 'You're trespassing. Go away.'

'Forgive me for intruding,' Hannah said apologetically, 'but—'

'Go away!'

'Where to?' she asked logically enough.

'Hawksley,' he said, 'where I presume you were heading, is in its right and proper place – in Lindell.'

'Perhaps you'll be kind enough to direct me?'

'It's a mile and a half away.'

The lightning was jumping like fire-crackers in the sky. Thunder rolls grew more guttural. The storm was getting close and all Hannah could do was gasp, 'Oh!' She stared helplessly into the face that from where she was standing was just a patch of light etched with black lines. She felt out of her depth, standing before him dripping rain on the floor. Then she became angry.

'I think you're being really rotten,' she said tightly. 'And also very rude.'

The man laughed at that, sending rough cracks of sound echoing round the room.

'And you are impertinent. This is private property.'

'I'm sorry,' she replied, and her anger went, leaving only the weary emptiness inside, and the tiredness, and the utter grey blackness of the ball of horror now encircling her life. She about-faced and stepped back into one of the splattering pools of light.

There was a moment of intense silence between them broken only by the monotonous drumming of the rain. Then from on high, the noisy sound of a plane, engine coughing, ceasing, then dramatically flaring into life once more before cutting out for good. Hannah froze. Time seemed to stretch for ever and then came a heart-stopping, reverberating thud.

Hannah was unaware of the fact that she had half-turned to the man, and had begun to shake. She heard herself moan and felt the blood draining away from her face.

'It's from Matching Airfield, I expect,' the man told her crisply. 'It sometimes happens when they limp home like that.'

Oh my God! Hannah thought. Is there no end to all this? I'm jinxed, I must be! She began to move towards the door, stiffly, like a mechanical thing.

Raven and Ginnie stepped out of the shadows, concerned for their friend, determined to let her see that she was not alone. At that moment a whiplash of lightning was followed almost at once by a fierce gun-crack of thunder. Hannah ducked, her nerves jumping like popcorn in her head.

'Wait!' The man's voice spoke with authority. 'This storm's turning into a corker and you all look done in. You had best stay here for a while.'

'Thank you,' Hannah stuttered and felt rather than saw him rise from the piano. He came forward, towering over her. His face was mature, plain and held bitterness. He was hawk-nosed, had an arrogant air, and was instantly unlikable, until one saw the very real pain at the back of his eyes, and remembered his music.

'Now before I leave,' he said, 'is there anything you need?'

'No, thank you. I – we really don't know how to –'

'Thank me?' His tone was wry. 'I don't suppose Mrs St John will be too happy either. You are not due for another ten days.'

'My letter said ninth of the ninth clearly enough,' Hannah sparked up.

'So did mine,' the others agreed in unison.

'I see.' The voice remained grim. 'Well, I must sort this out. Though I doubt whether Mrs St John, the person who owns "Hawksley" will be amused.'

'Beg pardon?' Hannah asked and glared. 'As for being amused, after this little lot, we're hardly laughing our heads off!'

He shrugged. 'There would have been someone to meet you at the station, had you arrived at the right and proper time.'

'As far as we're concerned,' Hannah was getting ready to have a go at this sarcastic man, 'this *is* the right and proper time.' She jutted out her chin, eyes flashing. 'I said we're sorry for butting in. What more do you want – blood?'

'Perhaps we'll meet again before you leave,' he went on coolly, totally ignoring her outburst. 'If not, Hawksley is well-situated in the village. When you leave here, turn to the right and you'll find the path, then it's just a case of walking along it. In the meantime, you will find the couch and armchairs quite accommodating.'

Since they remained where they were, not replying, he went on ungraciously, 'Oh, and there are plenty of blankets. They're in the large cupboard over there. I advise you to wrap yourself in them – after you've taken off your wet, and if I may say so, extremely unattractive uniforms.'

His cheek made them gasp, and Hannah's eyes blazed. He went on, clearly trying to explain his remark: 'I never did like to see women in breeches, and there's nothing earthy or horsey about any of you.' It was probably his way of trying to make amends, but the shock of his initial attitude left them dumb. He smiled briefly. 'My apologies. Well, good night, ladies. There is food in the larder. Now I'm off to the village to try to find out what the hell's going on.'

'Can't we go too?' Hannah asked quickly. 'After all, if Hawksley's in the village and—'

'Sorry. I came here on horseback, not by car.' And he swung away from them, impatient to leave.

'Good riddance to bad rubbish!' Hannah said the moment they heard the door bang behind him. She tried to smile, but her lips trembled as she added, 'Talk about God's gift.'

'Oh, do forget him,' Ginnie said in her no-nonsense way, 'and let's find those blankets. I'm freezing!'

'All right. I'll make us a cuppa,' Hannah replied, determined to act as though she was not feeling like a raging coward. 'I bet it'd be too much to ask, that he wasn't joking about there being something to eat.' She looked enquiringly at Raven. 'I've just spotted your wedding ring. Is your old man an officer or something grand?'

'I thought you were going to make us a pot of tea?' Ginnie cut in, seeing Raven's expression. 'For goodness sake take a candle into the kitchen and have a look round for the teapot and things.' She turned to Raven 'Are you all right?'

28

Raven just stood there and said nothing at all. It was Hannah, deeply apologetic now, who came out with it.

'He's dead, isn't he?'

'Yes,' Raven breathed through lips that looked starched enough to crack.

'I'm – I'm sorry,' Hannah said with all sincerity. 'I always seem to put my foot in it. I shouldn't have asked. I should have guessed.'

'War is a dreadful, awful nightmare,' Ginnie added evenly. 'Forgive us for butting in.'

They were looking at her, their warmth and sympathy so genuine that Raven did not try to hide her grief. She said quietly, 'Francis did not die in action. He was very ill and—'

'Loss is loss,' Ginnie replied. 'And Hannah and I are very sorry to have intruded on your grief.'

'I – I think that you'll both help me through it,' Raven told them quietly. 'I mean that . . . It seems such a long time since I had friends.'

'We'll stick together like glue,' Hannah told her. 'You know, like I told Ginnie here. We'll be The Three Musketeers and stay that way through thick and thin.' She swung round to Ginnie. 'Agreed?'

'Of course!'

'And we're going to need to be tough as old boots,' Hannah was back to being herself, 'if that bloke's anything to go by. Miserable sod. I ask you! We've all got problems of our own, but we don't walk about with them like millstones round our necks. Know something? If the locals are anything like him, I—'

'I though we were going to try and find tea?' Ginnie cut in. 'I could certainly do with a cup.' Lightning flashed again and Hannah covered her ears. 'Never mind,' Ginnie told her. '*I'll* make the tea. And Raven, perhaps you can look and see if you can find blankets and things?'

Later they wrapped themselves round warmly, drank tea and ate bread and fishpaste. The storm abated and they gradually relaxed. They spoke together, got to know a little about each other, discovering that each and every one of them felt badly in need of friends. Ginnie was scared for her brother, but was otherwise on an even keel. Raven was grieving for her husband and also for parents recently lost. Hannah was just plain Hannah, bright and sparky and ready to take anyone on. The other two looked at each other, knowing full well that something or someone had made her very afraid, but that she would drop dead rather than admit it.

'It's a good job we get on,' Hannah burst out defiantly, 'but you'll have to put up with me. I know I tend to talk back when perhaps I shouldn't, and . . .'

'You say what most people think,' Ginnie said crisply. 'Oh well, I wonder what tomorrow will bring?'

'Too much mud,' came the reply and they all laughed.

James St John decided to walk to the village. His horse was sheltered, fed and dry; no need to disturb him now. He'd collect him first thing. Besides, he needed to stride out, to let off some steam after being confronted by those damned girls.

He hunched his shoulders against the rain that was persisting even though the storm had gone. His excuse about leaving to investigate the crash had been a mere getaway. The three young women appearing out of the blue like that had unsettled him. Land Girls, he thought disparagingly. What a damned nuisance they were going to be. City people with city ways – with about as much feeling for the land as whales at sea.

It had taken all of Endercot's powers of persuasion to get him, the boss, to accept that feminine help was necessary. Ye gods! Women, young or old were crosses to bear and that was a fact. A man would never be able to understand them, never. Why, even his own hard-hearted mother was a hard-as-nails enigma. When she had heard about three young Land Girls coming to work on the Estate and needing a place to live, she'd laughed. Then she had looked him up and down in her usual calculating way.

'My God, James,' she had drawled at last, in that mocking way she had, 'whatever next? You having to put up with girls treading among your beloved beet. Poor dears. They will be taking their lives in their hands, with you around.'

'It's no joke, Mother.'

'I have never known you to joke, James. As for the girls, we shall have them here, of course.'

'No, Mother!' His tone had been as brittle as hers. 'They would never survive your biting tongue.'

'My dear boy,' there had actually been icy humour glinting in her eyes, 'there are certain things you should know about females. We can all be bitches, devils or saints as the mood takes us.'

'Females are a mealy-mouthed spiteful species more often than not.'

'Really – mealy-mouthed? Don't judge us all the same as that woman! As for the rest of us – of course we love to let our hair down and be all girls together.'

That had made him laugh for a start, Mother actually believing she could ever be one of the girls. Phew! She had been drinking again and was as usual deluding herself.

30

'Of course we relish tittle-tattle.' She had ignored his derisive snort. 'And think a juicy scandal is the most exciting thing out.'

'Typical, Mother. Absolutely typical!'

'You must admit, you provided an all-absorbing furore, James. You were the subject of innuendo and a great deal of mud-slinging. Actually, dear boy, you were a spell binding five minute wonder – that's all there is to it. But that was a long time ago and you should have forgiven and forgotten by now.'

He would never either forgive or forget, James thought. His mother least of all. And now he was lumbered with three more of her ilk. Land Girls.

James smiled sourly. Lord help them, he thought, specially stuck with Mother. She'd offered to have them, of course she had! There was no other choice. There was a war on and folk gave up their homes to the forces, to evacuees, to anyone who needed a roof over their heads. Besides, Mother had probably offered to billet them because she was bored. Or because she had been approached by the Min of Ag Office working in liaison with the WLA. But something had gone wrong. There had been a bad mix-up with dates.

He saw the village policeman cycling along. 'Evening, Dalton.'

'Evening, sir.'

'One of ours?'

''Fraid so, sir. Crashed over Norseby way. It's all in hand. The Matching lot were quick off the mark as always.'

'Poor devils.'

'Sir.'

Dalton cycled on, and James continued furiously towards Hawksley, his mother's place.

Chapter Five

Dawn was just breaking when Hannah, Ginnie and Raven left the old farmhouse that had sheltered them the night before. Now it did not seem awesome, and the lopsided carved wooden nameplate bearing the legend *Knollys* looked rather raffish. All three girls were quiet as they began the walk to Lindell. Hannah, still troubled by the memory of nightmares, managed to smile or wink every time either Ginnie or Raven looked her way. When she felt that she had been quiet too long, she carried on about the rotten snotty pig they had met the night before, his superior attitude having incensed her a great deal.

'He let us stay,' Ginnie pointed out. 'He didn't have to, you know.'

'And he didn't have to be so rude either,' Hannah retorted. 'Next time I meet him, I'm going to get in first! Arrogant old swine. What do you reckon, Raven?'

Raven did not reply. Once again she seemed to be trying to hold on to reality. Documenting events as best she could, thinking about anything and everything. She had to, to hold the grief at bay.

It was September and Hannah breathed in shakily, deeply. The air was like wine after the unexpectedly fierce late summer storm. Just to inhale, she told herself, was more intoxicating than anything that was sold in the Duck and Drake.

Before her stretched miles of rural Essex, overlaid with what looked like scorched handkerchieves of ripened grain, else fallow ground where grain had only recently grown. Further on, there seemed to be many acres of dark green leaves that looked like turnips. Here partridges were anxiously calling. There was a blaze of saffron yellow from wild rape, interspaced with bright scarlet pinpoints. There still seemed to be poppies everywhere. It had been a good summer which had overflowed into September, Harvest Festival time.

Hannah saw Raven's closed face again, not realising that as the older girl looked upwards, she was trying to picture three souls floating free as thistledown, perhaps holding hands. Wishing that she could be with them, flying alongside, at peace.

Something about Raven's expression just then reminded Hannah of Miss Pitt. Yes, she thought, the morning was as spiritual as Miss Pitt could wish. The war and Ram Rawlins seemed very far away.

The track the girls were walking along widened into a down-sloping lane. From this vantage point, the village came into view. It consisted of a miscellany of dwellings – thatch, elderly brick-tiled places, and a few newer-looking buildings. They were mostly centred round the Green. Even from here the blacksmith's was recognisable; there was an inn, and well beyond, rising above a screen of trees, the spire of a church.

'It looks lovely!' Hannah breathed. 'Makes London and bombs seem like bits of black hell.'

'Last night you called it "the sodding country" and told us that we could keep it,' Ginnie observed.

'It's because I hate storms. I'm scared stiff of them,' Hannah replied. 'And I don't like the dark either. Last night we were out in both.'

'So now all's well?' Ginnie teased. 'Aren't you the changeable one!'

Ignoring their light-hearted wrangling, still feeling not quite part of the everyday world, Raven was looking at the view as though through someone else's eyes. Blackbirds were hopping about and greenfinches gregariously flitting from hedge to hedge. Gorsebushes were richly spangled with gold, and rabbits kicked up their heels, showing white scuts as they scampered away.

'Are you all right?' Hannah asked.

'Things could be better,' Raven admitted in her quiet, well-modulated voice. 'I rather think I'm experiencing the aftermath of shock. I felt that time was standing still just now.'

'It never does in the country,' Hannah replied. 'Someone's at it already.'

'So will we be – tomorrow,' Ginnie said.

'I'm sorry.' Raven's voice was barely a whisper. 'To be a wet blanket, I mean.'

'Just shut your eyes for a minute,' Hannah told her, 'and listen to the morning.'

Raven smiled. She could hear farm machinery droning on the land nearby, cows plodding through a field, their lowing a gentle sound drifting through space. Not even the droning of planes from Matching Airfield could mar the serenity of the scene. And as a breeze, sweet with the scent of wild flowers, tilted against her face, she remembered

Francis's words and closed her eyes. Believing that it was as he had promised. That he was kissing her . . .

It was the blacksmith, Mr Cyril Stitson, a merry man with a russet face and huge hands, who pointed out the way to Hawksley. They thanked him and trooped off along a lane winding to the right. Now the rising sun sent down its bounty of excellence.

'It's getting too hot to march along like this,' Hannah said. 'Talk about donkeys going well-loaded – the handle of my case is wearing a ridge in my hand. As for you, Ginnie, what *have* you got in yours? Everything bar the kitchen sink?'

Ginnie merely shrugged and looked rueful.

The lane widened, then ended before a large, low wooden gate that led to open land. They opened it and walked through, carefully closing it behind them. Surrounded by fields, alone in its splendour, they at last saw the house standing against a backdrop of poplar trees.

Hawksley was early Victorian, large, grey and imposing. As they neared it, they could smell the perfume of the wide flowerbeds that were at the base of a walled garden.

'To think I imagined this place to be like something out of a creepy Bella Lugosi picture,' Hannah observed sourly. 'I don't know how I'm going to fit in. Talk about posh!'

'You'd fit in anywhere,' Ginnie told her. 'You're a natural. I'm going to have to cure your inferiority complex.'

'I don't feel inferior. Quite the reverse.'

'Ah.' Ginnie smiled and looked wise. She glanced across at Raven. 'What do you think of the looks of things?'

'My husband Francis would have written poetry about all of this,' Raven replied. 'He would have experienced emotions and dreams, felt things like . . .'

'Ghosts?' Hannah's brows rose. 'Raven, for Gawd's sake leave it out!' She glared at Ginnie. 'All right, so I'm superstitious and yes – I'm just scared I won't fit in, that's all.'

'If you don't, then neither do we. All right?' Ginnie's very blue eyes twinkled as she added, 'Should we find the tradesmen's entrance, do you think?'

At Hannah's explosive snort, she chuckled, then pulled a face, the weight of her suitcase now fully taking its toll.

Raven moved with quiet dignity, unmindful of her small leather hold-all that contained the little she had been prepared to bring with her from the old life.

Hannah marched towards the front door, bristling like a turkey cock, her second-hand cardboard suitcase clutched determinedly in her hand. She lifted the large scrolled bugle-shaped knocker. It fell with a resounding bang. They waited, clustered together before the door, tall, taller and short, expectancy on their faces.

No one came.

'Ginnie's right – it's the back door for us,' Hannah said pithily. 'Come on, let's find it.'

'Hang on,' Ginnie objected. 'You flare up at the drop of a hat, don't you, Hannah? We'll let Raven handle this.'

'I forgot,' Hannah replied without rancour. 'She ain't used to back doors. Sorry!'

Just then, the door opened and they found themselves looking at a young woman with bright ginger hair. She was full-lipped and full-bosomed. Her pinafore was jazzy with bright colours, and her smile was wide and warm and welcoming. She did not fit in with her grandiose, surroundings at all. She was a young-mother type and seemingly full of the joys of spring.

'Here you are!' she greeted them in a honey-warm voice. 'Had a bad time of it, haven't you? There's been quite a mix-up, I understand. Never mind! You come with me to the kitchen, and I'll put the kettle on.'

'That'd be nice,' Hannah replied, blossoming. 'We could all do with a cuppa. It's been quite a walk from Knollys.'

'Really?' Again that brilliant smile. 'Inside a week you'll be crossing half the county in the time it takes a duck to shake its rear portion. Life round here is all about walking and working and wandering down to the inn. You'll fit in, I'm sure.'

'I hope so,' Hannah replied with feeling. 'I'm Hannah York.'

'And I'm Lily Ainsley. I'm afraid that the war's taken up most of the staff. We lost Josh to the Army and Mr Foulds to the coal mines – which meant we had to shut our own stables and use the Drew's instead. Mrs Madeira the cleaner, and Vincent who's worth his weight in gold, and little old me try to run this place as best we can. I'm the chief cook and bottle-washer, by the way.' She called over her shoulder, 'Vincent? Vincent, they're here!' She turned back to the girls. 'Leave your things. Vincent will take them up to your room.'

'Ta ever so.' Hannah was grinning now, mock posh and more at ease. 'Who's Vincent when he's at home?'

'Vincent Blackstock. He's the man that sorts out just about everything, and he's been doing so for donkeys' years. He saw to the room you'll be taking over until the end of the war. You don't mind sharing, do you? It's very large and it's been made really nice.'

'Thank you.' Ginnie spoke for the first time. 'You're very kind.' Raven said nothing, just smiled.

35

They were trooping after Lily now, conscious of graciousness and luxury, all throughout the house. There was lots of red carpeting everywhere and hall-stands of dark polished wood, and a marble bust or two that could have been of anyone but looked predominately Greek. Most striking, over all, was the scent of furniture polish mingling with that of flowers. Fresh and sweet-smelling and very pleasant indeed.

Lily, a swift, nimble-footed person, queried: 'Did you make yourselves breakfast at Knollys, or did Mr St John have an empty larder?' She was leading them along a wide hall, to the right and into a large, old-fashioned, more than adequate kitchen. It was lofty, faced east and had a stone floor. A large wooden table was placed at the centre; round it were high-backed chairs. Through a half-opened door could be seen the scullery with its huge stone sink and an old-fashioned mangle.

Lily seemed to have taken to the three newcomers. Smiley and rosy-faced, she ordered, 'Sit down at the table and make yourselves at home, ladies. It won't take five minutes before you've all settled in.'

A name previously mentioned stood out like a beacon to Hannah. Her eyes snapped.

'Mr St John?' she asked. 'Don't tell me *he's* got anything to do with us. Gawd, he's not this woman's old man?'

'Her son actually. This is his official residence, but he prefers Knollys – says it's quieter there. I don't blame him. Mrs St John can be a handful at times.' While she was speaking, Lily had been bustling about, making tea and getting some breakfast on the go. 'Just make yourselves comfy. This won't take a jiff . . .'

Soon they were all leaning back, warm and comfortable, having enjoyed a scrumptious meal of tomatoes, egg and bacon. Rationing was apparently easier to bear in the country, since most people had their own chickens and grew their own fruit and veg. Hannah was in the middle of a sentence, telling the others how good she was at growing her own mustard and cress, when without warning the door flew open.

A tall woman with silver-blonde hair, high cheekbones, and a tight-skinned beautifully complexioned face, swept in. In spite of everything being in short supply, she was wearing lots of eye make-up, plum-coloured lipstick, a lavender blouse and black skirt. She had on silk stockings and black patent leather court shoes. Ebony beads gleamed round her neck and at her ears. She was clearly rich, and looked bad-tempered and arrogant.

'Lily! Where the hell have you been?' she enquired in a cut-glass voice.

36

'Looking after the Land Girls, Mrs St John,' Lily replied, adding, 'have you another headache? Shall I make you a fresh pot of tea?'

'Oh my God!' Sophia St John snapped. 'How prissy you sound. Tea? Is that the be-all and end-all cure? More to the point, have you seen that son of mine?'

'No, Mrs St John. Not yet.'

The woman frowned and ran long nervous fingers through her hair. Her eyes were green and, at that moment, blazed with pain. She was slim, sophisticated, tigerish in grace and mood. She seemed the hard and ruthless sort who did not like anyone, and didn't give a damn if they loathed her in return.

Now she said waspishly, 'All James thinks about is agriculture,' and, totally ignoring Raven, Ginnie and Hannah, she continued, 'and to that end I must put up with having three Godawful strangers in my house!'

'Oh, excuse *us*!' Hannah spiked up, cheeks flaming. 'And do pardon us for breathing, missus. On our part, we're pleased to meet you, I'm sure!'

Sophia St John's reaction was strangely unpredictable. After her initial shocked glare at Hannah, she threw back her head and laughed in a high, brittle way, then: 'We can't call you prissy, can we?'

'Never that,' Hannah replied and a dimple danced momentarily in her cheek, though her eyes remained angry. 'Well, shall we pick up our bags and buzz off right here and now?'

'You will go to your room,' the woman returned, loathing them with her eyes. 'And thank your lucky stars that it makes no difference that you're not supposed to be here yet. You will unpack and put your things away. You will then have to amuse yourselves as best you can until my son arrives, or better still, Endercot our Estate Manager. One or the other will tell you what to do.' Dismissing them, she turned to Lily and flared, 'Damn! Doesn't it matter that I still feel half-dead? I will have that tea, and some aspirin.'

'Yes, Mrs St John.' Lily was already busying about.

The woman went on fretfully, 'I waited three-quarters of an hour for those aspirin last night. All that time for the man to get to Kitts and back! Tell Vincent he's sacked.'

'He was late back because Briggs was blocking the road with his sheep, Mrs St John.'

'My God! Since when has Vincent Blackstock let a flock of sheep get the better of him? Take these – people up to their room, then fetch my aspirin. Then see to Vincent. At once, Lily!'

'Please come with me, ladies,' Lily said calmly, and once her back was turned to her employer, she looked into Hannah's still frostily glinting eyes and winked. Then she turned back to her employer, saying, 'Oh, and I'll tell Vincent if I see him, Mrs St John, but I did hear that he was thinking of going to Matching Village – to see about that cottage to let. He was saying only last night that it's about time he retired.'

'Rubbish! He has been with me for over twenty years.'

'Exactly,' Lily replied easily enough, and began swiftly ushering the girls out of the kitchen.

As they went upstairs, to a large pleasantly decorated yellow and brown room, Lily seemed quite unmoved over her employer's behaviour. She's probably used to it, Hannah thought. Well, it wouldn't bloody well suit me.

She looked around. The room was comfortable, tasteful in the extreme, as unlike the Spartan hostel in Colchester as chalk from cheese. It held three single beds, three single wardrobes and three mirrored chest-of-drawers. There was a bedside cabinet each. Old-gold eiderdowns matched the colour of bobble-fringed velvet curtains, and there was a large central red and yellow-beige rug of Indian design on the polished wood floor. Hannah, impressed in spite of herself, sniffed.

'All very nice I'm sure, but decent things ain't everything. It looks like the rich are as pig-ignorant as the poor.'

'What on earth made you think otherwise?' Lily replied. 'Sophia St John is her own worst enemy.'

'How come?'

'She treated her youngest son Miles badly. He was wild and usually kicked over the traces. I liked him. He laughed a lot, played a lot, and didn't bow down to her wishes. He flouted authority. Strangely, he and his friend, Deacon, ran off to sea together, joined the Navy. They must have had to come to terms with plenty of rules and regulations there.'

'I wouldn't have minded meeting him if he was tough enough to defy his marm-stink mum,' Hannah said stoutly. 'But the bloke we burst in on last night, phew!'

'Mr James? A cold fish if ever there was one. But he was very fond of young Miles. All three were real close – Mr James, Deacon Reeves, and Miles. The younger two led James a fair old dance, I can tell you. It must have broken his heart when . . .'

'Don't stop there,' Hannah insisted, when Lily paused. 'We might as well get the picture of these people. Bloody hell! The two we've met are hardly a pretty pair.'

'Miles and Deacon were on the *Courageous* when she was sunk by a German submarine. Miles went down with his ship, as did just over

38

half of her crew of a hundred and ten men. Mrs St John acted out the stiff-upper-lip thing, but she's had these furious headaches ever since. And that's even though she's always professed to have no time for her boys.'

'And her husband?'

'Great teddy-bear of a man, he was. Mrs St John was dotty about him. She wanted to be the only one in his life. So she married him, and though it went against the grain, had his two sons. She inherited his fortune when he died, but told me she'd live in a hovel and eat dried bread very happily, if only she could have him at her side again. She gets very confiding when she's drunk, you see.'

'Oh Gawd, a sozzler' Hannah groaned. A swift vision of her stepfather came before her eyes. 'I know all about them.'

'I don't think she ever forgave Mr James and Miles for being the apple of their father's eye. Literally doted on them, he did. Used to spend hours with them, horse-riding, sports, work on the Estate, that sort of thing. She felt like an outsider. Mr St John never knew that, of course. He loved her very much. As it was, Mrs St John was left behind during their shenanigans, to get on with her painting. She's a very good artist, you know, and was well-known in her field before Mr St John married her.'

'She has sad eyes.' Raven spoke for the first time. 'I think I know how she feels.'

'She's a bitch,' Ginnie said flatly.

'She needs someone's toe up her arse,' Hannah put in, determined not to be outdone.

'Well, I'll love and leave you,' Lily told them. 'I prepare lunch for one o'clock. Evening meals will be waiting for when you come back from the fields. I might be gone by then, to my place, Rose Cottage – and yes, I do have roses round the door. Oh, and don't worry about Mrs St John. You'll probably never have to lay eyes on her again. Keeps herself to herself, she does, and likes it that way.'

'Thank Gawd for that.' Hannah raised her eyes heavenwards. 'I prefer her room to her company any day.'

'Oh, and you needn't think you'll be stuck away up here. A nice sitting room is being prepared for you. There's to be a gramophone, records, a wireless and everything. If you had arrived on the nineteenth it would have all been in place.'

'We have been prepared for as guests,' Raven observed. 'How very kind.'

Lily nodded, then added, 'Mrs St John has been known to do the decent thing on occasion, but don't be fooled. She doesn't stand any nonsense.' She laughed wryly. 'I get away with murder – all but. However, I've been warned very clearly to keep my brats out of sight and sound. And Mr Moses mustn't dare put his nose beyond the scullery.'

'Your brats?' Hannah's tone brightened. 'I love kids. How many have you got?'

'Twin boys, Charles and Christopher. Chook and Chris to you. They're pickles, I can tell you, and all of seven years old. Maud, I mean Mrs Madeira, is their number one enemy. She was nasty to Mr Moses, you see. But then, the woman's a menace. She treats young Lenny badly. Some say that she beats him, but it never shows. The boy never breathes a word. Lenny's her nephew by marriage, an orphan, and thought to be a bit slow. I think he's just a dreamer and a bit nervous and shy. My boys like him and that's good enough for me. Lenny's father was Walter Madeira's brother. As I've said, Maud Madeira wants no truck with Lenny. And as for my Mr Moses . . .'

'Who's he when he's at home?'

Lily laughed. 'The twins' dog! They named him that because they swore they'd found him abandoned in the rushes. They think they saved him from drowning, of all things. The water's all of two inches deep at that spot. They were begging and pleading for me to allow them to keep him.'

'And you played hard to convince?' Ginnie wrinkled her nose. 'You sound like my mother.'

'They had their way, of course.' Lily grinned. 'I have never told them that I knew Moses was the last of Mrs Kitts's dog Brandy's litter. Really gorgeous little things, all now having good homes. Beautiful Golden Retrievers like their mum. The twins had asked Sam and I could they have one of the pups when they first knew of their birth. We said no, but we might as well have saved our breath.'

At that moment a man with a gnarled-looking face, clear grey eyes and grey hair, popped his head round the door.

'You'd better move sharpish,' he warned. 'She's working up to a fair old tantrum down there.'

'I know.' Lily remained calm. 'Vincent, meet the girls. I'm sure they'll liven things up around here.'

Introductions were made and Vincent, a quiet, steady-seeming man, left them all to it.

'It's not fair,' Hannah burst out. 'He seems a nice old thing. Imagine getting the sack just because he was late fetching her aspirin! It's really rotten. And I for one—'

'Don't worry about it,' Lily soothed. 'There are days when Mrs St John's treatment of Vincent really seems inhuman, yet she looks to him – yes, even clings to him – with an almost desperate air. His devotion is the one thing she can count on. He knows it and so does she.'

'Then what was all that talk about the cottage to let?'

'So much hot air, but she mustn't know that. Now I'd best go. Good luck!'

There was a whisk of colourful pinafore and Lily had gone.

'Phew,' Hannah whistled. 'So many unfamiliar names and people to get used to. It's always the same when you go to a new place, isn't it?'

Chapter Six

'I'm really looking forward to meeting Lily's boys and their dog Mr Moses,' Hannah said. She hastily pushed away the memory of old Meg and her master being buried alive in Walker Street. 'And our room is really and truly grand. I never expected anything like this, did you?'

'Birds in a gilded cage by the sound of things,' Ginnie laughed. 'And for what it's worth, I wanted to die when you sparked up to Mrs St John.'

'Shall I tell you something?' Hannah admitted. 'So did I!'

They looked at Raven, who seemed to have heard nothing. She was sitting there, still and quiet, just looking out of the window.

'Let's unpack our things,' Ginnie went on. 'Raven, are you with us?'

They were all quiet after that, busy with their things. Ginnie placed photographs of her family on her bedside cabinet, also one of a dark good-looking soldier.

'Is that Aiden?' Hannah asked.

Ginnie nodded. Hannah went over and looked at Raven's photographs of an elderly couple, and one of a young, thin, fair-haired man with a nice face and large guileless eyes.

'No wonder you are as you are,' Hannah said quietly. 'He looks special and – and sort of silvery.'

'Silvery? Oh yes!' Raven breathed. 'Hannah dear, how nice!'

Suddenly, all three stiffened. They could hear a distant throbbing in the air. They hastened to the window. Planes came into view, the noise from their engines growing louder. There were gaps in the formations.

'More lost,' Ginnie said. 'More death and grief.'

'Stirlings,' Hannah noted. 'All bombers. Where are the Spits?'

'Back to base, I expect,' Ginnie said. 'They've seen the heavies home and . . . Damn! Looks as if he's had it. I don't think I can bear to watch.'

But watch they did, hypnotised. The last plane, well behind the formation, was barely limping home. Smoke was pouring from it, making malevolent plumes in the sky. Then it began to drop, too quickly, the mechanism screaming through air. It seemed as though it was darting straight for Hawksley. Nearer, nail-bitingly nearer. Then in an instant its high tormented shriek faded, cut out. The plane plummeted behind the trees. A second later there came a throaty explosion. A thick pall of smoke belched upwards.

'Look!' Ginnie gasped. 'Thank heavens they're alive.' Parachutes were moving downwards gracefully. From the girls' vantage point they looked like translucent jellyfish afloat in a sea of sky. One, the last one, well behind the plane, was heading straight for them.

'He'll land on this roof!' Hannah goggled. 'Bloody hell! . . .'

Sergeant Air Gunner Matt Sheridan remembered thinking, 'This is it!' Before he took firm hold of his parachute and leapt head-first out of the plane. For an instant there was a void, then the world seemed to turn into a inferno as the plane jerked and veered away. He looked downwards and saw vague outlines of rural countryside . . . Then the earth began to leap up at him. A line of poplar trees tried to ensnare him. He kicked out and noticed that his foot and leg were streaming with blood. 'Damned lucky to still have a foot,' he thought out loud. 'Hope old Titch got away – and I didn't see the going of the pigeons. Tich liked them and . . .'

A gust of air sucked him downwards with irresistible force, straight on course for a roof. Matt Sheridan hit something hard. For a split second he saw a galaxy of stars, then he passed out.

When he came slowly back to consciousness, he found he was lying in a strange bed. An old man and a young girl were anxiously leaning over him. The girl, in Land Army uniform, said: 'He's opened his eyes, Doctor.'

The old man smiled. 'And about time, too – eh, young fellow? Well, well, I'm afraid the roof came off best. You'll have to stay where you are till your MO's come for you, and no doubt they'll get you as good as new in the end.'

Matt, conscious of a pounding in his head, smiled shakily. 'Thank you, sir.'

'That's all right, my boy. Oh, you've broken and badly injured your leg. Your spine's not in too good a shape, you must have been dragged along on your back. It's going to take a while, son – and you've gathered yourself quite a few other minor injuries, but nothing that can't be put right. Miss York will stay with you until your oppos arrive.'

'Wizzo!' Matt tried to be heroic, especially in front of such a pretty little thing, but could not hold back the groan.

'Now drink this,' the doctor said. 'It will send you to sleep. I'll be along later if your own chaps don't arrive first.'

'Thank you, sir.'

Matt obediently drank from the tumbler the young girl held to his lips. He liked the way her brown hair curled round her face. She had twinking hazel eyes and a delightful little snub nose. It seemed too much effort to swallow, but she insisted that he did.

'I'm so glad you are awake at last,' she told him. 'How do you feel?'

He merely groaned.

'Think nothing of it,' Hannah said blandly. 'It was nice of you to drop in.'

He slept, then, half-waking, felt a pinprick in his arm. He drifted away again and woke up a great deal later in the RAF hospital, near to base.

The weeks dragged by. Matt was fixed to a board and messed about with, and knew some real pain. He decided that the only decent thing that had happened since the prang had been waking up and seeing that girl. But the rest of the world habitually drifted away. There was only the war, the men, and thank God, Titch.

He had not recognised Titch at first. Half his face was bandaged and a nurse was pushing him around in an invalid chair.

'What-ho, Matt,' Titch wheezed. 'Glad you reached terra firma.'

'You too, old chap.'

'The birds made it. Didn't want their feathers to get singed like mine.'

'You don't look too bad,' Matt told him, even though Titch's face was swollen and blackened with burns. 'And for your sake I'm glad the pigeons got back.'

'Crew didn't. Neither Guy nor Donkin, poor bastards. As for the others, I'm not sure. They baled out and I haven't heard. They reckon I've had it so far as the RAF's concerned. After treatment I'm going home. Something to do with my lungs, old boy.'

'You should not be speaking so much,' the nurse said firmly. 'Really!'

'It's all right, sweetheart,' Titch gasped. 'This is my mate.' He ignored the nurse and continued: 'Matt, Richard's landed with hardly a scratch, at least ones that showed. You'd never think he was with us when we pranged.'

'Your lungs, Titch?' Matt was horrified, but kept it casual with: 'I say, bad show! Still, enjoy your leave. I'll miss you.'

44

'I won't miss this lot – bombing ops, I mean. And I'm not too happy about the idea of the Burns Unit either. I understand that they're going to mess me about and give me a Clark Gable face.'

'Impossible to change that ugly mug,' Matt tried to grin. 'It's better-looking now, burns and all. Have they given Richard a new kite?'

'Sent him on leave. He's all shook up, as they say. He came to see you, but you were out like a light. Still, they'll soon patch you up and shove you back upstairs.'

'And I've got to be grateful?'

'You're needed, old chap. Still, Richard will be back before you by the sound of things.'

'Good,' Matt said slowly. 'Very good. I've got a job for him when he finally condescends to show his face.'

'And that is?'

'To find this girl.'

'Now that's enough,' the nurse interrupted crisply, addressing Titch. 'You promised to behave. You're not even supposed to be here!'

'She loves me really.' Titch tried to laugh, but it was hard. 'Bung-ho,' he wheezed. 'Good luck!'

The girls felt quite at home in Hawksley now. Things were rather better than expected. Mrs St John kept herself to herself, and her son was away more often than not, at Ministry Headquarters. Lily was a gem, and Vincent as solid as they came. Of course, the dreaded Mrs Madeira was another matter. A plump little woman with beady eyes, a determined chin and a high colour, she always had a very dictatorial manner. She wore her fruit-festooned hat with a kind of dogged determination – almost like a knight's helmet, Hannah thought and smiled behind her hand.

The Manager of the Estate, Mr Endercot, a tall, wiry man who had a permanent love for his cherrywood pipe, was brusque, but a decent sort. Hannah had no quarrel with him. Kind and helpful, he saw them through general fieldwork, but it seemed that sugarbeet was the order of the day. Hannah's birthday came and went and she never breathed a word. Eighteen now, she thought briefly. Nearly a woman. Ha bloody ha!

It was morning time. Hannah, Ginnie and Raven walked along a lane to their place of work. Today they were to hoe. Recent rain had made the weeds rampant, for all that the year was getting old. Now the morning was brilliant with sunshine, but the air breathed in spicy and cold. They wore black working boots rather than wellies. They had believed that hedging and ditching was to be today's job, but at the last minute the order had been changed.

It was all the same to them. Lily had fed them plentifully as usual. They had been given their lunch tins and a flask of tea each liberally sweetened to the hilt with saccharine. All was well with the world.

High above they heard the drone of planes returning, one engine faltering, spluttering, but this time bursting into renewed life. Hannah thought of her dashing blue-eyed airman, wondered how he was getting on, then pushed the memory away. Matching Airfield might as well be on another planet on a clear bright morning like this. Then Nature suddenly changed her mind. The sun went in.

The lane in which they now walked was in deep shade. It was low-lying and became increasingly difficult to move along because of a water overspill. Mud clung to their working boots.

'It's like being on stilts,' Hannah said. 'Thank goodness they gave us black boots, and these brown dungarees to work in. Our uniforms would have been done-in in double-quick time.'

'I like our uniform,' Ginnie told her. 'All the rest of the women forces have skirts. I really enjoy wearing breeches.'

'And poking your thumbs in your belt like a man,' Hannah teased. 'You look ready for business and no mistake. I still feel like sticking pins in James St John every time I remember his remark about the way we look. Talk about like mother, like son! And – oh, just look at that poor thing!'

'It's a goat and there's nothing poor about it,' Ginnie observed.

'But it's wound itself round and round that tetherpost. It'll choke itself to death.'

'No, it won't,' Raven put in. 'Please don't worry, Hannah.'

Hannah clutched her chest in mock delight. 'She speaks! Music to my ears. The Land Army Lady speaks!'

'Shut up,' Ginnie told her without malice. 'We can't all be chatterboxes like you. I don't know who's the worst, Lily or you.'

'Sorry.' Hannah was looking at the goat again. 'I wonder if I can unwind that poor dumb animal?'

'I shouldn't interfere,' Raven advised. 'They are not the friendliest of creatures, you know.'

'How would you like to be tied to a post like that?'

Hannah slowly approached the animal, making soothing clucking noises. The Nanny had a very mean look in its eyes. Undaunted, Hannah moved in – only to shift out again sharpish. The goat had belligerently lowered its head and made a loud and defiant noise. There was no doubt about its intentions.

Defeated and red-faced, Hannah walked away, saying forcefully, 'Bloody thing!'

Ginnie was convulsed. Even Raven's lips twitched.

46

'And to think I thought him all lonely and miserable,' Hannah snapped.

'She,' Ginnie pointed out. 'It's a Nanny goat.'

'Well, it looks like a hateful old man, or a devil! No – it reminds me of darling James. Fancy seeing him this morning, after not seeing hide nor hair of him since that night. I was looking forward to a bit of ditching too.'

'What?' Ginnie jibed. 'Knee-deep in sour water, cleaning out all the rubbish, not forgetting a drowned rodent or two? Shame on you for a fibber, Hannah York.'

'I hate the way he comes down here just when he thinks he will – lording it over us mere peasants. Rotten sod.'

'He is our boss and son of the woman who owns the St John Estate.'

'Yes – *and* he knows it. Ha! Why couldn't he have left things to Mr Endercot like always? After all, that's what farm managers are for. It spoilt my breakfast, having St John barging into the kitchen and ordering us about as if he's God – the same God his mum's always yelling out to. I nearly told him what to do with his hoe. I would have, if I hadn't remembered all those wireless messages about digging for victory.'

'Hannah,' Raven put in, 'don't get so het-up. Stop carrying on and just enjoy!'

Hannah exhaled in a sharp explosive way and trudged on with the others. The sun grew warmer. Gorse hedges still held tints of blazing gold; late dandelions held their fuzzy yellow faces up to the sky. In no time at all Hannah's good humour returned. This was laborious work and they were filling in today during what could only be described as an Indian Summer. Later it would all be Go Man Go, because they had been informed that their main task would be back to the sugarbeet.

They reached their allotted field and standing astride the lines of winter cabbages, began to hoe the weeds. By the time the sun had reached its zenith they were sweating, their hair clinging to the back of their necks. Worse, flying insects worrying a mare grazing in the next field, left the animal to cloud over them every time they neared its vicinity.

'They bite!' Hannah moaned. 'And I still hate these boots. After all this time I should have worn them in. I'm sure I have blisters on my blisters.'

'This handle's rough for all I tried to sandpaper it down,' Ginnie said cheerfully. 'It's still hard on my hands. Never mind. They say that the first ten years are the worst.'

'Oh, I'm not really moaning, Gin,' Hannah apologised. 'It's just

47

that bloody goat made me jump out of my skin. I've never been scared of hard work.'

Raven quietly worked on. Remote, consistent, uncomplaining. 'She looks like she's doing penance again,' Hannah joked. 'She's got a Miss Pitt look on her face. Raven Gray ain't of this world!'

Raven looked up at that and smiled. 'Yes, I am,' she told them. 'Thanks to both of you.'

'It's time for our break,' Ginnie beamed. Happily in charge, since she was the only one of them who had been away on a week's training course. 'I wonder what Lily's given us?'

Lily had turned up trumps again. Cheese sandwiches in spite of the shortage, a large tomato each. And a huge slice of apple pie.

'Talk about heaven!' Hannah said blissfully. 'This is the life.'

'Talking about life,' Ginnie told her, 'I hear that airman of ours is getting stronger by the day. One or two of his crew didn't make it though, I'm afraid. I heard Vincent telling Lily all about it. He was speaking about Mr Endercot's pigeons really.'

'Pigeons?' Hannah raised her brows.

'Aircrews take them up,' Ginnie explained. 'They fly home with messages, photos, things of that kind. Our Mr Endercot supplies the Air Force with some of the pigeons. Breeds racers he does, and knows them all by name. Anyway, he told Vincent that he never lost a single bird. In fact, every one of them turned up right as rain.'

'Bully for the birds. Shame about some of the crew!' Hannah said pithily. 'Anyway, I'm glad my airman's all right.'

'*Your* airman? No one else stood a chance. Up there like a shot you were,' Ginnie teased. 'Nosy little devil.'

'Only because the doctor asked for help. No one else stepped in.'

'I know,' Raven put in seriously. 'And I feel so guilty about that – particularly as I was once determined to be a full-time nurse and had trained as such. But – I just couldn't.'

'Even if you could have,' Ginnie told her, 'you wouldn't have stood an earthly, and me neither. In fact, we didn't stand a chance because of young pushy-pants here. Good-looker, wasn't he?'

'Fair hair, blue eyes and so handsome I could die just thinking about him. Still, after all this time . . .' Hannah shrugged. 'I don't suppose we'll ever see him again. Here, what shall we do tonight?'

'Fall flat on our faces as usual, at least for an hour or two,' Ginnie yawned. 'After sweating this lot out it will be nice to be home and dry.'

'And feeling just like wrung-out dish cloths.' Hannah's dimple danced, then she was eying the food still remaining in Ginnie's lunch-box. 'Don't you want that?'

'Here you are. Waste not, want not.' The sandwich changed hands. 'Now let's make the most of this and rest while we can.'

'No rest for the wicked,' Hannah said joyously. 'Look – we've got visitors.'

Tumbling over the stile, laughing and calling out to their dog, came the twins. One dark, one fair, two young wretches who were the bane of sniffy Mrs Madeira's life, but openly adored by all three girls.

But, for now, the larger-than-life Maud Madeira, with her 'Dickensian' ways according to Raven, and 'Witchy' ways according to Hannah, was forgotten. Instead there were lots of jokes, and games all accompanied by the joyous barking of their excited young Retriever, Mr Moses.

Chapter Seven

Ram Rawlins walked slowly along Jamaica Street. It was a cockeyed little road lined by two-up and two-downers with boarded-up windows. Its small houses were pathetic under their weight of war damage.

All over London, people 'in the know' – ordinary people in the street – would say of various bombs or groups of craters, 'Lumme, the sods was aiming at the Town Hall!' or else, 'Stone me! That lot was meant for the station,' or, 'Strewth, the swines're after the docks again.'

On another occasion: 'The bastards got the coalyard and missed the rent office next door. Wot a shit! That means old Mallard's still got his book in his hand, and wig on his head.' Then, amidst laughter; 'Worse, the old bugger's still got his *head!* Ain't that a shame?'

People repaired what they could, swept up the broken glass and doggedly got on with what they had to do. The Blitz was aimed at civilians, but Britishers didn't give in to bullies. It was as simple as that. Life went on and sometimes it was good, and places like Jamaica Street could be Paradise. It was to Ram.

Ram reached number 10. Here the windows had survived and glittered as defiantly as a spinster's pince-nez. Val had put a blue china bowl filled with yellow paper chrysanthemums in the downstairs front. Val had class, Ram thought, and smiled his skull-like smile. Val made him feel alive, but mostly she also made him feel muddled and uncomfortable. She could say wounding things, but then she had always been the same. He had to be near her. Had suffered her jibes in silence even from the earliest days at school. But it was worse than torture when she sent him away.

He entered the house. It smelled of damp and decay and mice droppings, but it would do. He removed his overcoat and hung it up. Val would kill him if he failed to do that. When he walked into the kitchen, he found her sitting in the chair near the range, her high heels balanced on the fender. Her blue woolly jumper was tight across her breasts and her black skirt rode up, almost reaching her thighs. She was greedily eating chips from newspaper.

'Yours are keeping warm in the range,' she told him. 'Twopenn'orth, so you can make a real pig of yourself. I've put salt and vinegar on them already – all right?'

He smiled a catfish smile, then felt his mouth water. Christ, she was a looker, he thought, noting how the chip grease was making her full lips shine. No wonder she had been able to make her living taking her clothes off and dancing like Salome in that tatty Blue Lotus Club. Good old Biff had soon put paid to that! Biff was the only one that Val never dared argue with. Biff was, Ram suspected, the only person on God's earth that Val really cared for. Him and p'raps that weed Neilson. But Neilson was dead as a dodo, thank God.

Ram took his packet of chips out of the range oven, unwrapped the newspaper, then sat opposite Val and began stuffing himself. He stopped for a second, conscious of Val watching him.

'You eat like a pig,' she told him with her own mouth full. 'But I'll forgive you.'

Chips were chips and he was starving. There was no time for mucking about. He crammed more in, enjoying the vinegary taste, feeling content. Then his stomach lurched. Val was screwing up the empty chip wrapper in a suggestive, deliberate way, and she was watching him with that certain expression in her eyes.

She was still glancing at him sideways as she poured out two mugs of tea from the pot keeping hot on the top of the range. Ram almost choked himself in his haste. He was impatient to get on now, to enjoy the delights of this glorious woman. He was going to be in luck – yes, luck, for all the sarcastic remarks Fatty Blythe usually made. His head was clearing of its usual confusion. He was alive, anxious, checking the signals one by one. The pulse beating in her throat, the rise and fall of her breasts, above all that look, almost a glare, in her eyes.

She handed him tea. He swallowed it, untasting, his eyes fixed on hers. Then she moved in. The mug went flying, but he was capable only of looking into her eyes. Then it began. Her hands were everywhere, beating, scratching, drawing blood with an urgency and determination that at first delighted him then set him on fire.

At last he gripped those dangerous hands and forced her back against the kitchen table. She was making fierce little growling noises now, deep in her throat. They tangled together, forgetting everything about the world outside.

51

Finally, when it was over, Val pushed her bleached hair out of her eyes and gave him a knowing smile.

'All right?'

He nodded, watching as she straightened her skirt, tucked in her jumper, then began powdering her nose.

'Don't say much, do you?' she asked nastily.

'No need,' he grunted and smiled, though his bruised lips hurt.

'Well, I've got plenty to say,' she snapped. 'You owe me! I want you to find that cow and do for her. Understand?'

He looked at her, perplexed. 'Dunno what you're on about, Val.'

'Yes, you do. You let her get away!' Her voice rose; she was getting really worked up. 'It was all your fault, Ram. Some bleeding fine guard you are! That cow saw it all, yes – all of it. She knows enough to have my brother hanged – hanged by his neck until he's dead.' She clenched her fists until the painted nails bit into her palms. 'Dead, d'yer hear me, you stupid sod? Dead! 'Sides, I've got me own points to score.'

'Thought you'd forgot all that lot what lived in Walker Street.'

She sprang at him, eyes blazing. 'I ain't never going to forget, d'yer hear me? Biff don't want you to neither. What's more . . .' She stopped short as the fierce wailing of an air-raid siren began. 'For God's sake get a move on!' she yelled, and shoved him hard. 'We need blankets for the Anderson. It's bleedin' monkey's out there.'

'I ain't stopping,' he told her, looking blank. 'I've got fings ter do.'

'You've gotta stay with me. D'you hear?'

'I'm on me way. Biff said as how I've gotta be with him ternight.'

As he lumbered away down Jamaica Street, Val's voice followed him like a ship's siren gone mad.

'Bastard!' she was screaming. 'I told you, you've got to stop here!'

He wanted to stop with Val. Never wanted to leave her. But like his sister, Biff needed to find out about Hannah York. Good ol' Biff, so skinny and quick, and with such sharp darting eyes. Some called Biff a living snake. Slippery he was, they said, cunning and treacherous. Ram had half-killed the last stupid sod what had flapped his lip that way. Biff knew how many beans made five, oh yes! Like tonight, for instance. What was it he'd said?

'It's like this, Ram my old son. Ma Carpenter don't know you like what I do. So she thinks you're a bit, you know, thick. We all understand you're nothing of the sort, but that don't matter. Ma thinks you've got a bootlace missing, so here's what you do. Buy her gin. Lots of it, an' 'ere's a quid to do it. Fill the old moo up, get her sozzled. Then you ask her, careful-like, about Hannah York. If anyone knows where that little bitch is, it'll be Ma Carpenter. She'll be in the Duck and Drake tonight, so I heard. Got it?'

52

'Yers,' Ram had replied. 'I know. I'm to act like I've gotta screw loose and get round old Ma Carpenter all careful-like.'

'That's it, sunshine,' Biff had said, and the way he'd grinned and slapped him on the back had made Ram feel warm inside . . .

Chapter Eight

'Hannah is young for her age, for all she's so streetwise. I think she will always be an innocent at heart,' Raven said pensively. 'Just look at her.'

'I know,' Ginnie replied, watching as Hannah's whippet-thin figure ran around with the twins and their dog. 'That little group are like one, and have been from the moment of meeting. I'll never forget how Hannah knelt down and kissed Mr Moses so enthusiastically on the nose.'

'On top of that, Lily told me that there's only one person in the world the boys would have allowed to call their dog Ol' Mo. But there's something else underneath all her fun-filled ways. In spite of her roguishness, I detect something not quite right.'

'I believe it's fear. You feel it too?' Ginnie looked at Raven straight, adding slowly, 'And there was I thinking that you were too sad to notice very much.'

'I notice a great deal.' Raven smiled. 'It's just that when Hannah's around, no one else gets a chance to say much!'

'You don't often voice opinions though, do you? Hannah and me reckon you've always been the silent type.'

'I was a trainee nurse in a very efficient teaching hospital. We had a tutor-sister rather like Mrs Madeira, only Sister was top dog and had the power to make our lives a misery. So we students had to let go – or die! We managed to get our own back, – though in subtle ways . . . '

'Then there's hope for you yet,' Ginnie teased. 'In the meantime, shall we keep a weather-eye open for Hannah?'

'But of course!' Raven's warm slow smile lit her face. 'After all, as Hannah keeps telling us, we are The Three Musketeers.'

That evening, after a bracingly good wash and brush-up, and one of Lil's fabulous meat pies made with pastry containing more potato than flour, they got themselves ready for an evening at the Rookwood Inn, where they occasionally enjoyed a game of darts. The locals had come to accept them. The males ungrudgingly, since the Land Girls had proved themselves to be good workers. Some of the women were not so sure. Still, they were mostly Mrs Madeira's sort – the kind who wouldn't be seen dead in the Rookwood anyway.

Hannah, sipping shandy at a side table with Raven and Ginnie, felt her stomach flip over. Then the man with the bald head who was standing at the bar, half-turned. She relaxed. It wasn't Ram. She could breathe again.

These days, Hannah was happy and her life full. She had her two friends, and also the twins and Ol' Mo. For Mrs Madeira, she had a hearty dislike, because the woman was unfriendly, a mischief-maker and a bitch, – and that hat! At the thought of it, her dimple showed and her eyes danced.

'Now what?' Ginnie asked.

'I was wondering if Mrs Madeira wears it in bed, that's all.'

They immediately knew what she meant. Mrs Madeira habitually wore a black straw hat, set four-square on her head in typical no-nonsense style. It was festooned with artificial grapes coloured a particularly bilious purple, and dark green vine-leaves. The hat all but glinted as maliciously as the wearer's eyes. Mrs Madeira loathed and detested the twins, and all but hated Mr Moses. This, according to Hannah, showed how warped the woman was. She blithely dismissed the fact that Moses had jumped up at the woman in joyous welcome – and had all but knocked off that hat!

Ol' Mo was new-chestnut colour, clean and shiny, with soft brown eyes. He was sweet-mannered and affectionate, patient and gentle. He adored the twins with all his heart and soul, and given the chance, followed them everywhere. According to Lily, he would sit outside the school gates for hours waiting for them.

When Chris, the dark-haired, most daring of the two, had broken his arm, Mr Moses had carried Chris's Oxo tin for him. Oxo tins were invaluable at school. They stored the coloured counters used to help learning sums. At Lindell Primary, Oxo tins and also mustard tins really came into their own. Mustard tins were just the job for holding the damp sponges necessary to clean chalk off school slates.

Ol' Mo couldn't stand mustard tins getting thrown in the bin. This, no matter whether they were from Lily's cottage or from Hawksley. He would rake through the rubbish and rescue them, then take them in his happily slobbering mouth, to the boys. Getting caught earned him a regular and thorough clumping from Mrs Madeira, usually with the head of the broom. The twins had caught her at it, and declared war from that day. It had run off Ol' Mo's back, of course, and he remained his calm, sunny self, but the lads were a different matter.

If a prank could be played, it was played on Mrs Madeira. If a duster or scrubbing brush, or anything else necessary to her chores could be mislaid, it mysteriously vanished. Stinkbombs found their way through Mrs Madeira's letter-box. And rant and rave though the woman did, there was never sight nor sound of the twins. They could and did all but melt away. And if a whisp of red tail could be seen disappearing round Duckpond Corner, who would listen to tales that held no proof? Certainly not Mrs Kitt, proprietor's wife of Kitts General Store.

Mrs Kitt, a warm and motherly long-term member of the Women's Institute, had often listened stoically to Mrs Madeira's tirades. Her favourite subject was dogs in general – the Hawksley daily always adding that her husband, Mr Madeira a farmworker, fully agreed with her. He, it seemed, felt that all dogs, sheep-chasers, flea-ridden, dirty and destructive creatures, should be shot on sight, and that puppies should be drowned at birth.

Mrs Kitt always continued calmly weighing up and bagging Mrs Madeira's order. She knew, as her customer knew, that there were usually four to six small russet beauties waddling about in the kitchen. The fact that Chris and Chook, habitual visitors, were often found sprawling on the floor playing with Brandy's new family, merely meant the continuation of the war.

Hannah, having seen Ol' Mo receive a spiteful bang on the nose from Mrs Madeira's shoe, found herself heartily disliking the woman.

Because of all things Mrs Madeira seemed to love her hat best, it became the one target on the mind of the twins. The woman herself was formidable, and she was never seen without her hat. She scrubbed her doorstep with it planted firmly on her head, worked through the day at Hawksley under its weight of grapes and leaves, wore it at village hall meetings of all kinds, and went to church in it, and now the twins and Hannah alike wondered whether she went to bed in it.

Chris and Chook wanted to kill that hat stone dead . . .

Just then a newcomer, an airman, entered the Rookwood and strode towards the bar.

'He looks nice,' Ginnie observed.

'Not as handsome as mine,' Hannah replied, thinking of the man who had dropped on the roof. 'My one was fair and had a sort of devil-may-care look about him. He had blue eyes that—'

'Oh, *do* shut up!' Ginnie broke in without malice. 'This one's a dish.'

They all watched as the airman, who seemed to know Mr Endercot, Hawksley Estate Manager and pigeon-breeder, joined him at the bar and accepted a pint. They stood together, drinking companionably, but Hannah sensed the glance the young man flicked their way.

Hannah could tell by his uniform and badges that he was an Air Gunner. He stood about five feet eight inches tall. He was deep in the chest and broad at the shoulders – good-looking in a dark-haired, dark-eyed way. When he smiled, which he seemed to do often, he flashed white even teeth. He was, she had to admit to herself, a real corker.

The Rookwood was quiet, except for the buzz of conversation, and so it was easy to listen in. Hannah learned that until a recent 'prang', the young man spent up to twelve hours at a time in the turret of a bomber. This mostly over Germany, either going or coming from Danzig.

Hannah watched him swallow two pints of beer, then carry the third refill with him, and begin to beat everyone at snooker. Every so often he would continue his conversation with Mr Endercot, who had been the first to be vanquished at the game, but who stayed to watch.

With one accord, the girls rose from the table to watch the game too. Also to eavesdrop. For the first time ever, they learned that their boss's Christian name was Ellery; the young airman was Richard. Surprisingly, at this stage, the conversation was mainly about pigeons. Apparently, a chap named Titch, whom both men knew, had been particularly fond of pigeons. Titch had been burned in the recent prang.

'You'd be surprised how many go up,' the airman said to Mr Endercot. 'I suppose you know Manny Gee from Norseby?'

'I do at that.' Mr Endercot nodded grimly, and held a lighter to the bowl of his cherrywood pipe. He puffed once or twice before adding bitterly, 'He beat me in thirty-nine. He's got a champion he calls Sandy. Bloody ugly thing it is. It looks scruffy and it's small – small but fast. Too fast for my Macfadden, dammit.'

Hannah opened her eyes wide and grinned at Ginnie and Raven. 'Macfadden?' she whispered, so that only they might hear. 'Macfadden, a pigeon? Macfadden owned by an Ellery? Oh my Gawd!'

During the following snippets of conversation, the girls learned a great deal. That pigeons from local lofts were delivered by van, strung up in a hamper, all the time cooing away happily enough while they were placed in bombers. They were indifferent to speed, or shrapnel, and released only by day when stationary, or sometimes when at sea. And by official order, accompanying the airman during 'bale out' if the machine was shot down.

'Marvellous, eh?' Hannah said, once all three girls had drifted back to their table. 'Stop going all goggle-eyed, Ginnie. You seem to be smitten. I prefer the idea of your lovely Aiden.'

'Don't be silly. What's so marvellous?'

'That common little things that fly two-a-penny round Piccadilly and practically everywhere else, are actually important. I mean, ones that are owned and trained by blokes like old Ellery! Pigeons part and parcel of the war effort – strange, isn't it! If pigeons are tickety-boo, there's hopes for me yet.'

Ginnie did not reply. She was too busy watching the airman. It was Raven who replied.

'You are very important indeed, Hannah. And yes, it is amazing *and* curious, modern manmade machines for air warfare being coupled with natural things like birds. I think Francis would have—'

'I know – written a poem about it,' Hannah said and gave Raven a huge twinkly smile. She turned to look at the table again. 'There! Mr Magic Airman's done it again. Good player, isn't he? Corks! He's coming over.'

The RAF chap, smiling his wide white-toothed smile, was striding towards them, his eyes fixed on Ginnie. He was taken with her, and it showed. She was taken with him; that showed too.

'Hello,' he said, 'I'm Richard Neville and you're the girls from Hawksley, I presume?'

'Yes,' Ginnie replied, in her usual polite but no-frills way.

'Good show,' Richard said, then turned to smile again at Hannah. 'And you must be the young lady I'm looking for.'

Hannah's brows rose high and her finger pointed against her heart. 'Me?'

'You're small – like a doll, he said – you're pretty and have brown curly hair, so yes, you.'

Hannah's grin flashed out. 'Are you something to do with the airman who sprayed himself all over our roof? I could tell at a glance that he'd have the gift of the gab. Am I right?'

'Hit the nail on the head.'

'No. He hit Hawksley,' she chuckled. 'Why are you looking for me?.'

'Matt asked me to. Sergeant Air Gunner Matt Sheridan, actually. He is fed up to the teeth and badly needing a visitor. Preferably you.'

'Why me?'

'Why do you think? All right, I'll tell you. Because apart from bods like me, he has no one else.'

'No girlfriend – no family?'

'He's an ex-Barnardo's boy. And to my knowledge, there has never been someone to take his fancy like you. So?'

'I'll be happy to go and visit him,' Hannah said quickly, 'And so will Raven. Ginnie here goes home weekends, but—'

'I don't need to go home,' Ginnie cut in easily and gave Hannah a warning look.

'Than that's settled,' Hannah told Richard in a businesslike way. 'So it's our turn to pay him a flying visit. All right?'

'Good show! He's at Air Base Hospital. You can't miss it. He'll be waiting for you with both thumbs up.'

Mr Endercot was beckoning. Richard excused himself saying, 'I'll be back later,' and went to join the Estate Manager at the bar. The girls returned to the table and their glasses of shandy and listened to the masculine conversations around them.

There was no more talk of pigeons. It was all about THE MATCH – the glorious, fantastic happening that had occurred during the previous summer. The girls had heard it all before, and smiled behind their hands because the triumph grew with every telling. Lindell had won! And every man jack was determined to keep the delirious memory alive. It had happened well before the girls' arrival, but they had now heard it all, stroke for stroke, wicket for wicket, bowl for bowl, many times. It was all the more enjoyable because Lindell football team was non-existent since most of the active lads had been called up. But old Henry had taken a stand, and Cutts and Bingley, and what about good old Cyril? Who'd have thought Stitson could notch up forty runs before getting LBW'd . . .?

Now truly animated conversation swirled round them. Triumphant man talk. War or no war, nothing really mattered, it seemed, except the memory of that inspired cricket match, the contest between arch enemies Lindell Village and Little Norseby.

The boasting continued as everything else paled into insignificance. Preparations for flower arranging, the WI Sale of Work, the Ladies Knitting for Soldiers, prize-giving – even that for the little darlings at schools – early harvesting, late hay, baling, milk yields, flower, fruit and veg shows, anything and everything else that normally held full attention was, for the moment pushed to one side. Past glory was uppermost. It was The Match. For this one blazingly important annual event, the girls had been given to understand, absolutely every-one who could, downed tools to take part.

No one could remember how the rivalry proper had begun. It had all occurred in the mists of time. But Little Norseby were their adver-saries for every county competition, every rose, marrow, football match, darts game, jam, every single thing one could think of. It didn't matter if one took second or third or fourth prize, all highly com-mended . . . just so long as the first never went to Little Norseby! Over and above literally everything, there was the cricket. And after four years in the wilderness, with their best team members called up, Lin-dell had beat their enemies at cricket, and beat them well.

Just then Mr Briggs the shepherd looked over the rim of his pint and grinned, saying loud enough for all to hear, 'And it would have made things more perfect if you girls could have been here. Wearing your uniforms, all smart like. They ain't got no Land Girls at Norseby.'

'Nor young ladies as pretty,' round and red-faced Mr Kitt put in.

'Then let's hope we'll still be here next year,' Hannah, beamed. 'We're with Lindell all the way. And for jolly old Lindell I'll even wave my khaki passion-killers on high. They'll be enough to make the Little Norseby team drop stone dead.'

Everyone laughed and raised their glasses at that. The WLA had finally and fully arrived.

Shortly afterwards the conversation turned to the next great event – the flower arranging. There was keen competition among the ladies, and the WI used this particular time, too, to exhibit preserves of all kinds, cookery, knitting and needlecraft. Funds raised during this event went towards monies necessary for the upkeep of the village hall.

Now the men spoke of flowers grown to perfection, like old Jefferson's prize dahlias, Dene's chrysanthemums, Dredge's fancy potted ferns – or flowers and plants with unique foreign names that Hannah had never heard of before. She listened avidly, her heart and soul filled with delight. This was living to the full, she thought. This was the life!

She looked around at the welcoming fire, the cosy settles, scrubbed tables, Windsor chairs and benches. There were faded sepia photographs on the walls and slim ancient bricks showing here and there through the plaster. The Rookwood had the date 1775 carved above its lintel, and no doubt an inn existed on the spot long before that. Horse-brasses abounded, dark oaken beams added character, and pewter gleamed.

The Rookwood was a good old country pub, a focal point, a kind of club with its darts team, skittles, dominoes, shove ha'penny and – set apart in a place of its own – the snooker table. This typical country inn was as different as Walker Street's Duck and Drake as green cheese from the moon. Here she, Hannah, was safe and secure and utterly content. She would never come face to face with –

The old familiar palpitations in Hannah's stomach began again. She drew in a deep breath, looked at Ginnie and Raven and felt a surge of relief that she was not alone. That she had two such marvellous friends.

But walking back along the shadowy lane between them, hearing the wind soughing eerily among the branches and sounding like a lost soul made her skin crawl. When a cow behind the adjacent hedge suddenly lunged forward, and gave a plaintive moo, her heart leapt into her throat again. She instinctively grabbed hold of each of her companions. Ginnie and Raven, sensing it was necessary, each put an arm protectively round Hannah's waist.

Not a word was said . . .

*

Land Girls were allowed one and a half days off per week. The following weekend Ginnie decided to go home to Essex in spite of enemy action. The wireless let it be known that the bombing was still intense, the devastation of fire and high explosive persisting. But then every morning's news was of similar damage to Germany. The regular droning up above bore this out. Matching Airfield was clearly doing more than its share.

Hannah bit her lip, remembering how depleted the home-coming formations seemed at times. Then in spite of trying not to, she heard again the sepulchral groans of the old man who had lived in number 30 Walker Street, and she also wondered about his dog. She could smell the dry cindery smell of the remains of her room, feel soot choking her breathing, plaster dust hurting her eyes and clogging up her mouth. And she remembered with horror the mess the Krauts had made of the Duck and Drake – but before one reached that, there was the fetid smell of the Alley, and those three macabre figures dragging along the rag-doll figure of Frank . . . She shuddered and blinked the memories away.

'I think I'll stay here as usual,' she told her two friends. 'I like walking; I've covered miles. I often come across the twins and also Lenny, the Madeira boy. Then there's Mrs Kitt who'll always pass the time of day, and Mrs Endercot. There's so much to do, so many to see.'

'And places to go,' Raven said. 'I'm off to the Drew Stables, to see if I can fix up a ride or two. I used to be on horseback a great deal before I became a trainee nurse.' A thought struck her. 'Hannah, why don't you come along too? My treat, no matter what they charge.'

Hannah pulled a face. 'I'll come and watch, but get up on one of those great brutes? No, ta! Still, I promise you I'll go and see how good you are. I've found a perfect spot, an old gate that overlooks the open space. Oh, and watch it! Old Drew's a maniac about his private property – the twins' words, not mine. No trespassers allowed, so you'd best wave lots of pound notes in his face as you approach.'

'I will.' Raven's voice had a little lilt in it these days, especially when she was talking to Hannah. 'Who knows? I might meet your favourite person there. He rides on his horse Pegasus whenever he gets the chance. She's white and quite—'

'Then I hope Pegasus throws the old devil,' Hannah replied without malice, and chuckled. 'Better watch out for him, Raven. James St John looks the sort who would quite like having his horse trample folk to death.'

'Then I shall fly like the wind,' Raven promised.

Chapter Nine

Matt lay in the hospital bed, feeling like a fraud. He felt fine now, tickety-boo, but the Medic had said another few days, so patience had to be the name of the game. He couldn't wait to meet Hannah – yes, that was her name. His lips twitched and he looked down at the letters he had received.

Hannah had written to say that she would be along to see him very soon, that it was a case of trying to get away. Just about everything was going on. The Lindell WI Show, which involved just about everything from cookery, embroidery, knitting, wines and preserves as well as flower arranging, would be on within a week. Could he just imagine the scale of it all?

It was very important that someone named Lily beat a Mrs Madeira in the baking section, else die in the attempt. Lily therefore had to have lots of free time to concentrate. That being the case, she, Hannah, had been roped in as the minder of two fantastic boys – twins called Chris and Chook, who had a gorgeous dog known as Mr Moses. Boys and dog managed to get into mischief most of the time.

The first letter had gone on to say that she would have moved heaven and earth to get there, but his Air Force mate Richard had mentioned that a nurse named Madeline had now practically taken over all of Matt's free time. So, since he was not lonely any more, she would write to him lots and pay him a visit as soon as she could.

Matt grinned wryly. He was still going to punch Richard's nose for being a blabbermouth. Madeline was a cutesie, but that was all.

True to her promise, Hannah had written more. A letter a day, in fact. Her large writing sprawled across the pages in a lively way, full of news, of questions, and remarks about grey pigeons being worth their weight in gold. And shining over all, her sense of fun. Even admitting to calling her boss Old Celery behind his back, and innocently asking the chap about his salad days. She spoke of her two close friends,

Ginnie and Raven, and of the scrapes the twins managed to get themselves in.

For the first time in his life Matt had enjoyed writing back.

Now he was tucked in bed for afternoon rest and deciding whether to write another letter or not. He didn't want to push it. Something told him that young Hannah York was a bit like a cheeky bird herself, a robin happy to be daring, but ready to fly at even the most tentative advance.

He sighed and looked around. At cream walls, a pristine white sink, bedside cabinet with water jug, and a kidney-shaped dish ready for fresh swabs. He was in a side room, the main wards being kept for those in a bad way. Poor devils. The war over and done with for most of them, as in some cases was life itself.

He felt a mood swing, of gut-wrenching depression. In his mind's eye he kept seeing what was left of poor old Titch's face. He rang for a nurse, asked for and was given a tablet to help him sleep. When she whisked off, all starched linen and sensible shoes, he closed his eyes.

Later he awoke. He thought he heard noises, someone warning, 'Shush! Be quiet!' followed by stifled boyish laughter.

Hannah came in then. With her, two boys who would have been identical had they had the same coloured hair. They came to a stop by his bed and gazed at him with awe.

'Hello,' Hannah said, and smiled into Matt's eyes. 'You're looking better than you were when last we met.'

'Thank you,' he replied and grinned. 'It's not often I try to break through people's roofs.'

'And it's even worse when the roof wins,' she told him mournfully. 'Still, you're here to tell the tale and I hope you'll be out of hospital soon. Where do you go home to? I mean, when they grant you leave?'

'The East End,' he informed her. 'I have digs in a nice woman's house. Mrs Gibson's her name.' He smiled ruefully. 'She mothers me.'

'Oh!' She looked dismayed. 'You won't go back there, surely?'

'Because of the Blitz? It can't be much worse than what we come across upstairs. The Luftwaffe are no laggards, you know.'

'It will feel worse in the city,' she told him, 'because when you're in shelters or the Underground you are so helpless. Just sitting there, waiting. I . . . I mean, you can't fight back!' She laughed in a self-deprecating manner. 'Blow me, this is a fine way to talk to a patient. Let's forget the war. You got my letters, I see?'

'Yes. Thank you. They saved my life. I read them over and over on the black days.' His rakish grin blazed out then. 'Did your friend Lily win?'

'Two firsts and a third, and a Special Award of Excellence for her

63

Mock Almond Paste.' Hannah enthusiastically warmed to her theme. 'She makes it with dried potato powder and dried egg, you know, and—' She halted, aware of the mirth in his eyes. 'Oh well,' she chuckled with him, 'let's just say that our Lily won the day. Here, Matt, I must say that—'

She was stopped in mid-flow as Mr Moses padded determinedly into the room. Sleek and friendly his tongue hanging out and his luxuriant tail wagging, Ol' Mo took one look at Matt and it was love at first sight. To show his devotion he put his large paws on the bed and flicked Matt lovingly round the ear with his tongue.

Matt jerked away from this unexpected affection and his leg, plus its magnificent plaster, was exposed. The twins looked at it in wide-eyed fascination.

'Gosh!' Chris exclaimed – Matt knew it was Chris because he had brown hair. 'Can I touch it?'

'If you like, old boy,' Matt said, and Chris tentatively touched the plaster.

'It's hard, isn't it? Can you feel that?' Chris beat a lively tattoo on the plaster with his fists.

'What happens if they can't get it off?' Chook asked – Matt knew it was Chook because he had fair hair. 'Will they use hammer and chisel, or go at it like Mr Stitson does when he's fixing horseshoes?'

'I don't know exactly,' Matt replied, playing along.

'Don't be silly, boys,' Hannah said. 'They'll probably hold Mr Sheridan upside down and saw right through it.'

The twins enjoyed this joke so much they collapsed on the bed and laughed with boyish fervour. Matt, loving every minute, but very aware that boys and dogs were not necessarily welcomed by Matron, let alone Sister who was an ogre if there ever was one, tried to quieten them.

'Okay chaps,' he began crisply. 'It's time we—'

At that point, Mr Moses, cocked his head on one side, wagged his tail even more frantically, and slurped all over Matt's ear and face with joyous abandon. Matt began weaving and ducking, protesting loudly but laughing like mad. It was joyous pandemonium until Sister appeared – when even Ol' Mo froze. Without further ado, Hannah, twins and dog were shown the door.

They waited inside the gates for the return of Vincent who had given them a lift. Vincent's very ancient mother lived in the area, and Lil had sent her six of her light and airy tea-cakes. Mr Moses should have stayed with Vincent, but had clearly made a rapid exit through the van window.

Boys and dog were unrepentant. As for Hannah, scuffing her toes along the gravelled path, she was thinking of Matt Sheridan. How his eyes sparkled when he laughed, in that devil-may-care manner. And how brave he was! He had been shot out of the sky. His plane had gone up in flames. Yet even in Hawksley, in terrible pain – even then he had tried to smile. Oh yes, that had shown courage, but not half so much as he'd used on his handling of Sister back there. However, the woman had had her way, even though he had called her Sweetness.

'Cow!' Hannah thought aloud. 'She's worse than old Ma Carpenter of Sedgewick Street.'

'She's even worse than Mrs Madeira,' Chris said pithily.

'Her mouth curled up all rotten when she saw Mo.' Chook's tone was hot with indignation. 'Mean thing. She's as bad as Dragon Drawers.'

'I shouldn't have sneaked you two in,' Hannah told them, 'but I'm glad I did. You certainly put a smile on his face, so perhaps I wasn't so wicked after all. Still, boys are against the rules, and Ol' Mo turning up like that just about put the lid on things.'

'Fancy having someone like her look after you when you're sick!' Chris exploded.

'She's enough to make anyone want to puke up,' Chook agreed. 'Just imagine being given spinach by someone like her. All the spew'd be green and slimy and—'

'Stop it!' Hannah remonstrated. 'Keep on like that and I'll be ill. But I agree with you. That woman should have been more understanding. After all, Matt's a hero! He very nearly died up there. When I think of all the mean people who are not only surviving but making money out of this war . . .'

A vision of the last time she had seen Biff Marner and his clique swept into her mind again. She bit her lip, then added, 'Still, we'll forget all about the spivs and drones and Black Marketeers, and just think of our hero, eh?'

'My dad ought to see him,' Chris put in fiercely. 'Then he might not be so down in the dumps about being in Balloon Command. Poor old Matt's leg! And those scars on his arm and chest – and I know his back's been bad. Here, I hope the hair grows again on the back of his head.'

''Course it will,' Chook replied stoutly. 'He said it was growing already.'

'If Dad copped a leg like that,' Chris was still thinking of the plastered limb, 'he might never be able to bat against Norseby again. Besides, I like barrage balloons.'

'So do I,' his brother agreed. 'They do a jolly good job, tangling up

65

the hostiles and stopping them from diving down with their bombs. Here, I don't half like old Matt.'

'Me too.' Their faces looked enquiringly up at Hannah. 'Do you like him?'

'Yes,' Hannah said. 'I do.'

Vincent appeared then and they all jumped into the van. 'Well,' Vincent asked them. 'How was the lad?'

'Getting better,' Hannah told him. 'It was good of you to wangle us time off to visit him. I didn't think anyone would dare to ask James St John any favours.' She laughed, adding, 'Though we got short shrift from Sister. She made us all buzz off because of Moses.'

'Sorry about that – he was too quick for me. Damned fool could have broken his legs, I was going a fair old pace. When I saw he was fine I pressed on, time being short. Still is, so I'll drop you off at the house then take this little lot of scamps straight to the village.' Vincent gave his quiet, grey smile. 'And as for Mr St John, he's not so bad. Had a rough deal, that's all. Now, tell me more about the airman.'

'He'll get convalescent leave and then it will be back to active duty, I'm afraid.' A thought struck Hannah. 'Vincent, Matt lives in digs in the East End and we all know what's happening there! Do you think we could find somewhere in Lindell for him to stay?' She coloured, hastily adding, 'If he were agreeable, of course. I mean, the twins have taken to him, and even Ol' Mo, so . . .'

'If that's what he wants,' Vincent told her calmly, 'It can be arranged.'

Hannah sat beside him feeling happy and excited, knowing that she wouldn't half mind seeing Matt again.

When Raven and Ginnie returned from the field and had washed and brushed up, they sat together in the sitting room that had been set aside for them. They were listening to Carol Gibbons and his Orpheans playing from the Savoy Hotel. The music was beautiful, and violins added a kind of lushness to the song about a nightingale singing in Berkeley Square.

'Do tell us how it went,' Ginnie said. 'And stop looking so soppy.'

'I've asked Vincent to—'

The sound of Lily's voice cut in. 'Come and get it, girls.'

They headed for the kitchen. One would never waste a second before sitting down to one of Lily's meals.

The parsley pudding was a dream. It was a special recipe approved of by Marguerite Patten who worked for the Ministry of Food. The Ministry controlled the distribution of victuals and was responsible for giving out information on rationing. The recipes and Food Facts leaflets enabled people to make the best use of the provisions available,

66

and augment them with *un*rationed nutriments. These included potatoes, oatmeal and seasonable vegetables. But as far as Lily was concerned, Marguerite Patten was the goddess of them all. She quite outshone the Minister of Food, Lord Woolton. This, even though his recipe called Woolton Pie was a great favourite with the twins.

After the meal, Ginnie decided to go to the Rookwood, Raven to the bedroom to read through her husband's poems, and Hannah stayed in their sitting room to listen to the wireless. This because her favourites, Bebe Daniels and Ben Lyon were on. Hannah loved the wireless and adored the Crazy Gang, laughing uproariously at all the jokes.

Later she listened avidly for Big Ben and the announcer saying, 'This is the BBC Home Service, and here is the News.' Clearly the wrecking of London was continuing and she decided that she would do and say everything she could to keep Matt Sheridan safely in Lindell. The man had become a friend.

Next morning, before they set off for the fields, Mr Endercot called to tell them where they were to work. He seemed more disposed to talk than usual and accepted Lily's offer of a cup of tea. They sat round the kitchen table, listening obediently.

'Mr St John mentioned that it might be interesting for you to learn a little about beet,' he told them. 'He is determined to be part and parcel of the process of producing the sugar ration for the entire nation – that's why he had us plant so many acres. From now on it will be your job to top, tail and cut the beet.'

'I thought we got our pathetic ration from sugar cane,' Hannah remarked, adding honestly, 'when I thought about it – which was about once. And that was only when this wireless gave out about U-Boats sinking so many of the ships in our food convoys. Besides, sugar's hardly life and death!' She looked ready to add a few more comments, but fell silent when Ginnie gave her one of those looks.

'*Beta vulgaris* is of the same family as beetroot, and it was well-known even in Roman times,' Mr Endercot said as pompously as any schoolteacher. 'A German chemist proved the plant to be capable of producing sugar as far back as 1747.'

'Well, I never!' Hannah replied, tongue in cheek. 'But why are you telling us all this?'

'To give your work all the more significance,' Mr Endercot told her, adding, 'not my idea at all. It's Mr St John's special interest, and he likes to share his enthusiasm. For your information, he would have preferred to be in uniform and on active service – but the Powers that Be considered he was more use at home. So sugar beet's his war effort. All right?'

'Sorry,' Hannah replied, suitably chastened.

'Napoleon had two hundred and thirteen sugar-beet factories in operation by 1816.' Ellery was warming to his theme. 'But the fall in the price of cane led to most of the factories going out of business. But now, here in Britain, the Government reckons the beet will eventually make us independent of imports which are so imperilled by the war at sea. Thankfully our British Sugar Corporation's been going since 1934. So, ladies, your contribution to the war effort is very important indeed.'

'That's nice,' Ginnie told him, 'but since we've been hoeing winter cabbage and crops like that I don't see . . .'

'The Felsted factory has been open since September and going at it day and night. We cannot deliver our crop when we like. The whole operation is carefully planned and controlled. The beet is collected from all over, by a strict timetable, so when harvested it must go into a clamp to await its turn for collection. Some of our acreage is not to be expected by them until the middle of January. Mr St John decided on a rotation scheme for Hawksley. All experimental at this stage of course, but that is nothing to do with us. We,' he darted a swift but friendly look at Hannah, 'we merely have to do what is asked of us.'

'So we wait until January to . . .'

'No. Some is ready and we get cracking now, for our first crop.'

'I think Mr St John has the right idea.' Raven spoke for the first time. 'I have found all of this immensely interesting, Mr Endercot. I find it hard to credit that such a mundane-looking plant can be so important.' She looked down at the table, adding deprecatingly, 'But then we are not born and bred country people.'

'And like a breath of fresh air because of it,' Mr Endercot told her. 'And you're right about the importance of it all. It's been estimated that the average yield of an acre of sugar beet will provide enough sugar for a hundred and twenty people to have half a pound each for a year. And the tops can be useful too. An acre of beet tops will feed a hundred sheep for a week. And the dried pulp, which is returned from the factory, has been shown to equal oats in feeding value. So you see, young ladies, the work you are about to do, and will continue to do from now on until January, is very worthwhile indeed.'

'Mr Endercot,' Hannah said, looking wide-eyed and quite serious, 'Ellery! Thank you for telling us all of this. It makes me feel – so special. Almost as special as – as one of your pigeons!'

She pretended not to hear the choking noise Ginnie made.

'Young 'un,' Ellery told her easily, eyes twinkling. 'It strikes me that you're a damned sight more important than one of them. Even more so than old Macfadden, and my Eloise reckons that that bird's the only thing she knows that can bring a gleam into my eye.'

'That's it!' Ginnie laughed. 'Mr Endercot, you have just made Hannah your friend for life.'

'Yes,' Raven said, 'and I must tell you that Hannah has become intrigued by, and admires pigeons very highly these days.'

'As I do. And –' his aquiline features softened as he looked at each of them in turn '– Ellery's fine. Just fine.' He stood up. 'Ladies?'

They followed him out of the house and waited until he had lit his cherrywood pipe. He was their boss and their mate, and Mr St John had been right. Working in the beet-fields held a new meaning. They now understood the wider significance of what they were doing.

'Gawd, Ellery,' Hannah said, 'if you keep on like this I'll begin to actually honour pigeons and just *adore* all that beet . . .'

She ducked as Ginnie took a playful swipe at her.

Chapter Ten

'Bloody things!' Hannah exploded. She swung the bunches of beet, one in each hand, and fiercely banged them together. Earth flew away and then the cleaned-off beets were 'topped' by sharp field knives. The green leaves dropped, to be gathered later for fodder, the shorn beet making central piles between the rows.

'Now what's up?' Ginnie asked, brushing red hair away from her face with the back of her hand. 'As if we didn't know!'

'All I wanted was some time off to help make things nice for Matt.' Hannah's voice showed that she was more than het-up. 'After all, a welcome for a hero is not such a bad thing, is it?'

'Mrs Endercot has everything ready and well under control.'

'I know, but . . .'

'You can't wait to see him again? I thought you were off all men because of that chap in the menswear shop?'

'I am – in that sort of way. It's just that I like him as a mate and . . . Oh, Christ!' Hannah dropped the beet-knife, and raised her eyes heavenwards before saying forcibly, 'Shit!'

'What is it?' Raven asked, holding twin bunches of beet mid-air.

'I've bloody well sliced a lump out of my knuckle.'

'Let's see,' Ginnie said quickly. 'Come on.'

'No.' Hannah defiantly held her blood-covered hand against her chest. 'It's nothing – and I know what you are!'

'What Dr Dene is, don't you mean? Gosh, Hannah, you're bleeding all over the place. Let me look.'

'No!' Hannah hastily held her hand behind her back.

At that point Raven walked up, taking off the chiffon scarf she wore turban-wise to keep her hair out of the way while at work.

'Even from here,' she said calmly, 'I can tell that you need to hold your hand up. Let me put a sling round your neck. You'll be more comfortable.' As she spoke, she expertly tied the scarf round Hannah's neck. 'Won't you let me look – no? Very well, the doctor is called for. I'll come with you.'

'To hold my good hand?' Hannah laughed, eyes bright with unshed tears, but she was hurting and it showed. Even so she was determined not to give in. 'Thanks Raven, but no! I'm no milksop. I can manage by myself, and tetanus injections are nothing to me. I've already had more than my share. Almost every week at Colchester.'

'Don't exaggerate,' Ginnie said crisply. 'It's a bad cut, by the way you're streaming. Sorry, dear. You're on your way.'

'But . . .'

'And Raven will go with you, just in case you faint or do something stupid. I'll carry on here.'

'It's not . . .'

'No more arguing. I mean it!'

When Mr Endercot was not around, Ginnie was in charge, seeing how she was the only one who had gone through an initial WLA training course.

'So-called friend?' Hannah said tightly, eyes blazing. 'Ha! You're nothing but a bossy boots drunk with power.'

'Shut up. Scat!'

Hannah allowed herself to be walked off the field. Raven supported her, and although she would die before admit it, Hannah was feeling sick. Being angry, she had taken an almighty swipe at the beet, missed, and cut deeply into the knuckle of her first finger on the left hand.

'Hold on to me properly,' Raven told her. 'And just concentrate on how nice it is that Matt is here in the village and all but well again.'

'Well enough to be sent back up there in the sky,' Hannah replied and promptly burst into tears. 'Our airmen are taking a pasting. They're dying like flies and—'

'We all die when our number comes up. Try to think of it in that way.'

'I don't want to, and I never will,' Hannah snapped, upset and aflame with temper. 'If you must be such a clever-dick, you think about it. *You*, not me!' Then, seeing the shadow of grief cross Raven's face, Hannah quickly added, 'I'm sorry. I really am. Bloody hell, I'll always be a blabbermouth.' She laughed shakily. 'And I've just done it again.'

'What exactly?'

'Said something stupid and sworn like a trooper. Believe it or not. Raven, I'd give my eye-teeth to talk like you and not cuss all the time.'

'Then you wouldn't be you, Hannah. You would be a copy of me.'

'Which wouldn't be half-bad.'

Hannah closed her eyes and stumbled, but Raven held her secure.

'All right?'

'Oh Gawd,' Hannah admitted. 'My finger's throbbing like old Madeira's threshing machine.' She tried to smile, but it was a wobbly effort. 'And he's a sod if ever there was one. Just like his old woman, in fact.' She carried on gamely, ''Ere, talking about threshing, what about barley? I was standing by the containing sack and the chaff was going just about everywhere. It's prickly rotten stuff, isn't it? And when I say that barley yales get in every nook and cranny, I mean it. Know something?'

'Aren't you out of breath yet?' Raven queried kindly. 'You don't have to be brave, you know, Hannah, and try to joke and laugh as though nothing has happened. It's all right!'

'It hurts!'

'Then let's save our strength and just concentrate on getting to Dr Dene as quickly as we can.'

'Thanks,' Hannah choked and kept quiet from then on, her over-riding concern being not to vomit and show herself up even more.

In a heavy sort of way she was wondering what Raven was really thinking. She was probably deciding that number three of The Musketeers was the cry-baby of the year. No – Raven would never be like that. Nice, gentle Raven who was respected by everyone. Who was calm, and a lady at all times. Who, on the very rare occasions that she and that woman had met, Raven had remained gentle and coolly polite even to Mrs St John.

Hannah looked up at Raven's profile and wished that she had cut out her tongue before saying that it should be Raven who must be calm about dying. Death was one subject her friend knew all about. Losing Francis had just about broken her heart – and so soon after the demise of her mum and dad. Death? Raven carried the knowledge of it with her all of the time. Poor old Raven. Her loss had been so tragic, like having part of her soul removed.

On the other hand, she – Hannah – had experienced a different kind of emotion. She had witnessed a murder most foul. The demise of Frank had held horror for her, and terror, and a stomach-churning nausea. Even worse, there had been no grief as such, rather a dreadful distaste.

Hannah cast a swift look at her friend's face. Raven had gone awfully quiet. Was she remembering her husband and hating mouthy Hannah York who spoke a load of codswallop most of the time? She mustn't hate me, Hannah thought. I like her and I want her to like me. Oh bloody hell, when ever will I learn to hold my tongue?

It was amazing, Raven thought, how having friends put a different aspect on things. She no longer felt apart from the world. The grief was as real, but the actual act of living did not seem so pointless and grey. When had her mood begun to change? Really alter insofar as she was able to come to terms with things? She suspected it was when she met up with Hannah. The other girl had clearly always had a fight on her hands to survive, yes even from a very early age. Brave, bouncy Hannah was always ready either to do battle, or laugh uproariously at a joke. Hannah who, in spite of all the brave show she put on, was deep-down afraid. She needed them as much as they, in their different ways, needed her. Yes, even Ginnie.

Ginnie was comfortable with them. She maintained her regulated days with the calm assurance of a smoothly running stream. Ginnie, who spread level-headed confidence round her like a comforting cloud. Ginnie, who was as certain of the future as she was that night followed day . . . until she had looked into Richard Neville's sparkling dark eyes. These days, practical Miss Virginia Betts was becoming just a teensy bit unsettled. Aiden's photograph was now carefully placed in her cabinet drawer . . . and, amazingly, she had asked each of her friends in turn what they thought.

Raven remembered how she herself had hesitated to voice an opinion. It had been Hannah who, as always, had not been afraid to jump in.

'It's nothing to do with anyone else, Ginn. It's you that's got to live with it all. But from where I'm standing, I'd say that your Aiden's far away in India. That means he's got to cope with things over there. But Richard's here . . . and with a job like his, I'd say you had best make the most of that fact!'

How wise that was. How glorious had been Ginnie's smile. Yes, Raven thought, I think my life began to turn round for the better when I met Hannah and Ginnie . . . and I became the third member of Hannah's Musketeers. How strange, that the present can take over, and things past assume a distance, yet even so, stay so near. How long ago, actually, in days, hours, minutes, was mine and Francis's tragedy?

She took in a deep shuddering breath and began concentrating, documenting events. Her mind flicked back to two years ago – centuries ago. The grief and horror were still there, along with the aching loneliness, but the fine steel of Francis's words were as strong as ever.

'You are fortunate, darling.' he had told her. 'You have the opportunity to survive. Don't abuse that opportunity. Don't let all of this weigh you down. Recognise Life for the gift and the challenge that it is.'

Her beloved parents had certainly missed out on that one, she grieved, and felt her stomach plunge down like a lift out of control. Emotion left her shaken, beyond tears.

There had been a terrible storm that had held all the ferocity of winter depths. On that night Dr David Caine and his wife-nurse Elizabeth, died. Their daughter, Raven, a trainee nurse, received serious injuries. Previously they had all been attending a coming-of-age party held for the son of a family friend. It had still been going full swing when the doctor received an emergency call to a maternity case that had been causing some concern. As a matter of course his wife accompanied him. Raven had elected to go along too.

The car, of necessity, had been travelling at speed along a lane when lightning struck. A giant oak seemed to scream and fall very, very slowly. They had stood no chance. Her parents had been killed instantly. Raven herself had woken up a long time later in a London hospital where there were the necessary specialists.

Against all the odds she came through. Shocked, bereaved, she had been sitting listlessly in the bed when Francis Gray approached her.

'Hello,' he had said. 'We mustn't waste time, must we, Raven Caine? You and I are destined to be great friends.'

'I . . . I'm sorry?'

'Oh yes, we'll get on very well, you and I. Has anyone told you how lovely you are?'

'With part of my head shaved and all these bandages' She had smiled sadly. 'I rather think that you are overdoing the Good Samaritan thing.' Then she had added quietly, 'I know that you are trying to be kind, but I really would prefer you to go away.'

'No,' he told her, his grey eyes twinkling at her large hurt brown ones. 'We all know of the terrible grief you are feeling. It must be ghastly to be left alone in the world, and we're all at one with you. But . . . I do rather want to stay, you know. I badly need a friend, and I have chosen you.'

There had been something in his voice that had pulled her up short. She had looked at him then, really looked. He was not very tall; his face was pale but attractive. He had long slim hands and a studious air. She liked him.

'Tell me about your name,' he said. 'I will never look at that sort of bird in the same way again. I thought ravens rather predatory things with their long beaks and stubby tails. You are nothing like that.'

'When I was born,' she whispered, 'my hair was very shiny and dark. It parted in the middle and curved each side of my forehead, reminding my – my mother of raven's wings. I was to have been called Elizabeth, after her.'

74

Her tears fell and his arms enfolded her. He felt very slim and calm and comforting.

Their affair was immediate, born out of shock and despair. They had clung to each other and married secretly and in haste. Raven, now alone in the world, had no choice. Francis had a well-to-do family and more importantly, a twin sister named Fiona who swore that she always experienced her brother's aches and pains. He told Raven, quite seriously, that he had proved this to be nonsense long ago, but knowing and loving his sister Fiona as he did, he wanted to protect her from his final and most desperate agony. It was therefore his considered opinion that it would be best to keep his knowledge, and future whereabouts, to himself. His people would not think this strange. He had always been a wanderer, a would-be poet, someone puzzled about existence, who was trying to determine the meaning of the world.

Fully understanding his motivation, his desire to save his sister pain, Raven went along with his plans.

They had a simple ceremony at the Register Office. Everything had happened very quickly but no eyebrows were raised. Members of the hospital staff had glowingly witnessed the blossoming romance.

The small flat they rented near the hospital became their secret world. The past, for Raven, was taken care of by her father's solicitors. They saw to everything. Monies raised from effects and the leasing of the Surrey house to a new doctor, were transferred into Raven's account. In effect, she was able to walk away, at least physically, and think only of Francis.

She had clung to him and to the four walls of their home as if her own life depended on it. She went out only to shop, then she would hurry back to her husband, whom she adored.

Francis was interested in everything; his senses heightened in the extreme. They had spoken of Hitler and the aggressive mood abroad, but preferred to concentrate on more gentle things. And Raven had savoured every achingly beautiful word spoken.

They had held hands, lovingly smiling into each other's eyes. Treasuring their transient happiness; knowing that they only had a very little time.

'I cannot bear the thought of losing you,' she whispered.

'Sweetheart,' he replied, 'think of me as a newborn dragonfly that has left behind the grubby thing it was before. I will always be with you, in your heart and mind, for as long as you need me.'

'I won't be able to go on alone,' she had gasped. 'And we have so little time . . .'

'You will manage quite splendidly,' he told her, his voice growing

75

weaker for all he was sincere. 'And as for time, I have written a poem about it. Would you like to hear it?'

She nodded and listened while he spoke, in that quiet, elegant way he had. She had been holding on to him, adoring him with her eyes.

'Time,' he began, stopped and lovingly squeezed her hand before going on. 'Time, a manmade measure, means nothing at all, to red-wood trees, pyramids, the great Chinese Wall. We walk towards maturity, important things to learn. Which arches of life to cross, which broken bridges to burn. The hour is Now, the past long gone. The future's much too far. The reality of life is, quite simply, that – We are.'

She had looked up into his face, tears in her eyes. Thankful that God had given her the privilege of knowing and loving this man.

As she had known it would, the cancerous sickness in his blood had won. He had died, cradled and sleeping peacefully in her arms.

Gradually, as the numbness and nothingness of her life without him grew, she remembered one of their later conversations. He had spoken quietly of her need to fight for her own survival afterwards – for his sake.

It had been Francis who wrote down the address to contact when the need arose: WLA Headquarters, 6 Chesham Street, London SW1.

'Raven,' Hannah said in a strained voice, 'please come back to me. You seem to have gone away – and it's all my fault, isn't it? It's what I said.'

'Nothing is your fault,' Raven told her. 'In fact, Hannah, you and Ginnie are my two lifelines. You are immensely important to me because, before meeting you both, I was utterly and absolutely alone.' She smiled reassuringly down into the ashen, large-eyed face. 'Now, how are you feeling?'

'Sick.'

'We're nearly there. Hang on . . .'

Lindell was set before a marshy slough, where Mr Moses had, sup-posedly, almost met his doom. Hannah, now unashamedly holding on to Raven, trudged on, past a stretch of rough grass where horses grazed, past the huge sprawling buildings of the classy Drew Stables, and a pond where children fished for minnows. Then came the Green and the cricket field, and beyond that, the swerve of Duckpond Cor-ner. Here stood the ivy-clad domicile owned by Dr Dene.

'Not too far,' Raven told Hannah again.

There were only three other people in the waiting-room when they went in, all of them women. One was Mrs Madeira – a regular on account of her veins.

'Bulging!' she was wont to say. 'Bulging like balloons!'

All three ladies had been talking nineteen to the dozen, but stopped the minute Hannah and Raven walked in.

They stared at the girls and at Hannah's bloodied hand.

'That looks bad,' one of the women said. 'I'm next one in, but you go instead.'

'Thank you,' Hannah replied.

'The airman's in there now,' Mrs Madeira said, and sniffed. 'Thought they had their own doctors nearby at Matching. It comes to something—'

Suddenly there was a commotion at the window. The twins looked in, cheekily ignoring the stiffened figure of Mrs Madeira who was sitting directly beneath them.

The window was open and Chris stuck his head through. 'Hello, Hannah. Are you all right? Matt's in there – did you know?'

'He's staying with Mrs Endercot and we're waiting for him,' Chook called. 'That's really fine, eh?'

A deep throaty bark sounded. Mr Moses decided that windows were a great way to come in, except that his masters barred the way.

'Please take him home,' Raven pleaded, conscious of Mrs Madeira's glassy-eyed stare.

Chris saw the blood on Hannah. He waved an incredibly dirty hand, holding a large tin, in her direction.

'Hannah, what have you done? Hannah, shall I run and tell Mum? Golly, that looks awful and—'

At that moment Ol' Mo leapt. He was too large to get in by the window but his full weight went on Chris's back. With a yell Chris dropped the tin. It burst open and a goodly amount of fishing bait spilled over, down onto the waiting-room floor.

Then came two boyish roars of laughter as they saw hundreds of maggots wriggling towards the petrified patients. But there was even greater delight at the sight of the things, massed and writhing, all over Mrs Madeira's hat. As the woman moved in horror, some showered down and onto her nose. She gave out a short, sharp scream.

The boys vanished as Dr Dene and Matt appeared at the opened surgery door.

Mrs Madeira was about to faint. One swift look and Dr Dene had registered all. Nurse Jones was called to calm Mrs Madeira, the Denes' gardener to sweep up the offending wrigglies, and Hannah was whisked into the surgery in double-quick time.

Two stitches, a sip of sal volatile, a professional armsling and one tetunus injection later, Hannah left the surgery. Raven was waiting for her, and also Matt.

Raven nodded when she heard about the stitches. 'I thought so,' she said. 'Well, I'll be off, back to Ginnie.' She turned to Matt. 'And perhaps you will walk Hannah back to Hawksley?'

'You bet!' Matt was grinning all over his face. 'And here was I thinking it'd be a quiet life in Lindell Village.'

Halfway home the two boys and Mr Moses appeared from behind a hedge. All seemed unrepentant.

'Hey, Hannah!' Chris called. 'Are you better now?'

'Heaps,' she replied.

'You've got blood all over your dungarees,' Chook commented. 'It's a good job it's daytime.'

'Why is that, old son?' Matt asked, intrigued.

'Vampires,' Chook told him stoutly. 'I believe in them.'

'Shut up!' Chris ordered and turned back to Hannah 'Did she? I say, Hannah, did she?'

'Who and what?' Hannah asked, and tried to ignore the headache that she could feel coming on.

'Ol' Dragon Drawers. Did she actually take off her hat?'

'I'm sorry, boys.' Hannah was feeling guilty now. 'I wasn't there, and I just don't know.'

He turned enquiringly to Matt.

'I can't say I noticed,' Matt had to admit.

'She'll never take it off,' Chook said doggedly. 'I told you she wouldn't, Chris. I bet I'm right.'

Even Matt was curious at this. 'May I ask why?' he asked.

'She's bald,' Chook said darkly. 'She's as bald as an egg and that's why she's always picking on Mr Moses. She can't stand him because she's so jealous of his lovely long fur.'

The lane rang with Matt's deep, dancing laugh.

Chapter Eleven

London streets were sombre in the night, sullen for all it was All Clear. Sleet sliced down – cold, hard, vicious. Where paving stones were uneven it made miniature pools. It beat against bowed heads and splashed against trouser legs, turning alleyways into ebony rivers.

At their posts, like black shadows themselves, tin-helmeted ARP men, on guard for all the moonless night meant safety, watched and waited. At the ready, inside buildings, fire-watchers consoled themselves in their lonely vigils with cups of cocoa sweetened with saccharine.

A huge man, shrouded by darkness, shambled along the street, following the torchlight that bounced along before him. Ram Rawlins hunched himself up against the icy-cold sleet and swore long and hard. He was fed up – bloody fed up – and it was nothing to do with the weather.

He was bewildered, muddled, mixed-up. How could someone change so much and in such a short time? The love of his life was like fire one minute, ice the next . . . and then a volcano spouting venom – directed against his own confused self. All this – for having failed to kill that girl. It wasn't enough that they'd done for the Neilson bloke. It had to be the York chit, too.

'I dunno what's up, Biff,' he said once in his slow rasping way. 'Can't please her, and she hates my guts half the time. The York girl won't talk about what she's seen; she can't without splitting on her old man – what Frank was, who he was with. She wouldn't dare! But Val won't have none of that. She thinks I'm wrong for letting the kid get away. Val reckons . . .'

'Val don't know when she's well off, my old son.' Biff's reply was always the same, and he'd give that chilly smile, his eyes holding looks that could cut like a knife. 'You just carry on same as always. All right?'

'But you don't understand, boss.'

'Leave it out, mate. Just put it down to the fact that my sister's like all women. A bit gone in the head. Now forget it. We're doing all right these days, eh? Spondulicks are rolling in. You'll be able to buy her a fur coat and pearls the way we're going on.'

'I never knew she'd have me.' Ram said low. 'Didn't think no one would take me. I want to keep her.'

'You're mad, you are!' Biff's eyes glinted with derision. 'She's the only one on God's earth you'd allow to bash you. Bleeding hell, Ram, just look at the state of your bleedin' physog!'

'She blames that girl for lots of things.'

'No, mate, she blames Hannah York for being Neilson's excuse not to get married. Still, his loss is your gain, eh? 'Sides, what she don't know is that I'd never have allowed it. I'd have done Neilson in a damned sight quicker if things had looked like going that far. Now, for God's sake, shut it!'

The conversation always ended like that, and with Biff telling him to button his lip and get on with it. Reminding him that he was the Heavy and didn't need to think, just act. But Ram did think and it hurt his brain because all the thinking these days was about Val.

Ram's cadaverous face grew tight at the memory of how Val had been just now.

'Get that stuck-up mare for me,' she'd yelled. 'You owe me!'

Then she had flown at him, nails bared, fists flailing, and he had let her take it out on him, until breathless, she had thrown herself down on the sofa and sobbed. He had tried to kiss her better in his clumsy way, but she had glared at him so viciously that he had slunk off to find Biff, the only one whom he could call friend.

He thought he heard footsteps behind him. Was Val following him? He peered over his shoulder into the unbroken darkness. Nobody. Not a living mortal soul.

'Christ Almighty,' he muttered. 'I dunno. I just don't know!'

He heard the footsteps again and waited. A thin little runt appeared out of the gloom.

'That you, Ram?'

'Yers. That you, Weasel?'

'S'right. 'Ere mate, a message from Biff. You're to go to the meet. Something's come up, he says.'

Ram turned away without a word and left his previous destination, the Duck and Drake, behind him. He went down an alleyway, then through a back street that in spite of the sleet still stank of wet fish. Further along stood a group of bomb-damaged terraced houses. They were boarded up, grey-black monsters, seemingly empty of life. Sucked dry by an enemy in the sky.

80

Ram made his way over a pile of rubble, slipped through a broken fence and lopsided back door. The passage he negotiated stank of stale unmentionable things, odours that the thick curling up of cigarette smoke could not obscure.

Biff and Fatty Blythe were sitting at a table in a back room. Wallpaper peeling, ceiling cracked, plaster fallen down, it was a sorry place in spite of being lit by many candles. It was claustrophic too, because of tobacco smoke and the shortage of space. The four walls were piled high with crates and boxes. All rationed stuff worth its weight in gold on the Black Market.

Pink, piggy-eyed, wet-lipped Fatty had ins with the blokes on the Docks. Biff knew a Mess Sergeant who could get him unlimited supplies of Army fags and grub. Between them there was a steady and growing river of goodies to be had. As Biff had boasted to Ram, they were all on the up and up. The profits were gilt-edged. The spondulicks were mounting and getting to be as splendid as the treasures of King Tut.

'Been at it again, 'as she?' Fatty smirked, as he looked at Ram's face.

'Shut it!' Biff snapped, then back to Ram, 'Glad you're here, mate. We've got something to sort. What I've just found out ain't no bleeding good.'

'It's something what could mean curtains for us,' Fatty put in, and squinting, looked evil.

'That's right,' Biff agreed. 'Curtains! Ram, my old son, something is definitely bloody well up. We've got to talk. We've got to make plans. Got to get down to brass tacks'

'Yes, but Val—'

'Shut up!' Fatty and Biff snapped in unison.

'It's like this, my old son,' Biff began . . .

Chapter Twelve

It was late. Fourteen-year-old Lenny Madeira sat on an ancient milking stool in the flagged kitchen of his uncle's home. Lenny was alone and engaged in peeling potatoes, which he dropped one by one into a large enamel basin of water at his side. Into a bucket between his legs he discarded the peelings destined for his uncle's pigs. The boy was not sorry that his bad-tempered aunt had gone to bed, but he wondered vaguely and a little uneasily where his uncle was.

It was ten o'clock by the big clock that ticked stridently against a far wall in the shadows. An oil-flame, burning in a tall, highly polished brass lamp, was the only light, except when a log shifted in the ingle nook and sent sparks flying.

Larry felt afraid. He longed to finish his work and climb up the stairs which were behind the thick oak door in the wall opposite him. He wanted to shut himself inside the small bedroom which was his refuge from the world. It was always the same. When alone at night he hated the kitchen. His aunt knew this, but cared not a jot. Every night he had to prepare all the vegetables for the next day's use before going to bed. He had admitted to his fear of the kitchen once, when younger, and got a clip round the ear for his pains.

'Going soft, are you?' his Aunt Maud had snapped. 'Trying to act up? We all know your ma died in this kitchen, and that your dad was dead with a broken neck when they carried him in to join her. But it was all his fault.'

'Don't, Aunt Maud,' he had pleaded. 'Please don't!'

'Can't stand to hear the truth? Grow up! He should never have got so Christmas drunk that he couldn't manage the horse and cart. Killed his wife as clearly as if he'd put a bullet in her brain, he did. My one and only best friend! But you was thrown clear, wasn't you? You who's as like your dad as a twin pea.' There had followed another stinging blow, round his face this time. 'And it's me that has to carry the can back. Always did and always will.'

'Let me go back to Mr Allsop's house,' he had begged tearfully. 'He was my dad's friend and he said I might.'

'And expect us to pay for your keep? Do you think we're mad? That Allsop's a Norseby man good and proper. And with cunning Norseby Village ways. Your mum and dad came from Lindell, were born and bred here, and it was only work that took Bob away.' Maud Madeira had sniffed contemptuously.

'Please don't, Aunt Maud,' he had pleaded. *'Please.'*

'Not that it helped at all.' She was like a steamroller in her determination to spill out her bile. 'Always broke, your lot were, not surprising with their airy-fairy ways. But it's different here. I have me own rules. No more messing about with that violin of yours. It wails like a cat with its tail caught. You'll earn your keep while under my roof or I'll know the reason why.'

'Yes, Aunt Maud,' he had whispered, choking back a sob.

'And don't look at me like that, all quiet with your thoughts,' she threatened. 'They do say that Bob Madeira was soft as a brush. A dreamer what couldn't take a drink, and that it was my Walter's fault that he took too much that day. Well, I'll kill you stone dead if I ever see you with a drink, no matter how old you get. Understand? And as for Walt, one of these days I'll do for him too.'

She had looked evil, like a wicked witch, and she meant every word she said. If he was late doing his chores, if she just felt hateful, he was for it. She had a habit of beating him over the shoulders with either a copper stick or rolling pin. She was careful to do it where the bruises wouldn't show.

Uncle Walter hadn't been so bad when his brother Bob had been alive. They had been great mates. But the death of Bob, and of Lenny's mother, who came for a visit from their home outside Norseby on that dreadful Christmas Day three years ago, had left him melancholy and bitter with guilt. Under his wife's vicious tongue-lashing he had become weak-kneed as well. All his uncle was fit for these days, Lenny thought sadly, was to bully those people that he could. And God help any stray animal that got in his way. He especially hated dogs. It had been a dog darting in their path that had caused the accident, rather more than the drink. But try telling Maud Madeira that!

Now Mr Moses would be for it. Lenny felt an upsurge of panic at the thought. Aunt Maud had been raging on for hours and hours about Charles and Christopher Ainsley and their pet, insisting that the boys would be whipped and the animal shot, else she, Maud Madeira, would see to it that there would be hell to pay.

Lenny dropped his last potato in the water and carried the pan into the larder, where it joined the carrots he had scraped and sliced, and the three peeled onions that had made him cry. Afterwards he cleaned up carefully, lest his aunt should find a speck of dirt on her clean floor.

It began to rain and the large old cottage was full of night noises. Not loud noises, but stealthy, soft noises that Lenny found most terrifying. As ever, when alone in the kitchen at night, he remembered his mother, so white and still, gasping out her last on the kitchen table where she had been placed. And on the floor, by the far wall, as distanced from the fire as possible, the still, dead figure shrouded in gloom. Then a log had burst and light had shot across the room to flare up and illuminate his father's face. It had seemed skull-like, with sunken features and a strong out-jutting nose. Somehow, the sight of that nose had struck through the boy's sense of unreality, and he had accepted that his father was dead.

Returning to put the stool carefully back in place under the sink, after giving the matter deep thought, Lenny left the lamp burning as he started for bed. If his uncle came in he might stumble in the dark and wake up Aunt Maud. If that happened, there would be a third World War.

Lenny cautiously lifted the latch of the stair-door and opened it wide, revealing a flight of worm-eaten oak steps, and something truly awful. Something that bought the boy's heart into his mouth. On the landing above, wearing a long flannel nightgown and a white woolly bonnet on her head, stood his aunt. The candlestick and spluttering flame made shadows dance on her face. She looked like an evil witch ready to pounce.

'Lenny,' she said harshly. 'Where is your uncle?'

'I – I don't know.'

'Well, I'm going to find out,' she told him, her voice holding ice. 'Oh yes, I'm going to know here and now.' As she spoke she descended the stairs, which creaked under her weight.

Lenny watched her cross the kitchen and open the door which led out into the night, letting in a blast of wind and rain. The wind extinguished the candle and made the oil-lamp flame flicker and dance.

Undaunted, Mrs Madeira took a torch from the shelf and went outside. Her footsteps were sure of every inch of the way. Across the yard, thick with the gusting smell of Walt's pigs, she went. Angrily ignoring the weather, her slippered feet slushing through puddles, she made her way to the huge old barn that had been standing since the cottage itself had been built. It was used for drying purposes, for storing, keeping junk that might come in handy – Maud being a thrifty soul – including a bike and the threshing machine . . . and by Walter himself for when he needed to get away from his wife.

Reluctant to be left alone in the kitchen, Lenny followed Maud. He saw her flashing the wide beam of the torch around, then she opened the barn door. It made a tearing sound over the brick floor, for it was a heavy thing, and had sunk on its hinges.

Yes, Maud had been right. Uncle Walter was found, for the odour of shag tobacco came out into the night air. Maud went inside and Lenny crept nearer, pressed close to a window and looked inside to where the torch made a circle of light.

Walter Madeira was sitting on a bench, jacket undone, cap askew, his pipe in his hand. He looked unkempt and his mouth was twisted in thin bitter lines.

'Walter!' Maud exclaimed furiously. 'I'll not put up with this. Out here, smoking when you've got a good bed to come to, and when you've got to be up before five to get to work.'

'I'll be in good time,' he said, and smirked in a knowing way.

'You've heard what happened, haven't you?' Her voice was cold with fury. 'Down there sozzling in the Rookwood, sniggering along with the rest of 'em, I suppose. Well, you know what I'm going to say, don't you? What I'm going to expect you to do?' Her voice rose. 'Speak up for me, Walter Madeira and be a man for a change. In the meantime, you can put out that filthy pipe!'

'You won't let me smoke indoors, Maud,' Walter said weakly, smirk banished.

'No, I won't! Now put it out and come to bed. I'll catch my death out here. Not that you care. I don't know why I married you.'

The worm turned.

'Why did I ever marry *you*!' he retorted, and stood up from the bench, facing her with inebriated dignity.

'I'll tell you why.' She took a furious step nearer to him. 'You wanted a good house-drudge, a cook, and a general dogsbody. And on top of that, a nurse-cum-keeper for that slow-witted boy of Bob's.'

'It was you that dug your toes in and wouldn't let him go to Allsop's place,' he countered. 'Allsop's old woman took a real shine to the boy.'

'So they say,' she spat, 'but I won't have folk whispering behind my back about me not doing my duty by a young blockhead that makes me curl my lip every time I glance his way.'

'He's got a nice face. It's just his dreamy air you can't stand and well you know it.' Walter jutted out his chin, sobering with every second that passed. 'As my old father used to say, there's a bloody great difference between a cart-horse and a race-horse. Young Lenny's refined-looking, it's as simple as that.'

'Simple? How right you are – and we all know the sort you think my family are. Peasants. Well, let me tell you, a noble head isn't that much to shout about – it's what goes on inside. And you can forget Allsop. Yes, that Norseby pig's behind all this. I'm not giving in. It's like I said, I am not going to have villagers saying that Maud Madeira turned away a soppy ha'pporth of an orphaned kid. Him what needs loving care.'

'Love? Love, did you say? You don't know the meaning of the word,' he told her with the determination of a man now fully ready to burn his boats. 'You were a nice, gentle little thing once, but now? These days you're about as soft as a miller's stone.'

'I tell you, Mr Madeira,' the name was spat out with utter contempt, 'I'm the one what's respected round here.' Her voice was grating now, her eyes evil in her face. Her head, encased in the white bonnet, made a macabre dancing black shape on the spider-festooned wall. The torch-beam jumped as she jabbed it at Walter with every word she spoke. 'I tell you, respected and looked up to!'

'Not with maggots on your hat-brim,' Walter said, eyes narrowed, his words carrying more weight because his tone was even and quiet. 'You are not looked up to at all. In fact, you're seen as a bitter and twisted woman – a right old bitch being the general opinion. D'you hear me? A right old bitch!'

'How dare you, you bloody old fool!'

'And yes, old girl, they *were* laughing their heads off down the pub. It seems you forgot your marm-stink ways long enough to open your mouth and yell. And according to them women in the waiting-room with you, you kept your hat on, maggots an' all. You got the Doc's man to brush them off. A real picture that was, by all accounts. They'll cackle about it for years.'

'I'll see about that!' Maud Madeira was beside herself. She stamped her foot on the earth floor. 'If you don't put a stop to it, I will!'

Walter's eyes flashed dangerously. 'Hold your tongue, woman,' he said tightly. 'For the past few years I've never been allowed a moment's peace. You've changed since I married you. So, I say again, shut up! If you don't I'll not answer for what I'll do to you.' And he reached out for his rabbit gun, patience gone.

Seeing his aunt swing round ready to move towards the door, Lenny fled to the house.

Upstairs in his bedroom, he sat panting and puzzled, not yet ready to lie on his small bed. He was jubilant, although frightened. His uncle had at last shown fight. But what must he put a stop to? Why had they all been laughing at Aunt Maud? Something had made her furiously angry, something to do with Chris and Chook and the dog.

His eyes felt heavy. Suddenly he was aware of being cold and that his working clothes were wet. He took them off and crept between the crisp, clean calico sheets. It would be miserable, dressing in the morning, but he had things to do. There was wood to chop, eggs to gather, pigs to feed, and then it was wash under the pump and change into his more decent attire before breakfast-time.

All ready and waiting for him for the morning, there was a clean shirt and a woolly cardigan, and neatly pressed grey flannel trousers. Clean underclothes, ironed and aired, were folded and carefully placed on top of the chest of drawers. In spite of her hateful ways, Aunt Maud fed him well and clothed him decently enough. He knew that, and in a vague way felt this should make him grateful. It did not.

Before he slept, Larry had made a plan. He would rush through his chores and sneak off and wait outside the Ainsley cottage before his young mates went to school. He must warn them that something terrible was about to happen. If he could, he would run to Hawksley and tell the lovely Miss Hannah. She would understand more than any other grown-up. Miss Hannah talked to him and laughed with him and understood his thoughts. If anyone could help, she could. He'd tell the twins, and tell Miss Hannah too, that according to Aunt Maud, Mr Moses was to be shot . . .

'I'm going to miss you two,' Hannah said brightly, after cornflakes and sausage with tomatoes. 'If the rain keeps off, I might even walk over and join you – and all the acres of beet.'

'Golly,' Ginnie teased, brows raised. 'Are you crackers?'

'Matt is really nice,' Raven observed. 'Didn't you tell us that he was a hero?'

'Yes, he is,' Hannah agreed, 'and of course I'd like to see him.' She shrugged casually, but couldn't help her mischievous grin. 'And he did mention that he'll look for me in the Rookwood when they opened – if I felt up to it, of course.'

'He asked you to meet him – at the pub?' Ginnie's tone said it all.

'He wanted to call for me here, but I said no,' Hannah explained quickly. 'I told him that I might go along, and again that I might not.'

'Give me strength!' Ginnie looked up to the ceiling in disgust.

'I thought you were falling for him,' Raven remarked, 'because you told us that in your opinion, he is a real corker.'

'He is, and I do like him,' Hannah told her stoutly. 'He could turn out to be a jolly good pal – and that's all.'

'But I thought . . .'

'He's too good-looking, too popular, and too sure of himself. And don't forget dear Madeline!'

'Oh come now,' Raven teased in her quiet way. 'She was his nurse, for heaven's sake.'

'And I'm me, ready for a lark and a laugh and that's all. Besides, my finger hurts. No, really!'

'Hard cheddar!' Ginnie said.

They were still laughing and teasing her as they left to jump into Mr Endercot's waiting van.

'Well, now.' Lily began, whisking the breakfast things away. 'What are you going to do with yourself today? You could go home on sick leave, you know.'

'My house is a pile of rubble in the East End of London,' Hannah replied. 'And even if it wasn't, I wouldn't want to go back there! No, I'll stay here – and although I pretended, of course I want to spend all the time I can with Matt.' She looked uncertain. 'If that's all right?'

'What, staying here? Of course! Hawksley's your home while you want it. Until the war ends, in fact. And you're always welcome in Rose Cottage, too.'

'You're really nice,' Hannah told her and beamed, then added fiercely, 'I won't *ever* want to go back to London. If it's possible, I'll stay here in Lindell for ever.'

'Then we'll have to find you a nice marriageable local man. We have several who would suit you down to the ground, but—'

'I'll have to wait until they come home from the war?'

'Exactly.'

'Then I'll wait.' Hannah's tone was blithe now and her eyes twinkling. 'When is your Sam due home for leave?'

'I'll expect him when I see him. I miss him. He happens to be the most wonderful, most decent chap I know.'

'Don't boast!' Hannah laughed and ducked to escape the flying dishcloth.

At that moment Mrs Madeira came in. She stopped directly in front of Lily, her face thunder-black. Hannah saw Lily's silent signal and got the message at once. Without a word, she went into the 'Land Girls' Sitter' as it was now called. She was pleased to find that Vincent had lit a fire.

She was sitting by the hearth, reading an old *Picturegoer* magazine, when she had a visitor.

'Here you are,' Sophia St John said in her unemotional way. 'How are you?'

Fighting the impulse to jump up and salute, Hannah smiled politely. 'Very well, thank you.'

'Well done.' Then, commandingly: 'Tell me about yourself.'

Oh Gawd! Hannah thought. The old girl's acting like Katharine Hepburn. Worse, she's actually trying to make out she's interested in me. She heard herself reply: 'There's really nothing to tell, Mrs St

John. I was born in the East End, and brought up by a stepfather who is now as dead as my mother. I was a dunce at school, loathed every day I spent there, and couldn't wait to leave when I was fourteen. After that I worked where and when I could, and the moment I was old enough, I joined this mob. And that, I'm afraid, is about it!'

'The girl with red hair, what of her?'

'Ginnie? She's a very decent sort. Her parents are well-off – at least by my standards. They own a posh fruiterer's in Ilford. Ginnie won a place in High School and passed all of her exams, which shows she's got brains as well as beauty. She's level-headed, direct, talks tough at times, and works like the devil. Raven and me would go through fire and water for her.'

'Ah, Raven!' Sophia St John said meaningfully.

Blow me, Hannah thought, the penny dropping. The old girl's really interested in Raven, not me or Ginnie. Out of sheer pig-headedness, she remained silent, determined that the woman standing there so stylish and svelte in a silver-grey suit and pearls, would have to be open and ask. Then she felt uncomfortable and irritated because Sophia sat down on the chair opposite. She moved with grace. She crossed her legs, which in spite of the war were encased in fine rayon stockings, and settled herself. She was clearly intending to talk.

Cheek! Hannah thought. Toffee-nosed thing. She hasn't bothered to pass a civil word to any of us until now. Then she felt surprised because Sophia St John went on, 'Raven and I met and talked. I found her sitting alone in the rose garden soon after you came to stay. We spoke – briefly.'

'That's nice,' Hannah said, miffed. 'She never mentioned it.'

'Really?' Twin eyebrows were raised high. 'Strange! I find it rather odd that someone like her should engage herself working the fields.'

'The war's no respecter of persons, Mrs St John.' For the life of her, Hannah couldn't keep the sarcasm out of her voice. 'They call us all up for service, rich and poor, poets and peasants.'

'Poets? How odd that you—'

'I like poetry,' Hannah said through gritted teeth. 'And I don't find the idea odd at all, Mrs St John. In fact, I wish that I could have met Raven's husband, Francis. He was a poet and I'm going to learn his work off by heart before I'm through.'

'Is he in the Forces?'

'He's dead.'

'So that's why the girl is so reserved.'

'No, she isn't. Not to us anyway. She's just self-contained, that's all. There are times when she forgets, just a little, and . . .'

'Ceases to wallow?'

Hannah's cheeks blazed. 'Raven has *never* wallowed!'

'She was lost in a maze of self-pity when I came across her. She would not tell me why.'

'Couldn't that be because you're hardly the sympathetic type?' Hannah snapped, caution flying to the winds. 'And now I come to think of it, I shouldn't even be telling you things about my two mates. Just because we've been billeted here in your posh house, doesn't mean that you should know all of our business.' She laughed with furious tears in her eyes, feeling that Mrs St John was asking about them in a purely suspicious way. 'And this I will say,' she went on. 'I'm the low-class out of us three – but I do promise you, even I wouldn't want to pinch your pearls.'

'Don't be ridiculous, girl.' Sophia's voice was sharp with irritability. 'I'm interested, that's all.' Then, as Hannah jumped up, 'No, don't go.'

Hannah sat back obediently. Again she felt nervous tears threatening, and realised that cutting her hand, on top of everything else that had happened, had really put a tack in her nerves. She smiled wearily.

'I'm sorry for speaking out. I always was a blabber-mouth.'

'But everyone's favourite in spite of it, I understand.' Sophia St John's tone was smooth. 'Why, even my son admits to being intrigued by you. I believe you sparked up to him – and he can be a distant, very authoritative man. My dear girl, I was asking about Raven because I saw her a few days after she and I had talked in the garden. She was in tears.'

'There are times when she needs to be alone.'

'To cry?' Sophia snapped, impatient again. 'God, the world can and will walk over the Ravens of this world and not even notice the pieces. Can't she see that she must learn to be like granite?' She pointed imperiously to a painting on the wall, of a mountain hunching its back against the sky like a giant beast. 'I painted that, put everything I know into it. Do you know why? I saw it as something indestructible. Unlike jelly that melts the moment things get even remotely warm!'

That hit home. Hannah gulped, hating to admit even to herself how cowardly she felt when she remembered what she had seen back home.

'Mrs St John?' she said quietly, thinking of Frank, of how Val had looked with her bruised, bleeding chest and broken nose. Of how she herself had felt when that wicked, snake-like crack had wriggled round the ceiling only seconds before the ceiling had fallen down; of the bomb that had finished off 32 Walker Street for ever. Over and above all, jelly-like or not, she still felt ill remembering the malevolence in Ram Rawlins's eyes. He would never give up, she knew it. He would kill her when he found her. She knew that, too.

'Yes?' The question shot out like a bullet.

'Tell me how you went on whenever you were scared. Tell me what you did when – when your husband died.'

Green eyes glittered, cat-like. 'I went in and painted just about the bloodiest picture possible.'

'But most of us can't paint, you see,' Hannah pointed out gravely. 'We just have to plod on.'

'And sit in rose gardens and snivel?' So, the woman was back to Raven again.

'Oh dear!' Hannah drawled, herself again. 'Pardon us for being wishy-washy and oh so human.'

Sophia threw back her fine head and glared. In that moment she looked as if she could, and would, defy the universe.

'I will *not* allow her to sit and cry. Like it or lump it, you three have become part of my life simply because you are here under my roof. So no, I will not allow any of you to bawl.' Sophia leaned forward in her chair and stared straight into Hannah's eyes. 'Because if you do, I shall sit down and howl like a banshee myself!'

Hannah remembered then that this glass-brittle woman had lost a dearly loved husband, and a son who had gone down at sea. Realised too, that James the eldest child – had he ever been a child? – preferred to live at Knollys rather than stay at home. That must have been like a kick in the teeth to a woman stiff with self-pride.

To her own amazement, Hannah's voice held warmth as she smiled, saying: 'That wouldn't do, would it, Mrs St John – if you sat down and blubbed. Gawd's truth, you'd lose all your dignity!'

The older woman smiled, a tight hard little grimace, but her green eyes had ceased to glare.

'That is what is amounts to,' she agreed, and stood up. 'Now, what I really came to find out was, is there anything you'd like – a little treat of some kind? After all, we must spoil our invalids a little, don't you agree?'

Hannah beamed, mood changing. The woman was actually trying to be human, after all!

'Do you know what I miss most, Mrs St John?' she asked in a merry conspiratorial way. 'Fish and chips! Like you get from the shop, I mean. Wrapped in newspaper and covered in salt and vinegar. And if they care to throw in a few battered chitterlings as well – luvverly!' She chuckled, unashamed, adding, 'Common is as common does, eh?'

'Rubbish! Now, my dear, I shall ask Vincent to motor into—'

'Oh no! I was just sharing a wish for the past. We all do that at times, don't we?' The older woman frowned, but Hannah added emphatic-ally: 'Yes, *all* of us, Mrs St John!' She stopped burbling long enough to shake her head. 'Thank you for your kind offer, but I wouldn't miss out on Lily's parsley pud for the world!'

Sophia went soon after that and Hannah felt surprised because she found the woman not half so bad as she had believed. She set off to find Lily, just to chew over this astonishing enlightenment, expecting to be greeted by the smell of some mouth-watering dish cooking. There was nothing, and after a few calls, and a walk outside, she returned and realised there was nobody around. The place was quite empty. It was only then that she spotted the scrap of paper on the table. It was for Vincent. It read:

Dear Vincent, please help me. I telephoned the school, after Maud went on and on about visiting the boys' Head Mistress. The twins weren't there. I then found a note on my kitchen table at home. They've taken Moses with them and they have run away. They say they'll never be forgiven for what they did – even though it was an accident. They are sorry they laughed but Maud looked so funny with maggots wriggling round the brim of her hat. They've sworn to drown themselves before letting anyone shoot Moses. I'm off after them. They've have probably made their way to Marsh Lake. Please explain to Mrs St John . . . Lil.

Hannah's heart sank. Lily was on the wrong track. Marsh Lake was fine, but no hiding place. Then she brightened up. She knew where she'd find the twins! They didn't know she had discovered their secret spot a week ago. It was an old barn and she had come upon it and the twins quite by chance one Sunday afternoon. She had been by herself, since both Ginnie and Raven had gone to Ginnie's home for the week-end without her.

Hannah had been invited also, but had preferred to stay – remembering Ram and his evil intent. Who could dismiss the possibility that Ram and the Marner gang might be hanging round all the stations just waiting for her to show up? It was a stupid idea, but she was too afraid to take the chance. So it was that she was the only one who had found out the twins' secret. Knowing how boys loved hideouts she had kept quiet.

Now she left Hawksley and made her way along the lane. She turned right and cut across open fields. The old tumbledown barn came into view. She reached it, opened the creaky door and went in.

'Come out, you two,' she said firmly. 'No one's going to kill Ol' Mo, that I promise you.'

Even before the words had left her lips, her smile was replaced by a worried frown. She had been wrong. The boys weren't there. She walked about for what seemed hours. At last she decided to go back to find out whether Lily had news. She finished up almost running, forgetting her throbbing hand in her anxiety.

Lily had not found them and neither had anyone else.

Chapter Thirteen

Matt was disappointed. He had hoped that Hannah would meet him in the pub. Suddenly he knew that he missed her, that he wanted her, that although she didn't know it yet, she was going to have a fight on her hands to shove him out of her life. She was just a kid in many ways, her greatest kick being considered a dab hand at darts. She was not ready for love. She was a lively young cock-bantam with enough courage to take on Hitler, yes single-handed if necessary, but there was a vulnerability about her he couldn't understand. It made him want to protect her, though she was the sort to laugh and call him nuts if he so much as hinted at the fact.

He leaned against the bar, pint in hand, moodily wondering where the hell the other two were. Nice kids, both of them. Raven Gray, who was as cool as a cucumber and as self-contained. Then there was Ginnie Betts. She was a dead duck if ever there was one. He'd seen old Richard breaking in the fillies often before and they didn't come better than him. By Matt's reckoning, Ginnie would have the halter on well before summer set in – providing Richard made it till then. Ops were on for his pal and the situation was rough.

Endercot came in and Matt raised a finger for a further pint. He whizzed it along the bar so that it stopped before the Estate Manager, who was busily puffing on his pipe.

'Thanks, boy,' Endercot said. 'How's tricks?'

'Could be better. I'm not happy just hanging around.'

'You think there'd be more going for you in the Smoke?'

'No, here, given the chance.'

'So – which one?'

'Hannah. She was supposed to be here, but . . .'

'She's probably chasing about all over, looking for Lily's boys. She likes them two rascals – and they like her.'

'They're missing?'

'Seems so. Run off because of the trouble in the Doc's.' Ellery grinned round the rim of his pint. 'I'd give a year's wages to have witnessed Ma Madeira with her hair full of maggots. Mind you, the young tykes lead the old girl a dance. But then she shouldn't be so mouthy about their dog.'

'So the lads have buzzed off? I'd best help find them.'

'No sense in aggravating them wounds of yours. Supposed to take it easy, eh? No, leave the kids to it. They'll show up when they're hungry. Kids always do.'

'Think I'll have a go-see,' Matt said, shrugging, 'At least it's something to do.'

Matt made his way to Hawksley first, to see if there was any news. He knocked on the back door and received no reply. Tried again and turned away when there was no response. Evidently they were all out looking for the twins. He doubted whether the proud and arrogant Mrs St John was trudging the highways and byways, but then she was probably lying blotto somewhere. It was common knowledge that the woman was a lush.

He walked out into the night, and kept walking. Eventually he became aware of the pain in his side, that his back was killing him, and that his injured leg felt as if it was on fire, but he went on, trying to recall everything the boys had talked about. Trying to fathom some sort of clue, and cursing himself for a fool while he was at it.

The boys were wretches, bounders, mischievous and everything else he could think of. Their dog was a menace, stupid and chummy, but a menace just the same. So why should he worry if they had gone off on some daft escapade of their own? He determinedly pushed away thoughts of the marsh, the river, the old barns that looked as if they'd fall down at a mere puff of wind, of dangerous farm machinery, of the odd plane falling, even worse, bombs. Boys were boys the world over and probably were, right now, having the time of their lives. But Hannah?

Hannah would be dying a death, full of fear for the lads. She would run herself into the ground on the young wretches behalf. It was Hannah who was his concern. Perky young Hannah who, had she guessed how he felt about her, would hoot with laughter and call him plain daft. Hannah who had got right under his skin.

Ye gods! He wasn't searching for the kids, he was looking for the girl. For Hannah who was so chirpy and enthusiastic and full of fun. She who dived in where angels feared to tread, but quite clearly never had romance on her mind . . . at least where he was concerned. He found himself wishing he was dark and handsome like Richard. That

94

he had Richard's gift of the gab. That he was anywhere but stumbling along a path in a copse that led to Knollys.

It was dark and Matt was glad that he had brought his torch. Suddenly a dark figure moved from the shadows.

'Who's that?' Matt queried sharply.

'It's only me, sir,' Lenny replied.

'Good lord, the Madeira boy. What are you doing out here so late? You'll catch your death of cold.'

'I – I was keeping watch, that's all.'

'I see. Well, I think you'd best cut off home.'

'Yes, sir, only . . .'

'Only what?'

'I was hoping that Miss Hannah might come.'

'Did you say Hannah, boy?'

'I wondered if she might guess that . . .'

'You – you and the twins were hiding out here?'

There was a muffled, 'Yes, sir,' then silence.

One word out of place and the boy would cut off like a whippet, Matt thought. And the thing was that if he did, Matt would be the one at a loss. Clearly the boy knew what he was at. He had appeared from the bushes and seemed quite at home. No, if he wanted the twins back safe with their mother, he'd have to play it by Lenny's rules. He cleared his throat and said in a friendly, companionable way, 'You know Hannah then?'

'Yes, sir. She's nice. She sometimes walks here. Weekends usually, when the others have gone home. She won't go with them because she loves it here. She likes trees, she says, and wouldn't cut them down. When we meet up, she tells me things . . . and listens to me talking too.'

'What does she tell you?'

'How lucky I am to live here in the country. How evil it is in the city where everything's as smoke-grey as some people's souls. A few are really wicked, she says, as bad as Germans any day, with their killing and cruelty and treacherous ways. That you can't trust anyone up there, but it's different here. She said that she is my friend. You see, I told her that Chris and Chook are my only pals and she said rubbish. That she was my mate too.'

'That's good,' Matt said easily and found himself wondering what had upset Hannah so much that she hated going back to her own environment. Loathed and distrusted the people there so greatly that she thought of them as enemies. He stopped trying to figure it out and went on, 'Hannah's a marvellous friend to have, old son, and I'm her pal too. And right now I'm looking for her. She promised to meet me,

95

but never turned up. Shall we look for her together? She's probably worried stiff about the twins. Perhaps it might be a good idea to fetch them first, eh?'

'No, sir.'

'Oh?'

'My aunt says they're for it, sir, and that Mr Moses is to be shot.'

'I see! Well, old son, I promise you that the lads won't find themselves in water too hot to take.' He smiled. 'Not with Hannah on their side. And as for Moses, I swear that no one will dare raise a gun to him, let alone shoot him.' He laughed deep in his throat. 'In fact, if there's even a hair threatened on that darned dog's head, I'll take him on myself. All right? He's not a bad young fellow as mutts go. Now, shall we move on?'

They walked together through the gloom, feet scrunching over fallen leaves, and Matt was surprised to see how sure-footed and alert Lenny was. The lad was supposed to be a dullard, with more than one screw loose if you listened to the gossip his aunt put about. But there was nothing simple about the youngster walking so easily through the darkness . . . unlike the airman at his side. Matt was conscious of the clean smell all about, of leaves and trees and moss and fresh crisp air. He lifted his head up, to look at the sky through a gap in the branches, and his foot hit something hard. He swore, then pulled himself up short, remembering the youngster.

'Sorry about that,' he said. 'Not as used to all this as you. What do you and Hannah talk about? The squirrels here, and all other sorts of country stuff? Foxes and pheasants and things?'

'Yes, and about music.'

'Music, Lenny?' his tone betraying his surprise.

'Miss Hannah understands,' the boy told him. 'She says she doesn't know anything about music really, how to play or even to listen properly, but that since she's been here she hears music too, and she says I'm far from silly – that the boys at school and some grown-ups are the fools. Miss Hannah says that her favourite music is the wind in the trees.'

'I see.' Matt was intrigued. 'And what do you like best?'

Lenny had forgotten all self-consciousness now. He earnestly clutched Matt's arm. 'Just beyond the old house there's small stream. It's nice there, quiet and peaceful. I sit there often and listen while the water ripples over the pebbles. It makes music, hundreds of little rushing notes. It – it sings!'

'And you hear these notes and they make a tune, is that it, boy?' he asked, then thoughtfully, 'I think I know what you mean. Once, on a peaceful night when I was flying upstairs, I fancied I heard something quite nice coming from the stars.'

Lenny understood at once.

'That must have given you a good feeling, sir. Miss Hannah would say that too. She says that I don't hear music, I feel it. She likes me to play.'

'Oh?'

'I have a violin. It was my mother's. Aunt Maud was going to sell it, but my uncle stopped her. I was afraid after that, so I brought it here, to my hiding place.'

'Ah! And that's where the twins are?'

'Yes, sir. Miss Hannah's the only one who knows about it – and now you. You won't tell?'

'I swear, old chap. All right?'

'Yes, sir,' Lenny replied.

They came to a tangled mass of undergrowth that looked impenetrable, but Lenny carefully pulled aside branches of holly. Matt followed through to where there stood the dark outline of a tumbled ruin, clearly an old farmworker's cottage, abandoned when Knollys ceased to farm. It looked squat and forlorn, but there was a pallid chink of light shining through a window. As Matt stumbled and swore again, it was extinguished, then spluttered to life again as Lenny whistled, high and clear like a nightingale. At once a russet-red dart flew out and leapt joyously up at Matt. A tongue licked with gay abandon, slobbering all over his cheek. Then the twins came out, subdued, dirty and looking tired.

'Hello, lads,' Matt said easily. 'Nice place you've got here.'

'It stinks of rat's droppings in there,' Chris said, aggrieved.

'I'm hungry,' Chook announced. 'And I hate rats too. I'm glad Lenny's back. Now we can do as he promised – sit by the stream and—' his voice, trembling now, rose higher '– and eat?'

Lenny fumbled in a brown-paper bag he had been holding under his arm and brought out doorsteps of bread and fishpaste. Then, as the boys munched greedily, he looked up into Matt's face.

'It wasn't stealing . . . not really. There's always something there in Knollys and when Mr St John doesn't come it gets thrown away. I – I've often . . .'

'It's all right, matey,' Matt said carefully. 'I don't want to know. What's this about rats?'

'Nothing can get at my violin,' Lenny told him earnestly. 'I built it a sort of safety box with stones. And I come here when I can, and play. I'll get it now if you want.'

'He's jolly good,' Chris said round a mouthful of fishpaste, watching Lenny disappearing into the gloom. 'I say, salmon and shrimp! I think it's the best taste in the world.'

'I like lobster,' Chook began. 'It's—'

'Shut up moaning,' Chris told him. 'I'll give my crusts to Mr Moses, but you can give him all of yours if that's how you feel . . . thick-head.'

'He'll get my crusts too,' Chook replied, squaring up. 'And don't call me thick-head.'

'All right, bird-bonce.'

Lenny came back then and with one accord they sat down where they were, on the damp grass, while in the dimness, lit only by a shrouded moon and a trillion stars, the violin case was reverently unwrapped from a mass of black-out cloth.

The case was opened and Lenny took out the bow and the beloved instrument.

'They have been thinking about their mum, sir,' he said quietly. 'And I was remembering my mother and father too, so . . .'

He pulled the bow over the strings and Matt, sensing the lad's very real distress, said nothing. Mr Moses sidled up and rested his head on his lap.

Gradually, as Lenny became more sure of himself, a sad theme evolved. A theme that matched the desolate surroundings, and blended eerily with the darkness.

Matt stiffened then as a shadow darker than the rest moved near. Then he felt relief and pleasure as Hannah silently sat down at his side. He put out his hand and felt her fingers curl round his own. He waited, staring ahead, his senses alive as never before.

Suddenly the music changed until it was the rushing of the wind soughing through the leafless branches, which gradually whipped even fiercer until the notes became the great crescendo of a storm-tossed night. And although Matt knew nothing of two people killed on a Christmas night, of two bodies lying there stark and still in a stone-cold kitchen, he sensed a terrible grief, an urgency, a deep unrest. And there was something else. Something incredible and very important. He realised that a whole village had overlooked the genius within its midst.

High above, the moon escaped its dark shroud and sailed serenely in the sky. The stars in their myriads seemed to play hide and seek with silver-tipped clouds, and a hush fell as Lenny let the bow fall to his side.

'That was magnificent,' Matt said. 'Well done. You played brilliantly.'

'As always, Skipper,' Hannah added, and hastily took her hand out of Matt's grasp. She laughed self deprecatingly. 'Stone me, you're right little devils to find! I've been here, there and everywhere.' She turned to the lean-faced boy. 'The penny dropped the moment I learned that you had disappeared too, Lenny. What a young scallywag you are. Of course we are all going back – right now.'

'No!' Chris said fiercely. 'They're going to shoot Mr Moses and—'

'Over my dead body!' she told him firmly. 'Come on, no arguing, get yourself started. Your mum's going mad with worry back there.'

'We're going to be hung, drawn and quartered, Mrs Madeira said so.' Chook's voice was beginning to shake. 'And I don't want to be hung drawn and . . .'

'Don't be such a soppy ha'pporth,' Hannah laughed. 'Do you honestly think your mum would have anyone harm a hair on your heads? Besides, everything that happened was an accident – which, I might say, I saw with my very own eyes. So no more arguing. Home!'

'Cross your fingers and hope to die?' Chook was still uncertain.

'I can't die here,' Hannah told him blandly, 'in case your favourite vampire's around.'

'If Miss Hannah says it's all right,' Lenny told them, 'that's how it is. Go on, go back to your mum.'

'We don't want to, and—'

'I do, Chook!' Chris said fiercely, letting go of his brave façade. 'It's creepy and I hate vampires, and I want to see Mum.'

'Show them the way, old son,' Matt told Lenny. 'We'll follow in a sec.'

His tone was authoritative, and once Lenny had returned his violin to its hidden place, the three boys obediently began to walk back. Hannah made as though to follow, but Matt stopped her. She gasped, because his arms had gone round her and felt like iron bands. She tried to pull away, but it was impossible. Then the world was blotted from view and there was only Matt and the feel of his lips on hers. A surge of feeling rushed through her as wild as Lenny's music. She wanted to let go, and just for a moment kissed him back and clung to him – then sanity returned. She pulled away from him and glared.

'That was a rotten thing to do.'

'Not from where I'm standing,' he told her quietly. 'And it shows you what I feel. I'm prepared to wait until you grow up, Hannah York, but that's how things are and that's how they'll stay.'

'My name's not Madeline,' she sulked, 'and what's more . . .'

'I never wanted to spend the rest of my life with Madeline, but I do want to spend it with you,' Matt told her. Then he grinned. 'I never knew you worried about her.'

'Oh, stuff!'

Hannah flounced away, cheeks hot, heart racing, not knowing whether to laugh or cry. Then a fresh drama began as she joined the lads. Lenny had stopped dead at the clearing and was refusing to move.

'I'm not going back,' he was saying. 'I'm not going back there ever again.'

'Oh leave it out, lad,' Matt told him. 'Living with your aunt can't be so bad. Worse things happen at sea.'

'Not worse than living with old Dragon Drawers,' Chris said.

'It must be like living in black hell,' Chook agreed.

'Matt,' Hannah cut in, 'you take Lenny back to the Madeira place and sort of – sort of stick up for him, eh? I'll get these two young devils back to Lily and I'll wait for you there.'

The rest of the walk home was continued in silence. Glancing at his watch Matt realised the lads had been missing nearly all night. He found himself hoping that old Madeira was putting his missus through her paces. Damned old fogey needed to get her comeuppance for a change.

By the time he marched Lenny past the penned-in geese, and wrinkled his nose coming from the sows to the Madeiras' front door, Matt could feel the tension in the boy. His mouth went down at the corners. Bloody old bag, he thought, making a kid so scared he's gone stiff. They say animals and children know. What the hell's up with Walt? Doesn't see what's going on with his brother's son?

The door flew open before they reached it and Maud Madeira stood there, fully dressed and with her hat stuck firmly on her head.

'What do you mean by it?' she raged. 'You young swine, I'll swing for you yet.' She strode forward and gave Lenny a stinging slap round the face. 'I'll thrash you to within an inch of your life, that I promise.' Her voice rose higher, out of control. 'How dare you make me a laughing stock! How dare—'

Lenny cowered against Matt's side and began to sob.

'That's it,' Matt said coldly. 'You spiteful old faggot, that *is it!* Come on, Lenny, you'll be coming back with me.'

'I'm his guardian!' she screeched. 'He stays here and—' Then, as Matt was marching Lenny away; 'I'll have the law on you!'

'I hope you do,' he snapped over his shoulder.'And I'm sure that the whole village will join me in having plenty to tell the law.'

Matt's arm went comfortingly round Lenny's heaving shoulders. They walked to Rose Cottage and found the front door open. Matt went in.

They didn't hear him enter. Hannah was sitting on a chair near the fireplace, staring into the dead embers. Lily was on her knees, her arms about two muddy, subdued boys. Mr Moses, too, had his tail down. It seemed he sensed what was going on.

'Don't you ever do a thing like that again!' Lily whispered fiercely. 'Don't you know how much I love you both and how much I love Mr Moses? Your father would go mad if he knew you had gone missing. And I couldn't live without you, even if you are always in scrapes.' She looked tearfully over to Hannah. 'And I'll thank Hannah for finding you, thank and bless her for the rest of my days.'

'For the hundredth time,' came the chirpy reply as Hannah looked at the small group, 'it was Matt who found them first and—'

'So!' Matt said from the doorway. 'Here we all are. And with your permission, Lily, one extra.'

'Matt? Lenny?' Lily looked from one to the other. 'Then the balloon's really about to go up?'

'In all probability, yes. She walloped him one, and was threatening to kill him. She was beside herself and looking as though she meant to do murder, so I took matters into my own hands. I'm making him my responsibility until all this is sorted out. One thing though, I can't just walk him into the Endercots' place at this Godawful hour, so . . .'

'Lenny will stay with the boys, of course he will,' Lily said firmly. 'It's our fight, Maud's and mine. Shall you contact Walter, or shall I?'

'Leave it all to me. It's as I've said. From now on, I'm going to have a penn'orth or two to say. This here's a sensitive kid and that woman's scared him half to death. I want to chat up Walt. Man's talk, understand, Lil? All right?'

'Thank you, Matt.' Lil was smiling, the strain leaving her face. 'I'll get all three ready for bed – even though the night's through.' She looked down at the boys. 'I'll sort you out and make you some hot chocolate, then I'll have to dash off to Hawksley. Don't answer any knocks, do you hear me? Stay in bed. All of this will soon be put to rights. It's only a storm in a teacup so there's no need to be afraid.'

'Mr Moses . . .'

'Is as safe as houses, that I promise you.'

'Then I'll leave you all to it,' Matt said. He smiled at Lily and gave Hannah a long meaningful look, then saluting them both, he about-faced and took his leave.

'What a very nice man he is,' Lily said. 'And like a rock!'

'Oh, he'll pass with a push,' Hannah replied airily. 'Now, I think I'd best get on too.'

She left the cottage, but couldn't face going back to the house to sleep. She began to walk away from the direction of Hawksley, along an age-old track. The sky in the far east was beginning to turn pearl grey. All around, the clouds had dropped to ground level, and swirled about like great drifts of damp cotton-wool, bejewelling branches,

101

hedges and grasses, clothing them in a million minuscule moisture beads.

Hannah walked in the direction of the Drew Stables and then, in the silence and peace of the morning, leaned over the barred gate she had discovered, that was half-hidden by overgrown holly and ivy. The air was crisp and clean. It held the tang of wet leaves and mud and the briskness of coming winter days. Hannah stared ahead, feeling in a dreamlike state and still very confused.

She had never been kissed by a man before, at least not like that. It was disturbing almost upsetting. And what exactly had Matt said, about waiting for her to grow up? That was a damned cheek for a start! What was more . . .

Oh darn it, she was a silly fool to give it a second thought. Her cheeks went hot with embarrassment. But she couldn't forget how it had felt, how she had wanted it to go on. She pulled herself up, thinking that showed what a rotten mean devil he was, taking advantage like that. It was a jolly good job she had found this spot, this secret gate that was hidden from view, which in its turn hid her from view. From this vantage point she could watch the horses without being seen herself.

In the early-morning mists the horses moved like phantoms, some at full gallop, with tiny figures perched on their backs. Some were being led, blanketed and hooded against the raw chill, by shivering stable boys – or in this day and age, by anyone too young or too old, or too frail, to be called up for Army, Navy, Air Force, Munitions, Mines . . .

The sounds and smells of this place, the sight of magnificent beasts at their exercise, thrilled her. She threw back her head as if to drink in the champagne of the morning, then again the thought of Matt's kiss intruded – an ecstatic sigh escaping as her gaze wandered over the scene that was like a misty green sea where small woods loomed like fan-shaped islands.

She could hear the steady rhythm of approaching hooves. Hooves of a horse being led and not ridden. What's more, it sounded near the edge of the fields, not too far from the gate. Hannah stepped back out of sight. Mr Drew, a tough old devil the twins said, did not like people trespassing, and she, Hannah, was on his ground.

Horse and leader came nearer and Hannah peeped out to see. Was it by chance James St John's Pegasus?

It was not Sophia's grey, nor her night-black Belvedere. Neither was it the chestnut Tan-Tivvy belonging to Beatrice Drew, the stable-owner's daughter. Spoilt brat Beatrice who had been after James St John for years.

Some hopes! Hannah curled her lip at the thought. Beatrice and

James? Ha! Though the pair certainly deserved each other by all accounts.

The head of a beautiful white animal came into view. The leader, a shadowy figure on the far side, held the reins. It was Snow Queen, the mare that had once belonged to Miles St John – poor old Miles, who had been drowned at sea. Snow Queen was fussed over and cosseted as much now as she had been when her master had been alive. She was a glorious creature that Beatrice would give her eye-teeth for, but she would never, ever have her: James St John would see to that.

The horse was being turned, led further into the field, and now Hannah saw the figure of her leader. There was something familiar about the man. He was limping, seemed scrunched-up somehow, as if he had a curve in his spine . . .

Sudden terror turned her to ice. Her mouth went dry. Dear God in Heaven – it was Frank!

'No!' she was screaming in her heart and mind and soul. 'This is mad. This cannot be. Frank is dead. They killed him, Biff and Fatty and Ram. And anyway, how could he have found himself here?' Fresh horror came. 'Holy Mother!' If her eyes hadn't deceived her, if it *was* Frank, then Ram wouldn't be far behind.

She felt the world swimming round her. She held on to reason, fighting to retain her sanity until horse and walker were out of sight. Then she let herself fall to the ground and lay there, rigid, staring unseeingly up and into the ever-lightening sky.

A long while later, it seemed like an eternity, she slowly made her way back to Hawksley, no longer feeling either safe or at home.

103

Chapter Fourteen

The mist had cleared as Matt walked across the Madeira yard, making his way through ridges of mud. The smell of pigs made him want to spew. They reckoned that there was no such thing as a dirty pig – only dirty owners of pigs. Well, Walt's lot stank to high heaven and that was a fact. His geese were evil for all they were enclosed within a thin wire fence. The leader of the gang was ruffling its feathers, looking capable of breaking free and ready to attack.

'Stay where you are, Bonzo,' Matt said. 'Else I'll wring your bloody neck.'

Footsteps squelching over the ground, he reached the front door and knocked. Walter came, pipe in hand. He was stone cold sober and had a glint in his eye.

'Morning, boy.'

'Hello, Walt.'

'Wanna talk?'

'That's about it.'

'Righto. We'll go to the barn.' He grinned sourly. 'The missus a'nt too happy there.' He came outside and carefully shut the door behind him. 'The old barn's my place. Not all that safe these days, and the brick floor's about to give up the ghost. Still, we're better off in there for all that.'

They were walking side by side now, towards the barn. The air felt cold and puffs of white vapour were coming from their mouths as they breathed.

'Changed since yesterday,' Walter observed. 'Weather's as fickle as a woman.'

'And your woman scares the pants off Lenny,' Matt told him as they inched back the dragging door. The barn with its cobwebs and spiders and smell of rats' droppings enfolded them. It was crowded and claustrophobic with its old machinery, the thresher, various tools and rolls of wire.

'Scares me too sometimes,' Walter said evenly as he patted an upturned barrel and himself sat on its mate. 'Cider these held, and there's plenty more full 'uns lined up at the back. Somerset's got the name, but we don't do so bad with our apples in Essex. And you wanna taste our elderflower and berry wine – but our mead outstripped even that. Like amber it is, and sweet.'

'I'll have to try some. I like anything that's smooth and mellow.'

'I like the stuff that rasps the tongue.' Walt's smile was wry as he added, 'To drink, not to live with.'

'She's a bit cranky, Walt. Went off like a banshee, first thing.'

'Maud was as sweet as honey once, dainty and a good-looker too. It was a fight between me and old Stitson who'd get her. I bet he's laughin' up his sleeve about how lucky he was ter lose out.' He looked sideways. 'No one's heard me say a word against her till now. But things is different, because of my brother's boy. I'd made my bed and was daft enough to think I'd got to lie on all the lumps, but . . .'

'And you will lie on them, you milk-sop calling yourself a man!' Maud shouted as she fiercely pushed back the protesting, lop-sided door. She was scarlet with temper, wearing a black dress and that hat, looking menacing for all her lack of height. 'Don't know the meaning of the word loyalty, do you?' she flung at him. 'Well, you can pack your bags, you and that simpleton you brought under my roof, and neither of you never darken my doors again.'

'*Your* doors!' Walter told her, coming to his senses at last. '*Your* roof! This place is mine, Maud. Here I am and here I'll stay. And Lenny too – until I choose to let him go. Now get back to the house and stop making a fool of yourself.'

The passion of fury suffused her face. She raised her arm as if to strike him dead when she reached him. He stood up from the barrel, slowly, coldly, and gripped her wrist.

'I an't no maggot, Maud,' he told her. 'You can't have me brushed away.'

She seemed to swell, to gain enormous strength, and twisted away from his grasp. To the right, hanging on the wall, was a sickle and she made for it, clearly wishing to strike Walter dead. She was yelling threats now, beside herself, spinning round, knocking against a pile of heavy spades, rakes and hoes. They fell one by one, like dominoes, and landed heavily on the ground.

The floor gave way.

With a shriek of terror, Maud went down. Only her head was visible, and her hands, that were clawing into the yielding, treacherous crevices. From the yawning pit over which she found herself suspended, fumes, foul and suffocating, were rising. She began to gasp and choke.

Walter lay down full-length on the floor and firmly grasped her by the arms. Matt grabbed at the coil of rope suspended on the wall. While Walter hung on, Matt made the rope fast round under Maud's arms, knocking her hat off in his haste; then he passed the ends round one of the pillars that supported the roof.

Perspiration was pouring from Walter's face as he relaxed his grip and painfully rose to his feet.

'Don't fret, Maud old girl,' he said gruffly. 'We'll soon have you up.'

It was no easy job. Walter was far from young and Matt's injuries did not help. Maud was heavy, and their united efforts failed to bring her to the surface. She looked as though she was near to unconsciousness.

'Brandy. She needs brandy, boy,' Walter rasped. 'You'll find it in the kitchen, on the table, I was having a nip myself not an hour since.'

'You go. I'm stronger – I'll hang on here. Hurry!'

Walter vanished and Matt held on. The woman was a dead weight and her face was going blue. And there was something else. Bareheaded, though having a good head of hair, the lump showed. It was large and situated on the right side, above and at the back of her ear. My God, Matt thought, his body taut, his back agonizing, so that's what she's been hiding. The poor cow must be scared stiff! I bloody well would be . . . Then he began to sweat; he daren't let go, daren't. But his back was giving way, his whole body felt as if it were on the rack.

Walt was taking an age. Matt held on with every muscle in his body screaming until the old man returned. Walt began forcing drink down his wife's mouth.

'Come on, old girl,' he was saying in a soft, easy way. 'An't like you to give in. Come on, chin up, old dear. You an' me's a pair of bloody old chumps to be wrangling. That's it, Maudie, hang on. We won't let you go. I've phoned for help; it'll be on its way now. Maudie, come on!'

She swallowed, and seemed a little revived, but her face was white now, corpse-like. The rope seemed to be cutting into her, it was pulling so tight, yet she seemed unaware of it. And all the while Matt and Walter were trying to ease her weight. In spite of their efforts, her sagging head, the fumes, her hands turning blue-black because of the pressure of the rope, her body hanging over the unknown depths, it really looked like it was all up for Maud.

'Walt,' Matt breathed, 'Have you seen that . . .'

106

'Yes.' Walter's voice was grey. 'Right at the start, when her hat come off. Don't look good, does it? She's been clever to hide it. Poor old girl. Clever and daft and cunning – and I could bloody kill her stone dead.'

'She must be scared as hell.'

'I wondered why she took to wearing that hat – and them soddin' awful night-caps. Thought she was doing it deliberate to turn me off. I've not been on her side of the bed for donkeys' years, but this is a different matter. Poor old girl . . .' His voice roughened and he said again, 'Poor old girl.'

It seemed an eternity before help arrived, but just before Matt's back reached breaking point Maud was rescued and carried to her bed. Dr Dene was in attendance, crisply efficient, and cross.

'I suspected,' he told Walter, on examining the lump. 'I questioned, but was turned down flat. One cannot force a patient to have examinations, no matter how serious one suspects the condition might be . . . I'll telephone for an ambulance, of course. Damn good you have a phone, Walter. It would have been curtains else.'

'Has she got a chance?'

'We'll have to wait and see. X-rays and all that.'

'I'll go with her?'

'Naturally.'

Walter went downstairs and while the doctor was on the telephone, he said to Matt who had been hanging round, waiting, 'Can't thank you enough, boy. You look done in yourself, so best have Doc look at you before—'

'No, thanks. I'm fine. How's Maud?'

'Off to hospital and we'll see what we see. Matt, can you do me a favour?'

'Of course.'

'See that young Lenny gets to Norseby, eh? To the Allsops. Tell 'em that Walt sent him. That Maud's very ill and so, if they're still willing, p'raps they'll take the lad on for good and all.'

'He's a brilliant player on that fiddle of his. Did you know that, Walt?'

'Didn't, but I'm not surprised.' Walter's eyes went sad. 'My brother and his wife were all for things like that. Tell the Allsops to let him have lessons, proper like. He's to have every chance – and tell 'em I'll gladly pay.'

'I'll do that,' Matt replied and held out his hand. 'All in a night's work, eh?'

'Is that. Good on yer, boy. And thanks . . .'

*

In spite of being whacked, Matt made his way back to Hawksley. Lily heard his news wide-eyed and amazed.

'As big as an egg, you say? Lord, the woman's dead!'

'Not necessarily so. The X-rays will tell. Thought I'd let you know everything, mostly about young Lenny being off and away to Norseby. It will put his mind at rest when he hears that. I promised Walter I'd take him, but not today.' He smiled tiredly. 'I need a lie down. Bit of a strain all round. Poor old Maud was no lightweight. I suppose Hannah's asleep?'

'Yes, she turned up a while ago. She went for a walk and came back looking like death. Most people do when they've been up all night. You don't look all that healthy yourself. I'll make you a cuppa and . . .'

'No thanks, Lily, I'm off and away.' He turned at the door and added sheepishly, 'Tell Hannah I called, eh?'

'I'll give her your love,' she laughed.

'So, what do you think?'

'That faint heart ne'er won fair lady.'

'She'll not have me?'

'She'll not take you seriously, Matt. She's not that sort.'

'We'll have to see about that,' Matt told her and waved over his shoulder as he left Hawksley to return to the Endercots'.

The following Monday the girls were working hard, Hannah excessively so. She felt lost, bewildered and not quite certain whether she was sane or not. It *must* have been her imagination. It just couldn't have been Frank. Far better to try and forget the whole sorry scene. Her mouth felt inordinately dry. Her flask of hot tea had gone long ago. She needed a drink, would die for one, and told the others so.

'There's plenty in the tap in the yard we passed,' Ginny told her. 'Freezing water? Ugh! Sooner you than me.'

'Well, thirst is not only making me feel weak, but downright unwilling,' Hannah said and threw down her knife. 'And I feel really unsettled and quite horrible today. In fact, I think I'm fed up.'

'You said you loved this life,' Ginnie pointed out reasonably enough.

'I do, I do!' Hannah said stoutly. 'The country is fine – but even though sometimes the city seems like a cesspool, I think deep down I'll always be a Londoner at heart.' She jutted out her chin. 'But what's that got to do with the fact that I'm dying of thirst? I'll be back in a minute.'

Hannah walked over to fetch her empty flask and made her way down the lane. Because of the shock of what she had seen, or thought she had seen, Hannah did not hurry. Her blood was running hot and cold. Thoughts of that night, when the Germans had the docks ablaze, and Walker Street was in ruins . . . the terrible memory of the alleyway scene, lit by explosions, and that rag-doll figure being buried by rubble, was getting to be too much. She wanted to scream and run and keep going for ever. But it was no use.

Busy with her worries and woes she was unaware of James St John, who had been exercising Pegasus prior to returning to his city offices. The sight of one of his Land Girls, Hannah of all people, leaving the field and seeming to have such an aimless air was intriguing to say the least. Keeping Pegasus hoof-silent on the muddy ground, he remained hidden from Hannah's view, and followed her.

Eventually Hannah reached the yard and saw the tap. It seemed funny somehow, she thought, a tap perched on a bare pipe. There was no one around, at least, no humans, but there were lots of chickens scrabbling about. Hannah turned on the tap, rinsed, then filled the flask cup and really enjoyed the draught of cold water. Then she began filling the flask itself.

Suddenly she heard an awful sort of crow. She turned and saw a huge cockerel with a red comb sticking out of its head like a war banner, advancing on her and looking as if it meant business. Murder was in its beady eyes.

Hannah coolly turned the tap off, telling herself that it was a known fact: you only had to look savage animals straight in the eye to subdue them. She swung round and deliberately faced the enemy, breathing hard and steely-eyed. One glance assured her, however, that what might work with lions, rhinos, mad dogs and elephants, would get short shrift with this madly wing-flapping piece of poultry. Casting honour to the four winds, she swung round and ran hell for leather. The thing was following her! She could hear it! Imagining that awful beak pecking her to bits, blind panic filled her. Then suddenly, gloriously, she was safe.

A tall masterful man miraculously appeared. Then most wonderfully, he was sending the enemy packing as if it was a mere bit of fluff off a dandelion. And as she stood there, helplessly heaving and gasping, she watched as James threw back his head and laughed. His merriment, so unexpected – and so infuriating! – did wonders for him. It showed off his even white teeth, and the tanned column of his throat, and tousled his neat black hair.

He stood there, legs astride, hands on hips, face crinkled up with fun and looking younger by far.

'Hannah, Hannah,' he choked, 'You should never have run.'

'From where I was standing, I had no choice,' she retorted nastily. 'That thing was going to peck out my eyes.'

109

'I'm sorry,' he tried to look as straight-faced as her glare demanded. 'I keep forgetting that you're a young lady from the city and unsure of country ways. Would you like a lift back on Pegasus?'

It was only then that she saw the horse waiting patiently by the yard entrance, his reins hanging loose.

'No, thank you,' she said politely. Then, remembering that other horse, that strangely wizened old man leading it, she felt the return of her horror. Please God, she found herself thinking wildly, don't let it have been Frank. Not down here. Please, please, not here!

'Hannah?' James was asking her. 'Are you feeling well?'

'Fine, thank you,' she told him. 'Now if you'll excuse me, I'll get back – under my own steam!'

James stood there, watching her. Strange, he pondered, how the way she was trying so hard to walk away with pride and dignity seemed so touching. What a sparky little thing she was, what a little mate she could be. Yes, for a female, she was exceptional, and for an unknown reason, the youngster managed to get right under his skin. Pity he'd got off on the wrong foot with her.

He squirmed, remembering his first unfortunate remark about WLA uniforms. Socially he had kept himself away from most village women for years. Hardly knew how to talk to them, not that he wanted to after the hell he'd been through because of one treacherous female. Still, his 'uniform' remark the night the girls had come to Knollys had been meant kindly, but his lamentable attempt at flattery had sounded like sarcasm. And quite clearly, Hannah was never going to forgive him for it.

There came the chugging sound of Endercot's old jalopy. It pulled up and Ellery took out his cherrywood pipe, exhaled thin blue smoke, then enquired, 'You heard about the Madeira woman? I've been warning old Walt about his barn floor for years . . .'

Chapter Fifteen

For a while the whole of Lindell talked of the Madeira tragedy. But life flowed on, Hannah thought as she sat in the Hawksley kitchen one evening. There was work to contend with, the war, and wanting and wishing to know answers to questions – like had that really been Frank she had seen at the Drews' place? Had Matt really been sincere? And what of her bosom buddies, her chums? Things seemed to be going a bit haywire there.

Ginnie was getting more and more aware of Richard's charms – who wouldn't? But it was changing her character. Ginnie unsure of herself, Ginnie going dreamy, sometimes even acting downright confused, was not like the real Ginnie at all. She no longer seemed the sensible, down-to-earth individual one could lean on ... and it hurt. Ginnie the open-hearted was getting closed in on herself – and Hannah felt left outside.

How could she bare her soul to Ginnie now? Tell her a yarn about stepfathers, bombings and blokes called Ram who had mad murderous eyes?

On the other hand, Raven's regular rides now occasionally involved her meeting James St John. She had said so, in her cool, dismissive way. They had spoken together sometimes, and got on rather well. This made Hannah want to hit out – yes, all guns blazing! This because of the gossip she heard back from Lily.

Via Lily, Hannah heard again all about that cow Beatrice Drew being out and out awful to Raven; the snotty little devil acting as though Raven was an enemy of some kind. An enemy on a lower level, of course – since Raven was a monied no one from Surrey, whereas she, Beatrice, was the *crème de la crème*, born and bred in Lindell.

As if Raven could be interested in that sort of old-hat tactic, Hannah seethed. And as for James St John? ... That old stinker with Raven? Ha, that was a laugh for a start! But, according to Lily,

Beatrice Drew saw Raven as some kind of threat, which boded ill. The Drew girl had, over the years, managed to throw all feminine competition out of the ring.

It hadn't helped, Hannah thought smugly, that Raven on horseback looked tall and lady-like, almost too beautiful to be true. And Beatrice must have realised by now that all her snicks and snaps merely went harmlessly over Raven's head.

'Guess what,' Lily pressed home her point. 'In spite of her distant manner, I heard that Mr James can't take his eyes off our Raven. I reckon Mrs St John will hear the rumours sooner or later. *Then* watch the fur fly!'

'I've got fur too,' Hannah reminded her bluntly. 'Raven's got me and Ginnie on her side. Oh bloody hell, don't talk about Ginnie.'

'Right you are,' Lily smoothed down her sunflower and forget-me-not bestrewn apron. 'Do you want a saccharine in your cocoa?'

'Two, please.'

'Why aren't you in the Rookwood?'

'Can't stand the thought of watching Richard Neville chatting Ginnie up – and ogling. He gets her all goggle-eyed and confused. It makes me mad. I keep seeing that photo of her Aiden and, well – you know!'

'I thought you believed it was her affair? That Aiden was in India getting on with his life as best as possible, so the same must be good enough for her?'

'I still believe that . . . if it makes her happy, but she's not.'

'She's making up her own mind about things, I expect,' Lily said in her blithe, down-to-earth way. 'No one else must stick their noses in.'

'Point taken,' Hannah replied and grinned, shame-faced. 'I'm probably showing off because I miss Matt. He's a great mate and I got used to him hanging round waiting for me. Even Ellery says he and Eloise find the house too quiet without him.'

'You haven't heard?'

'Only a scribbled note in the post. Telling me that he received a posting to Bury St Edmunds. I don't even know where that is,' she added mournfully.

'Suffolk, north of here. Not all that far as the crow flies. It's before you get to Norfolk, anyway. Cheer up. Gert and Daisy's on the wireless later on. You like them.'

'Trying to get rid of Yours Truly?'

'Of course not, but I'm off soon. Would you like to come back to the cottage with me? I daren't be late. Emily's a darling the way she puts the boys to bed then sits there knitting until I get back. I'd never take advantage of a friend.'

'I like Mrs Kitt too, and her husband George. He's a very jolly old soul, isn't he? Lily, I don't half wish . . .'

'Go on, don't stop there.'

'It's just that I . . . I never know when Matt's teasing me. He told me that I'd got to grow up, you know.'

'Really?' Lily chuckled. 'I wonder why. Then what did he say?'

'Well . . . that he'd wait until I did.'

'And?'

'He never said any more! It was on the night I found him with the boys in the ruined cottage outside Knollys. He kissed me and . . .' Hannah bit her lip. 'I know this sounds daft, but I half-expected he'd say something else, something a bit serious. Or at least try to kiss me again before he left.'

'Ah! So that's it. Miss I'm-above-all-that, has suddenly changed her mind. He's fallen for you, Hannah, and he has probably let you know it in millions of ways.'

'He never did after that night. I suppose it's because I kept him at arms' length from then on. I mean, I couldn't take him seriously, could I? Blokes are all right, but . . .' She shrugged expressively. 'Anyway, he got all tied up with taking Lenny over to Norseby, and after that visiting him to make sure he'd settled in. Then he went with Walter to visit poor old Maud.'

'Walt's all right, and so was Maud before . . .'

'That lump started growing on her head? Matt knows that – now. He understands. He also knows that Walter only hates dogs because it was a yapping old terrier that scared the horse pulling the cart his brother and sister-in-law were in. They were both killed stone dead, you know. Lenny was lucky because he was thrown clear.'

'I know. Puts a different complexion on things, doesn't it?'

'Certainly did, so far as Matt was concerned. He managed to fill his days all right, with Walter, while I was working. Evening times, when me and Matt met in the Rookwood, he sometimes used to look at me as though he thought I was special. When we walked back here he'd tease me and laugh and ruffle my hair like he does to the twins, but that was it.'

'More to the point, how did you treat him?'

'The same. Like we're damn good mates. I feel at home with him, comfortable. It came as a shock when he got a clean bill of health and went back to Matching, but that was all right. I was glad for him in a way. He hated just kicking his heels. Then right out of the blue, he's posted and gone and—'

'Didn't he say anything? Anything at all?'

'Only that he was going. That I would be hearing from him soonest.

113

That I must always remember what he'd said.' She looked tragic. 'And all he said was that he was waiting for me to grow up. Charming!'

'You'll hear from him soon enough. He's mad about you and it shows.'

'Do you think so?' Hannah was pulling herself together. 'That's jolly decent of you to say so. I mean, I was feeling pretty humiliated. I'm not into romance or anything like that, but it's nice to have a bloke go gaga over you. Gives a girl confidence.'

'You're the last one that needs confidence, the way you up and lip everyone when it suits you,' Lily teased. 'Now I'll just put another log on the fire – and on yours too if you're going to listen to the wireless. Then I must dash.'

'Don't matter about the log. Goes quick that wood, eh? Not like lovely old coal. Let's hope your old mate who used to work in the stables here digs like crazy.'

'Miners are digging for coal for factory fires. There's huge furnaces in munitions factories and so on. No, young woman, we'll just be grateful that we're here where log-fires present no difficulties.'

'You can't half be a know-all,' Hannah complained. 'Oh well, I think I'll join Raven upstairs. It won't hurt to have an early night. We're on hedging and ditching now – ugh! You ought to see some of the things cluttering up the ditches. Dead rats for a start, and . . . Oh, you're off! Good night, Lil.'

Hannah went upstairs and found Raven asleep in bed, the book in which her husband had written down his poetry beside her. Hannah carefully put the book on Raven's bedside table then made herself ready for bed. But she was unable to relax, fretting over the thing uppermost in her mind.

She still hadn't breathed a word to her friends about Frank, what had happened, how things were. It all seemed too awful to be true. They would think she was mucking about, that she was having them on a piece of string, or that she had gone a bit mad. No, she'd do better to keep her mouth shut.

She had gone to the old gate again, of course she had, and seen no sign of Frank – nor the man she believed to be him. She had asked subtle questions, about the chaps who exercised the horses, but Raven hadn't been able to tell her much. She was mad on horses, apparently always had been. Surrey girls like her friend, Hannah thought fondly, lived in a totally different world to those that hailed from Walker Street.

Walker Street girls saw the magnificently tough old drays pulling the long carts laden with barrels of beer. Or else tradesmen's animals that stopped and started at command, and had such patient eyes. Horses, to men like those in Walker Street, were just names sneakily put on betting slips. They knew nothing and cared less about the beautiful animals that pranced and danced and ran like spirits of the wind over the grasslands around Lindell.

Hannah herself had come to love watching them, would have liked to get to know them, would probably become as soft on them as Frank had been, given half the chance. Her stepfather had really worshipped his old Firelord, by all accounts.

Hannah pushed the thought of Frank away, but before she slept she resolved to go back home to London the following Saturday. She only had to work until twelve and then she would be free. She would search for Frank's aunt – Ma Carpenter would know everything. In that way, Hannah would learn the truth of it for once and for all . . .

It was cold in the carriage: Hannah's feet were freezing. She sat there, her body rocking with the motion of the train, hoping that with luck it'd be a safe journey, no enemy planes about.

It was too much to ask for. The warning went. The train huffed and puffed, blew out steam with a high-pitched impatient shriek and came to a halt in a wayside station that looked little more than a cattleshed. Several of the passengers got out to stretch their legs, Hannah among them. She grinned wryly at a WAAF.

'Bloody good, eh?'

'All in a lifer. You're a spudbasher, eh?'

'Among other things. What do you do?'

'Drive a lorry and trailer laden with gas-tubes.'

'Gas tubes?'

'Barrage-balloons for the use of.'

'Crikey! That could be nasty – if a bomb hit, I mean.'

'It could: I don't think about it. I'll be in as much danger tonight – just like all the others sleeping in The Smoke. I don't suppose you hear or see too much of the war in the country?'

'Not too much,' Hannah nodded, not mentioning the bombing of Matching Airfield, of planes roaring off all proud and tremendous, only to return limping and growling like injured old men. Of the Kentish farm, cows blown to smithereens, and the old farmer's dead wife. The nice motherly woman who had made the best apple dumplings in the world . . .

'All aboard!' came the cry. A flag was waved. Passengers dived back into their carriages and found their seats. The WAAF travelling a little further on, waved a cheerful farewell. Hannah waved back, liking her, admiring her, knowing that she was just another ship passing in the night. She fell to wondering about her close friends, with whom she

115

had lunched not more than a couple of hours ago. She hoped that they would have a nice weekend. Raven had chosen to stay in Hawksley and admitted that she would spend most of her time hanging round the stables, given half a chance.

'Ha!' Hannah had snorted before pointing out, 'And dear old Sophia will probably haunt the place too, now she knows that devil James has got his eye on you. That woman rides a lot. Her horse Belvedere . . .'

'I know, Hannah.' Raven's tone was faintly surprised, her finely-arched brows raised. 'And please don't carry on about James. As far as Sophia is concerned, she and I pass the time of day when we meet. In fact, as casually as her son and I. There's nothing more to it. Oh, and for the record, Sophia is not so bad.'

'Strewth!' Beyond words, Hannah turned to Ginnie. 'Will you be coming to the station with me?'

'I shall catch the later train, I think.' Ginnie looked decidedly uncomfortable because of Hannah's glare. 'I promised to meet Richard first. I'll be going home after that.'

Poor old Aiden's had it, Hannah thought. Blow me down, you'd have thought Ginnie of all people could have seen through Richard Neville. So he was a hero, had been shot down. He was also a lady killer and he had Ginnie in his sights. The one girl who, up until meeting him, had everything in her life cut and dried, her emotions under control. She seemed to have gone deaf, dumb and blind where the airman was concerned. He's a wolf, Hannah seethed, and only Ginnie won't accept the fact.

She had dismissed them both, on her dignity, nose in air, leaving them looking bemused. They had no inkling of her secret terror. Hannah knew that she *had* to go back to Walker Street. Had to! She must know for once and for all if she had been seeing things, like misty visions of Frank.

Perhaps she was going crackers. Perhaps the war effort and everything was proving too much. Hold on! She told herself fiercely. Come on, girl – bloody well get a grip!

The train pulled into her station at last and she went outside and queued for her bus. On the way back to Walker Street she saw the latest results of enemy action. Collapsed homes, gutted warehouses, wrecked streets, but now with two new features. One, people were carrying water from public mains. Two, long queues were waiting for outer-city buses to take them away for the rest of the weekend. And here she was, going straight into whatever was going to be thrown down from above! Incendiaries at the very least; the Jerries loved the things.

116

At last Hannah walked slowly down the old street. The rubble was piled high – as high as her heart leaped. Suddenly she was smiling and delighted because there, just ahead of her, walking very slowly and carefully, was old Meg and her master, Sam Grimes.

Caution told Hannah to duck out of sight. To keep well away and conceal the fact that she had returned. Who knew where the Marners were, and Fatty Blythe and that God awful Ram? No matter. A flood of very real relief and joy made her run, and catch up, and call out: 'Hello, Skipper! Oh crikey, it's good to see you and old Meg. I thought you'd both had it!'

''Ello, mate.' The old man's voice was high and breathless, his eyes faded and watery. He only had one tooth left in his head; he was like a dried-up stick – brittle perhaps, but still tough. There was nothing wrong with his memory though. He recognised her at once.

'Han! Good on yer, girl. Fought you was a dead duck.'

'I thought you were done for, too. I heard you moaning and groaning, and you sounded so far gone that . . . Oh, Skip! It's grand to see you and Meg.'

'Still call me Skipper, eh? He weren't, yer know.'

'What?'

'Your old man, he weren't no skipper. He was a bloke what worked on the barges, and a real decent sort. I know because I worked alongside him once. Your Ma was nice too, and as pretty as a picture. Thought yer was her just then. Give me quite a start yer did, you've grown to look so much like 'er.' He began to mumble, then grinned a one-toothed grin. 'But she weren't the sort as would wear them trouser fings like wot you've got on.'

'They're breeches. All Land Girls wear them. It's our uniform.'

'Bleeding Krauts, getting ladies wearing them fings. I remember—'

'And so do I,' she cut in breathlessly. 'I've had nightmares remembering you being under the rubble, and hearing you moaning, and how I saw that just about everything had fallen round your ears. I told the chap you were there, you know. Buried under the rubble, though I didn't dare hope. But you're not dead.'

'Nah, it'll take more'n them bastards ter get ol' Meg an' me darn,' he told her grimly, his watery eyes defiant. 'An' we've got some bloody marvellous blokes wot come in rescuing, and I ain't got nuffink but praise for the firemen neither. Got that Docks lot under they did, when the whole bleedin' world fought it was impossible. Nah! We don't give in easy, us London lot.'

'I can see that,' Hannah laughed. 'But I really thought that you would want to keep away from this place. I mean, you must have had a terrible time.'

'Never been better fed in me life. Everyone wants ter help an ol' man what's lost everyfink. I've been given clothes and a new ration book, everyfink. They let me 'elp on the Council allotments, fings like that. Then me and ol' Meg come dahn here, regular-like. Just to see an' remember if yer know what I mean.'

'Good!' Hannah laughed. 'In other words, it's an ill wind, eh?'

He spat on the ground in a contemptuous way. 'I won't never forgive the Jerry bleeders for doing for the good old Duck an' Drake. The owners copped it, yer know, and several of the regulars wot lived rahnd here.'

It was the opportunity she had been looking for. Hannah held her breath, then asked, 'And – and Frank?'

The old man stood there, nodding and grinning, looking for all the world like a tatty clockwork doll.

'Ah! They got 'im out, the ol' sod. All half-dead he was. They found 'im in wot was once Walker Alley. Yers, got 'im free, patched 'im up and sent 'im off somewhere out of it, they did. I dunno where.' His grin was sly. His crackly voice became almost oily. 'And neither does no one else, girl. Make no mistake abaht that.'

She was shaking inside; her legs felt like two tubes of water. Her stomach was dropping to her knees, to the ground, was draining away, leaving her weak and trembly. She became conscious of her heartbeats, thudding like ack-ack guns in her ears. Even so she kept her smile glued on, her tone light.

'I'm glad he made it. I wasn't sure because as you know, I was shut in and he had gone away. So, he's safe. You can't keep a good man down, eh, Skip? You say he's gone and no one knows where – not even Ma Carpenter?'

'Don't know nothin' about that old cow. Stings people she does, in that Pop-shop of her'n. They give me this good suit when I got bombed out. Worth at least three quid of anyone's money it was. But Cissy give me this wot I'm wearing. It belonged to her old man before he went and died of TB. So I took the suit to Ma Carpenter an' she give me half a crown. I arst yer, ain't that the bitter end? What's more . . .'

'I've got to go, Skip. I really have.' On an impulse she knelt down and kissed Meg on her nose. 'But I'll look you both up again, I promise I will.'

'I'm at Cissy's place, all right? Know where it is?'

'Everyone knows Cissy. 'Bye for now.'

Hannah hurried away, all but running. She was in a panic and not knowing what to do. Frank was alive! They believed him to be the victim of that terrible raid – that was what Mr Grimes had said. She felt confused and deathly afraid – now seeing Ram and Biff and Fatty Blythe behind every pile of rubble. She wanted to make a run for it, towards safety.

Like her stepfather: he had cut off to safety too. She knew where he was, all right. He had found his way to Lindell, and that couldn't be mere coincidence, oh no! Now he was skulking with the horses at the Drews'. Talk about leaving a trail that would lead those rotters straight to her, let alone himself! How had he found her? Gone to the old Colchester address and spilled the warden, Miss Lawrence, a bibful of lies? But why hadn't he approached her, once he'd caught up with her? At least let her know he was around? What the hell was the bloody man up to?

Dear God in heaven, she thought feverishly, did Ram Rawlins know where he was? Had the bald-headed, evil-looking devil found Frank, and then her, and could he have actually followed her today? Was he hiding somewhere, ready to pounce even now?

Hannah walked along what was left of the Alley into Sedgewick Street, and breathed a sigh of relief. Ma Carpenter's grotty little house was still there. Windows blocked up, door askew, a large crack down the front, shrapnel embedded by the porch. It was large enough, that shrapnel, to have been a killer had Ma had been in the way. Was Ma still around?

Hannah knocked, waited, then knocked again. Suddenly the door flew open and there was Ma in her outdoor clothes, rolling-pin in hand and looking murderous. Her expression changed when she saw Hannah.

'Bleedin' hell! I thought you was someone after money. Don't half come it, some of 'em do. Yers, come it, war or no war. Who'd want ter pay rent for this shit-heap? I ain't even got a bloody back door. Where did you spring from?'

Hannah looked at the woman whose face was as brown and wrinkled as a burnt rice pudding, with a bulbous nose red with cold. Her dusty-looking coat had an imitation fur collar; matching moth-eaten false-fur cuffs fell below her wrists and almost reached her arthritic fingers. Her hat, pulled down low onto her forehead, did not hide her small, raisin-dark eyes.

From her head to her toes, that were encased in strong lace-up boots, Ma looked a right'un. She was rough, and could be more than tough. She was used to having her own way. She told you the truth, like it or lump it, and she expected to hear the truth right back. God help you if you lied and Ma ever found out.

'I've come from – from the country, Ma,' Hannah quavered. Then promptly burst into tears.

'Don't want no waterworks round 'ere,' the old girl snapped. 'Come on in. Got no coal, so you'll have to keep that coat of yours on. Right old bumfreezer, ain't it? What colour's it supposed to be?'

'Fawn. Mid-fawn.'

'Don't look like one thing or another to me. What else did they doll you out with?'

'What I have on. Green jersey, breeches, this Aertex shirt. Apart from these socks and brown boots I have been issued with hobnailed boots and Wellingtons, a sou'wester and oilskins – oh, and some really awful passion-killers!'

'Got gloves?'

'I do wear gloves sometimes but they get soaking wet at the drop of a hat, so the backs of my hands get red raw. I've had blisters on my blisters, but I'm as tough as teak now.'

'You look about as tough as warm milk.' Ma's tone was wryness itself. 'What's brought you back round 'ere?'

'I – I wanted to find out about Frank.' Hannah followed Ma along the dingy passage that stank of a tom cat's pee. Then into a kitchen gloomy with brown paint, patchy lino worn away with the years, and a gas-stove in the corner that was red with rust.

'Gawd help us,' Ma snorted. 'You'racked if you want to find out about him. He's a worthless piece of shit, if you ask me.'

'One that you've fought tooth and nail for, even so.'

'Blood's thicker than water. Sit down, girl, don't hover there like two of eels.' Another of Ma's hard, black calculating stares, then, 'So you want to know about Frank, do you? I thought you'd want the old bugger dead like some others round here.'

'I don't wish anyone dead, Ma,' Hannah said carefully, and sat down on a rickety kitchen chair set by a wooden table that had seen better days. 'But I – I heard that he was killed. I mean, I thought that he was. I just met the old chap who used to live next door and he said . . .'

'Old Sam says a lot of things, specially to that stupid dog of his. Talks to it he does, tells it things.' Ma grinned, showing strong but yellowing teeth. 'Especially about the Krauts. Seems he can't forgive the perishers for destroying the Duck and Drake. Anyhow, what other interesting things did he tell you?'

'That Frank was rescued.'

'That's right. ARP bloke found him. They patched him up marvellous. Went to see him, I did, in the 'orspital. Made a rapid recovery, did old Frank. Wanted to know where you were though. Kept on and on about you. He was worried about Biff and his gang wanting revenge on him, worse, on you just for being who you are. Didn't want none of that, he didn't. He always was fond of you.'

120

Hannah's lips curved in a sarcastic smile. 'I'm sure!' she said.

'Oh shut up, you stupid mare,' Ma Carpenter snapped impatiently. 'Never thumped you a fourpenny one, did he? He might have yelled and cussed and made threats, he always was a mouthy bastard. But he never chucked you out, did he? Even though you always have been a proper little madam aping that holy cow Pitt. Frank ain't never shown you no door.'

'No. He preferred to shut me in upstairs,' Hannah retaliated bitterly. 'I was like a prisoner and I hated it, which you jolly well know since you've saved me more than once. Even at seventeen I was treated like a two-year-old and—'

'That started when you was a bloody kid. You used to sleepwalk. He found you with your eyes shut at the top of the stairs once. You could have broke your neck.'

Hannah laughed disbelievingly. 'Now I've heard everything! I know nothing about sleepwalking, and I don't believe a word of it. He's always locked me in as a punishment. Why are you sticking up for him? He's a drunken spiteful old sod and well you know it.'

'He wasn't always like that.'

'I know that. My mother wouldn't have married him else.'

'He changed when she died. He thought the world of her, and of you too. Took you hopping in Kent he did, more'n once if I remember rightly. He was happy then. Life turned sour on him and that's a fact. Didn't help when Val Marner camped on his doorstep. That was shortly before that pore Firelord got done in. Doted on that ugly old devil, he did.'

'And that's where Frank is now, isn't it?' Hannah burst out. 'With horses. Pedigree animals that are trained to race and . . .'

Unwittingly, Hannah had opened the floodgates on Ma's pet theme.

'Now ain't that a turn-up for the book?' she ranted. 'Racers! Bombs might fall, castles might crumble, and young men die like flies, but the nobs carry on like they always do. The fact that London's flattened by night don't mean that jockeys in their colours shouldn't fight it out by day, does it? Gawd's truth! And stupid bastards like me and him next door, and anyone else with a few bob to flutter, have to sneak along to the book-maker risking actual arrest.'

'You've never sneaked, Ma. You crow like anything when you win.'

'All right, I'm a big gob.' A smirky yellow-toothed grin formed round Ma's words. 'Takes one to know one, eh? But I mean what I say. Talk about Them and Us! Monied classes use a commissioned agent wot keeps 'em within the law. Did you know that? Us masses have the coppers breathing down our necks if we even look like risking a shilling each way with old Foulks. Only the other day . . .'

121

Knowing that left to herself Ma would stay on this particular soap-box for hours, Hannah pointed out politely, 'We were talking about Frank, Ma.'

'You was. I wasn't,' she returned, then, relenting: 'Want a cuppa? It's like gnats' piddle, but it's still hot.'

'Thank you. Ma, do you know where Frank is?'

'No, and I don't care to. Can't split on 'im then, can I?' Ma went to the gas-stove in the corner and picked up a blue enamel tea-pot and began to pour out weak tea. Steam swirled up from the rim of an enamel mug as she spooned in condensed milk and handed it over to Hannah. She nodded when Hannah whispered, 'Thanks,' then continued. 'When he was in 'orspital, Frank asked about you. He heard about number 32 getting flattened, and about a Land Girl who'd got out. He made a bit of a scene, he did. Carried on about his missing stepdaughter and all that. Anyway, some do-gooders took it on themselves to make enquiries.'

'Oh dear. I wonder why? He doesn't really care about me, so . . .'

'He promised your mum that he'd keep a weather eye open for you. By his lights, he did just that. You want to thank your lucky stars he didn't bash you up like he did the Marner woman. She's with Ram Rawlins now – did you know?'

Hannah shook her head, conscious that the pulse in her neck was beginning its nervous tattoo again.

Ma Carpenter continued. 'Went to your old place in Colchester, them do-gooders did, and spilled some crap about Frank being at death's door and him wanting to see his dear stepdaughter just once more before it was too late. He kept whatever they told him close to his chest. Never said a word to anyone. Then he disappeared. Signed himself out of that 'orspital they said, as bold as brass. Now he's disappeared. Talk about like a thief in the night!'

'He escaped from Biff and Co?' Hannah said quietly. 'That's a risky business. He's braver than I thought.'

'I thought he'd gone to find you. If he's turned up near you and not let you know, I don't know what he's up to. Anyway, I know sod-all. That's what I told bully Biff, and then Fatty, then Ram. Told them all in turn, I did. I also pointed out that if they were that keen to find my nephew, they'd best do what I did, and make enquiries at the nearest cop shop. That caught them by the short and curlies. They thought the cops would get suspicious if – anythink sort of happened, know what I mean?'

'And did you – report it to the police?'

'Leave orf! Frank's no angel but I wouldn't put him in the shit with the cops. Give 'em an excuse to nose round, bastards. But I said enough to shut Biff and his mates up. They won't come no hanky-panky with me, that I promise you.'

Hannah sipped at the tea. It tasted horrible, but it was hot and sweet. She was grateful for it, and held the mug clasped in both hands. She looked around.

Ma's house was awful, like a dark and dingy box full of scruffy old furniture. Windows were blacked out, which made things more depressing. A side table was piled high with old clothes. The whole place stank of cats and kippers and boiled cabbage. It was rumoured that Ma Carpenter was rich as Croesus. If she was, it certainly didn't show in the way she lived. No one dared to try and find out if there was a hidden cache somewhere. Ma had made good use of her rolling-pin more than once in the past.

Suddenly, very desperately, Hannah wanted to go home. Yes, to Hawksley in the village of Lindell. That was where she belonged now, and it was nothing to do with the house or the place, but everything to do with all of her friends. Ginnie and Raven and dear old Lil. The twins and Ellery, Dr Dene and Walt. Mrs Kitt, Mr Stitson and every-one. Not forgetting lovely Ol' Mo, who wasn't a bit like Ma's one-eared battle-scarred old cat Tom, who was black as pitch, and who had a green and baleful stare. He swore and spat at everyone, even Ma, and he hadn't done his duty outside and covered it with dirt from the day he'd been born. Only someone like Ma could love an evil devil like Tom.

Hannah began to get to her feet, needing to smell fresh country air. Wanting to see the fields, and the lacy shapes bare branches made against the sky. To hear cows, and sense the freedom of vast open spaces. She wanted very desperately to cut and run to where it felt clean.

Outside, a deep-throated growling rose to a high-pitched scream, then zoomed down again, slicing through the air like a huge sickle of sound. The Alert repeated its wailing threat of imminent danger, then faded to a whine and cut out. And after that there was the listening, and the waiting for the aircrafts' drone, for the enemy who swarmed like wasps in the sky. And all the while the waiting brought about an awareness of one's own crazily beating heart.

'That's it for today,' Ma said, all matter-of-fact. 'It's the shelter for us. Looks like you'll be staying with me tonight.'

'No!' Hannah cried in her mind. 'Not here. Anywhere but here. No, no, no . . .'

123

Chapter Sixteen

Fortunately, London boasted the most comprehensive underground railway system in the world. Most of the stations were deep enough to offer virtual immunity from the bombers, and so they were commandeered by the people. Suitcases, brown paper carrier bags, string holdalls, anything and everything handy was trundled along.

Folk took bedding with them, food and clothing, books and newspapers, pyjamas and dressing gowns and packs of cards, mouth organs, even paper and comb. One needed to sing, to shout, to forget what tomorrow might bring. For the night-times at least it became the habit to live in a strange half-lit world, one that shuddered every so often and became filled with the roar of trains – huge moving monsters that stopped and started like glass-eyed, enormous science-fiction worms.

Folk with young children began their trek to the Tube during the early evening. They took their places, laughing and joking, knitting and nattering, taking no nonsense while settling down their kids.

Tube life was a separate existence; it took on a familiar shape and form. Makeshift catering arrangements ensured that people had neither to go up top to danger in order to eat, nor stay below and starve. You could watch the old chap playing musical spoons and the one-legged ex-soldier playing a penny whistle. Not forgetting the squeeze-box old Charlie Williams had. Everyone joined in singing *We'll Meet Again, Blue Birds Over the White Cliffs of Dover* and *A Poor Little Lamb That Lost Its Way*, absolutely everyone heartily bawling, 'Baa-aa, baa-baa, baa-baa.' Then the soulful mood would change and it was old favourites: *Tipperary, Bull and Bush, My Old Man Said Follow the Van, Nellie Dean* . . . Ma Carpenter liked that one. 'There's an old mill by a stream . . .' Her voice was loud and pretty awful, but no one gave a damn.

Hannah sat on the ground, her back against the coldness of the tiled wall. She looked around her, at the woman selling biscuits at tuppence a packet. Apples went for three ha'pence. A soldier, unable to finish his journey home for leave snored as he slept, a copy of the *Evening Herald* at his side.

Hannah saw the headlines. She craned her neck and read that the Luftwaffe was being knocked to pieces. That the great old bulldog Churchill was firmly holding the reins of the war. That the threat of invasion was a Haw-Haw fairy tale and by now, all but done to death.

The last train thundered by and the power was switched off. And now members of ENSA began their performances. Jolly, smiling, gesturing people, working with all their hearts and souls. Some were quite magnificently out of tune, but no matter. They were good-heartedly clapped by all.

Hannah watched and listened and smiled at the baby who was unnerving her with its unwavering solemn-eyed stare. Ma began to talk, inconsequential stuff about times long gone. In self-defence Hannah closed her eyes. She was thinking of Ginnie and wondering how she was getting on . . .

The Bradley Hotel, situated a stone's throw from Matching Airfield, was small and neat, set before a handkerchief lawn and evergreen shrubs. Ginnie looked round at their room. It was plain and clean, almost clinical with its white and blue decor. Ginnie undressed slowly, carefully; she felt nervous and unsure. Also she felt ashamed. The woman who had shown them to their room had looked at them in that smirky, meaningful way that said, 'I know what you're up to. I'm not bloody daft.'

Ginnie bit her lip, thinking of her mother, of her father's stiff back and straight gaze. Of Luke, somewhere out there, risking life and limb at sea. Was she being a traitor? Was she letting them all down? Dear heaven, after this night she could never wear the pure white of a virgin bride. That was her mother's dream, her father's desire, her brother's certainty. Not hers, not now there was Richard.

What was this madness that seeped through her blood? This unrest, the wild desire to give everything she had to Richard, the handsome, dark-eyed airman who could at any moment be shot down in flames.

She stared at her reflection in the tall mirror fixed onto the wardrobe door. She was glad that she had brought some dainty things from home. She had combed her hair out, so that it fell like a flaming waterfall to her bare shoulders. Her nightdress of palest pink rayon silk was held up by ribbon straps of the same colour. The garment clung to her figure and made it shine. She was slim and lithe and felt lovely. It did not matter that the room struck so cold.

125

She looked at the bed, pristine, like a prim old maid – but not for long. No, not for long! Her cheeks felt hot, her eyes were bright, and her breath caught in her throat as Richard came up behind her. She stared at him in the mirror and felt an unfamiliar emotion.

Dressed in his uniform he had been handsome. Now, bare-chested, dark-skinned, muscles rippling, he was the perfect man. His figure could be used as a model for a Greek sculpture, she thought, and wanted to die with love. He was not too tall, not too anything. He was just perfect in shape and form. And when she looked into his mischievously twinkling eyes she knew that nothing mattered. Nothing except this moment, this wonderful, magical *now*.

'I believe the term I'm looking for is peach,' he told her, and his voice was deep, resonant, making charm-bells ring in her ears. He added, 'You're an exquisite peach. One that I'm going to make blush even more. Virginia Betts, you are beautiful.'

'And you look like a film star.' Ginnie bit her lip, then added quietly, 'And . . . and I've never done this before.'

'I have. Lots of times, so you're in expert hands.'

Her cheeks flamed. She turned round to face him, eyes hurt.

'You . . . don't have to treat this so casually, Richard,' she told him. 'This is no joke to me, it's all new and strange and . . . I'm neither cheap, nor easy.'

'Sweetheart.' He was crestfallen, shocked. 'I never dreamed you'd take a joke so badly. I was trying to lighten things up a little, that's all. To make you feel not so . . .'

'Romantic?'

'Ginnie, it was my foolish way of saying that this moment is ours, but that I'm very aware that things probably won't – can't last.'

'You're married.' A very real fear flared in her breast. 'Is that it?'

'Good Lord, no! I love you and I always will. And if you're agreeable, we'll get married as quickly as it can be arranged. That, my darling girl, is just how dear you are to me. It's just that, in my job . . . Well, in this day and age, we can't be certain of having tomorrows, can we?'

'Oh!' Happy tears slipped down her cheeks. 'Of course I'll marry you, Richard. And I love you . . .' She paused then added shyly, 'I love you to bits, even though I know nothing about you. I've told you everything there is about me.'

'Ah!' he teased. 'So you want to make sure you know everything so that you can trace me in a trice? In case I feel the need to cut and run?'

'Richard!'

The smile left his eyes and he was serious. He walked over to the

126

gas-lamp and turned it off. It was dark outside, the moon covered by clouds. This was good. There should be no enemy raids.

Richard went back to Ginnie. She could smell the soap he had used to wash with, the hint of Players cigarette smoke, the Brylcreem on his unruly dark hair. He put his arm round her and led her to the bed.

They lay side by side and the thrilling feel of his body sliding down beside her made her gasp. She wanted him to kiss her. She wanted him to make love. She wanted . . .

'Very well, my sweet,' he was saying, 'here goes. I'm a Kentish man, born and bred. My father grows hops – fields of the things, and has done for years. I'm his only son and I know his hopes, but I also know that the life isn't for me. After the war, if I survive, I shall go into boat-building. Yachts. Graceful things that look for all the world like water butterflies.'

'Oh Richard! I didn't know, never suspected that—'

'An Air Gunner could have such an outlandish dream? One who's known as a clever-dick because he's A1 at Aircraft recognition? That he is also quite a dab-hand at Morse Code and is known in YMCAs and NAAFIs as a killer where table tennis is concerned?' He was laughing. 'Now let me see what other great attributes I have. Oh, I'm also a wizard at—'

She stopped him with her lips. Then he was holding her tight and whispering her name against her hair. She felt a delicious lethargy as his caresses began. His hands and lips roved over her body, teased and tantalised and led her on. Time had no meaning, it held only whispered words, and wild sensations, and a crying need such as she had never known before.

He entered her at last and every muscle and sinew within her tried to pull him in further, to hold and trap him. She thought he was going to pull out and moaned, but he pushed down hard, retreated, and returned even more forcibly this time. Then the rhythm began – fierce, strong, full of magnetic power. She became a mass of feeling, of burning, her movements matching his. And she was clinging to him, sobbing with joy and reaching a pinnacle of such heights that it became unbearable, and she had to let go.

They lay together, tight in each other's arms, then slept in contentment and peace. He woke her before dawn and they made love again, then once more before he had to leave and dash back to base. And as they wished each other goodbye, Ginnie knew that there were no regrets, only a singing delight at the realisation of a dream. She was now fully fledged. A young woman who knew everything about love and romance. She couldn't wait for it all to happen again.

As she cycled along the lanes towards Lindell she breathed in the cold crispness of the morning. The winter crops were still, weighed down, glittering with frost. Sprouts, cabbages, late beet. Tatty, bedraggled-looking, yet icily precious all the same. She thought of her father's shop, of its false grass that lined the shelves. The polished brass scales and little mountain of weights. In her mind's eye she pictured the colourful display of carrots and onions, turnips, cauliflowers, polished apples, even her father's potatoes looked clean. Clean and wholesome. Crops, most of which she had now seen grown. It was a satisfying thought, fulfilling. A part of life as it had always been lived, not part and parcel of a wanton world war.

Then she heard the high horror of a rabbit scream and the bubble burst. Nature itself was wicked and cruel; how then could man become any better than the law of Earth?

Suddenly she was sad. Ocean-deep sad. And she was remembering her childhood, sweet innocence, her parents and Luke – and Aiden who was in India getting on with a life of his own.

Right out of the blue, with utmost certainty, she realised that she never wanted them to know. They must never even suspect what she had done. Yet, back there, tucked up in bed with her man, she had been so sure. She had experienced no feeling of treachery, nor guilt. Now, in the cold light of day, all she could think of was the look on young Hannah's face if the truth ever became known.

Dear God, she thought in a tight panicky way, what have I done?

Ginnie began wondering whether Raven, with her calm dark eyes, would see the difference in her. After all, Ginnie had apparently gone back to Ilford yesterday and would not be returning to Lindell until the last train.

No. Raven would be her usual introspective self, reading her husband's poetry, finding a sort of companionship with the horses, as always completely unaware of the local girls' spite. The main backbone of the village – the mature, knowledgeable workers who rated the Land Girls first class, had welcomed the three with open arms. But unattached young village ladies had a different view of things.

Some had been openly hostile, some irritated to the point of rudeness. At times, at the wrong end of the treatment, Hannah had been moved to explode, 'Bloody hell!' But being fair-minded, she had grinned just the same.

On the other hand, Raven got quietly on with her life, seemingly quite unaware of unimportant events, or people. Particularly the few who could not come to terms with strangers in their midst. Those who were green because Hannah had taken over the airman, Matt, and she, Ginnie, had Richard in tow. Richard!

Ginnie pushed memories of the night away and felt her face flame.

128

Again her thoughts flickered back to Raven. Dear unworldly Raven who drifted through the days, which was just as well seeing that life had already hurt her too much. Thankfully the most bitchy of the local females never stepped inside the Rookwood. Neither had Raven ventured to the monthly hops in the village hall. Hannah had, naturally. Laughing and joining in, and jitterbugging, and thoroughly enjoying herself to the rhythm of *In the Mood*. Of course, those were the evenings when Hannah was wont to say, 'Bloody hell!' very forcefully, not once but many times. So perhaps Raven had been right not to go.

Ginnie smiled then, and looked at her watch. Her dear friend was indeed pretty saintly. It would never surprise her to find, when she finally got back home, that Raven had actually gone to church. Perhaps, if there was a chance, and the mood was right, she would let her hair down and confide in Raven. Tell her what had happened. About her love affair, and how it had all come to a head with her becoming a scarlet woman who'd stayed in a tiny Matching hotel. Clearly Raven would understand, since she herself knew all about true love. Dear Raven, just what was she doing right now?

Ginnie pedalled madly on the stupid old bike that had been issued by the Ministry of Agriculture. Terrible bit of rubbish it was, ancient, should have been thrown out of business years ago. Suddenly, very desperately, Ginnie needed the companionship of her friends. She began peddling even faster. The front wheel hit a large stone. Ginnie felt herself sailing over the handlebars . . .

Raven sat by the window in the room she shared with Hannah and Ginnie. She was thinking of the events of the day before. She had been given the full Saturday and Sunday off, since she had worked all through the previous week. It had been very early on the Saturday morning, she remembered, when she had set out. And very, very cold. Mists had made a wispy backcloth to the world. She reached Drew Stables and was given her mount.

She had been riding Blue Rinse, a silver-white mare, when James St John on Pegasus cantered up to join her.

'Good morning,' he had said in his stiff way. 'I must say, you have a good seat.'

'Thank you, Mr St John,' she replied politely. 'You ride well too.'

'James, please,' he told her, his voice more friendly. 'You've done this sort of thing quite often, haven't you?'

She smiled at that. 'Regularly. In fact, since my young days. I began with my own pony and was of course very, very proud of him. His name was Tutmosis, after an Egyptian pharaoh of that name. The person my father bought him from was very keen on Egyptology. All the ponies had quite glorious titles. I very nearly chose an Amenhotep, but Tut had such gentle eyes.'

'And yours are sad.'

The words had shot out almost like an accusation. She thought him brusque and rather cruel-seeming, with his hawk-like stare and arrogant chin. She did not like him very much, but tried to hide it. Her silence seemed to irritate him.

'Well?' He persisted rudely. Why have you got such sad eyes?'

'Because I don't feel particularly joyful.' Her tone was as frosty as the morning. 'Could that be it, do you think? Now, if you'll please excuse me . . .'

She turned Blue Rinse's head and rode off like the wind. She wanted to be alone. *Needed* to be alone. She headed away from the flatlands and into the rolling hills.

Here, as well as the grey ghosts of mist swirling about her, it began to rain, the light shower quickly becoming a downpour.

'The world's full of nothing but tears!' Raven announced dramatically, her mood in tune with the weather.

'Ye gods,' Sophia St John snapped, appearing out of nowhere, astride her satanic-black Belvedere. 'If you don't care about catching pneumonia, think of that damned horse!'

It was rude and uncalled-for. Rain ran off Blue Rinse's back. Twin patches of colour burned high on Raven's cheeks.

'And I suppose your next command will be for me not to snivel, Mrs St John?' she asked in a cool crystal-clear voice. 'How rude you are!'

'And how predictable you are. God, even your mental outlook's clothed in widow's weeds – and they were out of fashion donkeys' years ago. You know what you ought to do?'

Rarely for her, Raven became angry enough to retaliate in the like fashion.

'Drown my sorrows in a sea of Scotch on the rocks,' she suggested, adding pointedly, 'like you?'

'Certainly not. A prissy young thing like you couldn't hold liquor. No, to my mind you ought to thank God that your man died peacefully in his bed – unlike my son. And then set your sights on getting married again.'

'Really?' Raven stared at the hard-faced woman with wide, disbelieving eyes. 'And have you thought about whom I should choose?'

'That's up to you.' Cat-eyes were bright with sardonic amusement. 'What's the matter? Are you shocked?'

'No. I was just thinking what a hard and unfeeling person you are,' Raven told her. 'I couldn't understand how it was that your eldest son preferred your room to your company, but listening to you . . . your advice, says it all.'

Raven turned Blue Rinse's head in the direction of Drew Stables and urged her on. Infuriatingly, Sophia did likewise. Belvedere and Blue Rinse now trotted alongside neck and neck.

'So I'm rotten to the core,' Sophia shouted, 'but at least I don't give in! I try, dammit! Yes, I do at least try. You're young. You could marry, have brats – though on second thoughts perhaps that would *not* be such a good idea. Put a child in your arms and you'd smother it from the day it was born. My offspring did at least learn to stand on their own two feet.' Sophia's voice grew tight, held bitter sarcasm. 'I can imagine you with a child. God, you'd talk baby-talk!'

For one wild moment Raven had believed that this conversation could not be happening. It was bizarre. She had been remembering, thinking longingly of Francis. Now, because of this awful woman's intrusion, he seemed part of a dream – a gentle, melancholy unreality.

Raven's spurt of anger receded, leaving her calm once more. Then in a blinding flash understanding came. Sophia St John desperately needed to get things off her chest. And this was her way. To pick a fight, any old fight, just to be able to have her say. Just to let off steam, if not at fate, at the one nearest to hand. Today, on this cold, bitter morning, it was Raven's turn.

She heard herself asking, 'No baby-talk? That is wrong in your book? Tell me your preference. Just what did you do?'

'If they played up, I swore. I repeated every forbidden word I knew, and made up a few of my own besides. Ha! They soon had a damned good vocabulary, I'll say that!'

'And when they didn't play up?'

Sophia hesitated. Was that rain on her face or tears, Raven wondered, but the thought was swiftly gusted away.

'I ignored them,' Sophia said forcefully. 'They just about hated that turn of events.'

'Shouldn't you have given them some praise for being good?'

'Praise? Like, "You two dinky darlings"? "You dear sweet iddy-biddy boys"? Spare me! A good working relationship's more in my line. I let them know who was boss right from the start, unlike my husband. He treated them like equals, so they followed him around like puppy dogs. Not my way! My boys soon learned that they had to achieve things to get my attention. I have never fawned, nor grovelled. No – they had to earn my attention, damned-well earn it!'

'Even naughty things being acceptable, providing you, their mother gave them a glance? Oh, Sophia!'

'*Oh, Sophia!*' The mimicry was cruelly exact, the cat-eyes bright

131

with sarcasm. 'Really, girl, believe it or not, one mustn't always go by the book – pretty wishy-washy lot we'd get if we did.'

She wants to talk about herself, about her life, about her sons, Raven thought. Under the guise of putting me straight, she wants to talk about how things used to be, and how things are now. Poor old her. She's lonely! Even James lets her ride alone. Stuffy old devil. It wouldn't hurt him to soften up a little. After all, she is his mother.

They continued the ride back in silence. As they dismounted, stable-hands ran forward, ready to take off tack, rub down and care for the animals. Raven nodded and smiled, vaguely registering the fact that she had not set eyes on the new man before. He was quite mature, small and skinny, and he hailed from London – the East End; one could tell immediately by his voice.

'Shall we take a brisk walk back,' Sophia asked, 'rather than use the Morris?'

Raven nodded. Sophia was so proud of her motor car, a Morris-8 with built-in headlamps which could reach up to 64 mph. It had cost £139 and £1 extra for a sun-roof. It would be left to Ellery to bring it back.

As Raven and Sophia walked back to Hawksley and entered the house together, the older woman said brusquely; 'You could join me in my sitting room if you've nothing better to do. After you've changed out of your wet things, of course.'

'Thank you,' Raven replied, bemused. 'You're very kind.'

'Not at all. Lonely. I'll tell Lily that you'll be joining me for lunch.'

Later, as they sat together in a dramatically handsome room, Raven said quietly, 'Tell me about your son Miles. The one you lost at sea.'

'He was not cussed and dogmatic like James,' Sophia replied at once, seeming glad to talk. 'He was the dare-devil kind. Used to climb trees, trying to scare me to death actually, though I never let my fear for him show. He swam the river for the same reason; he challenged an absolute swine of a current and won through. He used to tilt back his head and laugh and say it was nothing. That he would be top dog, Sportsman of the Year one day. He was damn good at everything he tried. He would have kept his promise too, if . . . oh, God!'

Raven eyed the whisky decanter and asked, 'Shall I pour you a drink?'

'Yes, help me on my way to hell! Funny how I keep thinking of him as a kid, a dirty scruffy little devil with leaves caught in his hair. I'm good at hiding my feelings, you know. Had to be for the sake of survival. And for the record, love isn't a strong-enough word for the feeling I had for that boy's father. His sons, well – in my book, parental affection is a wishy-washy phrase. I felt a fierceness of a kind towards Miles and, by God, I miss him. Now pour me that drink.'

Raven wordlessly handed her a well-filled glass and watched Sophia down it in one defiant gesture. She had, Raven noticed, spoken in the plural regarding 'her boys', but had not mentioned James once by name . . .

All that had been yesterday. Now, this morning, she had promised to ride with Sophia again. She did not want to. Worse, she did not want to come face to face with James either. They were two of a kind, mother and son. Hard as nails and ready to ride roughshod over everyone else. If only either Hannah or Ginnie were here. She could make up an excuse, could . . .

'Phew!' Ginnie said from the door. 'It's quite a cycle-ride from Matching and that clapped out Min-Ag bike's a bone-shaker if ever there was one. I came off.' She limped in, rubbing her sore, jarred spine. 'I've scraped my elbows and my knees and I feel half-dead. Thank goodness for Ellery's old wagon. I wouldn't fancy going to work each morning on the rotten Ministry bicycles. They ought to be banned.'

All Raven could think of just then was that she had her longed-for excuse.

Chapter Seventeen

Mid-December, Richard came to Lindell. He was on leave and going to Kent to see his parents, but first he'd come to see Ginnie.

After they had kissed and were sitting in the Rookwood he told her blithely that he had shot up three supply ships lying line-ahead near the Scheldt. It was his usual job to scout over the Atlantic at night on the look-out for submarines coming up to breathe and recharge batteries. Hitting the supply ships was whizzo. All the crew had been keen as mustard; it had all been a jolly good show.

He drank three pints of beer, capped it with rum and seemed on top of the world. Eventually he grinned and winked. 'Usual spot?'

She nodded and wondered why he took things so much for granted these days.

'A short life and a merry one, eh Gin old girl?' he was wont to say, and she had gone along with it. Of course he was right. He could die tomorrow, just as could Matt and all the other millions of young men at war. So why was it that his absolute certainty about her made her want to squirm sometimes?

He left the table at which they were sitting, to order more beer at the bar. It was an empty gesture really, since the admiring audience was only too willing to buy.

Now I'm being really horrible, she thought.

Feeling guilty, she watched the way his cap slanted to one side in such a rakish manner, his attractive habit of tilting his head back when he laughed. He was so handsome, so worldly, so brave. And he was so sure . . . of her.

It would, she thought, be much more exciting if he attempted to woo her sometimes. To at least pretend to believe that she had to be pampered. That she was incredibly precious, and perhaps just the teensiest bit unpredictable? In other words, a young lady he had to put himself out for, to attain.

That was not his way. He joshed and teased, kidded and ribbed. He fooled around and bantered, was full of wisecracks and witticisms, and was all in all a jolly nice chap. Popularity was the name of his game. And, she had to face it, it worked. Richard was used to having his own way. And who could blame him for expecting her of all people to understand? He had to cram everything in while he could. By the nature of the here and now, he was unable to believe in tomorrows. Indeed, he considered himself lucky to have a today.

She watched him telling his story about the three supply ships yet again. Walter was having his ear bent this time. In her mind's eye she saw those crippled ships, the men fighting for their lives, afloat in dangerous seas.

Ginnie bit her bottom lip hard. She hated herself for having such treacherous thoughts. After all, weren't they the enemy? But she was thinking of sailors, ordinary men like her brother Luke, who was doing his service at sea.

What was it everyone was saying these days? That the only good German was a dead one? Her own father believed that! What utter and absolute bilge. There were good and bad in every nationality. And Germans or not, they were all someone's sons. There had been one evening in particular when Hannah had also openly gone along with those sentiments. She had been her usual forthright self, giving tongue to her thoughts against Richard's fiercest of arguments, saying bluntly, 'Sorry mate, I just don't feel all happy and triumphant when a Jerry plane goes down in flames. I don't think anyone deserves to be fried to a crisp.'

'That's what they'd do to our chaps given the chance.' Richard had been impatient, quite angry, and it had showed. 'In fact, it's being done to us on a regular basis. Remind me to tell you about Titch some day.'

Hannah had shrugged and looked sombre, but stuck to her guns. 'I know, and it's terrible. But it doesn't matter what side you're on, it's still not right. Our men, their men, both thinking they're doing the honourable thing for their country. Probably both even praying to the same sort of god. A Christian God to help them in their hour of need. Bloody hell! Who'd want to be poor old God these days?'

Richard had been really incensed at that. His normal sunny expression became thunderous as he exploded. 'We'll see how *you* feel if it ever gets to be between them or Matt.' Then, coldly contemptuous, 'Stop being such a stupid, thick-headed little bitch, Hannah. You don't know what you're talking about, so ruddy well shut up.'

'Richard!' Ginnie had remonstrated, immediately leaping to Hannah's defence. 'That's a bit much!'

135

Hannah had merely raised her brows in the expressive way she had, for once refusing to argue back. She even went so far as to attempt to change the subject. But Richard had been quite distant to her, refusing even to look at her for a while.

Everyone should be allowed to have their say, Ginnie had thought at the time, understanding that Richard could not be blamed for reacting as he did. Matt probably felt the same way too, as must all the boys in Air Force blue. It was a question of beating or getting beat. And yes, it was rather pompous of people who were safe on the ground to give tongue to their views. After all, they weren't up there, facing terrible death. Even so . . .

Hannah was far from being a thick-headed little bitch, Ginnie seethed. How dared he! It was odious of Richard to call her friend names. He had proved himself to be at the very least, ungracious . . .

Oh, what the devil! Ginnie's mind, back to the present now, raced on. What is wrong with me? Why am I thinking along these lines? So determinedly finding faults and picking holes? Why is it that I'm just not sure of anything any more?

Later, as she left the Rookwood with Richard, she was pushing away her doubts. He had such magnetism, such charisma. While with him she melted and was like putty in his hands. He had his arm round her waist, and paused from walking every so often, to kiss her and hold her close.

'I had to come today, sweetheart,' he told her in his normally good-natured way. 'Just had to. I couldn't let you down. But this once, this one time, I feel I need to see my parents, particularly Dad. He's such a dour old boy, seldom cracks his face, but he's a great mate all the same.'

'He sounds very nice, Richard, and your mother does too.'

'I feel I've rather put them in the shade recently and – Oh hell, you know!'

'Yes,' she agreed quietly. 'I have done exactly the same with my parents – when you've been free. Not gone home, I mean.'

'Do they know about me?'

'I'm sorry,' she replied hesitantly, 'but no.'

'And your two friends?'

'They suspect, I think. I almost blurted everything out to Raven after the first time, but the moment passed. She was too busy cleaning my wounds and patching me up. I had fallen off the bike, you see. So, no, I haven't actually said anything.' Her face went hot in the darkness.

She wished rather desperately that she did not feel so ashamed, but she did. Being furtive was not her usual way – and yes, she felt sneaky about her relationship with Richard. Things had become a habit – had gone too far. She was not happy, and did not like this regular hole-in-the-corner business. On the other hand it seemed to give Richard an extra thrill.

She remembered how it had come as a surprise when instead of returning to the Bradley, Richard had arrived the following weekend literally beaming.

'I've found us a marvellous place, old girl,' he had said triumphantly 'An unused bothy. Even better, it's near to hand – on the Hawksley Estate.'

'What on earth's a bothy?'

'A gardener's hostel.' He had ruffled her hair, acting as if she were a child. 'They're common on big estates. I thought you knew that, being a farm-girl now. I believe the Hawksley bothy-boys are all off to war. Or did you tell me they'd gone down into mines?'

'I don't know about the gardeners. Poor old Vincent does everything that must be done now. It was the head stable man who went north to the mines. He chose to, I believe. He's getting a whacking good wage, rather than the pittance he had here. Which is jolly good news for a *married* man.'

For the life of her she could not help underlining the married part.

'It doesn't matter, sweetheart.' Richard had light-heartedly brushed this statement away. 'I have found us a place. We can be alone and we can make love. Darling, I do adore you. You are the best thing that has ever happened to me.'

She had gone along with all their clandestine love-making, of course she had, but now . . .

'Richard,' she said carefully. 'Would you mind very much if we didn't . . .'

'Do what?'

'Go to the bothy?'

'Yes, I would mind,' he said, surprised. 'Sweetheart, I want to take off your clothes, look at you, kiss you all over, make love to you. And particularly tonight of all nights – before I go home and tell them the news.' His voice was full of teasing now. 'And I have, of course, got the same something to tell you.'

'Oh?' She was laughing with him now, because with Richard in this mood it was like being dizzily breezed along in a cloud of joy. 'Something to tell me?'

'Yes. That on my next decent leave we're to be married, Gin! I've already written and told Matt. We're mates and if it's possible, I rather want him with us on the day.' He squeezed her against his side.

137

'There's always something special about one's first crew. Matt and I have always got on.'

'Richard?' She was taken aback, felt that she was losing her footing. Now that she was hearing what she had hoped and prayed to hear, reality held a devastating sense of shock.

He blithely continued, 'Everything's cut and dried. Now, as soon as it can be arranged, I want you to come to Kent and meet my people.' He chuckled. 'I'm going alone this time – to prepare them. And you must put in a good word for me too, to your lot. Then it will be my turn, in Essex, to be under your Dad's scrutiny. I'm not too keen on that prospect, my sweet. Even though I'm sure you've made him sound like a Sergeant-Major just to scare me.'

'Richard,' she began, her mind seeming capable of registering only one thing at a time, 'you say you have written to Matt about this, and that everything is arranged? Even down to actually telling people – before even asking me?'

'Is that so bad?' he asked. 'I wanted Matt to share our good news.'

He bent down and kissed her again, fiercely, possessively, and she responded to his desire as always. Feeling that her heart and soul were reaching out to meet him. Knowing that near him she always felt on fire.

But the treacherous little question was there before she could brush it away. What of the times when he was not with her, kissing and whispering and holding her close? When he was not on hand with his hypnotic eyes and ready chuckle? When he was not around dishing out his charm?

While she was working with her friends or beside Ellery driving to the Felsted sugar factory, was Richard the only person on her mind, just as the silvery Francis was always there, in Raven's heart and soul? Did thoughts of Richard block everyone else out? *No!*

Her brother, far away at sea, was always on her mind. Her big, adorable teddy-bear of a brother Luke, whom she had looked up to from the day she had been born. And there too was Aiden. She wouldn't hear from him for ages – then the letter-box would rattle and all his mail would come pouring through. Censored, of course, and scored through with heavily blue-pencilled lines, but his signing off always clear. And always underlined. It was simply, *Yours ever*. She could tell by the dates that Aiden sat down and wrote to her at least three times a week . Before the war she had seen him every day. He had gone to school alongside Luke and they were the greatest of chums. Dear Aiden! He had been there for as long as she remembered.

Aiden was part of her life. The life she owed to her parents for its beginning. Her dearly beloved parents who were as staunch as oaks, who were such sticklers for right and wrong. Two people who had already been through one war and were now pacing their days through hostilities for a second time. Nice people, who in these worrying times tightened their belts and just carried on. What would they make of this turn of events, her forthcoming marriage? Would they look into her eyes? Could she look into theirs?

And there was Richard, of course! But somehow, these days, guilt and shame seemed synonymous with his name. Dear God, she thought wildly, that hurt. It really did. But theirs had been such a whirlwind romance, and because of the war one must take happiness where one could. Would her parents ever come to terms with that? She pulled herself up sharply. Richard said they were to be married. Once the deed was done, she need feel sinful no more. It was going to be all right!

But her doubts refused to go away. They were pricking into her consciousness like evil little djinns armed with spikes. Why was she still feeling so mixed-up? So taken back? She should be over the moon with what Richard had said.

That was it – yes! *He* had said what was about to happen. Had told *her*. Had it been a proposal? No, not really. Shouldn't he have gone down on one knee, and actually asked her? At least pretended to be uncertain of her reply?

Good heavens, she thought in a tight panicky way, why am I questioning everything like this? It isn't my way to sit on the fence. I *like* making decisions – I enjoy knowing my own mind! What on earth is happening to me? I feel as nervous as a kitten, not a bit like me!

'You're very quiet, darling,' Richard hugged her hard. 'This is not the reaction I expected at all. Didn't you think I'd keep my promise?'

'Yes – no – yes! It's just that you have told me so often that we must live for the day, which I have been doing, and . . .'

'What?'

'Nothing!' She laughed breathlessly, clouds of doubt lifting. 'Oh darling, nothing at all.'

'Come on then, sweetheart,' he said, his voice going deep in his throat. 'Let's hurry. If we don't, I might just throw you down among the brambles and make mad passionate love right here. And that, my sweet, would be quite unbearably prickly.'

He caught hold of her hand and they began running like gleeful children towards the lonely old bothy building.

'Brrh! It's brass monkeys out here,' Hannah said as she and the others got down from Ellery's lumbering mud-encrusted vehicle. Stretching ahead of them were the serried ranks of wholesome-looking Winter

139

Mammoth broccoli. This crop had been sown the previous April and the large heads were ready for cutting. The broccoli looked almost beautiful, glistening as it did under a fine layer of morning frost.

'I'm glad Ellery brought us,' she went on. 'What a good old stick he is. He always drives us when he can. I hate those bikes, I really do. My heart always sinks when we have to use them. On a morning like this, our hands would've frozen to the handlebars.'

Ginnie did not answer. She was pulling on her gloves, that would be soaked and useless inside two minutes, and looking unusually thoughtful.

'Ugh!' Hannah wittered on, 'My feet are like blocks of ice. I wish I was in Lily's place. Rose Cottage is so much fun right now.'

'Yes,' Raven agreed in her tranquil way. 'It is. It was nice last night, wasn't it? And I do so adore the boys.'

'Christmas mad, that's what they are.' Hannah's eyes were twinkling. 'And I understand that Lily is to have the whole holiday off. I'm glad about that. She told me that until four years ago, the St Johns had lots of servants and a professional live-in housekeeper. A bit of a tartar she was by all accounts, who ruled with a rod of iron. Still, Lily quite liked her, and learned fast. Lily has been with the family since she was fourteen years old. I reckon she deserves top marks for that.'

'Don't be so hard on them,' Raven told her. 'They have made us more than comfortable. I don't suppose there are any other LGs living in such a grand private house. In fact, who are downright spoiled.'

'Yes, we are.' Hannah gave Raven a sly questioning look. 'You like the old bat, don't you? Oh well, I suppose she's not so bad. She can't be if Lily's stayed on all these years. That old housekeeper must have thought so too. Anyway, Lily managed very well, because since Sophia's husband's death, and then that poor devil Miles's, socialising of any sort's been out. There wasn't even James to worry about since he spends most of his free time at Knollys. So staff were gradually let go, some through retirement, or because of call-up, and never replaced. The housekeeper was one of the very last to go.'

'Why did she leave?' Raven went along with the conversation out of politeness, simply because Ginnie was not disposed to join in.

'Retired,' Hannah said. 'When that happened, Mrs St John asked Lily if she'd like to step into the woman's shoes. Lily grabbed at the chance, provided she didn't have to live in. It was more money, which helped. Her Sam never earned much, being a farmhand. Lily reckons Mrs St John's been very decent to her. Kept her on even though she married Sam, and then had the boys, which means she has to fit in her duties with school hols, and all stuff like that.' She paused, then added thoughtfully, 'Don't add up to the drinking, swearing, hard-eyed old witch we know, does it?'

'What's going to happen to Mrs St John at Christmas-time?'

'She's going away.'

'Really? Somewhere nice?'

'Pretty near home. She and darling James are staying as honoured guests at the Drews'. According to Lily, old man Drew is mad about Sophia, always has been. She, of course, treats him like dirt. His spoilt brat of a daughter wants James, so there's method in their madness. But the pair of them are going to be out of luck . . . at least from what I've seen. Sophia don't stand any nonsense, and darling James is very much his mother's son.'

'Hannah,' Raven remonstrated, 'please get to the point. This conversation began with talk about our Christmas leave.'

'We're to please ourselves if we stay!' Hannah turned to Ginnie. 'What's up with you, misery guts? I'm asking a serious question here. Are you going home to your mum and dad, or are you going to take up Lily's invitation? I know you'll stay here if Richard's going to be on hand, but . . . Still, we won't know about that, will we? Anyway, the second choice is that we can stay put, in Hawksley if we choose . . . '

Since neither of her friends answered, Hannah continued, 'But who would want to stay in that great barn? There's not even going to be a sprig of holly, Vincent said. That's downright rotten! Especially when it grows like weeds round here.'

'Hawksley without Lily wouldn't be at all festive,' Raven said quietly. 'But I can and will cook if—'

'Oh, we won't have to fend for ourselves! Mrs St John has taken on two new people – Lily told me.'

'You're such a mine of information,' Raven teased. 'Hannah, you and Lily are gossips pure and simple. And why two people?'

'One to cook and the other a kind of all-rounder to help Lily. Lily said she could cope, but even self-centred Mrs St John's realised how overworked she is. I think it struck home to her when the twins went missing that time. Still, all that's neither here nor there.' She turned to Ginnie again. 'Here, Gin, are you going to Ilford or are you stopping here so that you can meet up with Richard, even if ever so briefly?'

'I – I honestly don't quite know,' Ginnie replied at last.

'Oh, come on!'

'I don't! I could be at home, or in Kent, or in Matching's Bradley Hotel.'

'Do what?' Hannah's grin was curious. 'Now what are you on about?'

'About you getting cracking,' Ginnie told her, momentarily funking telling her news. Then, adding firmly, 'Come on, we are supposed to be cutting broccoli.'

'All right. But don't change the subject. What's that bit about a Bradley Hotel?'

'Even I'm getting rather curious about that,' Raven put in. 'Do tell!'

Ginnie took in a deep breath, then, 'Richard and I are to marry – just as soon as it can be arranged.'

'Golly!' Raven's face lit up. 'How marvellous. What a secretive old thing you are!'

'A proper so-and-so,' Hannah agreed, adding, 'so Richard's won out? Corks!'

Ginnie pulled a face. 'Is that all you can say? Corks?'

'Will crikey do? What a dark horse you are, though I suppose it's no surprise.' Hannah threw down her cutter and her arms went round Ginnie in an all-embracing hug. 'I'm happy for you, Ginnie, I really am. When did all this happen?'

'This weekend.'

'Where did he propose?'

'When we left the pub. He just made a kind of announcement.' Ginnie looked at Hannah, eyes bright and twinkling now as she remarked, 'You look like a fish, Hannah, your mouth has opened so wide.'

'Whose wouldn't be? You've kept this little lot really close to your chest. Has Richard been so secretive with all his mates?'

'Yes, apart from Matt. He knew before I did, in fact.'

'Men!' Hannah laughed. 'They're all mad. Come on, tell us everything. What's it like? I.T. – *it*. You know!'

'Pardon?' Ginnie's face went scarlet.

'Don't tell me you haven't let him do it, not even once?' Hannah was in a high good humour and now out to tease. 'You've gone as red as a turkey-cock.' A thought struck her and she looked rueful as she moaned to Raven, 'Gawd help us, now I'm the only actual virgin round here.'

'Not really,' Raven told her with quiet dignity, 'just to put the record straight. But I will say this. Francis and I made love every time we smiled into each other's eyes.'

'And that,' Hannah replied, serious now, 'is about the loveliest thing I've heard.'

They fell to after that, cutting the broccoli and putting it in long wooden boxes that would be collected later. Raven and Ginnie were each busy with their thoughts. Hannah, on the other hand, was on top form. She always was when trying to hide her worries. Both Ginnie and Raven recognised the fact and said nothing. Hannah was singing

Arthur Askey's version of *Run Rabbit Run*, which went, 'Run Hitler, Run Hitler, Run, Run, Run . . .' And with each swing a white head fell, was swiftly gathered and placed in the box.

Listening to Hannah one would never have guessed that she, like the rest, got up at six and worked long hard hours, with only short breaks for a mid-morning snack, a further half-hour for dinner. Tea was a quick swig from the flask before cracking on again because daylight was so precious at this time of year. Usually the work was back-aching and monotonous, hard on the feet and the hands. Exhaustion was not uncommon, for life on the farm was a tough nut to crack for city girls, but crack it they did.

'Women's Land Army – bit of a joke?' Hannah was wont to say in tones of surprise. 'There's certainly no glamour. No honours abound, but who expects or receives gongs for muck-spreading or cleaning out pigs?'

'Hold on,' Ginnie had laughingly remonstrated. 'We're fieldworkers full stop. No animals! Our war effort's just good solid slog. And I personally would have it no other way.'

Hannah and Raven instantly agreed.

They also said that it was pretty boring stuff, particularly as they still hadn't seen the back of the beet. There was plenty, stacked up on the side of the lane, waiting to be taken to Felsted at the right and proper time. In the meantime, the broccoli was ready and waiting for the steady swing of cutting knives.

Hannah ceased to sing at last and to all intents and purposes was thinking only of what she was doing. But inside, her tummy was beginning to churn once more. She would get up extra early again tomorrow, and would keep on and on – until she came face to face with Frank . . .

Chapter Eighteen

After work, having washed and changed, then gone down to the kit-chen, the girls were introduced to the two new helpers who, Lily explained, were to live in the old servants' quarters, on the other side of the house.

'Meet Miss Peggy Powell,' Lily said. 'She and Betty have waited especially to meet you. Betty will be looking after you first thing, but it's Miss Powell here you can thank for your evening meal.'

The small woman with a silent watchfulness hovering at the back of her brown eyes, peered at them from behind cheap metal-rimmed glasses. Her scanty brown hair was brushed severely away from her broad forehead and screwed up in a diminutive bun at the back of her head. Her ears stuck out. Her coarse hands hung awkwardly at her side. She was very thin and wearing a dark brown serge dress that seemed too large. It was buttoned up to the neck in a no-nonsense way.

Poor old thing! Hannah thought. She's been through it, by the looks of her. She wants to cut and run – or at least to have the floor open so she can fall through it.

She reached out and took hold of the woman's hand. 'Hello,' she said. 'How do?'

Peggy Powell's fingers remained limp, but a muscle at the side of her mouth jerked a little in response. The woman nodded briefly, but did not reply. She seemed very humble and suddenly Hannah felt as uncomfortable as she.

'And this is Betty Joyce,' Lily went on, 'who you'll see lots of, because she turns her hand to just about everything.'

'Which sometimes ain't all that clever, yer know,' Betty said in a voice that was slightly plaintive, but held an underlying defiance all the same.

Betty was a very different kettle of fish to Miss Powell. She had a gutsy air about her, Hannah thought. Someone who might be down, but never quite out. The younger of the two new helpers was pleasant and clean-looking in her black skirt and white blouse. Her brown hair was naturally curly and nestled attractively round her ears. She had full lips, a generous nose and her dark eyes were smiling under heavily arched brows.

'Ah! Greetings even so, our fellow slaves!' Hannah said and beamed.

'Hello,' Ginnie said.

'So nice to meet you both,' Raven put in.

Betty smiled back. The older woman nodded again, but she was stiff and seemed very strung up. Bloody hell, Hannah thought, she's a lost cause and no mistake.

'Well, I'm off,' Lily told them, whipping off her apron that was covered today in a red and yellow daisy design. 'Miss Powell will sort you out, girls, once she gets to know how harmless you are. She's a real marvel at everything she does, specially cooking – which you're about to find out. Byesy-bye. See you in the morning.'

'Don't have to rush or nothing, yer know,' Betty told her. 'We're here to help, and looking forward to it.'

'Marvellous!' Lily waved in her bright and happy manner. She was away with no further ado.

There was an uncomfortable silence since everyone was ill at ease. It was Hannah who livened things up.

'Miss Powell,' she said, 'I think we're all feeling a bit shy, so we'll have to get to know about each other very quickly, won't we? In the meantime, I'm starving! Whatever it is you've got there is making my mouth water. Is it all right if we carry on as usual? Line up, hold out our plates and you dole us up our share? Or have we to sit at table very polite and wait? Or . . . Oh gawd, let's get stuck in, eh?'

'That's the ticket, Peg,' Betty told her. 'Let's feed our new mates, eh? They've been working themselves to death all day, yer know.'

The atmosphere was lightened at once. Miss Powell, now more relaxed and sure of what she was about, walked to the pots. The girls grabbed their plates.

'All mates now, eh?' Hannah carolled. 'Woolton Pie, luv-erly! Have you two eaten?'

'Yes,' Betty replied. 'How you three tuck in.' She gave Hannah a conspiratorial smile. 'I think Miss Powell and me's going to be very happy here, yer know.'

'Are you from the village, Bet, or anywhere around here?'

'No!' Miss Powell spoke for the first time, her voice quiet, but surprisingly firm. Her cheeks seemed to pinch in, her eyes behind her glasses suddenly bright and very wary. 'Mrs St John hired us from – the agency.'

145

'Well, I hope you like it here as much as we do,' Hannah told her, thinking, Corks! The old girl's going to be all right after all. She's just suffering from nerves. She heard herself adding, 'Mrs St John might seem a bit off-hand at first, but I promise you, her heart's in the right place.'

Hannah ignored Raven and Ginnie's startled looks, and blithely went on to tell how Sophia had actually offered to get her 'proper' fish and chips from the chip shop in town. This when she, Hannah, had all but chopped her finger off when cutting beet . . .

It was still dark the next morning and well before six when Hannah slipped out of Hawksley. She grinned and waved at Betty who was already lighting the fire. It was bitterly cold and Hannah's breath came out in spurts of white steam as she breathed.

She began to run, banging her gloved hands together as she did so. The cold air was stinging against her cheeks and making her eyes water. The moon shone down, a soulless white eye. The hedges held secrets – the trees, too. The fields were splodgy with dark shadows as cows wandered by.

If I find the old devil, Hannah was thinking, what do I do? What do I say? 'You rotten sod!' That'll be the first thing. Selfish old blighter, he can't put himself out enough to think of anyone else. And how do I look for him anyway? If I go over that fence I'll actually be trespassing. I'll get caught and put in clink. Old Drew's in with the local bobby who'll do anything Drew says. Oh damn! I don't half-wish that Ginnie and Raven were here.

Hannah reached her special place at last. She leaned against the gate and watched and waited. Gradually she saw the horses being exercised, among them Belvedere, Sophia's magnificent black mount, and James's quite splended Pegasus. Snow Queen, the beautiful animal that her owner had so loved, was not there. Perhaps she had not recovered from whatever it was that had made Frank lead rather than ride her that morning before.

Wait a minute! I'm a chump, I really am. Hannah pulled herself up short. Frank can't ride. How could I be so stupid? It was probably the shock of seeing him that put everything else out of my mind. He must be in the stables somewhere.

Her mind raced. Now how the devil can I go swanning in there? I've got to find him, I must find out what he's at. Dear God, why am I getting so scared? Now, just how must I go about this?

'Dammit!' she said out loud. 'Honesty's the best policy, they say. Oh well, here goes.'

She climbed over the fence and began walking across the field towards the Drews' place, trying to think about ordinary everyday things and banish the reality of Walker Street and the nightmare of her past.

So she concentrated on telling herself that she was glad of her thick jersey. That she had been wise to tuck her dungarees inside her Wellingtons. The rubber boots were a godsend, she told herself, a shield against the wringing-wet grass. Her gloves were good, thick and warm, a present from Ginnie whose mum apparently knitted millions of pairs with odd balls of wool collected by the local WI.

Soldiers, sailors, airmen, anyone and everyone who needed gloves, balaclava helmets, or blankets made from knitted squares ... Not only men of the Forces but also victims of bombs, refugees – just about everyone owed a debt of some kind to the homeliness of the WI.

Hannah tried to imagine Ma Carpenter in her kitchen with knitting in her hands. Even better, with the bug-eyed old Tom glaring and spitting at her side. In spite of her nerves, Hannah sniggered. Talk about looking like that old girl in the French Revolution – the one who sat laughing like a drain and knitting while nobility had their heads chopped off!

She sobered and sucked in her breath as the Drews' place came into view, its gates open, but imposing all the same. She marched forwards in a purposeful way, even though deep down, she wanted very desperately to run in the opposite direction.

Beyond the arched entrance to the stables was a wide cobbled yard, with many rows of stalls set at right-angles to it. Beyond this was another arch giving a vista of the paddocks and further meadows. A stable-lad carrying a bucket of water winked and whistled when he saw Hannah. 'Can I help you, miss?'

'Yes, please. I think you have a new worker here, a Londoner? He's rather been through it, I'm afraid, and—'

'You mean Frank. He's in that paddock over there,' the lad pointed. 'An' after that you can pay me a visit if you like.'

'I'm dead off luxuries,' she replied, but grinned in a friendly way just the same, adding, 'Ta!'

As she went through the arch she saw Frank leaning on a rail, watching Snow Queen being walked round by an earnest-looking man in a fawn overall.

Hearing her approach Frank turned, smirked, then asked, 'What kept yer?'

'Why did you come here?' she burst out. 'Thank you for nothing, Frank!'

'I've got me reasons and they're my business, girl. So shut it.'

147

'It's my business too.' She stepped towards him furiously. 'How did you find me?'

'Come off it,' he said, impatient now. 'How d'yer think? The hostel woman told them what asked on my behalf, of course. They hardly thought the questions were about some German spy!' He looked into her eyes and saw the fear and uncertainty there. 'Leaving Colchester weren't such a good idea, was it? You could have ducked yer head down better there because there's so many people about.'

'Frank, I don't need you to tell me—'

'That Ram's a bastard and he won't give in too easy, specially now he's took Val on.' He grinned sourly. 'I did hear as how he's going to get hitched to her, stupid sod.'

'You've probably led them straight to me, Frank.' She was getting really worked-up now. 'That was a rotten mean thing to do. Really horrible! And there was Ma Carpenter telling me that you – you quite liked me in your mean and selfish way. So much for that!'

Suddenly, in spite of his shrivelled figure and wizened looks she wanted to hit him, yell and scream and threaten to black his beady little eyes. Instead she heard herself asking lamely, 'Are you in very much pain?'

'It'll take a while, but I'll be as good as new.' He half-smiled and his tone mellowed into what for him could be considered some warmth. 'I did it deliberate, if yer must know,' he told her. 'Christ, anyone can do what them religious lot did for me. When they come back from Colchester and told me, shouting hallelujahs all over the shop, I thought it was best if got down here fast and kept me eye open.' He leered and winked. 'I made 'em swear to secrecy. Said you was in women's trouble, hinted that you were up the duff and that. Said that being your stepdad I was needing to find you and offer to help.' He sniggered. 'Bleeding hell, I left 'em on their knees praying for your soul!'

'Shut up, Frank!' she snapped, nauseated. 'What a wicked lie you've put your tongue to. And even that's not as bad as letting the whole wide world know I'm here.'

'For Chrissake, shut up! I've covered me own tracks good and proper. They won't catch me in a hurry – but you! Gawd, Han, why are you such a stupid little mare?'

'Charming!'

'I promised your ma I'd keep a weather eye open for you and that's what I'm trying to do. Look, mate, I promise you that at the first hint of trouble I'm off to the local cop-shop. I'll stitch 'em up. Yes, all of 'em, including that vixen Val. I mean it, make no mistake. But I'm hoping it won't happen. If it does, it's on the cards I'll be letting meself in for a stretch behind bars. So, since that's the case, I'd prefer to wait and see.'

It was incredible, but she found that she believed him.

'Why didn't you let me know you were here, Frank?' she asked quietly. 'Why was it that I had to find out for myself?'

He gave her a sour look. 'Why d'yer think? Can't hardly see yer putting a welcome mat down for me, can I? 'Sides, I'd 'ave preferred you not to know. I like it here. I was lucky that they needed an odd-jobber. I mainly do mucking out, all the dogsbody stuff. Still, I'm glad that most of their blokes got called up. I like the geese, they're luverly creatures. An' providing you keep out of trouble, I reckon I could get to stay on.'

Hannah was remembering his love for Firelord. That had been genuine enough. She resolved to try and meet him halfway.

'That was Snow Queen you were leading, wasn't it? Why?'

'Vet's orders. She ain't been on form, I dunno what's been wrong, but she's doing all right now. Gentle exercise, the vet said. She's a nice old thing, belonged to a young chap what's been killed in the war. I'm glad Drew's a decent sort. Sees to it that they're all looked after, he does. He's like our manager, Phelps. A bastard to us workers, but the horses do just fine. The old lady's a bit special, and she's spoiled by everyone, but there weren't no one else handy to exercise her the other morning, so Phelps let me do it – on pain of death if I messed up. He only let me because me an ol' Snow Queen kind of get on.'

There came the sound of men's voices and Hannah swung round, red-faced, a picture of guilt. The eldest of the newcomers was middle-aged, thin and silvery, huddled in a fur-lined overcoat, his beaky nose and tight-lipped mouth making him look like a bird. His companion was thick-set and craggy-faced and had salt and pepper hair. He had nice grey eyes.

'What's all this?' The older man's voice cracked out like a pistol shot.

'Oh, I'm sorry, sir,' Hannah said quickly. 'I – I know I shouldn't be here, but my friend Mrs Gray, who rides regularly on Blue Rinse, was telling our Mrs St John how she loves being here with all these beautiful animals. She was so full of it that I – I came over before work to ask if it would be possible for me to have lessons?' Hannah motioned towards Frank. 'This gentleman was being very kind and explaining that since he's just a worker here, he couldn't help me at all.'

'Madam,' the man snapped rudely, 'this is *not* a riding school. Good day!'

'And good day to you, sir,' Hannah replied and was suddenly back to normal. Gay and mischievous, and defiantly refusing to be bullied by the man, who was so clearly the big cheese, Mr Drew. This old stone-face actually liked Sophia, she marvelled. Fat chance!

Mark Drew stood there, glaring down at her, waiting for her to shrivel up and fade away, but she stood her ground, saying sweetly, 'Thank you *so* much for your courtesy! I can't wait to tell Mrs St John that I have met you at long last – and seen for myself how wonderfully Snow Queen's getting on.'

'Pshaw!' Mr Drew turned his back and stomped off.

The manager looked at Frank, said crisply, 'Carry on, Neilson,' then to Hannah in a warmer voice, 'good morning, miss. Sorry.'

Her heart sank. She was barely listening to Mr Phelps, too busy noting that Frank had given them his true name. He must have had to show his Identity Card in order to get the job. Being up-front wasn't all that good for a chap attempting to hide!

Without giving her stepfather a backward glance, Hannah walked quickly away. As she breathed in the freezing air and felt the wind whipping the blood into her cheeks, she wondered wildly how it was that fate never allowed her to forget about Walker Street. Damn Frank! she thought bitterly. Damn Val! And Biff, Ram, and Fatty Blythe. Damn them all to hell and back again.

She reached Hawksley just before Betty Joyce put all the breakfast things away.

'I'm so sorry, Bet,' she panted, 'I went for a walk and forgot the time. Is there anything left?'

A dish of porridge had been kept warm. To follow, two doorsteps of bread and home-made plum jam; God only knew where Lily had got the sugar from. Beaming gratefully Hannah wolfed the lot down.

Ginnie and Raven appeared then, both ready for work and very curious to know where she'd been. Hannah just laughed their questions away.

'I needed to think something out, that's all. Honest!'

Then Ellery came in, took one look at Betty's appalled expression and hastily took his cherrywood pipe out of his mouth.

'Ready, girls?' he asked.

'As ever!' Hannah replied, acting up as always. 'Come on, let's go. This morning's a bracer, wouldn't you say?'

'Very,' he replied. 'What were you doing over at Drews?'

Bloody hell, she thought, talk about nosy parkers round here! How did *he* find out?

'Thought I'd try to wangle some riding lessons,' she told him blithely. 'It was no deal, I'm afraid.'

'Hannah!' Raven remonstrated. 'Why didn't you tell me?'

'Why, are you so special?' Hannah was defiant. 'Have you got influence there?'

'No, but Sophia has.'

'Sophia?' Hannah grabbed at this – anything to divert their suspicions from the truth. 'Sophia now, is it? On Christian-names terms, are we? Crikey, what have you got that I haven't? Blow me down, Raven, I thought crawling was the last thing you'd do!'

Hannah saw the look in Raven's eyes and knew that she had gone too far. She was hurt; the jibe had of course been uncalled-for, and far from the truth. But Hannah was running scared. A vision of Ram Rawlins's murderous face swam before her eyes. She went turkey-cock red as she flared, 'Oh, sod all this gabbing on about horses and some stuck-up old bitch! I'm off outside. I'm ready if no one else is, to get on with some work!'

The day dragged by, with very little conversation, both Ginnie and Raven showing by their silences that for today at least, they did not like Hannah very much.

Visibility was good. High above they heard the planes from Matching Airfield going off to who knew where. It was a sad sound, Hannah thought, near to tears, and the whole wide world was a rotten lonely place.

The evening was no better. Ginnie made ready to go to the Rookwood, just in case Richard turned up. Raven sat quietly, reading a copy of *Woman's Own* magazine. Hannah had the wireless on, listening to *Hi Gang*, or was it *ITMA*, or *The Crazy Gang*? It didn't matter. She wasn't taking it in. She felt bereft, needing to apologise, but unable to. They might ask her again what she had been doing that morning, and she'd have to lie. She couldn't tell her two friends about the mess she was in. *Couldn't!* If they ever learned what an animal her stepfather was, the dregs from which she'd been spawned, they'd . . .

No! That was unfair. Her friends weren't like that. They would accept her even if she herself was a raggedy beggar from the streets. The reason she couldn't tell them, was simply because she herself was too afraid.

It was late when Ginnie came back. She looked worried and went straight up to bed. Hannah followed her, saying humbly, 'Am I too rotten to ask you what's up?'

'Don't be silly, Hannah,' Ginnie told her consolingly. 'You open your mouth sometimes and a silly noise comes out, that's all. As for what's wrong – well . . . She smiled in a trembly fashion, and pushed a strand of red hair out of her wide, frightened eyes. It seems that Richard is . . . is late back from ops.'

151

Chapter Nineteen

Matt sat in the Rose and Crown alone. He was getting drunk and didn't give a damn. He was holding a crumpled letter in his hand and wanting to swear his soul away. His mind was full of memories. He was remembering how he had met Titch during basic training. It had been at Bridlington, a seaside town that the RAF had more or less taken over. It was in a one-time smart private residence, now taken over for billets, that he and Titch had shared a room. They were very comfortable, and across the road, facing the sea, stood the swish seafront hotel where they had their meals. There was no Reveille in the morning, so they had to get themselves up, wash and shave and make their way to the hotel. They had to go to another part of the town for roll call, then were trotted off by a Flight Sergeant to their classrooms.

What a shambles it had been when they marched through the streets to their lectures. There was a long queue of bods, four abreast, with a Flight Sergeant leading the column. The marching pace for aircrews was in very quick tempo, and it seemed that not a soul could hold step. Titch and Matt, always tagging on at the rear, were forever running flat out just to keep up!

Often after lunch, if there was nothing of interest doing, apart from another endless lecture, he and Titch would gallop along behind the other bods until they reached the cinema. Do a quick right turn and double smartly through the foyer. They got the lecture gen from the blokes sharing rooms in their house during the evening.

Everything in those days had been a bloody great lark. When they finished instruction at Bridlington it had been off to flying training school at Inverness, Scotland. He and Titch had been as thick as thieves all the way through.

After their final exams, they passed out as Sergeant Air Gunners. There had been a big parade with bags of 'Bull', when they were presented with their Brevets and Chevrons. The parade over, it was

152

back to billets to sew on tapes. Nothing, Titch and he had thought, rejoicing, could hold them back now!

They were posted on for further training. They flew and swotted alternately. Then the day arrived when they were to crew up. Their Squadron went to Matching. It was inevitable that he and Titch had stuck together like glue. Titch had also palled up with Richard, who was as daredevil and headstrong as they. For the rest, they were a grand bunch of chaps. They had completed several successful ops. Then had come the night when he, Matt, had plummeted down onto the Hawksley roof; other crew members had been killed; Richard came out of it beaten but unbowed – and poor old Titch had been severely burned.

Now Richard had gone, just before Christmas last year. Hannah had written to say that they were heart-broken, especially Ginnie who had been expecting to marry him. But out of necessity they were all carrying on.

Matt felt let down. He would have banked on Richard, a survivor if ever there was one. Now Titch! Never in a million years would Matt have predicted that Titch would choose, voluntarily, to opt out of the game. Had his oppo, his dear old friend, gone completely bloody nuts? Had that sodding girl meant *that* much? Clearly she had. So now they had all passed from his life. Like ships they had sailed into the unknown. Titch and Richard, with the others, would live on only in memory.

Matt groaned and screwed up Titch's last letter, the scraggy epistle in which the burned airman had written that chaps dead and done for had had the best of the game. They were well out of it; unlike him, they would never get a 'Dear John' letter like the one he had just received from his fiancée, saying she was dreadfully sorry, but she could no longer bear to look at his face. Of course she knew that after a time, perhaps a year or so, things would get better, but even so . . .

Don't get caught up with a woman till this lot's over, Titch had written. *Play the field, old chap, but never the fool. Me? I'm cashing in my chips. Good luck and toodle-pip.*

Titch's mother had written to say that her son had taken an overdose of tablets. He had gone to sleep, and in spite of everything they tried, had never woken up. She added that perhaps it was kinder in the long run. The girl Titch had loved so dearly was all set to marry someone else. A civilian this time.

Matt thought of Hannah and knew in his soul that she would never change. She would look at him if he was burned and she would weep – but she would never let him down. Dear sparky young Hannah, on whom he had set his sights right from the start. Whose letters he clung to. Hannah, who was such a determinedly positive little thing.

He had been all set to propose marriage, had even gone so far as sweating at the thought of her laughing. Hannah had never taken him seriously. Even worse, she might take it too solemnly, think about it, then turn him down. He couldn't bear that idea. But it was worth a try. Yes, he would definitely try, but it was the devil's own job these days, to get young Hannah on her own.

Then out of the blue, Titch's letter had arrived. It had brought Matt up with a start. Had filled him with such a sense of foreboding that, for Hannah's sake, he had decided to play things down. The thought that had shaken him to the core, was that out of so many poor ill-fated bods, he had perhaps been *too* fortunate. Any day now, his luck could well run out.

It didn't help that his Squadron's aircraft were Stirling bombers. They weren't bad crates, but could only climb a mere 12,000 feet, not like the Lancasters that could zoom up to a neat 35,000. Enemy flak had done for quite a few Stirlings, so as kites went, crews felt they were a bit heavy-going. Titch had waxed quite poetical on the subject of Stirlings, and hadn't repeated himself once.

Matt groaned again. He visualised young Hannah, so bright-eyed and earnest, so full of the wisdom of her beloved Miss Pitt. What was it the woman had told her – that it all evened out in the end? That life turned out to hold more laughter than tears?

'Buggering hell!' Matt swore. 'Poor old Titch. Poor bloody Titch . . .'

Then he turned to the bar and roared out for another pint.

Hannah worked doggedly alongside her two silent friends. They were hoeing young beet, which was looking green and healthy in the warm May sunshine.

Being in a good mood, because she had found a cheery whacky letter waiting for her when she arrived back from work the previous night, she was disposed to actually *like* beet. Not half so much as James St John and Ellery did, of course, but it did look nice, growing like a green carpet.

She knew that sugar beet was of the same family as field-grown mangold, and that it originated in the Middle East, place and date unknown. She also knew where some of it ended up – shorn of leaves, being carried along on the factory's moving belt to be washed. Also sometimes on the grass verges of main roads – particularly at curves and bends where lorries leaned to take corners! There you would see the tumbled-off fruit, looking all forlorn, in little heaps turning black with rot.

154

Now, at the right and proper time, this new and lushly growing beet would be lifted and shorn. With luck Ellery would take her along as he had before, to help fork the fruit onto the moving belt. Once washed, the beet would be crushed, the extracted liquid put inside evaporators, and lo and behold, there were spoonfuls of the stuff that made the medicine go down.

Hannah breathed in the warm air and felt the sun on her face. It was such a nice fresh time, May in the country. She thought back to January when there had been snowstorms followed by ten degrees of frost. She had walked down the lane, over a little footbridge, and round by the brook that trickled at the bottom of the lane that finished up by Duckpond Corner. She had disturbed wild duck rooting in the sedge and gone on, powdery snow scurrying ahead of her. Drifts had curved round the banks of the brook which still managed to flow below snow-plastered tree-trunks; the same trees in their rime looking like lace-work against a clear sky.

Talk in the Rookwood had been of the harshness of a newspaper article that had been scathing about Irish 'neutrality'. Such columns afforded no comfort to the many thousands of Irish who *had* joined the Armed Forces. It was not their fault that Ireland was the only member of the Commonwealth not to be openly alongside.

'A typical Irish situation,' russet-faced Cyril Stitson had laughed. 'And I'll say this, they don't come no better than my cousin-in-law, young Paddy Reilly. Fighting his guts out he is, alongside our Tommies, and I'll take this moment to raise me glass to him.'

'To Paddy Reilly!' Glasses were raised to the unknown young man, Hannah's too.

It had been so good to be accepted by them all, she thought. Village life was just the ticket. Everyone knew everyone else. Oh, there was tittle-tattle. You knew what cottagers were having for tea even before they themselves sat down at table! There was cattyness, sly digs and scandal-mongering galore, but there was togetherness too.

The whole village had mourned with Ginnie and took her close to their hearts. And special words were spoken for Richard, a friend, in the pleasant little church.

Virgin St Mary's graceful arcades gave it a deceptive impression of spaciousness. And Hannah had looked around and loved its age and atmosphere, its tang of winter chrysanthemums and evergreen – the flower arrangers took great pride in beautifying their church. And Hannah had also breathed in the smell of old leather and hymn books and well-polished wood. It had been on the day they had all been thinking of and remembering Richard, that she had been filled with wonder. Winter sunlight suddenly blazing out and shining through the

155

stained glass windows had given everything a dreamlike rosy glow.

Hannah was not and never had been a church person. She had gone there that day, as had most of the village, for they knew the vicar was going to speak of Richard, the popular young airman who had died somewhere far away. He would always be remembered. A happy young man who, during his brief visit, had shared warmth and laughter with those he met. But at that moment, of silence and prayer, Hannah had found herself making childish bargains with God. That she would be good, would hold her tongue, become a saint! If only He could see His way to ensuring that Matt Sheridan would be spared.

It had been a service filled with comradeship and hope. It would perhaps have helped Ginnie just a little, but she had not been there. She had gone home, to her parents, and had not returned until Christmas was over and done. And because it felt right, Hannah and Raven had stayed together in Hawksley, rather than go to Lily's and try to join in with boyish fun.

So now they worked together, quietly and methodically, completing the tasks they were given. Closer than ever, grateful for the comfort and warmth of Hawksley at the end of the day; and the friendly companionship of the Rookwood. This on the evenings when they had energy left to want to venture out.

February held the memory of Churchill's appeal to the Americans. His closing passage, 'Give us the tools and we will finish the job,' was so intense that it had kept Hannah quiet for a full three minutes.

She continued her walking during free time. She kept away from the stables at Drews, had heard nothing and thought less of Frank. It was the countryside itself that saved her sanity. Her wandering by the wild brook, watching the sooty-footed lambs, seeing the slope of fields and dull browny-blue of the hedgerows as colour washes on old Chinese silk.

March, memorable for the twelfth's full red-yellow moon. Clear vision for night-fliers, a danger signal for those down below, it had brought to its peak the season's bombing raids. No hard news came through either from papers or broadcasts. They just heard the planes.

One day, there was a terrible crash when a Junkers 88 tore in flames past the village, landed in a field and burned itself out. The German crew had parachuted some miles away. Hannah had felt her heart lurch, remembering Matt floating down. What was he doing now? He never actually said. How she clung to his letters! Friendly epistles that never gave anything of his innermost feelings away. Yes, jokey, zany little sentences in his terrible scrawl. Often they would make her chuckle out loud, but secretly she was wondering, had she dreamed that kiss?

Then it was April and Easter, and the twins enjoying precious chocolate that everyone had helped get by giving up their sweet coupons. This had been when the sloe came out with tiny tufts of blossom, and the hawthorn leaves were beginning to appear. Hannah saw martens twittering and fussing, such garrulous little things; and the whole of nature was yawning and stretching and waiting for summer to be born.

Abroad, the Italians were routed in Abyssinia. There were retreats in North Africa and Greece. All the know-alls in the Rookwood swore that Egypt would be the next to fall. On May, the Devon city of Plymouth was raided yet again, very badly indeed – but as the wireless said, the people were staunchly carrying on.

The Americans now stationed at Matching were spreading themselves around. The village girls ceased to mind the Land Army now. They were too busy looking further afield. There were GIs in plenty – great guys who chewed gum, played crap, and handed out Lucky Strike cigarettes, nylons and wisecracks in equal amounts.

Several Yanks now make their way to our village, Hannah wrote to Matt. *They're charmers and full of the old toffee, believe me. They say 'Gee!' a lot, seem to be very well off, and are rather full of themselves. There's one, they call him Lofty, who has taken a tumble for Ginnie, but she's deaf, dumb and blind to everyone and everything these days. Raven and I just stay near her. We don't say much, but Raven, who understands, says that she'll come round eventually. We just have to be patient, that's all.*

Dear old Sophia St John's been brilliant to Ginnie. And something else, she and Raven actually seem to get on! The old girl just about puts up with me. Oh, the two women who came to Hawksley just before Christmas are really nice. But I think there's something a bit odd about them. Cyril Stitson offered to buy Peggy Powell a drink and by her reaction you'd have thought he was going to poison her to death! Betty's not so scared, but all the same, I don't think she's too keen on men. I said all this to Lily and she reckons that it's me that's odd. I hope you don't think so too. Why haven't you been down to see me? Have you been on duty all of this time? Or is it that you rate your London landlady higher than me? I miss your ugly mug. Love, Hannah.

It was getting late when the word came. Matt just had time to tuck the letter inside his jacket. She sends her love, he thought as he hurried along with the others to the Briefing Room. He sat before the platform, arms folded, attentive. He watched the pointer sliding, then stopping, on the large wallmap as the crisp no-nonsense voice went on.

'Here's your course, chaps. Fly at three thousand feet and return ditto. Steer clear of Rochefort, this island here, it's very well defended.

Nantes, there, will give you hell if you get in range. There's a large bulk of heavily-fortified Navy in and around there. You will lay your mine in the mouth of the Boreaux River in time for the convoy we are expecting. That's all. Good luck!'

That was not quite all, of course. Personal valuables were handed to the Briefing Officer, Matt and the crew collected parachutes and harness. Then grabbing up the rest of their gear, they jumped into the wagon that was waiting.

The Flight Sergeant in charge of ground-crew mechanics met them. Matt whistled wryly and grimaced at the rest of his crew. They weren't Titch and Richard and the old bunch, who couldn't be replaced, but he liked them a lot just the same. They were grand lads, just his cup of tea. All tarred with the same brush: here today, gone tomorrow, and the devil take the hindmost. Slap-happy, thinking merely of that hour, that minute, savouring it to the full. Would it rain next week? Would there *be* a next week? So what? Who cared?

There was David Deakin, the pilot, a nice bloke. Fair-haired, blue-eyed, conscientious. Pre-war he taught in a primary school. Ricky Davis, the Navigator, was a complete contrast. He stood tall; his hands were large with black fuzz on the backs. He was dark-haired, dark-eyed, and an ex-policeman. He looked it. Ron Rashley, Bomb Aimer, was a nice quiet kid – an ex-undergraduate. Always the same, blue-grey eyes twinkling with humour. You knew where you were with Ron. Pete Smith, Wireless Operator, fair, quiet left to himself, yet very sociable, ex-bank worker. Bruce Newman, air Gunner, red-haired and fiery, was usually with Pete. It seemed odd, but Bruce's previous work was with a vet. He had sensitive hands. Jack Baird, Flight Engineer, was dark, with near-black eyes that snapped with intelligence when he spoke of engines, his life-long passion. The crew called him 'Professor' behind his back. They called Matt himself 'Chippy' sometimes, because before call-up he'd been a cabinet-maker. Yes, Matt thought, looking round, they were a real decent bunch.

There came the routine inspection of their aircraft. The Flight Sergeant in charge of ground-crew mechanics met them.

'What ho, you chaps. Here's your old iron. G for George and you'll do me a favour if you lose the bloody thing on the way back.'

'What's the gen?' David grinned. 'No engines?'

'Oh, our chaps have banged them about a bit. They'll be okay . . . now.'

'Good show,' David said.

They piled in ready for take-off. Matt and Jack tested the turrets and checked their guns and ammunition. The four engines purred sweetly enough.

'Get up front for take-off,' David ordered. 'This mine's a stinker. A bit of a heavyweight.'

It was nearing time, ten o'clock at night. Matt felt the tension mounting. The others were dead quiet. David taxied G for George round to the main runway.

'Stand by for take-off.'

The kite took up speed, then the, 'Airborne, wheels up,' from David allowed them to relax. They took up their combat stations, and plugged in and tested the intercom.

Flying conditions were good; there was a clear sky and a full moon. Stirlings from other squadrons were on the same mission, but for the moment G for George was alone. Matt looked down and around. The world below was a mosaic of light and shade. Hannah was down there somewhere, he thought, helping to liven up the Rookwood, no doubt. But mostly he remembered her face, sweet and pensive, when she had sat with him that night while young Lenny Madeira had played his violin. Oh God, what wouldn't he give to be with her? What was she doing right now? He remembered her letter, her blithe mention of Yanks. They'd wonder what had hit them when they met up with Hannah! He hoped devoutly that she was not surrounded with GIs right now . . .

The wood fire was merely glowing in Rose Cottage kitchen. Hannah sat on the rug before it, hands clasped round her knees. Her lips were twitching.

'They're the bane of my life, Chook and Chris,' Lily was saying forcefully. 'And of course they blame it all on their rotten spelling. Actually I blame it on both pronunciation – and spelling.'

'I was always in trouble at school,' Hannah told her. 'Don't worry about it.'

'But I have double trouble,' Lily objected. 'And all over composition, their best subject too! Who would have thought writing about Moses's fetish over mustard tins would have caused so much trouble.'

'Mustard?'

'Yes. Mustard pronounced, according to them, musterd and written in their exercise books as musturd with a "u".'

'I don't quite see that as a terrible problem.'

'Ha! You don't know the half of it. The boys have school dinners. Miss Allthorpe kindly arranged meals for herself and children who live too far away from school to get home for lunch. Most children take sandwiches, but the twins sit down to something cooked. I prefer it that way.'

159

'Miss Allthorpe is the Headmistress?'

'Yes, boss of our primary, and one of the old school. You know, straight backs, stiff upper lip, all that sort of thing. You'd have thought I was asking for a couple of lowly peasants to sit at table. I mean, she was born in an era when one doffed one's cap to doctors and teachers and all of those one presumed were of a better class. Anyway, my kids eat as well as that woman! I pay through the nose for the privilege, of course, but it helps me out. I don't like taking advantage of my position here; I get away with quite enough as it is. But you can get the picture of old Allthorpe, can't you?'

'I've suffered a million stiff and starchy Allthorpes in my time,' Hannah agreed, and groaned. 'They'd die if they cracked their faces for a start. Miserable cows.'

'Don't I know it! Anyway, when asked what they wanted for afters my two said, get this, "Cuspoop, please."'

'Do what?' Hannah's face was alight with enjoyment.

'They told Miss that they mustn't say "turd" because it was rude. One of their mates told them so, in detail. Talk about looks of holy glee when they passed this information on to my own quaking self.'

'That's not so awful,' Hannah's lips were wobbling, 'is it?'

'It jolly well could be. Incidentally, I've dared them not to refer to what Moses does as anything except pooh.'

'Oh my God!' Hannah was trying hard to take it seriously, but her dancing eyes gave her away. Lily was not amused.

'I ask you! Apparently they went into a detailed argument about mustard and custard. Deliberately calling it muspoop and cuspoop, shrieking with laughter, naturally – you know them!'

'I do indeed!' Hannah was grinning all over her face.

'It's not so funny,' Lily told her fiercely. 'Now I've got to go on my knees to Miss Allthorpe and apologise for my moronic kids yet again. I could kill them both stone dead.'

'No, you couldn't.' Hannah laughed outright. 'You adore them. They're little rascals – but in this day and age it's nice to have something to laugh about.'

'Something vulgar?'

'Where I've come from,' Hannah told her blandly, 'the brand of real vulgarity would make your ears drop off.' She stiffened, smile dying. 'Damn!'

They both sat there, quiet, in the glow of firelight, listening. High above they could hear the drone of planes. Deep-throated, resonant. Bombers.

'Do you suppose that they're on the same op as Matt might well be?' Hannah asked. 'Oh dear!'

160

'I don't know, love.' Lily put her arm round Hannah in a comforting way. 'You're really taken with him, aren't you?'

'We're mates,' Hannah told her. 'He's a really nice bloke. It's just that I've never met someone who's flown through the air to land on a roof before.'

'You're smitten,' Lily told her. 'Just as I was with my Sam. Thank God, all my old man does is sort out a barrage balloon, although he would have liked to fly, and drop bombs, shoot guns and play the hero. . . Not a word about getting shot down himself, of course.'

'Men!' Hannah replied. 'What a lot of duds they are.'

'Just little boys who have been on the earth a long time.'

'I say,' Hannah said with open admiration. 'That's not a bad description of 'em!'

Far away they heard the deep-throated growl, then an upwards surge of sound as Moaning Minnie started up her warning.

Suddenly, Hannah was back in Walker Street, seeing the rag-doll effigy that Frank had become as the three would-be murderers had buried him in the rubble. She felt faint, remembering the implacable look in Ram Rawlins's eyes, and the nightmare sight and smell of that wall of smoke and flames. . . She shuddered, and Lily looked up, but seeing the young girl lost in her thoughts, she left her alone.

Biff, Ram and Fatty had probably caught Frank on his way to the Docks where he had been enlisted as a part-time fire-watcher, Hannah was thinking. Frank had avidly listened to old regulars' yarns in the pub, and Hannah had often overheard the things he passed on.

There were many different sorts of fires, he had said – all feared by those in the know. There were pepper fires, loading the surrounding air heavily with stinging particles so that when the firemen took a deep breath it felt like inhaling fire itself. There were rum fires, with torrents of blazing liquid pouring from the warehouse doors and barrels exploding like bombs themselves. There had once been a paint fire – an accident, Hannah remembered, that happened well before the Blitz; a cascade of white-hot flame had coated the pumps with varnish that could not be cleaned for weeks. Rubber fires gave out clouds of black smoke so asphyxiating that they could only be fought from a distance. A nephew of old Sam Grimes had died in one like that. Hearing these tales had made Hannah deathly afraid of fire.

Strange, she thought, listening to the air-raid warning now, how things never seemed so dramatic in the country. She loved it here, of course she did, it was so wide and wonderful, like Paradise! But London was her home-town. It had become part of her mental make-up, for it was there she had been born and bred.

161

You thought of the country as being green. You thought of London as being grey – grey buildings, grey pavements, a choppy grey river and regularly around November-time, thick blankets of grey fog. Even the town sparrows seemed more grey than country brown. And pearl-grey pigeons were as much part of the city as Pearly Kings and the dome of St Paul's. Above even that, huge silver-grey barrage balloons, sober and serene, brooded like waiting phantoms over the wartime scene.

Frank knew the Docks well. Since getting the sack from Hitchman's Dairy he had sometimes been a casual there, lining up with crowds of others, praying for a couple of hours' work. It had been Frank's fire-watching stints that had brought Biff Marner and Co sniffing round so eagerly. Before that, Biff had made his feelings known about his sister Val's adoration and desires in no uncertain way.

Everyone knew that the flanking warehouses held the precious cargoes that convoys had fought across oceans to bring safely ashore. Cargoes of things in short supply. . . Cargoes that would have a box or so missing here, a crate or two there, something else waylaid on its journey to the national store. Now Biff's gang were after Frank.

Ma Carpenter had imparted that little gem. She had spilt a bibful to Hannah, all but breathing fire and brimstone. She had come marching down Walker Street, boots flopping, hat set square, moth-eaten fox-fur, its eyes as glassy as Ma's, round her neck, and shoved open the door.

'Where's Frank?' she had snapped.

'I'm not sure, Ma. Probably in the Duck and Drake.'

'No, he ain't, I've already tried there. 'Ere, guess what I heard? That them Marners are trying to get round 'im to help 'em get past the guards. Frank ain't no tea-leaf and I ain't goin' ter stand by and let my nephew get it in the neck over them thieving sods.'

'He wouldn't. He *couldn't*! It would be more than his job's worth.'

'I know it, an' you bloody well know it,' Ma retorted, 'but that ain't the point, is it? If I've heard it, the cops will have heard it too. Gawd, that Frank's daft! Just wait till I get me 'ands on 'im!'

'I'm sorry,' Hannah had replied helplessly, and wanted to sink through the floor.

'Well, if he ain't here, I'm off,' the old girl decided, and she stalked out, stiff-backed, head high, ready to give anyone a mouthful who dared look at her askance.

Hannah had never heard the outcome of that one.

'What are you thinking?' Lily asked, bringing Hannah back to the present.

'That before September, 1940,' Hannah fibbed, 'four-fifths of London's auxiliary firemen had never fought a fire . . . And I was hoping that the Docks will be left in peace tonight.'

162

Chapter Twenty

The thin spread of the coastline appeared. Matt saw two other Stirlings, from this vantage point looking like twin ghosts. It was good to see them. They were on course and all set. Over the Channel David called through the intercom, 'Right, chaps, blaze away.'

Matt fired port and starboard into the sea and he and Bruce were satisfied that the guns were okay. They gave David the tickety-boo and he said, 'Good show, chaps. Approaching enemy coast now. Keep a sharp look-out.'

Dutifully Matt turned his turret to starboard and swore under his breath. The inboard starboard engine was sending sparks out of the exhaust. He reported it to Dave, and Jack Baird went along to have a look-see.

'How's it going, Jack?'

'No good. Bloody fine bone-shaker we've been saddled with.'

'Talk about we're coming so put the flags out,' Matt said sourly and tried not to think about it.

G for George passed over the French coast and the crew were on their toes waiting for the inevitable. Anti-aircraft guns opened fire to the port side. However, the flak was not too near. Searchlights threw out strong fingers that beamed white in the night. The plane dipped and wheeled, trying to avoid them. Matt felt apart from it all, ice-cool, almost as though this wasn't happening.

Their Stirling escort had disappeared and they were alone – or were they? Below them, quite clearly, Matt saw an airfield. A plane with lights on was in the act of landing.

'Watch out for Fighters,' came over the intercom.

Ricky Davis said to Ron Rashley, 'We'll be coming up to target.'

'All set,' Ron replied, then they were over the target and it was a dummy run. At the second go, Ron dropped the mine. G for George lifted considerably. Matt felt relieved, glad the mine was no longer on the doorstep, so to speak. Ricky's voice came over the intercom.

'Fly along the coast, please. We're off course.'

They stooged around, trying to get back on course. Suddenly, all hopes of sneaking away came to an abrupt end as all hell was let loose. It seemed a thousand guns opened up at once. Rockets screamed past the tail as the plane turned crazily, and they were away out to sea. Matt knew where they were then. Rockefort!

David Deakin turned the kite and got set on the course that Ricky gave him. Jack Baird called cheerfully over the intercom, 'Fuel's getting low. We'll have a job to get back to base.'

They began flying towards the coastline once more, then it happened.

Suddenly the world turned a somersault. G for George gasped and trembled like an exhausted runner who could see no end to the race. A shell had screamed into its side and the aircraft shuddered. In a flash the radio compartment was smashed. Another shell hit one of the petrol tanks and G for George became a bonfire. Matt and Bruce were working the guns overtime. Matt heard himself yelling, 'Damn you to hell! Damn, damn, damn!'

G for George died. He was killed, just like that, in a final scream of outraged engines, followed by a frantic whirring and winging off course.

Matt was surrounded by an inferno of light, noise, heat and the nauseating smell of burning rubber. He blinked and thought something exploded near his face, but the feeling faded to nothing. Momentarily there was a stinging in his chest, but it shut off. He continued sending out the ammunition as fast as he could.

Dave's voice came over the intercom. He sounded weary. 'Sorry, chaps. Can't hold it up any longer. Abandon aircraft.'

Matt swung the turret round. Then disconnected the intercom plug, climbed out, picked up his 'chute and clipped it on to his harness. He walked along to an escape hatch which he opened ready for jumping. Something else hit them. G for George bucked and shuddered, the hatch flew shut. Matt yanked at it, pulled hard, then swore as it jammed. It came open! He waited for Jack Baird as instructed.

The rear turret was empty; Bruce had left. Jack stumbled along the fuselage, his face bloodied and mask-like with strain.

'They've all gone. Get cracking, Matt.'

This is it! Matt thought. He looked down at the flak. It was like a gigantic, continually-flaring firework display. He took a firm grip on the handle of the 'chute and leapt head-first out of the plane.

For a few seconds he hung poised in eternity, or so it seemed. And in that strange timelessness Matt felt nothing, thought nothing, experienced nothing. Then the chute *whooshed*! and pulled him upwards as it billowed out, a giant pearl-like mushroom floating above his head.

The universe and all within it receded. He was in a silent void. In a strange way he was above his own body, not within himself at all. It was not dark, nor light, but a mixture of the two interlaced with deep scarlet. His heart was in his head, yet he had no heart. A voice within his negative body screamed, 'I am dead. I am infinitesimal, and death is this terrible, silent nothing.'

Just then, he received a stinging slap in the eye from the left-hand strap, which seemed to bring him back. He became conscious of a pain in his right leg and, exploring with his hand, realised he was minus a goodly lump of trouser leg, not to mention his own flesh. He believed his old wounds had also opened up again.

'Déjà vu!' For no reason at all, he was silently thinking something that Ron Rashley was wont to say. 'Bloody déjà vu!'

His leg was bent, he was holding his foot outwards and upwards and realised that he was trying to keep his flying boot on. Carefully, because he was swinging back and forth like a pendulum, he pulled his boot on, and then steadied himself by taking a firm hold of the straps.

Far below the river, Nantes looked like a murky glass hair-ribbon. He must have blacked out, because the next thing he knew, trees were jumping up at him. Caught unprepared, Matt fought for control. As the 'chute ripped and rustled then slowly gave, he found himself on the ground.

He looked around, feeling numb. Everything was still, and moon-light lit up the scene in a clear black and white way. He was in a narrow lane which was flanked on either side by a brick wall. There seemed to be a main road a few yards to the right. Matt blinked and looked at his watch. It was 2.30 am. He unclipped his harness, his only thought being to get hold of the 'chute and bury it with his other gear. Just as he began tugging at it he heard voices. German voices.

Matt stumbled to the opposite side of the lane where, in the shadows, he stood with his back to the wall. The parachute, in all its shimmering glory, caught and held the moonlight. If the Germans passed the lane from the left they could not fail to see it.

Matt sweated it out for a while and the voices steadily faded. He had to get his parachute down. Had to! He crossed the lane again and tried to tug. It was useless. He was in agony, but decided to try to climb up the wall to get a better hold. He scrambled up, experienced nausea, overbalanced and fell. There was an almighty row. It sounded and felt as though he had landed in glass cold-frames of some kind. A noise from the adjacent house made him freeze.

The back door was being opened. Silhouetted against a blinding

165

glare of light was a woman. She began shouting volubly to someone inside. Matt decided it was time to run. He tried, dear God, he tried, but his legs gave way. Then a black hole seemed to open up before him. He could not avoid it, and he was falling down, down, down . . .

The Rookwood was full of it. Rudolf Hess, Deputy Führer, the third man in the enemy's hierarchy, had stolen away in a fighter-plane.

According to rumour he was in Scotland somewhere, although a neutral country would surely have been better. Hess, doing a bunk over here, to the enemy? What was up? Was 'Orrible Adolf about to have his mate done in? No one knew, and after the first vain hopes that Hess had come with terms of peace, life went on. Clothes were rationed from 1 June 1941 and shops were banned from using wrapping paper and supplying bags. There was little or no tobacco in shops and cigarettes were now a commodity for which one bartered.

Returning from weekend leave, Ginnie mentioned that queues for sausages were growing longer and that when you got them they were mostly bread.

'Liver sausage isn't rationed,' she told Hannah. 'Mother fries it and all sorts of things go with it in the veggy line. I prefer Spam of course, and even the dried egg's not so bad the way Mum does it. Here, they're trying to get us to like whale meat now. Ugh! Still, beggars can't be choosers, eh?'

Hannah eyed her, seeing her cheeks were a better colour now; she had looked grey for so long, in spite of working outdoors. Even Ginnie's eyes were brighter. She seemed to be getting back to her usual aplomb.

'You heard from Aiden lately?' Hannah asked.

'A handful of letters arrived all at once. I found them rather comforting.'

'Wish I could say the same. I haven't heard a whisper from Matt.'

'No news is good news – so they say.'

'I'm nothing to him,' Hannah said quietly, 'not officially, that is. He could be in any amount of trouble and I wouldn't know.'

'He has friends, a crew! If it's ever necessary, one of them will pass on the word,' Ginnie told her. 'So, we will have to do what everyone else does – get on with things. Where's Raven, by the way?'

'With Sophia – talking about gee-gees, I presume. Good old Raven! There's something so consistent about her. I'd stake my life on her, wouldn't you?'

'Know something?' Ginnie replied carefully. 'In spite of all she has gone through, when it boils down to it, I reckon she's the strongest of us all.' She looked at Hannah. 'And in spite of us three being closer than sisters, we all have secrets from each other. Perhaps we should put that right.'

'Stone the crows, what's up with you? I ain't – I mean *haven't* got secrets.'

'No?'

Hannah coloured and jutted out her chin. 'Why – have you?'

'Yes,' Ginnie replied. 'And I think it would be best if we brought things out of the closet for a change. All for one and one for all, remember? Your line, not mine. If everything's out in the open, perhaps we can really help each other. I mean *really!*'

'I dunno.' Hannah shrugged. 'If I told you half of it, you'd think I was dreaming it all up. And I don't know where Raven would stand in all this, since something up my sleeve's also up Drews'.'

'The stables? Hannah!'

'There you are! You don't believe me already!'

Suddenly, gloriously, Ginnie was her old self. Her calm, steady no-nonsense self.

'We'll have a special meeting,' she said. 'This is an order. We'll go where we can be really private – in the bedroom and—'

'So even you've noticed how often Sophia barges in here? Bloody hell! You'd think . . .'

'That she'd know her place?' Ginnie asked dryly, which made Hannah flush up and then laugh.

'Gawd, Ginnie, I've got a nerve, haven't I?'

'Wouldn't be you, otherwise. Now come on, tell! Especially about the stables. You have me really curious.'

'I'll wait till our meeting,' Hannah told her, 'and then I'll spill the beans, and perhaps – perhaps if I'm not in this on my own, I'll not feel so out on a limb. So . . .'

'Scared?'

'You can tell?'

'Right from the beginning,' Ginnie nodded.

A few weeks later, over cornflakes and a smidgeon of milk, Betty Joyce broke the news.

'I was talking to Walter last night, yer know.'

'Ooer!' Hannah teased. 'You gabbing off to a man, Bet? Put the flags out.'

'He is all right,' Betty said casually. 'But that was not what I was going to say. There was a telephone call in the Rookwood for Walter. He had to go to the Cottage Hospital. His wife has died.'

Hannah looked the picture of guilt. 'I meant to go and see her. Lily and I thought we might manage it this weekend. Oh, blow me! Poor old Maud. Was it the lump that—'

'No. Things were going rather well in that direction, apparently. It was her heart what gave out.'

Hannah pushed her cornflakes away, her appetite gone. She was trying not to remember all the rotten things she had thought about the woman in the past.

'It's been a long haul for Walter,' Ginnie said. 'Perhaps it's a blessing in disguise. Apparently she never ever recognised anyone.'

'Death is never a blessing for those left behind,' Raven observed.

'Come on, you lot,' Ellery said from the door. 'On your bikes!'

'Good turn-out, eh?' Cyril Stitson murmured to Hannah as the congregation shuffled out of the little church and they all followed the bearers and mourners into the graveyard at Maud Madeira's funeral. 'Yep, like most of us,' the blacksmith went on, 'Maud was part and parcel of Lindell.'

'I can tell – just by looking at all of the people here,' Hannah said quietly. 'I suppose you remember her before she was ill?'

'I do at that. Strange how your mind travels back at times like this. When I was a boy I used to hang around and kick a ball about outside Maud's grandfer's old cottage. He died and I went to watch the proceedings. Saw Maud. All sniffy and crying she was, and pretty as a picture. The old cottage is still standing – just. Thatch and cob's all right so long as the rain don't get in it. I remember following old Grandfer's last do. There was only a rough track from his place and they had to carry his coffin across the fields as far as Old Road where there was a horse and cart waiting for them.'

Hannah did not know what to say to that. She wanted to walk away from the man, but did not have the heart. Ginnie and Raven were a little ahead, and like herself, were spruce and upright in their best uniforms.

Everyone came to a halt. Hannah had been thinking about Matt, remembering his roguish grin, his twinkling dare-devil eyes. Of how his attractive white teeth showed to advantage every time he smiled.

'Forasmuch as it hath pleased Almighty God of His great mercy to take unto Himself the soul of our dear sister here departed, we therefore commit her body to the ground; earth to earth, ashes to ashes, dust to dust . . .'

Hannah saw young Lenny standing stiffly next to Walter. What he was thinking was hard to tell. Then he glanced up and they exchanged looks, and Hannah knew that the boy felt the same as she. Wishing that it could be all over and done with, so that they could get on with the better things of life. However, Hannah told herself firmly, she loved the country, and wanted to stay for ever. She must accept that this was the village way.

Everyone attended village funerals. In the case of small communities like Lindell, everyone knew the deceased, and attended the ceremony out of respect and sympathy for the family.

Hannah looked beyond the grave as the coffin was lowered to the patches of golden lichen spreading over the church wall, the stained glass windows sparkling in a harsh, glittery way. And standing to the right was a solitary yew, massively dark and brooding. It had witnessed hundreds of such burials over the years. Christenings, marriages, funerals, birth, life and death. I must stop being so selfish, Hannah thought. I must stop worrying and wondering about Matt.

As they turned away from the grave with its surround of floral tributes, Hannah stole a glance at her friends. Her heart went out to them. Like most people, they were concerned with remembering the people they themselves had lost. But Matt was not lost, she thought in a tight, panicky way. No! He couldn't be. She would know, feel it – yes, even though she hadn't received a line from him for such a long time.

Back at the Rookwood, there was a buzz of conversation, mostly about, 'Ol' Walt's good luck in getting that Betty Joyce to take over the funeral grub. And a grand do it is, too.'

Bit of a genius Bet was, albeit like her mate Peg, a mite stand-offish at first. Still, her and Walt seemed to get on. Speculation was rife.

'Here we go again!' Hannah grinned at Ginnie and Raven, and lifted her cider glass. 'Cheers!'

Chapter Twenty-One

The Saturday afternoon was one of bracing autumn weather. It had brought roses to the twins' cheeks and to Hannah's. They had been rambling for hours, Ol' Mo having travelled twice their distance since he'd been loping backwards and forwards all the time, sniffing things out, busily chasing imaginary rabbits, or sticks thrown by the boys. Now it was getting towards evening time.

'Can't we walk any faster?' Hannah laughed. Her mind had been going round and round, like a squirrel in a cage, wondering about Matt. So it was that she was glad of the lads' company. At least their lively chatter kept her mind off things.

Matt had not written to her for ages and she felt sad. But then, lately she had sensed that his mood had changed. Oh, he hadn't written anything untoward in his last brief letters, but she knew something had happened, something that had jolted him off course. And he was not prepared to share it with her; she could tell that just by reading between the lines.

Had he met someone else? She could not face that idea.

'Hey,' she called out to the twins, who were now joyfully wrestling on the ground. 'We won't be home till dawn at this rate.'

'Let's march along like soldiers.' Chris jumped up, dark hair awry, face filthy.

'And sing marching songs.' This was Chook.

'Fair enough,' Hannah replied, pulling herself out of the doldrums. 'What shall we start with?'

'*Ten Green Bottles*.' Chris's choice was immediate. 'I like that one.'

'That isn't a marching song,' Chook objected. 'Everybody knows that, Fat-nut.'

'If I'm a fat-nut you're a thick-head!' Chris chortled. 'What about *The Quartermaster's Store* then? The bit about rats as big as pussy cats reminds me of Dr Dene's Felix. Ol' Mo nearly caught him last week.'

'You're telling whoppers,' Hannah teased. 'I saw Mo skid to a halt when Felix stopped running, and turned and faced him. When she spat at him, I've never seen a dog back away so fast. Some hero!'

Chook looked proud. 'Brilliant runner, isn't he? I bet he could win races.'

'Hey, Hannah!' Chris called from the nearby hedge. 'How does an elephant get down from a tree?'

Hannah went along with the joke. 'I don't know how an elephant gets down. You tell me.'

'He sits on a leaf and waits for autumn!'

Two boyish roars of laughter echoed down the winding unlit track. The light was fading. Hannah laughed too, while inwardly hoping that the twins knew just where they were.

'I've got one. Want to hear it?' Chook sniggered.

'I guess you mean to tell me anyway,' Hannah groaned, 'so shoot.'

'All right! How does an elephant get up a tree?'

'I haven't the foggiest.'

'He sits on an acorn and waits for it to grow!'

'Oh, charming!' Hannah laughed. 'Now I know why elephants live a long time. If they didn't they'd never reach the top of that tree. Is that all you kids do at school these days – tell elephant jokes?'

'Jolly good, aren't they?' the irrepressible Chris chortled. 'Everyone in class is thinking them up. Why do elephants wear red nailpolish.'

'I don't know! And Chris – are you quite sure we're going the right way? I don't recognise this place.'

'Of course we are. It's a short cut.'

'How short?'

'We only have to go about four and a half miles instead of five.'

'Oh, very good!' Hannah said and plodded on, thankful that she had her torch . . .

It was getting late when the dark silhouette of Rose Cottage came into view.

'Oh Lord!' Hannah said. 'Your mum will skin us alive, it's so late. What a time to get home!'

'We're for it all right,' Chris said, although he didn't sound too concerned. 'Mum will stick us in bed and threaten to tell Dad when he comes on leave.' He took the war into enemy camp. 'And you're almost as bad, Hannah. You wouldn't even listen to us, you were walking so fast!'

'I'm sorry,' Hannah replied, relenting. 'Incidentally, why *do* elephants wear red nail-varnish?'

'So they can hide safely in a cherry tree.'

171

'You're screwy,' Hannah told him fondly. 'Nutty as a fruit cake, and your jokes are getting worse.'

'I bet Mum won't want to hear jokes,' Chook said. 'I bet she's ready and waiting for us. Gosh, I'm tired and I wish it wasn't so late.'

Moses ran ahead and scratched impatiently on the front door. It flew open and Lily was there.

'Where have you been?' she demanded in a furious tone. 'Get inside, the pair of you. I was about to call out a search-party. I could kill . . . Is that you, Hannah?'

'Yes,' Hannah said, and followed everyone else into the little cream-painted kitchen that was a joy with its red and white gingham cur-tains, a dresser crammed full of crockery and bric à brac, and crayoned pictures on the walls. Wooden chairs were gay with home-made cushions, the large table was covered with a red chenille cloth, and there were rag rugs of many hues on the floor.

'I was on one of my walks when I met up with Chris and Chook,' Hannah explained. 'We began playing hide and seek and mucking about in general and we went down the wrong lane.' She sank grate-fully onto one of the chairs. 'It was an accident, Lily, and quite hon-estly no one's fault.'

'Well,' Lily's voice wobbled, 'the very next time I'm left here waiting and wondering, and being scared to death imagining all the dreadful things that could have happened, I – I'll . . .'

Two young heads were nuzzling against her, downcast faces hidden in her blue woollen dress. Her necklace of rainbow-coloured beads jangled as she gave in and flung her arms round the boys, holding them close.

'Honestly, Hannah,' she said, 'I could limb them! Tonight was as bad as the time they ran off with Lenny. The little devils just don't think!'

'Well, seeing that the devil usually looks after his own,' Hannah chuckled, 'I should think they're as safe as houses round here. They seemed happy and confident enough even when it began to grow dark, and they're so full of energy. Also Mo, who's just drunk his water-bowl dry, by the way. In the end we followed the old chap. Like one of Ellery's homing pigeons, he is.'

Suddenly Lily's expression changed. Became bleak. Hannah thought she had better go, but Lily stopped her.

'I'll just see to these two, then you and I will have a cup of cocoa and a chat. No, I insist!' She smiled down at her sons, who both had their eyes closed. 'Oh, they're nearly asleep!'

Hannah helped Lily to undress and settle the boys. Mr Moses was flaked out too, and snored and whimpered and jerked his legs.

172

'He's still chasing rabbits in his dreams,' Hannah said. 'One day I'm hoping to own a dog just like him.'

'Hannah,' Lilly told her quietly, 'I have something to tell you. Perhaps you'd better sit down.'

Oh God! Hannah thought, she's found out my association with Frank! She's going to tell me she doesn't want the likes of me near her two nice young kids.

'I try not to be a bad influence, Lily,' she began, 'and we really did lose our way. But . . .'

'Hannah, dear, listen,' Lily said gently. 'You know you have been saying that you have not heard from Matt for a while now? Well, Ellery has heard something. A young airman he met said that Matt's plane was one of those that did not get back. It was a little while ago, he thought. Ellery doesn't know anything official, at least not at this stage, but he thought I'd better let you know.'

'Thank you, Lily,' Hannah said very quietly, her face now as doughy-looking as the flour and potato pastry Lily made. 'If – if you don't mind, I won't wait for the cocoa. I'd best get back.' She tried to smile. 'We mustn't forget the war effort, eh? Must have our early start.'

'Stay here tonight. There's plenty of room.'

'Thanks, Lil, but I want to get back. Good night . . .'

It was Ellery who found out the true story about Matt. He knew who to ask, and had friends in high places at Matching – on account of his pigeons, of course.

'Sorry, love,' he told her gravely. 'It has been established that most of the crew are now prisoners of war. But the navigator, Ricky Davis, is dead, and they don't know anything about Matt. They're doing their best to find out about him, but so far no one knows.'

'You mean,' Hannah said quietly, 'that he is missing, presumed dead. Thank you.'

Back at her place in the field, she began wielding her hoe as if her life depended on it. Small, determined, just for once without her smile.

Ellery watched, pipe clenched between his teeth. He noticed how, when Hannah spoke, the other two looked up, listened and then drew near, comfortingly together. They were all different, all gorgeous, and as close as sisters, he thought.

He could sense their solidarity, even from here. And found that he could only marvel at the girls who before the war had known nothing of country ways. And Hannah? He had a special feeling for the youngster, for her vitality, her sense of humour and sheer guts. She hadn't moaned once at a Land Girl's normal working day. Up at dawn,

173

endless hours of hard, monotonous work, and ready to spark up in her own or her friends' defence at the drop of a hat.

Pity about young Matt. Dead as mutton, of course. Stuff God, stuff Hitler, stuff all the bastards that made war. And above all, stuff fate for making him the one to tell the kid the bloody awful news.

Ellery stomped off, his boots sending up scuffs of dry earth. He headed for the Rookwood. They'd all be gutted to have the rumours confirmed. Sheridan had been a handsome young devil. Rakish, clean-shaven, as popular as Richard – who'd gone the same way, by Christ. But there'd be no church sermon for Matt. He was missing, which wasn't dead. Maybe he'd have a word with the vicar. There ought to be words said for the missing. Helpful, meaningful words. Not much use perhaps, but worth a try.

Ellery took his pipe out of his mouth and spat on the ground. Then he swore, long and powerful and hard. Usually a peace-loving man, Ellery found himself fiercely needing to tear Hitler from limb to limb.

'No, I don't want to go out,' Hannah said bluntly after dinner that night. 'I want to sit up here, be all quiet, and just look out of the window, and – and watch the moon.' She glared over at Ginnie who was putting on a thin layer of orangy-coloured Tangee lipstick and staring at her through the mirror. 'All right?'

'Fine,' Ginnie replied. 'If that's what you want.'

'I'm not licking me wounds.' Hannah's voice rose just a fraction. 'It's just that I've sort of leaned on the idea of Matt. In the back of my mind, I mean. And I'm always half-expecting him to come down here to visit me and the twins. He really enjoys the boys' company and laughs like a jackass at their scatty jokes. He's really fond of Ol' Mo too.'

'Didn't you ever consider going to see him? There must be places to stay the night near where he's stationed, so why did you leave all that up to him?' Ginnie was really curious to know the answer. She added, 'After all, the journey itself wouldn't have taken too many hours, and you could have left here on a Saturday. Gone straight after midday dinner.'

'I was never invited,' Hannah admitted. 'So I supposed that he didn't want me to go poking my nose in.'

'I don't and never could believe that!'

'Couldn't push meself, could I?' Hannah shrugged. 'I looked for-ward to his letters though, and accepted that sometimes he just didn't feel like writing. When I didn't hear, I felt sure he'd write when he was good and ready. Besides, we're only mates.'

Raven, who had been sitting on the bed, shook her head.

174

'You don't accept that you're sweet and attractive and very desirable, do you? You are, you know, Hannah. Matt thought so – even a blind man could see that.'

'Then when he comes back from being missing,' Hannah retorted, 'we'll have to find out all proper-like, won't we?' She added defiantly, 'In the meantime, life goes on.'

'Hannah dear,' Raven told her, 'you don't have to pretend. At least, not to us.'

'She's right,' Ginnie put in. 'By the way, couldn't it be truth-time all round for a change? Couldn't we come clean just for this once – tell each other our real worries and woes? Try to help each other with our problems instead of keeping them all locked up inside?'

'No!' Hannah said tightly. 'Do you mind?'

'We're all holding something back.' Ginnie's tone was firm. 'You in particular, Hannah. I think that if you just told us what has been bothering you for so long, it might ease things a little.'

'Shut up!'

'Oh?' Ginnie raised her brows. 'What happened to the all for one and one for all thing? Are you telling us to mind our own business now?'

'Yes. No. Bloody hell, I don't know!'

'Neither do I. That's unlike me, eh?' Ginnie impatiently tossed her red hair out of her eyes. 'I'm used to having things all cut and dried, but let me tell you, nothing's further from that right now. Unlike you, Hannah, I need to get something off my chest. But I want someone else to be brave enough to break the ice first. To be honest, there are some things that even my mother doesn't know.'

'Suit yourself,' Hannah flared. 'Me – I've got nothing to hide.'

'Then why act as though you have?' Ginnie persisted. 'Honestly, if you tell us about whatever's scaring you half to death, it will help. And at least you wouldn't feel that you had the whole darned world on your shoulders.'

'Just the really rotten bit about Matt – is that it? Ha! That's all you know.' She choked on a sob. 'Leave me alone!'

Raven unwound herself. Yes, unwound. She never seemed to make a sharp movement. Hannah found herself giving the unimportant matter deep thought. Yes, Raven was as fluid as silk, as lovely, and as graceful. Oh, to be like her! Or to be like Ginnie, a dramatically raving beauty who'd had Richard eating out of her hand since that very first glance. Ginnie, who was usually so competent and calm.

Beside her two friends she was a nothing and a nobody, with a stepdad who was a drunkard; even worse, a woman-beater.

And she herself was just rotten Hannah York from Walker Street who'd mixed with people like Val Marner, nymphomaniac. Not forgetting the woman's brother Biff who was part and parcel of every crooked deal within miles. At his side, like a sick-making slug, the vindictive Ram Rawlins. And with them all the way, slyly rubbing his dimpled hands together, the oily rapacious Fatty Blythe.

What an evil bunch, Hannah thought, clenching her fists. She would continue to fight them every inch of the way – later, when she had the strength and actually knew what to do for the best. She could always spill the beans, of course; tell the East End police what she had seen. But that would bring them rozzers down here. They would want to interview Frank. Then the whole horrible business would come out, and mud would stick. Everyone would presume that she, Hannah York, was like her stepfather. Shifty. A liar and cheat, one of the dregs.

Suddenly, very desperately, she felt the need to scrub herself clean with carbolic soap. To try, as she always had, to wash the grime of Walker Street away.

Who, Hannah asked herself bitterly, in all the years she could remember, had ever been on her side? There was just one person ever to put out a tentative helping hand – the old crone Ma Carpenter. Ma, who liked proving to the world that she could handle anyone, even bloody old Frank.

Previous to Hawksley, the only living soul who had seemed to be genuinely fond of the stinking kid from Walker Street, was Miss Pitt, the plain little lady who had a heart the size of the dome of St Paul's. And now?

'All right!' Hannah shot at her friends, who were looking at her with compassion. 'So I'm sitting here feeling sorry for myself – and not only about Matt.'

'My dear . . .' Raven began, but Hannah ignored her.

'You asked for it, so I'll tell you what I've been hiding. Who I am, and what I am, and just the kind of mess I'm in. And after that little lot you'll be jolly pleased to walk out of here and leave me alone' – she jutted out her chin – 'which will make a sodding marvellous change.'

It all poured out then, the unabridged story of her life. The dirt and degradation, the pettiness of those around her. The fight to survive but remain decent just the same. The last terrible scene in the kitchen of number 32, with Val Marner bleeding from the nose, and whining. And standing over her, unsteady, the staggering, drunken thing that had once been a man.

'And d'you know the cream of it all?' Hannah finished and laughed through her tears. 'The joke of the century? Ma Carpenter thought I ought to be grateful to the swine! This because he never actually bashed me, and he never chucked me out. What a blessing, eh? Well, now the old sod's here. Yes – *here* – working in Drews. And I've already told you why. The only thing that can be said for him is that he loved my mum, and an old horse called Firelord what went to the knacker's yard.' They were watching her, stunned, and she added fiercely: 'So now you know!'

'You silly little devil,' Ginnie said slowly at last. 'Hannah, I thought better of you.'

'Now what's wrong?' Hannah furiously brushed her hand across her eyes.

'What happened about our three Musketeers pact?' Ginnie asked.

'I dunno what you're talking about.'

'Yes, you do, dear.' This was Raven, cool as ever. 'How is it that you would go through fire and water for either of us, but can't accept that we would do the same for you?'

'Because she's daft as a brush,' Ginnie said bluntly. 'I vote that we don't mull over what Hannah has told us – yet. I mean, I badly need to get something off my own chest. So I reckon we should all spin our yarns, then talk them over, and try to work out what's best to do.' She turned to Raven, adding fondly, 'Though I don't suppose for a minute that you've committed any sins.'

'My in-laws believed that I had,' Raven told her quietly, and smiled in an apologetic way.

'Never!' Ginnie said.

'The wicked old sods,' Hannah breathed, momentarily forgetting her own troubles. 'You of all people. How blind can they be?'

Raven's mind flicked back to a year ago – it could have been a century ago; she still couldn't quite bring herself to work it out. The memory was always the same. The cold winter sunlight shining through stained glass windows making the brass handles on the coffin gleam in a malignant way. Raven remembered that at the time she had believed she could actually smell death. It was a subtle cloying at the nostrils, wispy, at times barely definable. As horrifying and as distressing as the stiff wreathes of laurel, mosses and decapitated flowers. Flowers that had been cut and killed before their time for the sake of a ceremony. The same ceremony that was officially proclaiming to the world that one Francis Griffith Gray had gone from this life.

Raven put her hand to her ears, but she had gone back in time, could still hear the church bell tolling, and out-of-tune voices groaning in plaintive song. A dirge for the deceased. Then a holy man's words, meaningless, holding cold comfort, because she could not accept that death was a pre-ordained plan that was, according to the speaker, somehow Divine.

There had been the scuffling sound as knees touched the floor. This then was an abasement before an absent God. A deity Who had been deaf to her heart-felt desires, her desperate supplications. A God Who was supposedly now about to receive Francis Griffith Gray's soul.

Raven remembered wanting to scream out, to rant and rage against the Almighty. She had wanted to run and keep running for ever. She could not stand the sham of it all!

'I remember Francis's mother crying at the funeral,' Raven said quietly, 'and his father blowing his nose and crying too. The rest of the Grays were standing round like a collection of black hawks – or vultures. Yes, vultures. And I have never felt so alone, nor so loathed.'

'But why?' Hannah asked, puzzled. 'I don't understand.'

Raven seemed not to have heard. Her oval face was still, her eyes wide and sad. Her long fingers, roughened now by her Land Girl's life, were tightly entwined.

'The day after the funeral,' she told them, 'I was called to the study. They were all there, hating me with their eyes. Francis's sister wanted to kill me, I could tell. Then Francis's will, his last will and testament, was read out – in which I was exonerated from any suspicion of being a fortune-hunter. Dear God, how I loathed just sitting there, feeling like a disgraced schoolgirl!' She smiled pensively. 'Their utter relief when it didn't happen made me feel nauseated. They could not hide their pleasure, not from the solicitor, themselves, nor even me.'

'I'm sorry,' Hannah said again. 'I still don't get it.'

'Francis and not his father, had inherited the family home and all that it entailed. I understand that previously my husband had never acted as if he owned it. Indeed, he travelled around a great deal, seeing the world through a poet's eyes, and writing things down. His parents had continued as though they owned the place. When Francis died and his people learned that he had married, they feared everything would come to me. But Francis left the property to his parents – with my approval.'

Raven's lips trembled and she faltered a little, then continued. 'I saw triumph on their faces. Yes, naked triumph for all of their very real grief. They thought they had achieved victory over an unwelcome outsider. Francis left me comfortable, but I was not poor when I married him. Anyway, that didn't matter.' Raven hesitated, then went on, 'I think that my unforgivable sin was having Francis all to myself, and worse, for keeping the knowledge of his illness away.'

'Why did you?' Hannah asked.

'His twin sister believed that she suffered everything he did. Francis never accepted that, but he wanted to spare her as much pain as possible. His concern was for her more than anyone else. He explained this to me and I agreed.'

178

'You must loathe and detest them all,' Ginnie said bluntly. 'I would.'

'It all felt so unreal,' Raven told her. 'I loved Francis so, and I found myself asking God why couldn't I have died too? I walked away from them, and went back to my flat. I felt so lonely, so bereft, and all I could think of was that I was without Francis. I felt that my own life had come to an end.'

'And now?' Ginnie asked.

'I have both of you.'

'Which is all very well,' Hannah told her, 'but it just ain't enough!'

'Hannah,' Raven said apologetically, 'my story is nothing, compared to yours. And we must—'

'Hear Ginnie's yarn?' Hannah finished the sentence for her, then added, surprised: 'Gawd, just look at her face!'

'To put it bluntly,' Ginnie told them and flushed scarlet, 'Richard and I slept together. When I went home before Christmas I was six weeks' overdue. I wanted to die the death. You know, grief, guilt, fear of what everyone would say . . . Then things righted themselves. I had a very heavy period, and a right old stomach ache to go with it. My mother believed it was just one of those bad times. She refers to periods as "not being well". She gave me a hot water bottle and insisted that I went to bed for a while.'

'She never even suspected?' Hannah sounded amazed.

'It never occurred to her that her goody-goody girl could be anything less than perfect. My only failing being that I had fallen in love with someone she had never met, and that I was going to marry him. That he died a hero's death was a comfort, of course. Oh God! My mother put my being under the weather down to shock and distress.'

'No doctor?' Hannah asked, then her lips pursed in a silent whistle, 'My Gawd, Gin, you took a chance.'

'Perhaps,' Ginnie replied, 'but now I'm relieved that things happened as they did.'

'Glad?' Hannah's voice held disbelief. 'Relieved?'

'That Richard never learned the truth,' Ginnie said flatly. 'I had become uncertain of my feelings for him. I went along with his plans because – because it would have been too cruel not to. Do you understand what I'm saying?'

'Yes,' Hannah said crisply. 'You're saying that Aiden's still in with a chance. What's the problem with that?'

'Should I be perfectly honest and write and tell him the truth about what has happened?'

'No,' Hannah told her. 'Poor old Aiden don't deserve that!'

'I . . . I was sorry about the baby,' Ginnie said. 'I would never have . . .'

179

'Don't worry,' Raven told her. 'We know.'

'Yes, we're sure you wouldn't have done anything stupid about that,' Hannah agreed. 'And for what it's worth, you would have made a bloody fine mum. But from where I stand, you mustn't breathe a word to your Aiden. What he don't know he can't grieve over.'

'I agree with Hannah,' Raven said.

'Ain't fair, is it?' Hannah's voice was now ragged with feeling. 'Life is a shit. Raven lost her lovely Francis. Ginnie's lost poor old Richard, and my Matt's missing and presumed . . . No, I refuse to believe it. He's around somewhere, eyeing up the girls and making a right old nuisance of himself.' She turned to Raven, 'And you, me old China, you've got to find someone else. Someone who can look after you. Someone as unlike your sweet silvery Francis as chalk from cheese. You've got to work at making my Miss Pitt's principles come true. You know – more laughter than tears.'

'A beautiful thought, but unreasonable,' Raven decided. 'Besides, you weren't all that jolly yourself a while ago.'

'Oh, I was being a Moaning Minnie, that's all. The shock of hearing about Matt threw me, even though I can't make myself believe what they say. As for Frank, I can handle him. But you, Raven, you've had too much grief already. And now, Gin, so have you.'

'It was fate.' Ginnie sighed.

'Not on your nellie,' Hannah grinned, 'Look – I know how we can alter things. For starters, Raven here needs one of them happy-go-lucky Yanky-doodle officers in tow. To that end I reckon that we'll have to visit Matching and find out who we can pick up.'

'No – we have to sort out your problems, which are very serious,' Ginnie said. 'Stop trying to change the subject.'

'Shut it!' Hannah warned. 'We'll cross my bridges when we come to them. But I will say this, it's bloody marvellous to have you two for mates. I'm glad you know everything. I don't feel half as scared now. My biggest fear was that you'd find out and then chuck me.'

She ducked as pillows flew towards her from both beds. After that they spoke freely together, told more secrets, shared hopes and dreams, and like Hannah said, were indeed all for one and one for all.

It was not until much later that Raven and Ginnie slept. Then Hannah let herself go. She put her head under the pillow and thought of Matt, her handsome bosom-buddy. Matt Sheridan, Sergeant Air Gunner, who had made her feel so special. Who had actually kissed her, then shied away like a startled stallion ready to run. Well, he'd run all right. Oh, she could tell by his last letters that he'd distanced himself from her. That all he wanted from her was to be a good friend. Not that she wanted anything more.

She, Hannah, had never been in love like Raven, nor even half believed it, like poor old Gin. But she had come to consider Matt as someone important. Now he was over there somewhere, lost and alone.

'I'm with you, Matt,' she whispered in the darkness. 'I'm with you wherever you are.'

Chapter Twenty-Two

Matt had no idea of just how long he had been ill. It could have been days, weeks or even months. The immediate past remained dreamlike, the only reality having been the scarlet flashes of agony that had at least proved he was still alive. He'd had a vague sense of people all the way through, of quiet French voices . . .

Now, at last, he was strong enough to take notice, to try to communicate. With the aid of an English-French dictionary, he learned that he had broken the glass-houses belonging to a farmer. That the farmer's wife had been alone and afraid, and warned her young daughter to stay inside, had gone back in to telephone her husband. By the time he returned, bringing with him his baker friend and also the baker's son, Matt had disappeared.

They had searched – under stealth, for the enemy were hunting too – and it had been the baker's boy who found him. The friends had carried Matt between them, and put him into a van. Because they didn't dare start the engine, they had quietly pushed the vehicle back towards a hiding place where he had been lodged since then. It was a small space, used for stores, that led off from the bakehouse. They had risked their lives, these people – yes, faced death with wry smiles and expressive shrugs. They openly hated the Gestapo who were never very far away.

Now it was nearing evening, and after a final surreptitious visit from a woman doctor with an old-young face, Matt was declared strong enough to get up. He accepted some shabby, well-worn civilian clothes handed over by the baker's son, a good-looking youngster of thirteen or so with serious brown eyes, an oval face and a shock of dark hair.

Shaky, still weak, Matt dressed and followed the lad through the bakehouse and into a charming living room.

'Monsieur,' the baker introduced Matt to the family in careful

English, 'this is my wife, my grandmother, my grandfather, and my son. He delivers bread, you know? It is he who found you.'

'Thank you,' Matt replied, shaking hands in turn with each of them.

He was now able to look at his benefactors properly. Before, in the dimness of the store-room, faces and voices had intermingled in a rather alarming way. The baker's wife, whom everyone called *Maman*, was round and rosy and her brown hair was tinged with red. Grandma was very old and brittle-stick thin. The grandfather was white-haired, wrinkled and quick on the uptake. The baker himself, thick-set, mature, with alert near-black eyes, was clearly the son of his father, and the father of his son. Apart from age-gaps, the men of the family were very alike. At first, Matt had believed the baker to be much older – this because of his black hair had been powdered with flour.

The family were smiling and nodding and acting as if he was an honoured guest. He was offered white bread, a wonderful sight after the brown cardboard handed out in England, and too, there were eggs, also wine.

The meal completed, Matt began to feel stronger. He and the baker began to converse. It was a halting conversation, pleasant and strange. Names were not exchanged, nor questions asked. But Matt learned that the family lived reasonably well, bartering bread for meat and wine. It was a simple enough system and clearly worked.

There came the throb of aircraft and the young boy ran to the window and opened the shutter. He called out, '*Boches.*' Joining him at the window, Matt looked up at the two aircraft. Messerschmitts, he thought, and clenched his hands until the knuckles grew white. He stood silently watching them until they disappeared from view. He was thinking of his new crew and wondering how they had fared. Then he was remembering Richard and Titch, and his face worked in an uncontrollable way. Suddenly, *Maman*, began to carry on. He turned, shocked, as the torrent of words continued. The woman was clearly ticking them all off. Matt heard an authoritative, '*Allez, allez.*'

Smiling and shrugging the family obeyed.

'Maman, says that you are still weak,' the baker told him. 'That you have done too much already, and that now you must rest.'

Matt was led back to his hiding place where flour and empty sacks were stored. His bed, a pile of flour-sacks, was a very welcome sight. He all but fell upon them, grateful and needing sleep. Instead his mind began going over the past.

In vivid pictures he saw his crew skylarking back at base. How were they faring now? Had they been caught and even now stuck in POW camps? He must get back to England, he thought, as soon as possible.

183

He desperately needed to see Hannah again. Funny – he could not remember her face . . .

He slept at last, despite the gnawing of rodents around him. What was a mouse or a rat between friends? He was lucky to be alive . . .

Suddenly it was morning; he was awake and feeling quite good. He remained there, lying on the sacks, listening hard. It seemed hours before the boy popped his head round the door.

'Come!' he said.

Matt was taken to a room to tidy himself. He took advantage of inferior soap and brackish water, and washed as much of himself as possible. The lad brought him comb and mirror. Looking at his reflection, Matt grinned wryly. His face was scarred, but not too badly, though he looked old.

'Not a pretty picture, eh old chap?' he asked.

The boy laughed and mimicked haltingly in English, 'Eh, old chap?' Then added, 'English soldiers say, "Wotcher, cock". RAF say "old bean". Very different, eh? You understand?'

Surprised, Matt found himself enjoying the joke. Later, he ate bread and drank wine for breakfast, and then the men left to continue their business, which began in the early hours.

Matt insisted upon helping the women with household chores. It was the least he could do, though he was not much used to movement now. His back and heavy-as-lead legs ached consistently, where he had opened old wounds. And there were some deep wounds on his chest. His face felt stiff on one side. He had, he learned, received multiple cuts when falling through the farmer's glass. Some of them had become infected, had filled with pus. Subsequently, fever had developed. This as much as everything else had led him to be so debilitated. To use his own words, he was a bit of a mess.

Hobbling through his duties, he became conscious of *Maman*'s quick glance. She smiled but her pointing finger was firm. He obeyed her, went back to the store-room and slept.

Then someone was tugging his arm. He woke up, and blinked his eyes until he was able to focus. Beside *Maman* was a very old, fragile-looking lady dressed all in black. She had a sharp-featured face and eyes very like Grandfather's. She also had abundant silver-white hair.

'How do you do, Monsieur?' she said in a high thin voice, her English excellent.

'How do you do, Madame?' he replied.

The little old lady looked at him keenly. Her expression was bright with suspicion and yet Matt found himself liking her.

'Your plane was a Spitfire, no?' she said abruptly.

'No, Madame. It was a four-engined Stirling bomber.'

'How many were there of your crew?'

'Seven, Madame, including myself.'

Matt knew that the visitor was no enemy; the baker would never have allowed her in otherwise. Besides, the old dear looked like a relation. It was irksome though, the way she eyed him, and continued her interrogation.

'Will you tell me their names and describe them to me, please?'

For a muddled moment he nearly said Richard and Titch. Then it became even more confusing. Under the old lady's gimlet gaze he began to feel that perhaps he was not a Sergeant Air Gunner belonging to the RAF after all, but a despicable creature posing as one. All the time Madame was watching him keenly, noting his reactions. Suddenly she smiled.

'Forgive me, monsieur. We must be quite sure. You understand?'

'Of course.' He grinned ruefully, 'I only hope I passed. I feel like a schoolboy up before the Headmaster.'

Madame chuckled and held out her hand. 'You are a very nice, how you say, schoolboy? Tomorrow, I shall come again. Be ready to leave. You understand?'

Oh he did, he did! At last he was in contact with the Underground movement – the Resistance. With luck he would soon be going over the mountains, heading south on the long journey to Spain, and from there back home.

Madame did not arrive until well after midday. Matt was given a shabby but warm jacket, a pair of boots and a beret. All of his own things, including his RAF identity disc, had long gone – most of them disposed of in the baker's ovens.

'You are now a civilian,' Madame told him. 'If they catch you, you cannot be a prisoner of war. The most you can hope for is to be shot quickly and mercifully as a spy. The worst is torture, so much so that you would beg for mercy. You would want to die. This you know?'

'I can guess.'

Suddenly it was time for goodbyes, and as he shook hands with his friends Matt made a silent vow that one day he would return and thank these brave people properly.

Madame handed him a shopping bag to carry. She then held his arm and they left the baker's shop together. Matt found himself in a small country town, full of people. It must be market day. For a moment he wanted to bolt back into the safety of the shop. Madame began speaking volubly in French as some people passed them. Matt nodded and leaned down in an attentive, listening attitude. The people went by, noticing nothing amiss; so did many others, including a German or two.

185

More confident now, Matt kept up the charade – a Frenchman listening to his grandmother, helping the old lady by carrying her shopping bag. Then Madame nodded towards the opposite side of the road, saying, 'Now many Boches. Further along is a military camp. There will be many soldiers about. They will not be so relaxed, you know?'

They came to the wide main gate. Madame's hand clutched at his arm more fiercely. Two soldiers were leaving the camp. They began crossing the road towards him and Matt's heart banged hard. Madame continued her conversation. She even managed a dry chuckle and looked up at Matt in a coquettish way. Matt grinned down at her, although it was an effort. Mingled with his fear was an overwhelming admiration for the old lady.

The Germans went by, speaking loudly, not even noticing them.

Not far from the German military camp they stopped at a large block of flats and went inside. Madame lived on the ground floor. Her flat was small and poorly furnished, but it was safe. Before Matt could voice his gratitude Madame held up her hand.

'*Non, mon ami!* That I can help pleases me. Now this you must understand; my husband does not know that I am a member of the Resistance. Neither do any of the people in this building.'

'I get the idea, Madame.'

'Good. Now you may come here for food only when my husband has left for the day. I will give you a blanket, a pillow and some fruit to be going on with. Your hiding place is not very comfortable but it is the best I can do. We must go now. Follow me.'

They left the flat and began to climb a flight of stairs. Madame pointed out the door that led to the toilet. Nearby was another door – Matt's hidey-hole. It was little more than a cupboard, clearly no longer used, and crammed with junk. There was no room to stand up, and Matt had to move things about before he could lie comfortably. The old lady left him then and he settled down as best he could, trying to conquer his sense of unease.

Gradually pain-filled time passed and Madame returned to take him downstairs and into her flat. The meal she gave him was sparse, composed of bread, fruit and cheap wine. It was noticeable that Madame was not nearly as fortunate as the baker's family.

'It is not much. I am sorry,' she said.

'It is more than enough, and I thank you.'

'Someone will come to see you tomorrow. You will then make one more move towards your home. Now, back to your hiding place – and the waiting, *mon ami*.'

He lay in the dark. He was cold, cramped, and still far from strong, but he was on his way home. Home! The word assumed unreality. Where *was* home? His lodgings in London's East End? Lindell? This bloody cupboard? He could only think of Hannah – young Miss York who would never in a million years take him seriously. He thought of his scar, how his battered, unshaved reflection had looked in the mirror – which in turn made him think of dear old, hideous Titch. Alone, where no one could see, Matt wanted to give way and weep.

He did not.

Two days later, Matt learned that home was still a distant dream. He was to go to a remote spot and then with others, cross over the Pyrenees Mountains into Spain. How long it would be before they set out was hard to tell. A lot of it was to do with the weather and how fit he could get. He would have to be moved regularly, he was told. It was too much of a problem to have him stay long in one place. There would be much danger.

'Of course, *mon ami*,' said Claude, the merry little fat man, who had appeared from nowhere it seemed. 'There are some very difficult German guard posts to get by. We will have to keep our eyes open, you know?'

'It has been done before, *monsieur*?'

'*Oui!* I have managed it many times.'

Ye gods, Matt thought, he doesn't look brave. He doesn't look especially tough either. Nor fit enough to walk round the block let alone climb the heights. He found his thoughts immensely humbling. His admiration for these people grew. Above all, hope was dawning. Perhaps, one day, he would indeed be walking once more on English soil . . .

Hannah's love affair with Lindell continued. She enjoyed watching Cyril Stitson at his work and given the chance would just hang about on Saturday afternoons. Intrigued, she would see the sparks fly from the anvil and sniff in the queer pungent smell when the hot horseshoe was put on the hoof.

She also loved Kitts, with its little brass bell that tinkled over the door whenever one went in. The general store had stood in the same position for over a hundred years. It had a character all of its own, with its variety of goods for sale, the aroma of paraffin oil, firelighters, apples and pears, candles, mothballs, and sacks full of biscuits for dogs. There was soap, sweets, Rinso washing powder, dolly dyes, and starch. The shelves were crammed to bursting with all sorts of things, plain and fancy.

Kitts was a shopper's delight or despair, according to how many coupons had already gone on your ration book. In the far corner, behind glass, was the Post Office section, where you bought airmail letters, and stamps, or put in money to save for a rainy day. Kitts was a wonderland; and Mrs Kitt herself a wonder of calm in her plain blue overall.

The one place that Hannah did not visit these days was her secret gate overlooking the flatland where the Drew horses exercised. She wanted to keep her stepfather at a distance; it was safer that way. The wonder was that he never turned up at the Rookwood. She breathed many thanks to God for that mercy at least.

Another reason for distancing herself from the Drew Stables was the fact that the St Johns habitually used the place. She could take Sophia's moods with a pinch of salt, and when the woman was being reasonable, she quite liked her. But darling James? She thought him arrogant and a bore. 'Stuffy swine wants to loosen up for a change,' she had said to Raven once, but Raven had merely smiled.

One very nice thing happening was the fact that Lenny often came over to stay with old Walter. The boy, so much more confident these days, usually made a beeline for the twins. All three young people plagued the life out of Hannah, given half the chance. She moaned and groaned and made a fuss, and loved every minute of it.

Like them, she enjoyed the walk to the small station, and watching and waiting for the arrival of the steam trains. They were few and far between these days and more important for that. Now the huge chuffing monsters were packed with Americans, a lively gum-chewing bunch who all seemed to have mouths full of gleaming white teeth, bouncy walks, and a vocabulary of Hi! and Gee! Guys and Dolls and Wow!

They whizzed about in Jeeps, gave gum to children, grinned a lot, flirted a great deal, and puffed at Lucky Strike or Camel cigarettes. They thought thatched cottages were 'great' and village girls, 'dames'. They were, Hannah considered, a pretty interesting bunch.

One night a group of them wandered into the Rookwood.

'Go on,' Hannah nudged Raven with her elbow, eyes dancing. 'Go to the bar and flay them alive with your aristocratic air.'

'No!' Raven, knowing Hannah of old, settled herself even more firmly in her chair and lifted her half-full glass of shandy from the table. 'Egg me on as much as you like it simply will not work. Picking up fellows in bars is not for me.'

'Oh go on, Rave!' Hannah nagged. 'You're so marvellous, and they'll believe they're talking to Elizabeth or Margaret Rose at least.'

'You're incorrigible,' Raven replied, lips twitching. 'Besides, I'd be no good at it.' She laughed in her low, enchanting way. 'You go and do your worst, Hannah. Or what about you, Ginnie? You are the two unmarrieds. I want to see you both in action.'

Hannah giggled. The three girls often joshed like this when together. They had indeed grown closer from the time they'd exchanged secrets. There was now nothing to hide, so there was no reason to keep up ones guard. They were at home with each other, close enough to poke fun and tease. They had all solemnly agreed to accept poor darling Francis's words: That life was a gift; it must be lived to the full.

Raven had come a long way out of her shell. She could even be something of a scallywag at times, albeit always in a ladylike way. These days too, Ginnie was able to speak openly and lovingly about Richard. She never mentioned her brief pregnancy again. As for Hannah, she played her part as always – bright, brave, always ripe for a laugh. With her friends around her, and even tough brittle old Sophia on her side, she was beginning to feel safe from the wolves of Walker Street.

Now, here in the Rookwood, she was openly going out of her way to rib the socks off Raven.

'You're just plain scared,' Hannah jibed.

'Perhaps,' Raven, twinkling, agreed.

'Well, at least you admit it,' Hannah told her loftily and turned to Ginnie. 'Well, what about you, Gin?'

'No,' Ginnie said promptly. 'But what's holding you back, Bossy Boots? This American business has always been your idea.'

'Not for me – for you two! I'm faithful to Matt.'

'And Aiden is my cup of tea,' Ginnie told her. 'I know that now.'

They both turned expectantly towards Raven who made them speechless when she replied, 'I rather like James.'

'Flipping hell, James St John?' Hannah scoffed. 'I'd as soon try to flirt with a lump of cold cod.'

'I should imagine that a lump of cold cod could withstand even chummy old you,' Raven observed. 'I can picture it now. But then, Hannah dear, you're such a brave little devil, and you'll try just about anything once.'

'I'll take the cod before the man,' Hannah replied.

'I believe you would,' Ginnie chuckled.

'He can be very nice,' Raven told them, then because of their outraged expressions, she laughed low and sweet. 'That's knocked you both for six, dears.' She turned to Hannah. 'I will say this. If you think picking up American airmen is hard, imagine trying to make an impression on him. I dare you!'

'Sorry!' Hannah quipped. 'I'm dead off luxuries, you know.'

The conversation turned round then to the St Johns who were so difficult to understand, who always seemed to find it hard to get along with people. Both alike in character, mother and son had moods which altered at the drop of a hat. Each of them, according to Hannah, alternating between bombastic, overbearing and downright rotten, to being halfway friendly and yes – talking about Sophia – sometimes even nice.

'All that keeps that pair going,' Hannah said disgustedly, 'is painting on the one hand, and sugar beet and agriculture on the other. The one I'm really fond of back there is our Lily.'

'We all feel like that,' Raven agreed. 'We adore her as much as we do the boys.'

'I quite like Peggy and Bet,' Ginnie added. 'Even though they don't seem to trust anyone but us very much.'

'Bet's coming out of her shell at last,' Hannah noted, looking at Betty who was standing shoulder to shoulder with Walt. 'I've been egging her on, you know. Now she and old Walter seem to be getting along rather well.'

'Pity he's got her standing at the bar,' Ginnie observed.

'Bet feels safer there – out in the open,' Hannah told them. 'I have explained all that.'

'What is she afraid of?' Raven asked.

'I don't know, but there it is.' Hannah looking over Raven's shoulder, went pink. Her eyes rested on a tall red-headed man and his two pals. Then looked under her lids at Raven, and said, 'Whoops!'

Without even trying they found themselves being chatted up by three GIs. The rest of the evening passed in a happy carefree way. But the girls' refusal to be escorted home when Time was called, was polite but of the definitely 'No thank you' kind.

'My name is Spence, peaches,' the very pleasant red-headed Yank told Hannah. 'And I'll be looking for you toot-sweet. I didn't catch your name.'

'Perhaps because I didn't throw it?'

'Gee honey, you're cruel!' Spence was in no way put out. He beamed down at her, his brows raised in an enquiring way.

'All right then,' Hannah pertly replied. 'I'm Ivy.'

'Gee honey,' came the reply, 'where I come from, that's poison! So why not give out with the truth?'

'Because it's hardly necessary, seeing that I've been referred to as Hannah all night long,' she told him blithely. 'What – you didn't know? Gosh, are you deaf?'

'No, sugar. I am in lurve.'

'I say, jolly bad show,' she mimicked Matt and laughed up at Spence, liking him a lot, then said hurriedly: 'My friends have left and so must I. Bye bye for now.'

She ran to catch up with the others who had already reached the lane. She was pink-cheeked in the darkness, over the moon to have a young man so openly impressed with her. She thought of all the things he had said. She had been called peaches, and sugar, and other similar things.

'Gordon Bennet,' she whispered joyfully. 'I feel like a dish of afters!'

Chapter Twenty-Three

When she thought about it afterwards, Hannah was quite amazed that Ginnie and Raven had decided against meeting the Americans halfway. Not that she was too interested herself, she maintained fiercely, and tried to dismiss thoughts of Spence who had taking to lounging outside the Rookwood, waiting for her.

Men were unnecessary as permanent features in her life, Hannah held. Frank had put paid to that idea long ago. Who on earth would want to be saddled with a loser like him? No. The only male she was actually fond of, and that since coming to Lindell, was Matt. Her heart yearned for news of him. He was the nearest thing to a brother she had ever known. Yes, a brother! Someone she could love as deeply as Ginnie loved her Luke. Of course, Spence was marvelous to flirt with, he was good for a lark, but Matt was a different matter.

Hannah firmly dismissed the thought of Matt's kiss, but the memory of that night, of Matt's arm round her waist, clung to her senses, like perfume left floating in the air when the wearer had gone.

How magical that night had been, and so emotional. The experience of wild yearning had shaken her through and through. It had all been something to do with the music young Lenny had played. Yes, Lenny, Walt's nephew, who was such a very nice boy. She would go over and see his uncle again. This coming Saturday afternoon, in fact . . .

It was a bright and breezy Saturday. Hannah walked across the yard, now quite used to the smell coming from the sty. She ignored the geese, a gaggle of them, wandering free. They had long ago decided to leave each other alone.

Hannah was a welcome visitor these days. She and old Walt had become used to each other, he dour, she a dancing spirit. He a man of earth, she a child of air. Both happy to accept each other's point of view.

Walter was grateful to Hannah because she and Matt had taken Lenny under their wing. This when the boy's friends had been thin on the ground. The bond had recently grown stronger, because of Betty Joyce. In their diffident ways, both Betty and Walter had sought Hannah's help, mostly by questioning her about each other. Hannah had finished up by suggesting to each of them in turn that they get together. It was she who had set the date, time and place.

The pair were now growing close, had become good friends. Maud Madeira was never mentioned these days – though, Hannah noticed on her visits, a picture of the lady, in her younger days, still held pride of place on the wall.

Hannah liked talking to Walter, even though by most villagers he was still considered to be a crabby old sod. To Hannah, he was the epitome of the countryman.

'Look you here,' he said to her as she joined him outside. He stooped to grab up a handful of splendidly friable soil to show her, and let it run through his fingers and fall back onto his potato patch. 'This is the result of generations of careful tending. Remember all I tell you. That's if you're really set on staying on here after the war.'

'I am. Oh, I am!'

'Yes, girl, I can believe it. What's more, you're a natural, I'd say.'

'Am I really, Walter?' Hannah's face glowed. 'That's nice! How would I get my dirt like that?'

''Tain't dirt,' he ticked her off firmly. 'It's the Lord's good earth. You can sweep up dirt from a kitchen floor.'

'Sorry,' she chuckled and squeezed his arm, ignoring his grumpy look. 'You can't half be a miserable old devil at times. What Betty sees in you I'll never know.'

'Ah.' Walter shrugged. 'Mebbe it's because it's well known in the village as how I was walked all over by a certain good lady for years.' He gave her an accusing look. 'Just like you try to do with your sauce. If you'd have been mine, I'd have tanned your backside.'

'You're all mouth and trousers,' she teased. 'And I know that in spite of all them dirty looks you give out, and all your huffing and puffing, you wouldn't harm a fly.'

'Well now,' he gave her a half-grin, 'p'raps that's it. Question answered. Mebbe it's 'cause Bet don't see nothing in me to be scared of – like she was with folk elsewhere.'

'Is that so, Walter?'

'I'm talking out of turn,' he told her, 'but yes. Since she was a young'un, in fact. You'll have to ask her about it and learn for yourself.' He stroked his chin in a solemn way, adding, 'Of course, on the other hand . . .'

'What?'

His face crinkled up like a walnut as he grinned. 'Of course, on the other hand, you could put it all down to me fatal charm.'

'You know Walt, I'll go along with that,' Hannah laughed. 'In fact, I quite like you myself. Especially when you teach me such interesting things. You were telling me how to go about getting good earth?'

'Rich feeding does it, lovey, with cow, pig, and horse manure. Muck spreading ain't all, though. It goes along with back-breaking effort – like what you know about, eh? Digging, raking, hoeing, weeding, all the stuff you do now for the Hawksley Estate. Gawd bless your heart, I don't have to tell you that! But there it is, hard work and nature, meaning the sun and the rain. The land can't do without either.'

'Oh I know. I know!'

'There's many a tip I can give yer, so bear that in mind.'

'I'll have my own place one day,' she told him earnestly, 'and there'll be colour and perfume.'

'Ah! You prefer pretty flowers, eh? Well, you'd best give your full attention to a vegetable plot. There'll always be plenty to think about, and it's worth putting your back into things what'll do you good. All year you'll be hard at it. Look at us last February, remember? Getting broad beans in, stamping and rolling the onion bed ready for the setts. Then there was—'

'I love roses and sweetpeas, Walter.'

'And so you should,' he told her. 'They do say you can find God in a garden – but I reckon He can be found in a pod too. Round and green and perfect. Like pearls, peas are. Good-looking enough to make a woman's necklace, eh? And have you seen the colour that glows from a bunch of young carrots? My dear, I reckon you can find the Almighty Himself in my vegetable patch.'

Although Walter was teasing, Hannah knew that he really did feel that he was speaking the truth. On top of peas and carrots, his pride in newly banked-up potatoes was legion. And as for the giant marrows – he always won prizes for those.

Walter chuckled then, determined to egg her on. 'I've even got a feeling for my compost heap,' he imparted in his dry way. 'Everything that breaks down is suitable. Not a single thing's wasted for my compost – or the pigs' bucket, and that's a pure fact.'

'Walter, I know things have to be useful,' she protested, 'but – I mean, there must always be room for the beautiful!'

'Well, me dear,' he winked, but looked solemn just the same. 'I'm sure you'd like to go and see out back. There's marigolds, Sweet Williams, pinks and nasturtiums . . . anything and everything that'll gladden your heart. Bet's heart, too. To my mind they're pretty as

194

paint, but you can't chop 'em up and add 'em to dinner like you can with a handful of mint.'

'Oh, you are awful!' Hannah nudged him in a playful way. 'And I do know some things. You can eat nasturtiums, I read that in *Woman's Weekly* magazine.'

'Peppery they are,' he told her, wagging his finger. 'Just like you.'

As she walked back to Hawksley Hannah found herself wondering about the things Walter had said, or rather left unsaid about Bet. He had hinted that Betty Joyce had something to be afraid of. Well she, Hannah, knew all about fear. Perhaps she could have a heart-to-heart with her at some time, though in all probability, Peg had already done that. Hannah thought Peggy Powell was rather nice, even though she was even harder to fathom than Betty Joyce. Peggy kept herself very much to herself. Oddly, Sophia St John seemed to have a special understanding of the two newcomers. This, now Hannah came to think of it, was truly strange.

Hannah breathed in deeply. Her surroundings were full of country smells, of rural scenes and sounds. She could feel the breeze on her face and all but taste the air. She looked up at the sky, it was clear and cobalt and held no threat today. She thought of Matt and felt her throat grow tight. And then she held her head high and pulled her shoulders back. She must never accept that he had died. Never! He was missing, and desperately missed, but that only meant that one day, one wonderfully glorious day, he would be found. She began to hurry. Raven would be back from Drews by the time she reached Hawksley. It would be nice to have a chat.

Good old Raven. She had rented out her family home. And as for Hannah herself, well there was just a pile of rubble where her home used to be. Ha! she thought. Good riddance to bad rubbish. I wonder if Frank will ever find his way back home? No not on your nellie. It'd be too dangerous for him back there. But what was she doing, thinking about all that? It was over and done with. One should never harp on about the past. She must must talk to Betty, and at the very least tell her that.

A little further along, a lanky red-headed man unwound himself from against a tree and grinning, walked to meet her.

'Hi there, cookie,' he told her. 'I could eat you, you look so sweet.'

'Spence!' She was beaming, and thinking he looked a bit like Gary Cooper. 'You say the weirdest, but nicest things.'

He held out his crooked arm. 'Grab a wing, chick.'

She held his arm and walked beside him feeling small and feminine, and quite desirable when it boiled down to it. He began speaking easily, about his home town, and Mom, and her blueberry pie. About his kid sister who was a cheerleader for the Hawks and his Pop who was a great guy and someone who did brilliant things on broken-down machinery used on farms.

'Oh! So you're a country man?'

'You ain't kidding, sweet pie,' he told her. 'And when I tell them back home all about this, I'll explain that they ain't seen nothin' yet. It's all so Goddamn small!'

'Haven't you heard?' she asked him, eyes narrowing. 'That the really good things come in small parcels?'

He laughed down at her. 'Looking at you, honey,' he drawled, 'I can only agree.'

Prior to parting, at the gates of Hawksley, Spence swooped down and kissed her firmly on the lips. Before she could yell at him, he about-faced and was off. Hannah stood there, watching him, a tinge of excitement wriggling her toes. He liked her, he really did. Hurrah for the US of *A!* . . .

James St John tramped over the grass, frowning and deep in thought. He would have preferred to be in uniform, doing something tough and heroic, instead of dealing with crops and masses of forms; and seeing to it that every acre in the county produced more than twice the amount it had before. He had wanted to duck old issues, to tuck them neatly away, but it had loomed large in his mind lately, the past. The lousy memories . . .

So, for once, he had left the lads to exercise Pegasus and he had made himself walk the same old path, go the same old way, look at the same old back door. It had always been open in the days when he and Miles had gone to call.

Good old Miles, jolly, likable, damned wonderful all-rounder Miles. A chap couldn't have had a better brother. This even though Miles and his best mate Deacon always put him through hell. He smiled darkly, accepting that his young brother and his pal had made him feel like a rank outsider at times. But he was not, he knew it and so did they. It was a game they played, that was all. They were close, always had been. And knew they could call on each other at the drop of a hat. Could and would defend each other to the death, should it be necessary.

A part of James's own soul had gone down with Miles and the *Courageous*. A huge slice of his own life. If he could have changed places with Miles, he would have. He had loved him like that. What his own mother felt about it was hard to tell. Guilt, probably. She was as guilty as hell. She must know it – else why should she drink so much? Women! He loathed and detested them all.

196

He cast his mind back, to the earliest days. When summers had been long and winters wonderful. In those days he had a young and demanding, very spoiled, beautiful mother. The point was that he liked her, truly liked and loved her with all his boyish heart and soul. It was not much good, simply because she never ceased to make it clear that she did not like him, and could barely tolerate Miles.

It was different with his great lumbering full-of-life father. The man that he and Miles would have cheerfully died for. The sportsman, the countryman, the man who was top dog in all things. He and Miles, and Deacon too, had shadowed Robert St John like adoring slaves. And the great one would throw back his head and laugh and ruffle their hair each in turn, and act like a grown-up kid himself.

James, the quiet one, would stand a little apart, happy and part of it, not minding that Miles had the edge where Father's love was concerned. Miles was the rapscallion; the dare-devil always up to his neck in pranks. The huntsman, the shooter, the all-round good chap, in character as much like his father as a fellow could be. On the other hand, it was reckoned that James took after Grandfather St John, the renowned agriculturist who above all things had loved good Essex clay.

In his young days, James had a special liking for Deacon's mother, Mrs Jan Stiles. She was slight and fluffy and rather a bunch of nerves. However she was also warm and gentle, and always seemed interested to hear what a chap had to say. She made time for the three boys, gave them fresh lemonade and home-made buns. Always happy to welcome the St John brothers whenever they came bounding through the door.

Jan Stiles had been especially understanding where James was concerned. She had known how it was. She had been kind to him, seeing him as the more quiet, the patient but strong older brother, who was always at the butt end of the younger pair's jokes. She spoke in a soft, sweet voice. In short, she was the kind of mother that his own could never be.

The Reverend Stiles's religion was somewhat obscure. His services were attended by cranks from all over. They believed in crazy stuff of the Ancient Egyptian kind. Magic and mystery and sacred pyramids entered his teachings. Lighted candles and mumbo-jumbo, and chants for the good. 'White magic is godly magic!' he would thunder, and such had been his personality, that for many, his every word held sway. Tall, lean, angular, dressed in black, he was a hypnotic man. Women believers were one hundred per cent under his sway. Even the non-believers of Lindell were rather fascinated by the man, and did at least believe him to be sincere. Because of his character, his popularity even, his shy wife Jan was welcomed by women's groups everywhere. This pleased and delighted her. She glowed.

The Stiles lived very well. It was whispered, by some of the more down-to-earth people, mostly males, that this was thanks to his wife's private income. However, no one knew for sure.

'Who gives a damn about that?' Robert St John would laugh, eyes alight, hands on hips. His father, James thought, had always been such a decent, very jocular man. He remembered him continuing. 'Stiles's daft believers now see to it that he is kept in clover, by all accounts. At least that must let his wife off the hook.'

On another occasion James remembered his father speaking about the Reverend Stiles.

'I don't know about the man's right to use the title Reverend,' he had said, and grinned. 'But it does no harm. However, don't be taken in by him, even though young Deacon's the best mate you chaps can have. Beware of Stiles's kind. Oh, they're genuine enough perhaps, but I'm not sold on men who persist in shoving their opinions down other folk's throats.'

'Father!' Miles had begun, but Robert St John had shut him up with a look.

'Your mother feels the same way, and she's not often wrong. So, if he tries any of his rubbishy talk on you two, he'll be run off the Estate.'

He had roared out with laughter at their faces, James recalled. Miles in particular had gone turkey-cock red.

'Oh, all right.' Father had let them off the hook. 'Have it your own way. I'll not banish the family of your best friend. Come on, you two, we'll be late for the cricket match.'

Yes, James thought, Father had looked on the whole thing as a joke. But since Stiles was decent, even though something of a nut, there was no reason for him not to.

Then the good days were gone.

James remembered how bad things became at Hawksley when his father had died. Robert was there one day, absent the next. The light had gone out of all their lives.

His mother had always been jealous of the time her husband and sons spent together. Things grew worse when he died. Sophia became bitter and twisted, and had put a stop to the get-togethers Miles and his friends arranged, even fourteen months after Father's demise. She banned their parties, dancing, their music, and Hawksley had become a mausoleum. His mother was particularly loathesome to Deacon because he and Miles were so close; and even more awful to Miles himself simply because she could not browbeat him. Miles had always stood up four square and lipped her back. In fact, gave as good as he got – until the day Mother had snapped, 'Oh God! Why do the good people die, and empty-headed creatures like you live?'

She hadn't meant it, of course, but that was it so far as Miles had been concerned. He had joined the Navy, and Deacon had gone with him. It had been left to James, with Ellery Endercot's help, to take over care of the Estate.

Before the would-be matelots left, Deacon had asked James to look out for his mother, and James had instantly agreed – not thinking anything of it at the time.

I was too young, James thought. Too damned foolish, too blind and too honourable! I should never have done what I did, nor kept my mouth shut about it all. I just stood there and took it, which makes me the clown. I trusted her, would have staked my life on her. Well, I've learned my lesson. I'll never believe in a woman again.

His lips tightened. They're all tarred with the same brush, he thought, and that includes members of the WLA. Their coming had made him uncomfortable. Yet he had asked for them out of need. Too many of his men were now in the Armed Forces – where he would have chosen to be. He smiled bitterly. That was the price of getting too clever at his job, too interested, and just too darned keen to keep up his grandfather's good work. So here he was, scuppered, and stuck with his three girls. Town types who irritated him just by being there – and even harder to bear, by doing so well.

And the small lippy one? She got under his skin the most. Sometimes he wanted to strangle her just because she was such a sunny, bouncy little thing. She never seemed to have a care in the world. Just went sauntering through life. She'd been knocked for six when the Air Gunner went missing though. Had seemed quiet. But she'd carried on, worked like the devil, and these days the twinkle was coming back to her eyes. And she just about adored the other two. It showed in the way she looked at them. And they stuck by her, great field-performers all.

Yes, he had to admit, his Land Girls had managed remarkably well. They were an asset all round. But they were *women*! Treacherous for all that they were really lovely in their different ways.

He swore and moodily kicked at a tuft of grass, glad that he'd taken up residence in Knollys, his mother's old house. The Land Girls still made him edgy, even though he knew them better now. As for Ellery, the old fool thought they were smashers all round. To be honest, James agreed with him!

The red-head, James thought, had the looks that most girls would die for. Her long flowing hair was enough to drive a man wild. Then there was the tall, stately Raven who rode like a dream, and reminded him of the sad princess in *Swan Lake*. She had the face and form of a ballerina, all right.

And then, of course, there was the young twerp who upped and lipped him every chance she got. She glared like a trooper ready to down tools and fight if he dared to say a single word out of place. He wanted to take her down a peg, but no longer had the heart. She had been so thick with the Airman who had been shot down. They had seemed fond of each other. Poor young devil, it must be devilishly hard for her. She must feel as gutted as he himself still felt over losing Miles.

He neared the gates of Hawksley, meaning to pass them and go on his way, but he stopped, legs astride, glowering.

There she was, making sheep's eyes at a Yank, and not grieving over the Airman at all. Then, as James watched, himself unobserved, the Yank kissed Hannah full on the lips – and she was just standing there, looking stupid, watching as the GI walked away.

By God, James seethed, they're all the same, women. All the bloody same! Cheats and liars and too devious to be true. Look at her, rotten to the core. I'd like to wring her skinny neck.

Chapter Twenty-Four

Raven had not yet arrived so Hannah made her way down to the kitchen. Betty was there, busying about. Peggy was nowhere to be found and it was Lily's day off. Hannah plonked herself down at the table and wheedled, 'There wouldn't be a cuppa going spare, would there, Bet?'

'For you, anything,' Bet replied. 'You're my real favourite, yer know.'

'And Walter?'

'He's a good man.' A muddy flush tinged the older girl's cheeks. 'He really is, in spite of what folks say.'

'I know. He's a special mate of mine. He does lots of good things – but doesn't shout it from the rooftops like some. The only thing wrong with him, so far as I can see, is that he won't tolerate dogs – and you know how I am with Mr Mo.'

'He has his reasons.'

'My! Now we're sticking up for him,' Hannah ribbed. 'Getting under your skin, is he, Bet?'

'There's no harm in him.'

'Well, I understand he threatens to shoot all dogs.'

'One killed his brother.'

'Correction, the owner of a dog let it run loose. It darted out in front of the horses and caused them to rear. There was a terrible accident and Lenny's parents died. So, to my mind, it was the dog's *master's* fault. I believe there's no truly bad animal, only bad animal owners.' She poked Betty in the ribs as the woman handed her a cup of tea and a dish that held saccharines. 'Oh, and while I'm at it, them pigs of Walt's don't pong so much now. What's up? Have you been scrubbing their backs? I know Walt lets you loose inside his house, but the pigs!'

'I ain't got to take none of your nonsense, my lady,' Betty replied without malice. 'Seen him lately, have you?'

'Been over there a while ago. There he was, bold as brass, crowing over the earth on his potato patch. Yes, me and old Walt had quite a chinwag. Mostly about you. He sort of hinted that you had good reason to be a bunch of nerves. He told me to ask you why.'

Betty's face went a deeper colour, like ripening sloes. Her eyes were sombre, her lips tight. 'He shouldn't have said nothing.'

'Perhaps, but him and me are mates. It seems he'd like to think that you and me are mates, too. So, if you're in trouble, is there anything I can do to help?'

'Can't turn the clock back, can you?' Betty asked evenly. 'And you can't strangle a lily-livered, evil old dad either, can you?'

'No. And don't talk to me about dads, or at least a stepdad. What did yours do?'

'When I was ten years old, I needed new boots. My mum asked my dad. She had to ask him for everything, even for a box of matches. He took the small amount of money she earned, so she never had a thing that she could call her own. She did as she was told, yer know. He'd give her a sound thrashing else. She was scared of him, an' pregnant at the time, so by the look on her face I knew I could kiss them boots goodbye. So it was a surprise when he pipes up that he'd give me threepence a week to pay the tallyman. So I got me boots.'

'Well, what's so wrong about that?'

'Now then, I'll tell you. After I got the first threepence and me nice new boots, I'm in bed all happy, ain't I? And all of a sudden there he is, creeping up and getting in beside me. I didn't know what to do. I felt daft and I tried to get up, but he was all over me, pulling up me nightdress and that. And I thought to meself, bleeding hell, this is rude! What's my Dad doing? And then I felt this hard thing what was pushed between me legs and – I didn't know, did I? He was on top of me and I couldn't move. He pushed his thing into me. It hurt, but I couldn't yell because he had his hand over me mouth.'

'You're joking, Bet!'

'Wish I was. He didn't bother to try and shut me up after the first time. I thought it was what I had to do for my threepence a week, and I hated him. I'll hate him till the day I die. I hope as how he's in hell right now, yelling and screaming in agony. I hope he rots for the life he led Mum. He threatened to kill me if I told her, and do for her too. But I reckon she knew. She used to give me them haunted looks, yer know.'

'My God,' Hannah whispered, all laughter now gone. 'And I thought Frank was bad.'

'My mum worked all hours, charring and half-killing herself. She'd

202

be out of the house for hours on end, but my dad was always there, waiting. And he'd follow me about the minute I got in. I tried to refuse once, but it was no good. He took his belt to me, yer know? I finished up black and blue.'

'Oh Bet! I never dreamed . . . '

'And the worst thing was the waiting. My heart used to thump and I'd try to get indoors without him hearing me, but he always did. Me mum died having the baby and it died too. Lucky it did, seeing it was a girl. Unlucky for me. Though she never dared say nothing, I knew Mum was on my side. With her gone there was no one at all.'

'Couldn't you have run away?'

'And starved? At least the old bastard fed me to keep me quiet. And keep quiet I did. My dad had his way with me regular for all them years. And I felt dirty. I ran away once, when I was about twelve, but he followed me. Took me back he did, kicking and yelling, but people watching just laughed. He told them I was his daughter what had gone wrong. That it was his duty to take back a heathen runaway kid what was heading for a life of sin. That was a laugh for a start! He half-killed me that night, threw me down the stairs. I broke my arm, but that didn't stop him. *Nothing* did!'

'Betty, I don't know what to say. Honestly!'

'Cor, that makes something of a change.' Betty's tone was lighter now. 'But I'm grateful that you're listening, Han. It's helping me, just by getting it off me chest. Though it's our secret, eh? It's gotta be, because Mrs St John wants it that way.'

'Really? I don't understand where Mrs St John comes into it. I never dreamed she was a caring person at all.'

'Well, she is, make no mistake. She founded the Sanctuary and gives money to help keep it too. She's from good people, bloody good people! But on the other hand, I'm evil and belong in hell.'

'Oh shut up, Bet!'

'I am and I do, because I wanted to sing and dance, I was so glad when my dad died. Then, when they'd shoved him six feet under, the rot set in. The relief and joy I felt went and I got ill.'

'My poor old Bet. Was you very ill?'

'They put me in the nut-house.' Bet paused, swallowing a sob. 'I didn't go much on that. Then Mrs St John heard about me and had me sent to the Sanctuary. I've been there a long time, but not as long as Peg. She's got her own tale to tell – about being messed about by her dad. There was twenty of us there, all been abused by our old men. Makes you think, eh? Anyway, me and Peg are here now, and Mrs St John says we can stay as long as we want.'

'I'm so glad!' Hannah jumped up and impulsively hugged Betty

203

hard. 'We're friends eh, Bet? We can have a few laughs together and a chinwag or two. And you can be quite certain of Walter. He's a pussycat under all his old guff. And know something else? You've got living proof of how greatly he wants to please you. He made you that special flower garden, didn't he? He planted it instead of the lettuces and things he loves so much. He did it purely for you!'

She left Betty soon afterwards. What she really wanted, was to do some serious thinking herself: to get things in perspective regarding Frank. Her stepfather had been a wicked rotten swine, but never in a million years would he molest a child.

Raven still had not returned and Hannah sat in the WLAs communal room listening to music on the wireless. She was feeling nauseated by Betty's story, and yet it had happened to Peggy Powell too. And where did Mrs St John fit in? A sanctuary? What an unpredictable woman she was! Over and above all, she Hannah, had learned a lesson or two. Frank hadn't been so awful after all – at least, not to her. He had kept his hands off her. What he had done to Val was unforgivable, but *she* was not Val. She was Hannah York and proud of it. And in time she would learn not to be afraid of Biff Marner and his terrible gang.

Billy Cotton's signature tune struck up – *Somebody Stole My Girl!* and Billy Cotton shouted out, 'Wakey Wakey!' and it was fun-time.

Hannah tapped her foot in time to the tunes, determined to be positive in thought and deed. It was nice here in Hawksley, she mused, and it was getting to feel like her own home. Over and above all, she was actually liking dear old Sophia. Yes, for all the woman was like a hedgehog with steel spines.

Right out of the blue, Hannah found herself wishing that, like Peg and Betty, she could be sure of never having to leave the graciousness of Hawksley House.

Betty popped her head round the door. 'Message for you. Raven won't be back just yet. She'll see you later on – all right?'

'Thanks,' Hannah replied, not minding at all. It was nice sometimes, just to be alone – and think. And remember some good things for a change. Like the fact that Matt had kissed her and it had been sweet. She would never give up on him, never! In her mind's eye she could see him now. Wonderful, devil-may-care, blue-eyed Matt. Now Spence had kissed her, and it had been an exciting surprise. Yes, two men had actually kissed her. And meant it for real. Talk about scarlet woman! Hannah mentally hugged herself and smiled.

Raven did not return, so Hannah made her way to the Rookwood alone. She heard planes leaving Matchwood and thought of Matt. In spite of her determination to be positive her fear for him was so great that it made her feel dizzy, along with her deep concern for all the people daily facing death through war.

She hoped there were to be no more raids carried out by enemy aircraft on Matching airstrip, or on the city, nor on the districts sprawling all round. It was a faint hope really, because there was a moon. Large and light, literally beaming, it was treacherous, for it showed the Luftwaffe the way.

It was always worrying when Ginnie was on leave, Hannah thought. Oh, her best bosom-buddy lived in a quiet, very decent spot, but airplanes with bombs to drop, got shot of them when the ack-ack held sway. The Civil Defence boys were getting to be spot on, and the enemy cut and run when the barrage got too hot. Especially when the Spits whizzed all round them like busy little gnats. Still, no one was safe, not really. She knew that only too well. Please God watch over Ginnie, she prayed.

Right out of the blue Hannah felt pulses beating in her stomach. She felt sick with nerves all over again and began to pant, for it was suddenly hard to breathe. Oh Miss Pitt, she thought, help me. It's still happening.

Her imagination was playing back the same old scene. And once more she had the suffocating feeling of being buried alive, of choking on plaster, of mortar dust clogging her mouth and nose. Then the nightmare of flight, and of struggling along Walker Street with her case. And of seeing them. All three jerking and jigging like characters in a silent picture show. Biff, Ram and Fatty, all intent on getting rid of Frank.

Far away in the distance Hannah heard the siren begin to wail. She bit her lip, needing to run and run and never stop. But she didn't know where to, so it was all quite futile. She drew in a deep shuddering breath and walked on, following her torchbeam that was, as always, pointed low, for all there was a moon. She saw the old inn that leaned against space like a black comforting mass, and quickened her footsteps.

The Rookwood was busy.

Hannah was among friends. Kindly familiar faces, villagers whom she had come to know. And of course, there was Spence, smiling his wide white-toothed smile as he unwound himself from the bar.

'Hi there, good-looking, tell me what's cooking,' he said, then added, 'Hey! You look like you've seen spooks. Hang loose, kiddo. Just hang loose.'

'I'm fine,' she told him and tried to laugh, but it was a wobbly sound. 'The warning's just gone, by the way.'

He shrugged. 'It's going to be tough on some poor slobs tonight. Adolf's a son-of-a-bitch. Now, where's that smile? Come on, split your lips like always. What'll you have, honey – the usual?'

'Yes, please, a shandy – and Spence, thanks.'

He grinned and went back to the bar to order her drink, while she stayed where she was, standing with her back to the wall just inside, where there was a space to the left of the door. She was fighting for self-control, but her jangled nerves remained taut.

She remembered the cacophony of gunfire, of exploding bombs and the mad crackling of uncontrolled flames. And the persistent sense of unreality that overhung everything because the impossible had happened only minutes before. There had been a catastrophe. She had been in her house, and an explosion had sent it falling and sprawling and splattering all over and all around her. Then, like a zombie, she had all but mountaineered down what had once been a flight of stairs – and outside, someone was screaming for help because her husband was buried and caught up by his legs somewhere.

Hannah fought for self-control, hating herself for thinking the same things over and over again. But the present was blotted out. The crazy pictures of the recent past would not go away. There seemed to be a blood-red wash behind her eyes that was threatening to turn black at any minute. Black that would make her give way, fall and look a fool

Once again she knew that there was indeed a hell, but it wasn't reached after death. It was all around – here on earth. It was only one's friends, male or female, and nice little boys, who helped to keep insanity at bay.

'Sugar!' Spence came back holding a glass in each hand. 'Are you all right?'

'Yes,' she whispered. 'I'm fine, honestly, but—'

'After you've had your drink you would like me to take you back?'

'No, Spence,' she told him. 'I mean it, I really am all right! It's just that – I'm not thirsty after all. I have to go, and I would rather manage alone.'

Before he could argue, she had turned on her heel and made her escape. Her torchlight jogged before her in a crazy fandango as she ran, but she was barely conscious of the fact. All she knew was that she needed to get back to privacy, needed to go through a lone battle with her nerves.

It did not work out that way. Raven was there, in their bedroom. The blackout was drawn and the light on, while Raven read. She looked up from her book, concern swiftly replacing her welcoming smile.

'What is it?' Raven hurried over to put her arm round Hannah's shoulders. 'Has someone frightened you?'

'No. It's just that I have been remembering and . . .' She held onto Raven's hand hard. There was desperation in her eyes as she continued. 'I must – must fight this fear by – by facing it. And to start with I must accept that I can't ignore Frank. Trying to forget him won't make him disappear. So . . .'

'Hannah! Hannah dear! Sit down, here, on my bed beside me. Now calm down. Please explain.'

'It's been going over and over in my mind. I want to run away, but I can't run away from myself. I'm determined to go and see Frank. I don't know what visiting him will do to help, but something tells me I've got to start somewhere and he's my best bet.'

'Why not leave it for a little while? We can wait until tomorrow night and get our heads together with Ginnie. We can—'

'No! I want to go tomorrow morning and I need to go alone. A favour, please, Raven?'

'My dear?'

'Telephone Mr Drew in the morning, or better still ask him for me when you go riding. I want permission to go and visit Frank.'

'Frank is ill in bed, Hannah, in the men's hostel. He was quite bad when he went in, with summer flu or something of the kind. He's not all that strong, is he? Anyway, he's on the mend now, but I don't think you visiting him will—'

'*Ill?* Why didn't you tell me?'

'Think about it,' Raven told her. 'Didn't you spend some considerable time telling us that you never wanted to set eyes on the man again?'

'I'm seeing sense now,' she said urgently. 'Raven, please try and get permission for me to visit him. Old man Drew warned me off before, and I . . .'

'Why not go and knock on Sophia's door? She has far more influence than I do. It's quite early and she'll still be up, I know.'

'I can't ask *her* of all people.'

'Why not? She's very decent when you really get to know her. I have been with her all afternoon. She had enough petrol to drive into town and she invited me to go and see *Gone With the Wind* in the little fleapit they have there. We went to a very nice café afterwards. Since you had already arranged your day and had decided to visit Walter, I was jolly glad to accept the invitation. Sophia is approachable, Hannah, honestly, and her bark is far worse than her bite.'

'I'll not grovel.'

'No one expects you to. Go and speak to her now. I'm sure that

Sophia will telephone through to Mr Drew directly. They are old friends.' Raven all but pushed her out of the room.

Hannah found herself knocking on Sophia's door almost before she had the chance to think. The butterflies were beating their wings in her stomach again when she heard the brittle voice calling out, 'Come in.'

Chapter Twenty-Five

Hannah stood just inside the door, heart sinking. The half-empty whisky glass in Sophia's hand told its own tale.

'Well?' Sophia snapped. 'God, don't stand there on tippy-toe. I thought you of all people would never do that!'

'Invite me in then,' Hannah told her bluntly, chin jutting out, immediately accepting the challenge. 'I've come here because I'm at the end of my tether, I'm desperate and I need your help, but even people like me know when to wait to be asked.'

'Oh, for heaven's sake! Come in and sit down and have a drink.'

Hannah walked in, sat down, but refused the proffered bottle.

'Well?' the older woman looked marvellous in pale blue, but was her usual impatient, bad-tempered self. 'Spit it out.'

'How are you on fathers?' Hannah asked and waited for Sophia to explode. She did not, but stared at Hannah hard.

Then: 'My father was an artist, Emrys Wray-Evans to be exact. His pictures were landscapes mostly, and very well received. He bought Knollys because he so adored painting Lindell and the surround. While he was painting he forgot everything. One winter he painted the village, and the surrounding view, from the church end, right through to the stretch of view that swerved round in a semi-circle ending with Dredging Fields. It took him ages; he was out all hours for days on end, uncaring that the weather was particularly bad. Everything was very lovely and covered in frosted snow. My father caught influenza. Complications set in and he died.'

'Oh! I'm sorry,' Hannah said quietly. 'I didn't mean to remind you of – of grief. That's so very sad! I expect your mum—'

'My mother never caught flu, even though there was an epidemic. She nursed Father night and day. My mother and I were very alike in character, in an all-or-nothing way. When he died she grieved so badly that the doctor insisted that she went away for a while. She was far from home when pneumonia set in and she died.' Sophia shrugged. 'I rather suspect that was what she wanted. She had lost Father and he was the one who counted. She liked me – just, but it was Father who was the be-all and end-all of her life. It is not so good, being second-best.'

'I know. Oh, I do know that.'

'Anyway, I lost them both, and until I met Robert, my husband, I never thought that I would feel complete again. Does that answer your question?' Sophia threw the whisky down her throat in a single violent gesture, the empty glass being swiftly refilled. 'I am a one-hundred-per-cent person where allegiances are concerned. Robert accepted that, and understood. That is why he went along so wholeheartedly with any schemes I took up.'

Hannah remained silent. It still did not make sense, she thought. And she still felt unsure of admitting to links with Frank. She couldn't bear the idea of a put-down from Sophia St John. Oh, she could stand toe to toe with anyone in a stand-up fight, but humiliation was another matter, and right now . . .

'Mrs St John,' she asked quietly, 'Sophia, how is it that Peggy and Bet are so beholden to you?'

'That's my business.'

'Forgive me. Betty will kill me for admitting to this, but she – she told me about her life before she met you. In confidence, of course.'

'Did she now?' Cat's eyes narrowed. 'Remind me to have a word or two with her. Doesn't she realise that people can be cruel? That if it came out about her and poor Peggy, people would whisper behind their backs? Make them feel uncomfortable? I saw and heard first-hand exactly what happens when news of that sort of thing leaks out.' Sophia looked at Hannah straight. 'Hannah, have you a reason for asking about all of this?'

'I – yes, as it happens. About fathers, I mean.'

'Very well.' Sophia's expression became thoughtful. She seemed to be looking into Hannah's soul, then decided for her rather than against. She cleared her throat in an irritated way and continued, 'My father was an artist, very unconventional and a law unto himself.'

Oh Gawd! Hannah thought. Don't tell me that Sophia had that sort of trouble with her own dad!

Impervious to Hannah's suddenly wary expression, Sophia went on: 'There was one summer when he was out and about walking, to his favourite spot, Dredging Fields – that was before the houses were built beyond Duck Pond Corner. Quite unexpectedly he came upon a huge carpet of buttercups. They were stretching as far as the eye could see. Absolutely masses of them, all open, face upwards to the sun. As he

210

put it, they looked like cloth-of-gold. They, and the trees, and a clear blue sky, were such a marvellous sight that he knew he had to put it all on canvas. He began to sketch and was there for a long time. Before going back to Knollys he walked further along, passing a hovel, a pig of a place near where the old Madeira cottage still stands today. And then my father saw her. He told me afterwards, that she took his breath away, she so fitted in.'

'A lovely lady?'

'He saw a child standing there, Hannah. A sweet and lovely child with hair the same colour of the buttercups, and eyes that matched the sky. The full and final canvas leapt into his mind then. Everything, he thought, would be perfect. He could see the whole creation in his mind's eye. Full of enthusiasm, he approached the child's father, who, with his eyes on the main chance, literally haggled.'

'Over money?'

'What else? Anyway Father paid him a great deal in order to have the child pose for him. She was a year younger than me. That little girl, whose name was Mary, became my dearest friend.'

So, Hannah thought surprised, old Sophia had a soft spot after all! She didn't seem the sort who would actually have a dearest friend.

'I had someone I thought the world of once,' she confided. 'Her name was Miss Pitt. She used to look after me, explain things. Try to put me on the right track.'

'Really? Well, your Miss Pitt seems to have done quite a good job,' Sophia said dryly. 'However, Mary was very unlike you. She was only a wisp of a thing. She was tiny and fragile and looked as if a puff of wind could blow her away. She was very timid and her eyes were like the blue-est of crystals. She was unsure of my father, too, and she used to flinch if he approached her. Silly old me – I wondered why! She sat there, doing as she was told, because she was too scared not to. But she would, and did, turn to me. I was a mere child myself. Even so, I started out by just wishing to defend her – from what, I didn't really know.

'After that, I used to see to it that she had food, as she was always near to starving. With Mother's permission, I gave her some of my best clothes, and above all, books. She loved nursery stories, and pictures of the Flower Fairies.' Sophia laughed harshly. 'God! Can you imagine me being patient? I even taught her to read!'

'You were good to her, Sophia. That was nice.'

'*Nice?*' Sophia impatiently took a cigarette from a gold case, lit it with a matching gold lighter and inhaled, then went on, 'What a wishy-washy word that is. Nice!'

'I'm sorry. I didn't mean—'

'Mary and I became like sisters, we were so close. Know something? In all that time, several years in fact, I heard her laugh just once. *Once*, Hannah – would you believe? Think about it. We were watching kittens at play. I will never forget the sound of Mary's laugh. It was sort of tinkly, I recall. Like bells.'

'What of her relatives? Didn't they care about her?'

'She only had her father. I loathed and detested him. He was a lumbering ox of a man. But Mary and I were as thick as thieves and always remained so. When she was fourteen years old she became ill.'

'And she died,' Hannah said flatly. 'I can tell by your tone.'

'Not then, not exactly. She had a miscarriage, Hannah. There was not a ha'pporth of her, and she still looked so young and innocent, but she was actually with child! I could not understand what was happening. My mother explained. It was a wonder that Mary did not die there and then. It all began to happen while she was with me. We were painting pictures, in Knollys. She gave a sudden terrible gasp and doubled up. My mother called the doctor. Even he was shocked at what he found. Mary was torn and in a terrible state underneath. Her poor fragile little legs were black and blue with bruising. It all came out then. Mary had been abused, and very cruelly abused, for years.'

'Oh dear Lord!' Hannah choked. 'And when just fourteen she was actually pregnant? Sophia, who was it?'

'The doctor got the truth out of her. It was her own father. When I became very angry and asked her why she'd never breathed a word to me, she admitted to being too afraid. Later, the story got out. I don't know how. I certainly never breathed a word. People were vicious, specially the women. They said she must have egged him on, no smoke without fire, that sort of thing. That was what her father said in his own defence, of course. They ran him out of the village even so.'

'Good!'

'From then on Mary stayed with us in Knollys, and the scandalmongers started whispering even more horrible things. I believe "whore" was one term consistently used – to her face, Hannah! In the end, my poor little Mary wanted to die with shame. One day she did just that. She drowned herself. I grieved and still do, over losing her.'

'And I thought it was awful when Miss Pitt decided to go to do Christian work abroad,' Hannah said thoughtfully. 'But I at least knew she was alive. Still is, as far as I know.'

'I thought the bottom had dropped out of my world when Mary went.' Sophia's tone held bitterness. 'And then the following very hard winter, I lost my father, then my mother . . .' The whisky glass was emptied at a gulp and filled yet again. 'Are you sure you won't drink with me, girl?'

'No, thank you. It's very kind of you. I'm not against it, but . . . So when you could, you founded the Sanctuary?'

'Yes. Because when I was cross with Mary that day, she whispered that she had found Knollys to be like a sanctuary. That if it hadn't been for our friendship, she would have gone mad. She also said that it must be terrible for girls in her position not to have anyone.'

'Like Bet?'

'Yes, and the many others we never learn about.' Sophia narrowed her eyes again. 'But that's not why you're here, is it? Come on, tell me. While I'm full of the good spirit, in fact. Had it not been for the drink I would never have given you house room, and certainly never told you about the one person in the world who actually loved me over and above everyone.' Another drag on the cigarette, more whisky, and a ferocious stare. 'But you know that, don't you?'

'My story's not near so bad as Mary's,' Hannah began stoutly, 'but I need your help all the same. You see . . .'

She told Sophia everything then. About her childhood, her life. Everything from start to finish. Ending, 'But I need to see Frank if he is ill, Sophia. In his way, I believe that he tried to help me. I would like to try and help *him* now.'

'He needs shooting. He sounds an evil swine.'

'Mrs St John!'

'Sophia will do.' She shrugged and looked at Hannah in a speculative way, then, 'Oh very well, you both need help.' She snapped her fingers. 'And as far as the louts in London are concerned, it's simplicity itself. Get your stepfather to write a full confession. Let him name names, give dates and places, and in short, dish as much dirt about those odious creatures as he can. Then he must sign it.'

'It would be a warrant for his own imprisonment!'

'No, girl. His safeguard. Stop arguing and listen to me. The same thing applies to you. You must set down exactly what you heard and saw on the night of the raid. Name the three people who treated your stepfather so brutally. Tell all! Then put your signature against what you have written. Even more importantly, give the letters from your stepfather and yourself, to me. They will go in the safety-deposit box in my bank.'

'Oh, but—'

'The next step will be to let that man Marner know about the letters.'

'Oh, but he might—'

'Be quiet, Hannah, and listen!' Sophia would brook no interruption. 'He must know that they are in very safe hands, and it must be made very clear to him, that if anything happens to either you or

Frank Neilson, the epistles will be immediately delivered to the police.' Sophia glared and said impatiently, 'And believe me, they will!'

Hannah was feeling pole-axed, hardly able to believe she had heard aright. She had come to this lady for help, but she had never in a million years believed that Sophia St John would take matters so firmly and capably into her own hands. She had listened to Hannah's sordid story and known exactly what to do. What was more she would do it, make no mistake. Gawd! Hannah thought, near to tears with relief. Just let Biff Marner, Fatty, and Ram Rawlins watch out!

'Oh Sophia,' she stuttered. 'What can I say?'

'Not much, since you are opening and shutting your mouth like a fish. Now please leave while I telephone Mark Drew. If you wish to visit that detestable Frank, I will see to it that you may. When I speak to Mark I will ask him which of the hostel rooms Neilson is in. I will leave his number on the kitchen table, so it will be unnecessary for you to bother me further. Oh, and by the way . . .'

'Yes?' Hannah whispered, still feeling unnerved.

'We will keep all of this to ourselves. Do you understand? All of it! I do not wish either yours, or Betty's or Peggy's stories to be put about. Have I made myself clear?'

Hannah stood up and looked at Sophia, who stared back in a hard, mouth-twisting way. Then Hannah, recovering her voice, said sincerely: 'At the risk of being called prissy – your own term not mine – I'd like to say thank you. Thank you from the bottom of my heart. It's as marvellous to have you on my side as it was to have Miss Pitt.' Then, because Sophia continued to glare, Hannah's courage failed her, and with a strangled, 'Good night!' she fled.

She was grateful that she did not have to say a word to Raven. On entering their bedroom she found that the other girl was already settled and sound asleep.

It was very early when Hannah made her way to the Drew Hostels. They were outside the stables enclosure, and Frank's place, number 22, was easy enough to find. She knocked on the door, found it unlocked, so turned the handle and went in.

As she had half-expected, the place was a mess – small, damp-smelling and claustrophobic. It comprised a kitchen-cum-living room, with a boxroom behind that held merely a single cupboard for clothes, a small chest of drawers and a narrow bed.

What Hannah did not expect was to find Frank looking so wasted and ill. He was sleeping and his breathing was laboured. He awoke with a start as she bent over him.

'Wotcher, gel,' he said huskily.

214

'Frank, I'm so sorry. I didn't know.'

He struggled to sit up and she helped him.

'Didn't wanna know, more like,' he told her without malice. 'Can't blame yer though, ducks. Too ashamed to come slumming in your uniform, were yer?'

'Silly! I like to wear civvies at weekends.' She laughed softly. 'And Mr Endercot will tell you that I have been known to wear my hair tied back with bows and things even on the fields. But that's neither here nor there. Frank, did I really scare you just now?'

''Course you did,' he admitted surlily. 'I ain't no bleeding hero. An' I wouldn't put nothing past that toe-rag Ram.'

'Well, cheer up,' she told him. 'I have good news. I know how we can stop them in their tracks. Stop them for good and all.'

'An' pigs might fly!' he wheezed. 'Look mate, put the kettle on. I'm 'alf dead with thirst here.'

'I'll make us both tea, and something to eat if you've got anything in, and after that you are going to write down lots of things.'

'Gawd 'elp us! Now what are you on about? I've been under the weather, wished I was dead, and you want me to sit up and write? Don't know your arse from your elbow, do yer?'

'For goodness sake, Frank. Just be quiet and listen.'

It took a while to convince him, and to give him something to eat, bread and watered-down condensed milk. It looked horrible, was a soggy mess in fact, but it had to do. It was all she could find. While he ate, she whisked round and tidied up the place. When she turned to look at him she saw that he was not up to doing much at all.

She picked up her cardigan, it had been chilly first thing, and slipped it round her shoulders. She looked neat and trim in her white blouse and black skirt.

'I'll be here as often as I can from now on,' she told him. 'And as soon as you're able, start working things out in your head, Frank. I know that you can't think straight just now. But we need to tie that lot up so tight they'll never get free. I'll help you put everything down. All right?'

'What I can't fathom,' he gasped, 'is how that bastard Biff's going ter get to know.'

'Easy! When everything is signed, sealed and settled, I'll go back and see Ma Carpenter. She'll soon put the word round. Knowing Ma, she'll add on some spicy bits of her own. Talk about the cat among the pigeons, eh?'

'Right you are,' he replied, closing his eyes. He opened them again to say, 'Ta, Han. Good of you to come, mate. I dunno as how I deserve it, but ta all the same.'

215

She smiled, still shaken at the sight of him. He had never been a huge person, but now he was gaunt and stick-thin. The beating he had received at the hands of Biff Marner and Co must have done an awful lot of permanent damage. His recent illness had done the rest.

Hating herself for being a daft fool, she had to admit to feeling sorry for him. And sorry for herself, too. Her mind went winging away, not to the East End, but to some foreign spot, and Matt. Had the pigeons on his plane survived? Far more importantly, had he? Where was he now?

She was brushing away her tears as she walked out of the hostel and straight into the path of Beatrice Drew. She knew it was her since she was on the back of the aristocratic Tan-Tivvy, a very recognisable horse. No one but Beatrice was allowed to ride him for pleasure. Loyal and long-serving stable-hands exercised him when she could not. This honour apparently turned them into bundles of nerves.

Tan-Tivvy was pulled up. A haughty voice drawled out: 'Who on earth are you? And just what are you doing here?'

At a disadvantage, Hannah found herself looking up at a blonde who was wearing impeccable riding gear.

Beatrice Drew was quite startling. She had white-gold hair cut in a thick fringe, which made her smooth skin look a richer, deeper gold by comparison. She had a heart-shaped face, a full red mouth, and large blue eyes, which were now deeply suspicious. Even so, Hannah thought, when she was not being insufferably arrogant, the other woman could probably be very provocative and interesting. She was a stunner all right. Enough to catch old James? Nah!

At Hannah's first glance she assumed the stable-owner's daughter to be about twenty-five. Now, on a closer look, she judged that she was in fact thirty or older.

Beatrice began tapping her thigh impatiently with her whip. Her words cracked out like pistol shots.

'I asked what you are doing here?'

'Minding my own business,' Hannah replied.

'*My* business,' Beatrice snapped. 'You are trespassing on *my* land. I can have you all but—'

'Put down?' Hannah's tone held sarcasm. 'I do assure you, it wouldn't be easy. I'm not the cringing type. Now, if you'll excuse me?'

'No!' The whiplash came down to flick against Hannah's chest. 'You will explain yourself!'

'Know something?' Hannah smiled sweetly. 'I'll explain *this*. I'd just love you to use that whip again.'

'Oh really?'

'You wouldn't half learn something quick, dear,' Hannah replied perkily. 'Like I'm no horse. Like I'd fight back, and just about give you the hiding of your life.'

Before things could get out of hand, there came the sound of horse's hoofs and James rode up on Pegasus. His quick glance showed surprise at seeing her, and contained questions that she couldn't answer in front of a third party.

'Good morning,' James said in a cool authoritative way. Then his manner became even more overbearing. 'What can I do for you?'

Hannah smiled and raised her brows, but said nothing. James went on almost silkily now. 'Have you two been introduced? Beatrice, this is Hannah York, one of our girls.' He gave Hannah an icy smile. 'Hannah, meet Beatrice, usually known as Trixie. Trixie Drew.'

The rotten swine, Hannah seethed, he's doing this deliberately. He doesn't like me and it shows, and by broadcasting that woman's pet name, pretending she and I could meet on common ground, he's just asking her to hate me.

Beatrice's cold blue eyes raked Hannah from head to toe. 'I have heard of you,' she said in an offensively off-hand way. 'You lodge in Hawksley, don't you? As a farm-labourer – or something.'

The "or something" managed to sound extremely insulting. Hannah went very red.

'My friends and I are members of the Women's Land Army,' she said evenly. 'Tell me, just what kind of war effort do you manage to achieve?'

'With these hands?' Ten beautifully manicured nails fluttered out to be flaunted and Beatrice's laugh was an open insult.

Hannah ignored her and turned to look up at James, conscious that she had to look up a very long way too.

An imp inside her made her stand to attention and salute.

'I came here to visit someone who has been ill, sir! One of the workers here.' She saw his disdain and glared up at him defiantly. 'Mr Frank Neilson, in fact.'

He was openly looking down his nose. 'You have been visiting one of the casuals here?'

'Why not?' she asked, eyebrows raised. 'He's a fellow Londoner.'

'Ah!' His tone held sarcasm. 'Another string to your bow, Miss York. Forgive me, but aren't you rather scraping the barrel with Neilson? Have you forgotten your American so soon, and wasn't there the Royal Air Force fellow before that?'

She was livid at his cheek. Eyes flashing, short dark curls dancing as she tossed her head, she was about to give him the gobful of the century, but changed her mind. This because she became conscious of

217

the bitchily leering Beatrice. It suddenly became very important to wipe the sneer right off her face.

Hannah smiled and tilted her head in a coquettish way. 'Good heavens, Mr St John,' she cooed. 'How is it that you seem to know so much about me? You must be watching me all of the time. How flattering! The American is Spence Farraday and he wants me to be his GI bride – isn't that sweet? My airman had serious intentions too, but we must wait and see if he gets safely home. Still, in the meantime there has been . . . Oh, but I won't bore you by listing all of my friends.' She darted a meaningful look towards Beatrice. 'Sufficient unto the day, don't you think? Luckily I have quite a few chaps to choose from. You see, I'm determined not to be on the shelf when I'm over thirty years old. Thirty is so old, don't you think?'

One swift glance was sufficient to tell that her barb had hit home. Giving them both a cheery wave, she walked away, acting as if she hadn't a care in the world. In some ways she hadn't. Her only concern for the time being was that Frank didn't get the sack because of the things she'd said.

Further on she saw Raven, who was wearing her riding habit and looking tall and willowy and absolutely gorgeous. Raven could give Beatrice a run for her money any day. They met and smiled.

'Are you all right?' Raven asked.

'Bearable.'

'Was Sophia able to help?'

'A great deal, but mum's the word, eh?'

'Is that Sophia's wish?'

Hannah grinned. 'Not wish – command, more like! Oh, and something else. There's a couple of real charmers back there. I'm talking about James and bitchy Trixie Drew. They think, and they must continue to think, that I'm actually smitten with my stepfather, although they don't know that's what he is.' She laughed heartily. 'Don't look at me as though I'm mad. It's true! They actually think I've been visiting a bloke I fancy! One of the "casuals". I don't mind, really. It's better that way.'

'But no one sane would believe that, Hannah. You're far too young and no one would ever dream . . .'

'Oh no? You should have seen Mr High and Mighty's face. And as for Miss Snooty! She'd swallow anything she wanted to. I said it was because he's a Londoner.' Hannah frankly giggled, adding, 'We Londoners stick together, you know.'

'It won't wash!'

'It's got to, Raven. At least for now. Now go on, enjoy your ride on Blue Rinse. Tata for now.'

'You're incorrigible!' Raven rebuked her, then continued on her way.

By the time Hannah reached the village she was in a high good humour. Thanks to Sophia, she need fear Biff Marner and his crowd no more. All that remained was for the letters to be written, hers and Frank's, and once they'd been handed over, Sophia would do the rest. That achieved, she would go back to Walker Street and find Ma Carpenter. Old mouth and trousers Ma who would know exactly how to let Biff learn that he'd been had.

The twins appeared from nowhere, it seemed. They were both quite filthy and enthusiastically chewing apples. Mr Mo jumped up, slobbering.

'Hello, you lot,' Hannah greeted them. 'Where are you off to?'

'We came to meet you. Lenny's over here, with Walter and Mike Allsop,' Chris said, adding joyfully, 'Hey, Hannah?'

'Yes?'

'You know Lenny likes Matt an awful lot?'

'Yes. Shows how wise he is.'

'Well, he wrote to the Red Cross, someone really high up, asking about Matt. He did that ages ago, but didn't tell in case we got upset. Mike helped him write it all down, how important Matt is to Lenny an orphan, and all that kind of stuff. Guess what, he had an answer! A letter yesterday morning, and he'd almost forgotten he'd written too. They did their best to find out, and think he's alive, and still somewhere in France.'

'Oh!' Tears flew into Hannah's eyes. 'After all this time? Oh, how wonderful!'

'They think he might be with the French Underground. He was, the last time anyone heard. That's all they could find out. But not bad, eh?'

'Not bad at all,' she replied in the same vein.

'Hey, Hannah,' Chook said importantly. 'What's brown and wrinkled and goes round and round?'

'I – I don't know,' Hannah replied unsteadily. 'Do tell.'

'A clockwork prune!' Chook's roar of laughter rang out.

'It's not as good as my one,' Chris said.

'It is, it's better.'

'Well, before you both begin to batter the living daylights out of each other,' Hannah said, 'let's hear your riddle, Chris.'

'All right. What goes through a hole at a hundred miles an hour?'

'A train?'

'No!'

'All right, all right! What goes through a hole at a hundred miles an hour?'

'A mole driving a racing car!'

Hannah laughed simply because the boyish shrieks of joy were so contagious. Then Mr Moses bayed and went rather mad and it took Hannah to sort them all out, and all the while her eyes were sparkling ambers of delight.

Later, as she continued alone to Hawksley, she thought of Matt. Her heart danced with memories of that kiss! She tried to picture him, but all she could remember was his wide and wonderful smile. Yes, that smile! The most real part of him – just like the Cheshire Cat in *Alice in Wonderland*.

Chapter Twenty-Six

Matt was, he believed, on the journey to Paris, he and other passengers crushed together on the train like sardines. Matt began thinking back, to how this had all begun.

Two days after meeting Claude, the merry little fat man, Madame had tapped gently on the cupboard door. Once again, legs trembling and still painful because of bouts of cramp, his back on fire, Matt had returned to her sitting room. Claude was there, a huge smile spread over his features. He held out his hand.

'Hello to you, Charles-Philippe Cousteau, for that is who you are, and here are your papers to prove it.' He took the ID from his pocket. 'There is no photograph as yet, but that will soon be rectified, eh? A picture with the whiskers you now have, yes? Not a clean shaven Englishman at all.' He picked up a camera that had been placed in readiness on the table, and turned to Madame. 'A comb, *chère madame*? We 'ave an older man, you understand?'

A good hair-tidying later, the photograph had been taken.

'*Très bien!*' Claude said. 'I will see to it that the papers are completed all in good time. Now we must be getting on our way. You are no longer safe here, *monsieur*. Indeed, you are causing a great stir.' This was news to Matt. Claude's smile became more pronounced and there was triumph in his eyes. 'The Gestapo are buzzing like bees all round Nantes. They know that one of the airmen is missing. A good disappearing act, eh?'

Claude threw back his head and began to laugh heartily. The more he laughed, the more his English deteriorated until he was speaking rapidly in French alone. To him, the whole business was a great game, unless the man was as drunk as a skunk, Matt wondered dazedly, or perhaps a little mad? But his laughter was infectious, and even *Madame*'s worn face relaxed. Claude paused to take breath, then merriment was banished and replaced by a purposeful air. 'Come!' he ordered. 'It is time to leave.'

221

Matt remembered turning to *Madame*. At that moment she seemed so vulnerable and so small, yet he knew first-hand of the bright courage that burned within her fragile frame. He had put his arms about her and kissed her on both cheeks. Her two hands fluttered like speckled moths and momentarily cupped his face. Uncharacteristically he had wanted to cry. Then they had left her, Matt knowing that he would carry the memory of her standing there, in her doorway, all the days of his life.

He had followed Claude after that, hurrying as best he could, the agony in his back and leg increasing rather than the reverse. At last they reached a kind of warehouse – a safe place, Claude said. They would make further plans soon.

During the night, fever returned; and with it, Matt suffered hallucinations. He had learned later that he had been wrapped in sacking, and given heavy sedatives to keep him quiet. Claude said that he had nearly died. That he had been 'out of this world' for some time. Matt only remembered a haze peopled with phantoms of Titch and Richard, and planes and flames. A girl with dark hair and a madonna face had floated before him. She had seemed wise and kind, and her calm smile had seemed to say that it was going to be all right. That yes, everything would be fine.

When he was out of the fever and strong enough, he was able to leave the building. He continued to follow Claude, in a succession of visits to strange houses, ruined buildings, forsaken barn-like places, and once, the shell of a church. As the Gestapo searched one place, and voted it clear, Matt was sneaked into it. He followed German soldiers all along the line until he felt as if he was on some form of escalator. One that moved forwards rather than up or down. And all the while Claude was there, chuckling to himself, thinking what a game it was.

In permanent pain these days, Matt had begun to think the world around him had gone crazy. He was living on the edge of fear. He knew that he would ask Claude to shoot him, rather than allow him to fall into enemy hands. He knew too that he was a liability, unable to help himself because of his injuries. Some days he was scarcely able to move along.

So it went on. He was shunted around, from pillar to post, with the Resistance – or *maquis* as it was familiarly known – always just the one jump ahead.

Then things had begun to get hot. While he hid in cellars, stuffy back rooms, or outbuildings, ordinary people were being shot, to teach them a proper respect for the Fatherland. People were being indoctrinated, processed, presented with new sets of rules. Men van-

222

ished; young women, too. French Jews in particular were having very terrible times. It was happening all over. France was no longer France, but a crushed *fleur-de-lys* under a swine-hound's cloven hooves.

These days Claude's eyes were not laughing so much, and a tinge of angry colour burned high on his cheeks. 'Quisling' – a traitor who collaborates with an occupying force – became the most hated word.

People who helped these days kept their thoughts locked in behind tight faces: Matt thought wearily that it would never end.

He felt bad because the maquis members were prepared to risk their lives to help him, a useless crock. They treated him as someone special, yet he knew he was not. They acted as though they believed his life was important. He knew it wasn't worth a light. Someone gave him a walking stick which made him feel like an old man.

One evening, unexpectedly, he found himself hurrying along in the dusk as best he could. He was following Claude. They had entered a charming house and Claude's expansive smile had flashed out again.

'Welcome to my home, Monsieur Charles-Philippe Cousteau,' he said. 'Good news, eh? The immediate danger is past. You are now presumed dead and the search has been called off. So this evening we will have a little celebration. That will be good?'

Matt was taken into a delightful sitting room. In pride of place stood a magnificent bureau. Claude unlocked it and took out Matt's photograph with a flourish, saying, '*Voilà!* Now let us get your picture on the papers, eh?'

The job didn't take long, and just as it was completed a lady came into the room. She was pale-faced, golden-haired, petite: and most evident, a bunch of nerves. She greeted Matt in a friendly manner, but gave an expressive shrug when Claude went again to the bureau. This time Matt caught a glimpse of the contents. A profusion of false identity papers.

'It is not good to be so unafraid,' Madame Claude murmured plaintively.

Claude heard and laughed. 'Come now, *ma chérie*, the more furtive one is, the more suspicion falls upon one. Can you not see that?'

There was a knock on the door, then the first of a group of visitors appeared. Some of them Matt recognised as his benefactors in the previous house-to-house chase. All brought wine, others fruit, or long sticks of bread which they carried tucked under their arms. No one came empty-handed. Each one shook hands with Matt. Claude, who was now enjoying the whole thing hugely, explained.

'So, *mon vieux*, a great welcome you receive, eh?'

223

'It's bang on,' Matt replied politely, 'but I don't really understand.'

'It is simple. Yours is the first plane to be shot down over Nantes, and you are the first airman that this branch of the Resistance has helped. You are our first "Operation", so we all, how you say, want to get in on the act!'

'They'll kill you all, given half the chance.'

Claude shrugged expressively. For once his smile had gone. 'Every moment the German is in my country, we die a kind of death,' he said. 'Now, let us eat and drink, eh? Soon, when the time is right, perhaps in a day or two, we will go to the bottom of my garden, where there are railway lines. We have kept you here with us as long as possible because you have been so ill, so weak, eh?' He winked. 'But you are stronger now?'

Suddenly there came a pounding on the door. Everyone froze. Claude answered it. Immediately a tow-headed youth with an olive-skinned face hurried in. He began speaking with rapid excitement. About a train that had not been cancelled after all. That was in fact, due to arrive at the station quite soon.

Claude turned to Matt. 'Put on the beret, my friend. Come! It is time to move on.'

Matt obeyed. In a trice they had hurried out through the kitchen, into the garden. Matt stumbled, but was all-but shoved over the wall and on to the railway lines. Claude was running full out now. The youth who had brought the message stayed close to Matt who was following as best he could. He became conscious of the sound of their footsteps ringing dully on the metal, and thumping on the wooden sleepers.

On they hurried, following Claude, zig-zagging between stationary carriages, along straight stretches, then past more carriages, until at last they slowed to a walk as they went up the slope leading to a station platform. Claude said briefly, 'Wait!' He had put his finger to his lips. He then disappeared along the platform. Slowly Matt's breathing returned to normal, his heartbeats slowed. He stood there, beside the youth, hardly daring to lift his eyes. Claude returned, and handed them a ticket each. Then he nodded slightly towards the station entrance.

'Many, many Gestapo are by the barrier. They watch everyone going through. Be careful, my friend. Good that we came along the lines, eh?'

'Whizzo,' Matt replied, then took a second look along at a would-be passenger. He was standing, beret pulled well forward a few yards away from Claude, the youth and Matt. He glanced surreptitiously further along. The Gestapo were indeed out in force, but so were

224

members of the Underground. They were there, supportive, the friends and callers who had visited Claude's house.

In the distance came the faint rumble of an approaching train. It panted into the station like a medieval dragon snorting great clouds of steam. It stopped and in a trice Claude had pulled open a door and pushed Matt and the youth into a crowded corridor. Suddenly, the baker appeared. He pulled a shabby coat out of a bag and draped it round Matt's shoulders. Then he grinned, patted him on the back and vanished. And Matt, in agony, heart pounding, wanted to swear because it had happened too quickly. He had had no chance to thank anyone. No chance either to say goodbye.

So the train had pulled out. The youth stayed near.

'I am Henri,' the young man said under his breath, when no one could hear. 'It is better that we sleep.'

Feeling drained of all emotion, Matt obeyed the boy's sign and sat on the floor, where he tried to sleep, with the others, like sardines.

The journey seemed never-ending. Matt wondered how much further they had to travel before reaching Paris, which he believed to be their destination. As the train slowed prior to stopping, Henri gave the signal. A move at last. They had reached Le Mans, and had to sit and wait on one of the station benches, as bold as brass, as a busy rush of activity ebbed and flowed about them.

A crowd of German soldiers pushed by. Wine-flushed, swaggering, loud-mouthed. Watching them, Matt was unaware that his injured leg was stretched out before him. Then he winced as a large military-shod foot was placed fair and square on his instep. He instinctively drew his leg away and glared in pain and fury at yet another German soldier. For a split second he felt fear turning his blood to ice. To be discovered now was unthinkable.

The soldier bent down and apologised clumsily in French. Matt nodded, accepting the apology, and the German grinned in a friendly way. Matt smiled stiffly in return and felt surprised that a Kraut could be so young, so apple-cheeked and open-faced. It was infuriating to find himself thinking of this particular enemy as a half-decent chap. The soldier walked on and Matt heard Henri's sigh of relief, which was not half so loud as his own.

Caught by curfew, they and many others stayed the night where they were, in the station. Early the next morning there was a stirring among the people. Soon they made their way to the exits and gave up their tickets at the barrier and walked out into the street. The German sentry outside the station was a striking helmeted figure in an immaculate uniform of green and red. A fixed bayonet completed the picture. Matt felt more degraded than afraid as he limped past him and saw the

225

man's cold eyes slide impersonally over his filthy trousers and crumpled clothes.

Matt's limp grew worse. He put his hand on Henri's shoulder and remained silent. The resultant journey was a nightmare. There were few people about, mercifully no Boches, but there was pain. Oh God, Matt was thinking. What wouldn't I give for a cold beer and a sit down!

Gradually they left the town and reached open countryside. The sun shone on flat grazing land, broken by an occasional copse. The road stretched interminably before them. Still they walked.

Just as Matt was beginning to wonder how much further he could go, Henri said, 'We are here.'

They left the track and went into a field that led in turn to a wood. Once among the trees Henri pointed to a patch of grass.

'Rest. I will go on alone to make sure all is well.'

Matt lowered himself and gratefully closed his eyes, only to groan because in a very short while Henri reappeared. He was grinning happily.

'Come! All is safe.' He helped Matt to his feet. They walked through the wood and across more fields. Henri gestured about him. 'This land is ours. Soon you will see the house.'

Ahead Matt saw a large rambling farmhouse. As they approached, the door flew open. Beckoning them in was a small plump lady, unmistakeably Henri's mother. As they entered she held out her hands.

'Welcome,' she said and ushered Matt into a large, cool room. 'Henri has told me how ill you have been. You must rest, *Monsieur*. We can offer very little, but we are 'appy to give you all that we have.' She brushed Matt's thanks to one side. 'It is nothing. In a moment, when you are a little stronger, Henri will show you where you can sleep.'

During the next few days Matt learned many things from Henri's garrulous mum. That the Germans had been to the farm and helped themselves to all the available food and valuables. That they had destroyed crops that they themselves did not need. Henri's mother then went on.

'François is my eldest son. Indeed, this is his farm. He escaped from the Germans, and fled with many others to fight for France. He is with the Free French. Henri my youngest, does what he can.'

Matt was left in no doubt that Henri's mother was deeply patriotic. To see her beloved country under German rule was a personal insult, she said. To think of them goose-stepping through the châteaux that stood like ancient jewels in their history-steeped surroundings was quite unbearable. The tramp of enemy feet through the vineyards of

Alsace, Bordeaux, and Burgundy was nightmarish. It was said that the Boches swarming in the little old towns of Sarlat and Les Eyzies-de-Tayac were like devils from hell. And that hosts of guttural orders and conversations in the valleys of the Auvergne, all but drowned out the bells on the sheep. It was deplorable.

'*Oui, oui, Madame*,' Matt heard himself saying over and over again. He felt completely helpless. He was on edge every time Henri went away. On edge when he heard enemy planes growling overhead on their way to England, and also on edge when Henri's mother carried on. And carry on she did. Saying that the Hun filling his nostrils with the aroma of Grasse's spring mimosa and summer jasmine was heart-breaking. '*Monsieur*, eet is too 'orrible to be true!'

Henri's mother always finished in tears. Matt listened to the tirades in silence, and tried not to turn away from the disgusting soup, made from God only knew what. There was also hard black bread. Sometimes there was a fried egg and at other times a bowl of milk. Luxury. The Germans had left Henri and his mother in dire straits since after their visit there was very little left.

The sixteen days that Matt stayed at the farm seemed more like sixteen years. He was in pain all of the time, but he had to admit to himself that the walking stick helped.

These days, the thought of home was no more than a distant dream. But there was that face. That calm, beautiful face with its velvet-brown eyes . . .

'So you see,' Hannah excitedly told Ginnie and Raven, holding her hoe aloft, 'all I have to do is go back to The Smoke and see old Ma. She'll tell them, all right. Blow me, she'll not be able to wait! You know what I'm up to, of course, and you're with me every step of the way, I know. But it's to go no further. Mum's the word. Sophia's orders.'

'Don't worry,' Ginnie replied. 'Now for my news.'

Raven and Hannah stepped over the growing rows to draw close. 'There were four letters waiting for me at home,' Ginnie told them, 'all long and very important, but in one . . .'

'Yes?' Their eyes were bright with expectation.

'Aiden proposed!'

'Well, that's nothing different,' Hannah told her blandly. 'Since according to you, he always does.'

'I wrote back straight away and . . . I accepted!'

'Bully for you!' Hannah was ecstatic, and Raven glowed.

'So we'll celebrate tonight?'

'Of course!' they agreed, beaming.

227

'Last one in the Rookwood's a ninny,' Ginnie said, and it was laughing and teasing and wedding talk for the rest of the day.

That night there were many congratulations and lots of teasing in the Rookwood. But when that was done the talk reverted to the forthcoming cricket match between Little Norseby and Lindell.

A year gone already? Hannah thought. How could it be? Oh, it had been hard work, and frightening at times, and she never had been able to get round that miserable old goat – who she found out belonged to Eloise Endercot. But nowadays all was getting to be right with her world. Of course, James St John never ceased to irritate her – and that latest business with snotty Beatrice Drew had been no fun. But she had heaps of friends, even including Sophia, and now there would no longer be fear from those city pigs who had wanted to do for Frank. On top of that, it had been fairly good news about Matt. So all was right with her world. Back to the cricket match.

Everybody was taking part. Lily and her cohorts were to provide refreshments in the form of sandwiches and huge batches of eggless sponge, which would be rolled round homemade jam, or cut in small squares and decorated in many different ways. Everyone would be chipping in with the odd spoonfuls of precious tea to fill the two huge urns. Handymen and women were repairing deck-chairs to place them along the boundary.

Mr Endercot was to be the umpire. And excitement was high because this year it was established that Sam Ainsley would be there to play. Lily's husband, an immensely likable man who had the greyish look about him of fine steel, was slim and trim fighting fit. He was twenty-nine years old – and most important – he could outbowl the best for miles around. Cyril Stitson was the captain, and scratch team though the players were, their optimism ran high. Hannah was surprised to learn that James St John was the president. It really did look as though winning would once again be the name of the game.

'I can't wait to cheer everyone on this weekend,' Hannah told them, feeling on top of the world. She was thoroughly enjoying herself until she noticed that she was receiving some very odd looks from a few of the old blokes who usually played dominoes together in the corner. Load of gossips – bad as some of the village bitches, Hannah said to herself, and dismissed them without a second thought.

When Spence appeared, he had a queer glint in his eye. He was, she thought, being rather silly and over-attentive. At first she refused his offer to escort her home, but he made such a poppy-show about it that she finally relented – providing he behaved himself. Raven and Ginnie wished them goodbye.

228

Hannah and Spence were halfway home and had reached a particularly secluded spot when he stopped, turned to face her, looking intense, and put his hands on her shoulders.

'Well, honey,' he said in a smooth and meaningful way. 'How's about it?'

'I beg your pardon?'

'Aw come on, kiddo,' he drawled. 'What gives? If you can spend the night with a Limey, you can give me a go.'

She was nonplussed. 'Spence – what are you talking about?'

'What they're all talking about, the whole goddamn village. I might have figured some handsome guy, but an old bum hanging out in the stables – Jesus!'

He was furious now, coldly angry, and the moonlight made his eyes glint in a spiteful way. He was tall and tough and suddenly she was scared. She turned from him, feeling sick because someone had been saying wicked, untrue things. Worse, she was humiliated because Spence and others actually believed what they had heard. She wanted to run and run, and shout it from the rooftops that she had never done what they said. Instead she said coldly, 'Thank you, Spence. Thank you very much! They could have spun me terrible yarns about you, but I would never have believed them. Never!'

'Cute!' he snapped. 'But words don't mean nothing. Now it's my turn, huh?'

Then he was grabbing her, and forcing her backwards. His knee was nudging her legs apart, his mouth bearing down over hers. She fought him, desperate, writhing like an eel, escape her dearest wish. It was an uneven battle. She fell, he on top of her. With one hand he was tearing at her blouse. He was going to rape her, she knew it. She would die before that happened, she knew that too.

She began fighting him as best she could. Biting and scratching, trying to scream, but he forced his mouth down over hers, bruising her lips with his teeth. Her skirt was being pulled up. He was nearly home. Dear God in heaven, he was nearly there!

She twisted her head away and her scream was high and wild and terrified. Suddenly, in a split second, it was all over. Spence was reeling back. Spence's passion was done. The GI had keeled over, flat on his back, sprawled out on the ground.

Looming over him, powerful, white-faced and furious under the light from the moon, stood James St John.

Chapter Twenty-Seven

James felt exhilaration as the Yank sprawled on the ground before him. However, the man was already struggling to get up. Lord – the thought flashed in James's mind – on films they stay down! He was flexing his muscles to do battle again when a small firecracker flew into his arms. Hannah was sobbing, shocked, thoroughly distressed.

'Take me away, James',' she gasped, then again fiercely, 'please, get me away!'

He held her close and glared at Spence. 'Have you got the message?'

'Sure, you son-of-a bitch.'

Spence stayed down, scowling, aggrieved. He had done nothing wrong, apart from being determined to get his share of pussy. A sure thing, they'd said. So she'd tried the hard-to-get line? It was a kinda game dames played. Sure, he'd gone along. What else was a guy gonna do? Now this, Goddamn it. The Limey lunatic turning up was an unexpected turn of events.

He saw Hannah hanging onto the big lug like there was no tomorrow. Jesus! He gave up.

'I must warn you,' James was saying calmly to Hannah, totally ignoring the now apparently vanquished Yank, 'that I did not bring the car.'

'I don't care.' She was clinging onto him for all her life was worth. 'It's not his fault. It's me! Take me away – please?'

Keeping his arm around her, he about-faced and began walking away. Spence, watching Hannah's retreating back, looked frustrated and swore.

After a little while Hannah whispered shakily, 'Thank you.'

'Think nothing of it.'

'He – he is a nice person usually,' she was saying in a tight, frantic voice. 'He said . . . He thought . . . He was quite wrong!'

'What about?' he asked cryptically. 'You?'

'Yes.'

'But you egged him on, didn't you?'

'No!'

'I saw you kissing him. That sort of thing is bound to give a fellow ideas.'

He felt her stiffen. He tightened his grasp. She relaxed a little and continued to walk within the crook of his arm.

'Correction,' she replied, in a small firm voice. 'You saw *him* kissing *me*. A big difference, you know.'

'Really?'

Suddenly Hannah stood still and looked at him. She was glaring. Moonlight glistened on her face and on the teardrops still there.

'He had the idea that I was fair game,' she told him, and for all she was trying to be calm now, her voice shook. 'It seems that someone has been spreading wicked lies about me. Yes, me and Frank Neilson! And it also seems that these stories are believed.'

'Rubbish!' he told her. 'I know that is what you yourself actually insinuated, but bravado can be seen through any day. I am not stupid. I also know that Trixie's the sort to get your rag out. You're stiff-necked with pride.'

'I'm not – and how dare—'

'And no one in their right mind would believe that odious story – which you yourself began, my dear.'

'You old devil!' she said bitterly. 'Well, if it wasn't you yapping off, it must have been her. After all, it was only you two who saw me leaving the hostel.'

'And half the stable staff.'

'Oh stuff! Who else but that rotten woman would care?'

'Why should someone like Trixie Drew give a damn?' His voice had an edge to it; Hannah was irritating him now. Always ready to put up a fight. Didn't she know that the world could crush her and walk on, not even noticing the pieces?

'Are you deaf, dumb and blind?' Hannah was shaken to the core, look at the state she was in – and here he was pompous swine, sticking up for his own kind, naturally! 'I argued back, didn't I?' she went on bitterly. 'Me a common worker, dared to open my big mouth. And she didn't like it.'

'You're being stupid. Stop it!'

'She thinks I'm dirt between her feet.' Her voice lowered a little as she went on. 'Perhaps I am, and Frank too. I don't know. What I *am* sure of is that I'd never go out of my way to make someone feel small.'

'Oh Lord!' he snapped, exasperated. 'You're carrying on as if these are Victorian times. What happened to the common bond, the fight

231

against the enemy, the "We're all on the same side" idea? Don't you see—'

'I see that so far as manners are concerned,' she rushed on regardless, 'I could knock her into a cocked hat. And another thing . . .'

She had to stop here because hands like steel were gripping her shoulders and shaking her hard.

'How dare you assume the world's against you! How dare to believe you're worth so little?' he gritted. 'You're not dirt beneath anyone's feet – in fact, quite the reverse. And now we'll put an end to this nonsense and get you safely back home.' Coldly furious, brooking no argument, he marched her back to Hawksley.

The kitchen was empty. He plonked her down on a chair by the table and put the kettle on. She was looking at him with dazed, nervous eyes, and he suddenly realised that for all she acted otherwise, she knew very little of the man-woman thing. The Yank had scared her to death, and it showed. She looked washed-out and weary, then becoming aware of his gaze, she tried to smile, play her part. Whether that was brave or stupid he found hard to tell.

'Oh Gawd,' she said, in a light nonchalant way, 'I'll get over this in double-quick time, you know. He caught me offguard, that's all.'

'Well, we'll have to make sure he won't try it on again, won't we?' he drawled.

'Oh, I don't know.' She shrugged and tried to look blasé 'When I think back, perhaps I'll reckon I've had no end of a time, keeping an old bird like you hopping about with clenched fists, I mean.' Suddenly a tinge of colour returned to her cheeks. Her eyes twinkled. 'You didn't half clock him one.'

'No one is allowed to upset my people,' he told her calmly. 'You are one of a highly respected group.'

'Valuable asset to the Estate, ain't I?' She was getting back to normal, even to the point of lipping him. 'But there's no need to worry your hair white. And you don't need to listen to them stupid yarns neither. Ol' man Neilson's nothing to me – at least, not in that way.'

'My dear girl,' he asked, amused. 'What made you think I believed he was?'

'You were furious, that's why. You have a way of looking down your nose, and when something's really getting to you, you go grey. Yes, you do! Like putty.' Her old smile blazed out. 'Ellery and Walt, and blokes in general, go blood red. And you want to see Frank when he's had one over the eight!' As she mentioned the man's name her smile faded. She bit her lip, and again gave him that one quick scared look. 'I'm sorry for rabbiting on,' she finished lamely. 'Never alter, will I? It – it

232

was decent of you to come along and rescue me. I was frightened out of my wits, if the truth be known. I'll never be able to thank you enough, Mr St John.'

Without waiting for the tea, she jumped up and made her escape.

He sat there, fuming. The Mr St John bit had come like a punch on the nose. She had called him James when he had shown up back there. He had rather liked that . . .

A week later James sat in his town office still bemused with thoughts that had crowded into his mind from the night he had rescued Hannah.

Nowadays, on the rare occasions they met, she was more wary of him than ever. She must have kept her fracas with the American secret. The other two girls were always with her. They knew of the rumour-mongering and were going out of their way to show solidarity. Yes, even Raven turned up regular as clockwork at the Rookwood, and they would sit at what was laughingly called 'the Land Girls' table' and joke and act as though they didn't give a damn. But Hannah *did* care. He knew it. And the rotten thing was, that until this vicious mischief-making, Hannah had looked on Lindell as a kind of paradise. One certain thing was, Spence did not visit the Rookwood these days. James smiled wryly to himself.

James now saw that attempted rape would fill any woman with a sense of horror and shame. For Hannah, a girl who was very young for her age, at least so far as chaps were concerned, it must have been a nightmare. The knowledge that he himself had witnessed the sordid business must be making her feel even more humiliated.

Strange how he kept seeing her, as she had been one midday during the twins' summer school holidays. She had been perched on a stile, an urchin in brown dungarees, her short curls dancing in the breeze, eating an apple – a round red one, joking with the young Ainsley boys and calling their dog Ol' Mo. They had all turned as he strode up. Hannah had jumped off the stile in a flash.

'It's all right,' she had said and laughed up into his face. 'Usual break, all square and above-board. Ask Gin if you don't believe me – sir. Oh, and the boys brought me a prezzie. This!' The apple had been held out for inspection. 'Nice, eh?'

He had nodded agreement, wondering how anyone could make the word *sir* sound like the joke of the century. He had not let his face slip in case the young firebrand thought he was poking fun, and went on his way. He heard one of the boys whispering behind his back, 'Old Misery-Guts' followed by boyish sniggering, and Hannah telling them both to be quiet and behave. And he had continued to want to wring her neck because there had still been an underlying chuckle in her admonishment.

On the whole, she remained as prickly as a porcupine where he was concerned, and forever on her guard. He wondered why. Even so, the picture of her perched on the stile had stayed.

James scowled. Women were the bitter end! He would never understand them. Never trust them. Never look to them for help. It was a damned shame that a chap had such strong physical needs. Still, he'd found Veronica's establishment, thank God. Very decent, high-class and exclusive. A fellow got what he wanted there, for the price he could afford, and he could afford plenty.

There were no questions asked at Veronica's. He and she had met socially, at a posh do, raising funds for the War Effort. They had become friends. He had never bothered with Veronica's girls, top-flight though they were. He was one of the favoured few, for Veronica was always there for him.

Veronica was tall and red-haired and very handsome indeed. She was marvelously made-up. In James's fair opinion, she wasn't as good-looking as the fresh-faced Ginnie Betts, but then, 'his' Land Girls were rather special all round. Still, Veronica was easygoing, pleasant company. They enjoyed meals together, with wine from her own substantial cellar, stimulating conversations, and music. Piano music in particular.

Veronica truly believed that she and her team were supplying an important service to high-ranking service men who were lonely and far away from home. She believed she knew all there was to know about men, and scorned women who took them on for, in her words, 'Meal tickets and very little else. . . Girls get rings on their fingers and boys get rings through their noses,' she was won't to scoff. 'As the Americans say, James dear – Big Deal!'

'There are instances of women truly loving their partners,' he'd argued once, thinking of his mother. 'A chap would be darned lucky to find someone like that.'

'Yes, he would,' she had agreed. 'Mind you, it's rare. Most good wives mistake unswerving loyalty for love.'

'What about you?' he had asked, the word 'loyalty' bringing back bad memories . . . mental pictures of himself standing there before that crowd, being judged, found wanting, disbelieved. And hardest to bear, the triumphant looks on those women's faces. And something else – enjoyment! They were greedy for scandal, eyes alight, smirking . . . Remembering made him go hot under the collar even now.

'Me?' Veronica had tossed her red mane and looked proud and

strong, and rather dignified. 'Need you ask James, dear? I'm truly loving and loyal to only one person. Me!'

'And what about my sort of chap?'

'You're what they call a good egg.' Brown eyes had narrowed speculatively. 'You're a friend, and I hope we will always stay on the same footing. I'm fond of you, James. But, and here's the truth of it, I can carry on living very happily, regardless of anyone else. Do you understand?'

'Exactly.' He had thrown back his head and laughed. 'You are so good for me, Veronica.'

'I'm glad to hear it,' she had replied.

Oh yes, he pondered, Veronica was a woman of the world; perhaps she could give some small pointers towards understanding Hannah. He wanted to understand her. She was unique. Perhaps Veronica could explain . . . The idea was banished instantly. He knew that he would never speak to Veronica about Hannah, or vice versa come to that.

He decided that the following weekend, sometime either before or after the cricket match, he would have to have a long talk with Hannah.

Friday evening he boarded the train and made his way back to Lindell.

He found his mother in her private sitting room. She looked as stately and as distant as always. Keeping up her guard, he thought, and still unforgiving. Never accepting that Father's love for her had been as different from his paternal love for Miles and himself as chalk from cheese.

Suddenly James made a vow: the things left unsaid between them for years should now come out into the open. He sat down opposite his mother, folded his arms and looked her straight in the eye. Sophia lifted one eyebrow, stared straight back, then exhaled a cloud of cigarette smoke from between scarlet lips.

'He adored you,' he said bluntly.

'My dear James . . .'

'Don't use that bored tone on me, Mother,' he cut in. 'Listen for a change. Do you know that when we boys were out with Father, he was always talking about you? Wondering what you might think about any given situation. Carefully considering what he believed your opinion would be of certain people when weighing them up. He was remembering you all of the time whether you were with us or not. In fact, he thought you were the cat's whiskers. He always said so and admitted to wanting to please you most of all.'

'What's this?' she asked crisply. 'Are you mad? You're speaking bosh.'

235

'Am I? How else do you suppose he let the Reverend Stiles stay where he was if he hadn't listened very carefully to you?' In spite of himself adding sourly, 'Of course, I can't thank you enough for that, can I?'

Her colour was high. She lifted her chin. Her eyes were crystals alight.

'If he thought I was so wonderful,' she asked, ignoring his question, 'how was it that he and both of you were off at every available minute? How was it that I spent so much of my time here alone?'

'Because you wanted to paint,' he replied dogmatically. 'That was what you always said. You needed to become as good as Grandfather Wray-Evans, and to continue from where he left off. Father respected your wishes and understood that you needed to develop your potential to the full. The trouble was, you never could accept that one cannot hold onto a slice of cake and eat it too.'

'I detect criticism.' The strange green eyes glittered with amusement. 'You really are going over the top, aren't you? I don't know that my actions warrant this. My only crime, apparently, is that I fought to become an artist.'

'No one has to fight to *become* an artist, Mother,' he pointed out. 'One either is or is not as the case may be. No, you have talent, but it wasn't enough, was it? You had to be recognised. You had to receive acclaim. You were obsessed.'

'What are you trying to prove, James.' She was getting angry now.

'That you're a hypocrite,' he said harshly. 'Always wanting to blame everyone else for your bouts of isolation – when they were exactly what you wanted. But you liked playing the martyr, Mother, and you enjoyed throwing tantrums and being unforgivably rude, and you still do. My poor father ... he was so proud of your achievements. He was convinced there wasn't another woman like you on earth. He adored you.' James paused, full of emotion. Then: 'And if you would only take time out to forgive yourself for being a very stupid, extremely volatile and self-centred person all these years, you would believe it, too. Just as Miles and I believed it. Just as we both knew that he loved Miles better than me simply because he was the one who most looked like you. Jealousy is indecent, Mother! Childish and unkind! Jealousy has always been your greatest crime, particularly as it was always directed at your own two sons.'

'You are speaking about things that do not concern you,' she said painfully, and tossed whisky down her throat. 'Oh God! Why don't you just go away?'

'No,' he told her evenly. 'And now I've got that little lot off my

236

chest, I'd like to ask you a question, since I respect your judgment. What do you think about young Hannah?'

She raised her eyebrows in surprise. 'She's a girl who came here to work.'

'That won't do.'

'Ah! You've heard. There are some unhealthy rumours going round the village about her. However, she is coping very well and as only she knows how.'

He smiled bleakly. 'In other words, fighting back with her head held high. Bully for her. Now, Mother, think! About these rumours?'

'Very well, James.' She reached for the decanter. 'Since you seem so interested in this piffling affair, the Neilson creature who works for Mark Drew is her stepfather. Something, I might add, of which she is not particularly proud. Even so, when she heard he had been ill, she felt it only right to go and help him. That is the kind of girl she is. And that is how you and Trixie – what an absurd distortion of a perfectly respectable name – came to see her there. Any more questions?'

'Why Mother,' he said sarcastically, 'you could almost be defending her.'

'She's incorrigible – a cheeky little beast with too much to say for herself. Even so, she is the most difficult of all three girls to really get to know. Surprisingly, she grows on one.' She glared over her glass. 'Not that she's ever in my good books, you understand. She will allow that damned dog to sneak into their sitting room whenever she thinks no one is looking. But yes, I do like her. What's more,' she looked at her son defiantly, 'I am going to help her.'

'How?'

In short cryptic sentences, Sophia told James all there was to know. He listened in silence, allowed her to pour him a large whisky, and finally said, 'I think I'd best weigh in and help too. Had the end of the stick that stinks for most of her life, hasn't she? Where is she right now?'

'Gone! I asked Ellery Endercot to let her off early this afternoon. And believe it or not, I personally wished her luck before I sent her packing. It's necessary for her to get the message across to those brutes as soon as possible. Apparently there's an old woman, a Mrs Carpenter, who will be able to spread the word.'

'You mean, she'll be staying the night?' He was frowning. 'In London – with all the danger there?'

'Hannah will be on her own ground, James. She will know what to do. She told me that she will not be staying with this Carpenter person, but might just look up a Mrs Gibson who is the landlady of Matt

Sheridan. Remember him – the Air Gunner who is missing? Hannah is fond of him and believes that he is still alive.'

'I'm going after her.'

'Where? You know she has no home, at least one that is standing. Why do you wish to go, James? To protect her? And just how can you do that?'

'You're spluttering, Mother. As to why, she is my responsibility.'

'Correction. She is a worker on our Estate. That is all.'

'Is it?' he asked belligerently. 'You admitted to quite liking her a minute ago.'

They stared into each other's eyes, both strong-willed. Both determined not to give way. Then Sophia shrugged.

'James,' she told him, 'there is nothing you can do to help at this stage. And this weekend, everything must revolve round the cricket match. That will be the only thing on everyone's mind. No one will realise that Hannah is missing – and instinct tells me that it's better that way. Oh, and I suppose you know that Beatrice is gunning for her? It was she who started all the talk.'

'Damned bitch!' he snapped, his eyes holding flint.

She was staring at him contemplatively. 'My God!' she said at last. 'You are finally becoming human. You're actually going to step down from that high horse of yours to defend our young field-worker! You'll be telling me next that you are actually prepared to go further than being nominally pleasant to Raven when next you meet.'

'Mother!'

'Oh yes! It's there for all the world to see. That stately young woman is getting under your skin, and I couldn't be more pleased. But now for a naughty child like Hannah to be taken under your lordly wing . . . My God! You are getting soft in your old age.'

'I would do the same for any one of them.'

'Well, thankfully it will not be necessary. Ginnie is off home for the weekend, cricket or no. Letters from Aiden, her fiancé, are still arriving there. Raven will be keeping me company. Incidentally, if the rumours about Hannah offend you, why not go to the Rookwood and stop one or two of those clacking tongues? Both Ginnie and Raven have been down there, defending Hannah to the death every time they got the chance. Those girls seem to have a common bond of friendship that is quite unusual.'

'I will treat myself to a pint or two,' he answered, adding, 'and perhaps Raven will join me?'

'I am afraid not,' Sophia replied crisply. 'Raven and I are to spend the evening together; it has all been arranged. I do not have many

238

pleasures in life and speaking with Raven happens to be one of them. For this evening at least, she is wholly mine.'

'Then it appears,' he told her, 'that someone else in the family's getting human, too – doesn't it?'

Chapter Twenty-Eight

It was Saturday night. Hannah continued her search for Ma Carpenter. She had tried three of the local pubs already, and rather than go back to the old dear's smelly house and wait with the evil-eyed Tom, she decided to press on.

Up until now everything had been a resounding no-no. The worst blow had been to finally locate Mrs Gibson's house, only to find it a broken shell; the inside and back wall had been completely blown out. Neighbours explained that Mrs Gibson had died on the night of the raid, also two of her lodgers. Shocked, Hannah had wandered off, became lost for a while, and ended up in a nearby shelter.

Now it was her second night in London and undeniably the blackout was a bloody nuisance. Then the warning cleared its throat and began to whine up and down just as it had the night before. Talk about Wailing Winny, Hannah sighted tiredly. I wonder how many are as angry and as scared as me whenever they hear that sound. Not that I'd admit it. I'd drop dead first! She had to smile to herself at that.

Guns began pounding away in the distance. There came the faint droning of planes. Against the far horizon, pencil-slim beams of light began criss-crossing the sky. It was, Hannah considered, all quite appalling. During the previous night, in the same shelter that she was heading for now, she had heard accounts of life during recent air-raid attacks that had left her marvelling at the courage of her fellow Londoners.

In spite of the German's belief that victory over England was now only a question of time, she had seen not one ounce of proof. No one here even considered the idea of defeat. And so the people dug their toes in. There was endurance and courage as well as horror and humour, and above all, the determination to press on.

Right now, local searchlights were making great arcs, and explosions were happening one after another all around. Amazingly,

Hannah found it impossible to be feel frightened. This because it was all on such an enormous scale. It numbed the senses and made everything seem unreal.

History was repeating itself; it was Walker Street all over again. Incendiaries were falling like rain. Ack-ack guns were cracking her ears apart, leaving what seemed like dizzy spaces full of pins and needles in her head. The red-orange sky was awesome, obscene.

She began to run full pelt, reaching the shelter at last. It was claustrophobic and dully lit. Figures lay sleeping on the ground, shrouded with blankets, their shoeless feet poking out at the ends; strange grey log-shapes, breathing and snoring, looking like mythical creatures waiting endlessly in a vacuum. Above all, stubbornly refusing to die.

Good old Londoners, Hannah thought fondly. They drank some odd drinks and smoked even odder cigarettes. Young women painted black seam-lines on their legs simply because there were no stockings to be had. Food was scarce, apart from the 'British Restaurants', of course. Everywhere was bunged-up with sandbags. Queues waited with unbelievable patience. Dreaded telegrams arrived and grief was paramount. Yet even so, general morale remained high.

Hannah, born and bred in the city, was not too surprised at the stoical adaptability of everyone. Nowadays, war had simply become a part of their lives. People could and did laugh, sometimes at foul remarks about Hitler, at Tommy Trinder's jokes, and the Crazy Gang's pranks. They admired Ol' Bulldog Winnie, and adored the royals – the King and Queen and two young princesses who bravely stayed in the capital. Everyone knuckling down and doggedly doing their thing on the Home Front.

The brave became braver, the crooks more crooked; heroes were made, martyrs were born. Black Marketeers grew richer by the day. There were men called Spivs and some named Drones, and coolly superior wireless announcers held sway. *Workers' playtime* blared out, messages were given over the air and Vera Lynn became loved by every serviceman.

It's a Lovely Day Tomorrow, sang the Sweetheart of the Forces. Also *We'll Meet Again, There'll Be Bluebirds Over the White Cliffs of Dover* . . . sentimental songs that pulled at the strings of the soul.

Hannah listened as the people at the other end of the shelter started up a little party. Someone had a squeezebox and they were bouncing out *Run Rabbit Run, Rabbit, Run, Run, Run*, followed by other rumbustious numbers.

Hannah's lids became heavy.

'*London Pride has been handed down to us. London Pride is a flower that grows . . .*'

241

Far away in the distance she heard the All Clear. It did not matter. Nothing mattered except the overwhelming need for sleep . . .

'Oi, you!' The harsh voice woke her and she blinked because someone was shining a torchbeam directly into her eyes. 'Silly cow, what d'yer come down here for, eh? You know I always go up the Blackbirds.'

Hannah struggled up until she was resting on her elbows. 'You weren't in there when I looked, Ma,' she said sleepily. 'Goo' night.'

'Not so much of that, moo-face. I've been traipsing all round looking for you. I was told as how you wanted ter see me, and so help me, I'm bloody well here now, so talk!'

'Oh!' Hannah was fully awake now. 'Thank you, Ma. I – I have a message that has to be passed on. And . . .'

'Since I'm the local fog-horn, it's me what gets the pleasure?'

'If you don't mind, Ma!'

'As a matter of fact, I sodding well *do* mind. I've been going round all over the place trying to find you. Thought you might have word of Frank.'

'I have. Oh, I have!'

'Then spit it out. 'Ere!' A large flask was handed over. 'Take a swig of this, girl. It's hot and sweet, just how you like it.'

'Tea – you angel! Thank you, Ma.'

'Don't thank me,' a wrinkled face creased in a monkey grin. 'Give me a half a crown.'

'Will sixpence do?'

'Cor, bleeding hell!' Ma Carpenter said.

Hannah sipped gratefully at the hot brew, sweetened by milk, then told Ma, 'This is something very serious. You see, I know where Frank is. At the moment he is getting stronger. He has been very, very ill. Now the whole point is this. He has seen things, witnessed things, and is prepared to go to Court to spill the beans. He has proof beyond doubt, about what Biff Marner, Ram Rawlins and Fatty Blythe have been up to. He has written a full statement, naming names, times, places, everything! Anyway, all of this has been sealed in an envelope and placed in a bank. It will be delivered to the police if anything ever happens to Frank or me. That – that's the message we need them to get, Ma.'

'Bloody hell, mate, it sounds like you've got friends.'

'Frank has! And he wants you to make sure that they learn about the letter, and to keep out of our way if they don't want it to go to the law.'

'Gawd's strewth! Got 'em by the short and curlies, ain't he?' Ma's

242

grin went, then she shook her head. 'But I can't help yer, girl. I would if I could, but I can't.'

'Why?'

'Gorn up in the world, ain't they? Got bags of lolly with all them dealings they do. Made fortunes they have, make no mistake. And they've moved away from their common old haunts.'

'But you must know where they are?'

'No. Posh they are these days. Out of my class. Hanging out in them bleeding hotels where guests think their own shit don't stink. All togged up an' smoking cigars, the last I heard. I also heard that they 'ave half the rats in London working for 'em.' Ma winked meaningfully, and tapped the side of her nose. 'Vermin what are making sure faint hearts don't let 'em down. Like not doing what they're told. Know what I mean? All doing them dodgy deals. Black Market of course, and paying up, and keeping their bloody traps shut.'

'But it's important, Ma,' Hannah told her. 'Think about it. If they have so much to lose, they'll make sure they catch up with Frank one of these bright fine days.' She smiled wryly. 'Not that there's much of him these days: he's all skin and bone. Do your best to help him, eh? Spread the word.'

'Lor' luv yer, 'course I will,' Ma said stoutly. 'Now 'ave another cuppa char. Tell you what, we'll try up the Sunday Market tomorrow if you like. I can ask ol' Charlie, and there's Ginge, and Lou. We'll sort it, gel.'

'I've got to get back tomorrow, Ma.'

'Oh? Well, don't worry. I'll see what I can do.'

'You promise?'

'I promise yer!' Ma said.

Chapter Twenty-Nine

During the journey back to Lindell Hannah felt relief. Ma would get the message to Biff and Co. Once that happened she and Frank would be free of fear. Now she really could get on with living, put the past behind her – she hoped.

The motion of the train, the merry clackety-clack was soothing somehow. She was cocooned in a carriage filled to choking point with remote-looking strangers. All typically English, intent as ever on keeping themselves to themselves.

Hannah lay back against the upholstery and closed her eyes. A picture of James danced before her. How stern he was – how superior. It had come as a shock, the way he had put himself out to help on that terrible night – when poor old Spence had got it all wrong. Her lips twitched, remembering that mighty punch James had delivered. Who would have thought he had it in him to so nice! Which he probably was, when he forgot to be such a miserable old stick in the mud. He was not in the least like rakish, laughing-eyed Matt. Matt was a fun person, a don't-give-a-damn sort of chap that she felt at home with. Oh yes, she'd had some good old chuckles with Matt.

She frowned. It all seemed so long ago – that night with Matt, and Lenny playing the violin. Hannah suddenly found herself wondering just what Matt would make of Ma. Would they have liked each other? Probably. Yes, she was sure they'd find something to chuckle about. Dear old Matt. Nothing could get him down . . .

Another train journey, Matt thought, and fought to hold back despair. It was all taking so long and it was his fault. He should have been able to fight off the second bout of fever that had brought him so low. Thank God for all the helpers he had had on the way. They had ignored the fact that he was a dead loss, with a leg that splayed out, ulcers forming, and a back that permanently ached. The rare and hasty medical checks he had received had helped. Medicine, dressings and pain-killers had been delivered whenever possible, but the occasions were few and far between.

Matt knew that whereas other chaps had safely and rapidly been taken along the chain, his journey to freedom had been a long and painful affair. He still missed young Henri. The boy had left him and returned to the farm, having delivered him to a real tough-nut – the black-eyed, scar-faced Jacques. Jacques hadn't seemed to mind taking a cripple under his wing, though. He was neither friendly nor unfriendly, just matter-of-fact.

It was Jacques who had taken him to the crowded station platform where the train was ready and waiting. People were climbing aboard, cramming themselves inside carriages, but Jacques deliberately made for the corridor. There was a group of chaps already there – clearly workers, grimy, ill-kempt. Jacques looked from one to the other of them, searching with his eyes, then seemed satisfied. When the train pulled out of the station, Jacques murmured something to a small, stocky bloke wearing a white scarf. Instinct told Matt this was also a member of the Resistance.

All was going well until they slowed down and finally stopped in a station. There was a babble of sound and above it, a metallic voice making an announcement through a loudspeaker. *Achtung, Achtung,* and something about identity. Jacques sidled up to Matt.

'Gestapo,' he growled under his breath. 'Get your identification papers ready.'

Within seconds Matt found himself being stared at and subjected to an order rapped out in German. Wordlessly he gave up his papers. Blue, marble-hard eyes lifted from the photograph, unblinkingly scrutinising him. Matt felt his skin crawl. The stare became insolent and the papers were shoved back towards him with unnecessary force. Matt accepted them and the punch in the chest in silence – and felt old, old, old.

Three hours later, his group left the train, boarded another, and were told it was heading for Foix. Here fortune was with them. They had a carriage to themselves; they could speak, although few bothered. Jacques told them casually, 'This is your last train journey, Messieurs.'

'And then?' Matt asked.

'Why, the Pyrénées.'

Matt let his breath go in a burst of relief. 'Shouldn't be long now then.'

Jacques shrugged expressively. 'If you are fit, it will not be too long.'

When they arrived at the small town of Foix there was no real

245

station as such. Passengers jumped off, or in Matt's case, struggled down – and from there they walked into the town. Here, they were split into smaller groups. Matt accompanied by Jacques, was grateful to be taken to a café and served with a drink – the first thing to pass his lips for hours. He savoured each mouthful before swallowing and felt the world becoming a rosier place.

On the signal to leave, they were escorted along the street until they reached a house only half-built. In the cellar it was warm and the floor was liberally spread with straw.

'You must rest,' the guide said. 'Sleep, for in the early hours the Spanish guide will come. Then, my friends, you will begin your journey.'

Matt lay in silent contemplation. He was thinking of a beautiful young woman, one with large, dark velvety eyes. To his left he heard an exasperated, 'Goddamn it!'

'Ugh!' Matt burst out. 'One of the things has crawled up my trousers.'

He kicked out wildly with his good leg. The American beside him swiped out at a mouse, missed and hit Matt's injury. Pain seered through him, making him grit his teeth. The wound was really poisoned, had refused to clear up no matter what. The throbbing had become part of his life. Now for the first time he began to wonder whether he would be able to make it over the Pyrénées. This whole business had changed him, he knew it. The worst thing of all was the humiliation. Some hero, he thought, hating himself. Some buggering hero! They're all but carrying me!

He felt a movement against his cheek 'Bloody things!' he grunted, and jerked his head away and swore again. He knew that he would always remember the smell of this hiding places; warm, sour straw and the choking odour of mice.

Matt decided that his only chance was to forget his leg, his back, and his general debilitation. He must think only that every step he took would bring him a little nearer to the fantasy woman of his dreams. The one with the face of a painting he'd seen once, in the chapel at the orphanage. It was of the Virgin Mother – serene and beautiful.

As a lonely orphan his soul had cried out for someone to hold him as the Holy Mother had held that Child. He knew he would give his life to have someone wonderful to love him like that. To cradle him so that he could relax, forget the pain, sleep and let the whole lousy world go hang for a change.

Good Lord! he thought, and tried to pull himself together. What's up? I'm thinking like a chump. I've got to stop it – rise above it. Be the bloke I used to be. I bloody well must! What was young Hannah's creed? Life must all boil down to having had more laughter than tears. Jesus Christ! he swore. How wrong could you be?

In the early hours the rest of the group, French, Americans, two Jews and a Pole, all left the hiding place. They stood together, shivering in the grey darkness. The cold was intense. Matt pulled up the collar of his coat and thanked God and the baker for it. Some of the group were given loaves to carry on the journey. It was sheer luxury, just to smell the hot freshly-baked aroma of that bread. It made the belly rumble, the mouth water, it made one realise what the basics of life actually were. Those not carrying bread were handed out canteens of water, equally precious. Very often since the crash, Matt's mouth had been dry for hours.

A large man unwrapped himself from the shadows and walked towards them. He was wearing a white scarf. Satisfied that everyone was within hearing he said, 'Messieurs, I am happy to introduce you to Dieguito, your guide. He will take you to a meeting point on the Pyrénées, where the second guide will arrive from Andorra. Now, my friends, you will please be silent whilst leaving the town. That is all. *Au revoir!*'

The people who had brought them thus far shook hands all round.

'*Vamos!*' the guide said abruptly.

After that they set off at a quiet, heart-pounding pace. The houses were left behind, then they were in the density of a wood which ended as suddenly as it had begun. Now they slithered over dew-wet grass which sloped upwards in a gradual introduction to a high mountain. The grass gave way to rocks, the rocks to boulders.

They climbed higher and morning mists eddied round their feet like grey phantoms. Matt was feeling half-dead by the time Dieguito motioned to them to sit down.

'Rest while you can,' he advised. 'We wait for new guide. Then the real journey will begin . . .'

It was October already. Smoky nights abounded, and two young boys carried on to Hannah about bonfires. A real Guy Fawkes night was out of the question, of course, because of the black-out, but Lily had promised a sort of party night on 5 November with roast potatoes for all that.

Local cider-making was in progress. There were apples aplenty. Cider was a jolly good drink, Hannah discovered; so was mead. The local policeman, Jack Dalton, who lived in the station-cum-cottage that looked picturesque enough for a chocolate-box pic, kept bees. PC Dalton was also an expert distiller of mead, and consequently a very popular man! Mrs Kitt's sloe gin, put up the year before, was like nectar from the gods. She suddenly acquired a great many friends. It was an annual joke enjoyed by everyone.

Hannah just lapped up all of these country fun and games. She had returned from London feeling more confident, and had reported back to her friends, and to Sophia and Frank. She had also penned a letter for Lenny to send to his 'High-Up' friend in the Red Cross. In it, she reported that Matt's room in Mrs Gibson's house was, sadly, no more. But there was always a place for him in Mr and Mrs Endercot's home. Perhaps the letter would reach Matt. You never knew.

Hannah had also made it her business to go to Knollys and speak to James. Feeling like a kid up before the Head, she reported things as they had happened, then, just as she faltered into silence, he stepped forward and put a hand on each of her shoulders and stared down at her in a fierce, almost aggressive way.

'Don't keep things to yourself,' he told her sternly. 'We are here to help.'

'Are you?' she asked, then throwing caution to the winds: 'I wondered. Sometimes you look like—'

'Yes?' His question was a challenge.

'Well – I wish you'd explain something that's been puzzling me a lot. Sometimes you look down your nose and act as though you hate me.' His face was turning to stone; his eyes were pebble-hard. She heard herself ending rather lamely, 'But since you stuck up for me, and clocked Spence such a fourpenny one, I've been wondering lately why you seem to detest women so?'

A shutter closed over his face. He became once more inscrutable.

'Don't be absurd,' he told her in a clipped voice. 'Members of the female sex are not important enough for me to hate.'

She had coloured, feeling snubbed, wishing with all her heart she hadn't asked the question. Then she felt angry. The man was impossible!

'Cor blimey – pardon me for breathing,' she flared. 'Why is it that you make me feel like a useless kid!'

Then, infuriating to the last, he suddenly grinned. 'They don't allow kids in the Rookwood.' He had said it so meaningfully that her face had gone hotter than before and she had wanted to die.

But after that incident, James's duties seemed to allow him more time at home. Sometimes he even slept in his room in Hawksley and would join them for breakfast.

'Keeping an eye on us all,' Hannah sniffed. 'Pig!'

'He likes speaking about horses,' Raven said quietly, 'which is rather nice.'

Ginnie said nothing at all, which spoke for itself.

248

James rode Pegasus a lot. During her visits to Frank's place, Hannah often saw James and Trixie Drew riding together. Then she would make a grimace and feel cross – until she saw Raven riding up on Blue Rinse to join them. That was quite a different matter!

Frank was gradually turning back to the man she remembered from her childhood. Cheerful, kindly, and at peace with himself. A rough diamond, in other words, and still rather frail.

Things were not all right in the Rookwood yet, unfortunately. Little cliques of spiteful people would carry on with their censorious looks, snidey remarks, shoulder-nudging and sniggering behind their hands. Their topic was still the ever-fascinating subject of Hannah, and Frank. Yes, unbelievably, about her and her stepdad Frank!

'Are we going out tonight, dear?' Raven asked one evening after a particularly tough hedging and ditching day.

'Yes,' Hannah said without joy.

'Me too,' Ginnie said.

Hannah smiled. 'You are real mates, but you don't have to, you know. I can go alone: I'm not scared of that lot. Sticks and stones and all that.'

'To coin a phrase.' Raven's dark eyes glowed. 'The Three Musketeers?'

'Up guards and at 'em, eh?' Hannah's grin beamed over her face.

'Exactly!' Ginnie replied for them both.

Washed and changed, chatting vivaciously, they made their way to the Rookwood. Inside, it was alight, alive and welcoming – until one became conscious of little knots of people glancing at the Land Girls and obviously indulging in some serious tittle-tattling. Whisky Fran, a tough old bag of bones, and a couple of her dusty old cronies were sitting at the Land Girls' table. At the arrival of Hannah and her two friends, the old besoms got up and with wicked looks and turned-down mouths, pointedly left the table.

'Ignore them,' Ginnie said, smiling with gritted teeth. 'And sit down.'

They sat in place.

'The usual?' Raven asked, then at their requests for 'Shandy, please' she went to the bar. She was a lady through and through, Hannah thought, the epitome of grace.

The group at the next table were making suggestive remarks out loud, about supposedly innocent girls staying in old men's rooms until the wee hours – then walking home alone. Hannah and Ginnie were speaking quietly together, trying to ignore the talk, but the former's cheeks were red.

'You must let me tell them the truth, dear,' Raven told her, catching the tail-end of the gossip. 'This whole business is going from bad to worse and you must let me put a stop to it.'

'Let me put them straight,' Ginnie said bluntly. 'I want to!'

'Why should you?' Hannah asked. 'It's their problem if their own lives are so empty that they have to worry about mine. Why don't you two go and sit at one of the other tables? They'll treat you like lepers while you stay with me.'

'Shut up!' Ginnie told her. Raven merely looked hurt.

'Bloody hell!' Hannah exploded, 'Now look what the cat's dragged in.'

James walked in, the beautifully turned-out Trixie Drew on his arm.

'They're slumming, darling,' Hannah snorted. 'And doesn't James know it? As for dear Beatrice, she looks like she's got a smell under her nose. She's probably only here to keep tabs on James. And who on earth in their right mind would want *him*?'

'Oh, I don't know,' Raven teased in her quiet way. 'He has his points, you know.'

'Yes. On three prongs!'

This made Ginnie chuckle out loud.

James pretended not to notice Hannah, Raven and Ginnie. Then Hannah experienced a sense of shock. Walking directly behind James and Trixie was none other than Frank. Eyes wide and unbelieving, Hannah saw that her stepfather was more than usually tidy. For once in his life he was wearing a half-decent outfit.

James strode up to the bar, reached over it and grasped the hand-bell used for proclaiming Time. At once, all conversation stopped. Then James looked round at everyone – except for the table where Hannah and her friends sat. As soon as he was sure of everyone's attention he spoke.

'Good evening ladies, gentlemen. I have come to make an announcement – that will come as something of a surprise to even my closest friends.'

'Gawd,' Hannah whispered to Ginnie. 'I didn't think he had any close friends.'

'Shut up!' Ginnie hissed back.

James continued, unaware: 'I would like to introduce Mr Frank Neilson.' He pulled the unwilling Frank forward. 'He is currently working at Drews. Now before I go any further, I will mention this for the benefit of some of you here. It is not generally known that Mrs St John and I are shareholders in Drews, and have been from the moment we decided to stable our own nonworking animals there. I am stressing this point for specific reasons.'

250

There was a murmuring from some of the Drew employees, a shuffling of feet, and looks of discomfort. Everyone there was now openly wondering what James St John was going to come out with next. The man was usually taciturn , and any announcements were usually left to old Ellery or someone of the like kind to make. In other instances orders were pinned up on the Estate office wall.

'To continue,' James said, 'Mr Neilson was badly injured during a London air raid. He also lost his home and all of his possessions' His gimlet eyes swept round at them all in turn. 'However, he came to Lindell and settled among us quite happily until he became ill. It was then that Mr Neilson began to receive regular visits from Miss York, our young Land Army friend.'

'The rotten old devil!' Hannah seethed, going bright red. 'What's he up to now?'

James had everyone's full attention. He stood there, legs astride, arms folded, very much master of the situation. He seemed totally unaware of Frank's glowering discomfort, and of Trixie's look of horror and chagrin.

'Now I understand,' James continued coldly, 'that my girls have been suffering at the hands of gossips. This is to end here and now. I will point out that, as you and PC Dalton know, there is such a thing as the law of slander. However, it will not go that far. I am expecting all of you – particularly those in my employ – to set the village straight on a matter in hand. Mr Frank Neilson is in point of fact Miss Hannah York's stepfather. She will be visiting him whenever possible and vice versa.' Again that cold, fiercesome look. 'Do I make myself clear?'

Hannah felt that everyone in the world was looking at her. She wanted to die. Then embarrassment gave way to fury. How dare he turn up like an avenging angel and make a poppy show out of her and Frank?

She sat at the table, red-faced and glaring, hating him through and through. He seemed quite unmoved, merely gave her a stern look back. Then he turned round, shook hands with several people he knew, and coolly agreed to join Ellery in a pint. Frank, still looking awkward, asked for and received a soft drink at the bar. He must have changed his drinking habits!

Clearly infuriated, Trixie turned her back on James, having refused a drink, and imperiously ordered one of the Drew employees to escort her home.

James then proceeded to have a good time with his cricket-crazy friends. Bob Mitchell, the proprietor of the Rookwood, himself brought over a bottle of the inn's best fizzy white wine to the girls,

251

with Mr St John's compliments. Raven thanked him and smiled and nodded her appreciation. Ginnie did too. Hannah merely sulked.

Betty Joyce came over to join the girls.

'They're all cockahoop, yer know,' she told them. 'And now you're in their talk.'

'Really?' Raven asked, smiling and as calm as you please. 'Is that good or bad? Do tell!'

'Mr James says since the cricket team beat Little Norseby hands down, and we're going from strength to strength, that yes he would support the darts team. That he would like to see his girls also try their hand. Little Norseby's got a women's team, Ellery says, but Lindell hasn't been too bothered about it till now, being short of members and that.' Bet smiled her smudgy smile. 'Ellery was also saying that you three have all beat the best in this pub. Now Mr St John's convinced "his girls" will knock the socks off Norseby. He's a real proud person, yer know.'

'Bloody cheek!' Hannah said. 'And I wish he wouldn't keep calling us his girls.'

'It might be fun,' Ginnie remarked.

'I wouldn't mind,' Raven added, to everyone's surprise.

'Well, I'm not going to,' Hannah said fiercely.

'Yes, you are,' Ginnie told her. 'And stop glaring like that.'

'I'm going to kill him,' Hannah snapped. 'Kill him stone dead.'

'Shut up and grab another seat. Your stepdad's coming over. He looks half-dead. Now try to be nice!'

Frank looked tired but happy enough now that he was no longer the focal point of all eyes. Hannah introduced the girls to him and he nodded and greeted them, clearly on his best behaviour. Then Ellery gained Ginnie and Raven's attention, Hannah's too, but she merely smiled and continued to sit next to Frank. The other two joined Ellery at the bar.

'Sorry, mate,' Frank said gruffly, now that they were alone. 'He's a bit of a bastard, your guvernor, eh? Just marched in and told me to get meself changed. That you needed support and I was going ter give it to yer, like it or lump it. Honest Han, I didn't want ter show you up.'

'You didn't. He did.'

'He's a bit of a big 'ead, ain't he?'

'He's got every right, Frank. He socked someone once, on my behalf. Knocked him down flat! Mind you, he looks as though he could go ten rounds with Joe Lewis when he's really angry.' Her wicked but determined grin transformed her as she promised, 'And he's going to be good and furious by the time I've done with him over this little lot.'

252

'You shut your gob, Han. He's your boss. 'Sides . . .'

'Yes?'

'I like knowing you're not too far away. Know what I mean?'

'Gawd, Frank. Here – how is it that you're drinking orange squash? Or is it hiding a splash or two of gin?'

''Orspital's rules. I was knocked abart a bit, remember? And my insides got a bashing. They said me liver's a bit suspect, so here I am, no alcohol. I'm all right really, but I can tell you, they managed to put the shits up me good and true.'

Hannah was watching him closely. 'You really like it over there with those old horses, don't you, Frank?' she said quietly.

''S'right. But I ain't going ter stay at Drews.'

'Good! I think darling Trixie might make things uncomfortable for you.'

'Ain't nothing to do with her. It's His Nibs what said it. I'm going over to Cobbitt and work with Clancy. D'yer know 'im?'

'No, I don't.'

'Well, he looks after the Estate's working 'orses. Big old devils they are. Their stables are by the Cobbitt orchards. Ain't you been over there?'

'Not quite so far, no.'

'Well, we'll be picking apples next year, according to the guvenor. Yers, mate, he's said I'm all right where me job's concerned . He just wants me on the St John's part, nuffink like to do with the Drews. I'll miss old Snow Queen though. Miss her rotten. She and me get on. Like me and old Firelord did, in fact.'

'Did you tell Mr St John this?'

'Of course I did. He softened up a bit. Said I'm allowed to visit her.'

'It strikes me,' Hannah said pithily, 'that James St John just loves to play God.'

Frank gave her a look. 'Stone the crows,' he said, 'you look like you hate his guts. Yet you was sticking up for the bloke a moment back. Said as how he knocked some other poor sod down.'

'I don't hate him,' she replied. 'It's just that he really irritates me.'

'Bloody hell. Poor bugger. Now you've got me feeling sorry for him.'

There came a dry rough sound, a rusty croaking noise. It was the infinitely rare grating of Frank's laugh.

Chapter Thirty

They were together, standing on frosty ground in an exposed spot, with the wind whistling all around them. Their hands and feet were frozen stiff, in spite of woolly gloves, socks and hobnailed working boots. Their faces were chapped and noses red.

'My Gawd!' Hannah said, her breath gusting out in steam. 'I'm wondering why I joined this little lot. I must have been mad.'

'It's lovely in the summer,' Ginnie replied, and her eyes sparkled with humour, like emeralds caught in light.

Hannah shrugged at her, thinking, dear old Ginnie. She's her own calm, beautifully certain self these days. I wish I was as sure of things.

She lifted her pick to break the ice. They were busily taking the soil off the potato clamps that lined the edge of the field. Hannah wished nastily that she could get the chance to use her pick on darling James some time. He had returned to the city before she had been able to face him. Now she was hoping and praying that he would come back to Lindell at the weekend.

'Do you remember the looks on their faces when he went mouthing on about how he and Sophia are part-owners of Drews?' she said bitterly. 'And that Trixie's expression! She didn't like the bit about the St John's owning part of Drews, did she? Took her down a peg, that did. I could almost forgive the black devil for putting Madam Marm-stink in her place. But I won't forgive him. Never! And as for—'

'Shut up,' Ginnie said at last. 'You're being hateful and you know it.'

'How would you like it?' Hannah retorted fiercely. 'Having the whole world learn your private business?'

'The man was sticking up for you, for all of us, and don't you forget it. To my mind, he should be given three rousing cheers for what he did.'

'Frank wanted to die.'

'You mean *you* did. Yes, you! You went red as fire and just about curled up.'

'Well?'

'So change your record, Hannah,' Ginnie replied, quite unmoved. 'You're getting boring, which is quite unlike you.'

'Not boring,' Raven put in quietly. 'Ungracious.'

Hannah glared at them both in turn, knowing that they spoke no less than the truth. They weren't to know that she hated being beholden to James. Ever since he had come upon her, on the ground, pinned down by Spence, kicking and fighting, she had felt ill-at-ease in his presence. What a sight she must have been. Hannah cringed miserably. But she had been fighting for her honour, after all!

Of course it would have turned out terribly different if James had not been there, so why was she so angry? The plain fact was that James St John got her rag out more than ever these days. Unlike her dearest friends. Never them! She smiled over at them in her wide all-embracing smile.

'Sorry! I don't know what gets into me at times.'

There came a thunderous roaring overhead and they stiffened, knowing that their little concerns were piffling compared with what was going on. Heavy British and American bombers taking off on their missions to Europe, soaring up from runways like a flock of formation-flying geese. Huge predatory birds, stiff-winged, heavy-bellied with explosive, death-dealing eggs.

Far beneath them now, Matching Airfield, with its Nissen huts, corrugated-iron hangars and prefabricated sheds. Its sleeping bunks and private spaces were plastered with photographs of girls back home; of Mom or Ma, wonderful ladies brilliant at making blueberry or apple pies. And too, there were pictures of families, friends, and leggy pin-up stars. A hugamug of persona captured and held on paper and card, little things but precious all the same, all pinned up on the airbase walls that the fliers might never see again.

'Blow me,' Hannah said, smile dying, 'I can't stand that noise, and just thinking about things makes me want to either blub my eyes out, or swear.'

'No time to do either,' Ginnie said, 'Come on, let's get cracking. Bet said that Lily left a message saying that since we're near enough to cycle back midday, she'll make us some toast and hot soup. That means we can eat all our beetroot sandwiches in one go.'

'Now she tells us!' Hannah marvelled. 'I've been starving for hours. Let me get at the lovely grub.'

'When I'm an old married woman,' Ginnie said pensively, 'I swear I'll never give Aiden beetroot sandwiches. No, not for as long as I live.

They're not so bad with cheese, but when the ration's run out like now – yuk!'

'Don't worry.' Hannah was really cheering up. 'The soup will be tasty. Lily has been boiling that chicken carcass for hours and it will be as good and filling as always. She's a wizard at doing all them chopped carrots and things that go in the pot. They really make it nice.'

'Lily is a wonder,' Ginnie agreed. 'Miles better than Peggy even, and I won't even say a word about poor old Bet. It's Lily that's the real genius, and she's going to teach me all kinds of home-making things, including cookery. I have it all mapped out in my mind. Aiden will have no complaints, I promise you.'

'My old man, if I ever get one,' Hannah told her and chuckled in a merry way, 'won't know if he's on his head or his heels. Know why? It'll be because I'll be missing half the time.'

'Where will you be?' Ginnie asked, intrigued.

'Queuing outside the fish and chip shop, of course.'

'That means,' Raven told her, quietly teasing, 'that you'll practically be living in enemy territory – considering the nearest shop is at Little Norseby. That is, if you are still determined to stay here in Lindell after the war.'

'I don't want to move away from here – ever.'

'I shall go back to Ilford,' Ginnie told them with certainty. 'Aiden's parents own a shop that sells paint and wallpaper, paste, nuts and bolts, door panels and all kinds of decorating things. Before the war he used to work in it with his father.' She turned to Raven. 'Will you go back to Surrey after here?'

Raven shook her head. 'I don't think so, Like Hannah, I shall stay.'

'In Knollys, naturally,' Hannah jibed.

'Really?' Raven looked at her quizzically. 'Are you still trying to pair me off with James?'

'Well, you like him, don't you?'

'Yes, I told you that I do. A great deal, in fact. However . . .'

'Now what's up?'

'James is the opposite to Francis in every way. My husband was, well – a poet.'

'And James looks a very physical man,' Ginnie said bluntly.

'I was going to say down-to-earth.' Raven sounded slightly aggrieved. 'He is not a dreamer, so far as I can tell, so . . .'

'I'll tell you what he is!' Hannah began threateningly, and they both turned to her, laughing in unison: 'No, please don't!'

So grinning back at them, Hannah shut up.

After that they worked in silence, in the bitter cold. Later they huddled under a hedge to eat the sandwiches Betty had made, the beetroot tasting as cold as ice. Then there was the hot tea from the flasks. It was rather disgusting, without the magic of Lily's touch, and it left the taste of saccharine in their mouths. It smelled even worse, as though it had been stewed which was not the case; still, it was comforting just the same. But tea, hot, tasty or otherwise, was a two-edged sword. There came the moment each girl dreaded.

Hannah wandered round the edge of the field until she came to a thick clump of holly bushes. Feeling she was well out of view she proceeded to let her trousers down in order to spend a penny. It was a relief, since, like her two mates, she hung on for as long as she could. This was the most vulnerable moment for a Land Girl, something that had not been anticipated in the first flush of enlisting. Usually the girls went in pairs, so that one could keep watch. Today the world seemed empty so Hannah went alone.

Now, squatting there, shivering, she could smell the frosted clay, and the mustiness of rotting winter leaves. There was a fresh, stringy sort of smell coming from the holly leaves. The berries were still small and green and nowhere near red. There was a hint of animal odour on the wind. And the biting tongue of freezing air that had raced over open country for miles.

A holly branch brushed its prickles against Hannah's hair. She jerked her head away, hating the indignity of it all. Holly was great, she thought sourly – for Christmas. But for the real smell of Christmas it had to be peeled oranges and pine needles, and Christmas roast chicken. Frank's funds seldom if ever ran to turkey, but the large chicken he bought was always done to a turn. The stuffing too, and the potatoes baked to glistening brown, that were placed round the bird like a string of large beads. And after the meal, completed with Christmas pudding and lots of thick sweet custard, Frank would light up, savouring the one cigar he treated himself to every year. He would lean back in his chair and heave a contented sigh. Knowing that he had done well.

Yes, it had always been Frank who had cooked Christmas dinner for her, his stepdaughter. Frank who refused to go to the Marners for the festive day. Rough, miserable, down-at-heel Frank – whom she had thought she hated. That was until the day she had found him so near death at Drews. A silly sentimental old man whom she had come upon one day, cradling Snow Queen's head against his own skinny chest.

Hannah had already made her Christmas plans. She had decided that for once she was going to move heaven and earth to make a nice Christmas for Frank.

Suddenly she froze in horror. There was the sound of branches being pulled back behind her. Then a long low whistle.

'Bloody 'ell, you've got a fine arse there,' a male voice said. 'It's

257

glowing all nice and pink and round. I want to stroke it, and mebbe I will.' A gurgling guffaw clearly belonging to a slow-witted local youth known as Goofy, followed. 'Can't act the hoity-toity ter me now eh, Land Army?'

She almost toppled over as she swung round to look at the intruder, her heart in her mouth. A large lumbering figure peered at her from behind the bush. The face was round and red and blessed with little piggy eyes. Loose lips revealed unwholesome protruding teeth.

In her haste to pull her trousers up, Hannah swore and nearly fell over. Then she stepped forward, her cheeks on fire, words spilling out of her mouth.

'How dare you! And I've never been anything other than matey with you, so I don't know where you get the hoity-toity bit from. But now I think you're disgusting, and not fit to live.'

'Why's that, Land Army? 'Cos I've got eyes in me head? I like to see your arse, I do.' He was smirking, all but gibbering, and she wanted to strangle him. And would have too, had he been within her grasp. He was still laughing and leering and carrying on. 'I would walk miles to look at it, and I 'ave done in the past. I just love your round and rosy backside.'

'You mean—' she was shocked and so angry that she felt sick, '– you actually mean to tell me that you've done this before?'

Goofy's eyes glittered merrily and his body heaved as he continued to laugh. 'Of course I have. You're a little beauty, Land Army.'

'And you're a mean rotten devil, Goofy Harvey,' she yelled, hands raised, trying furiously to part holly branches in order to thump him one. 'Just like your dad. Yes, him who sits huddled up in the Rook-wood with his cronies that look like a coven of witchy old women. Just you wait until I tell him, and even better, Mr Endercot, that you've been spying on me.'

It wasn't fair, the way people always caught her out. Like when she was sprawled all over the ground fighting off Spence, her knickers on display, and now when spending a penny! It was awful, so embarrass-ing, and she wanted to kill Goofy Harvey stone dead. The holly bush finally gave way and she was in front of Goofy, her badly scratched hands ready to grab him, but he was too quick for her and jumped away.

'My dad won't listen to a Land Army,' he told her nastily, his mood changed. 'And I weren't here of me own accord. 'Twas Mr Endercot 'isself as sent me.'

'Why, you . . .'

Just then, Raven and Ginnie came running up.

'What's going on?' Ginnie asked sharply.

258

'Are you all right?' Raven's voice was thick with concern, her eyes almost black she was so angry.

'He's been watching me!' Hannah said furiously. 'Filthy beast. What's more, he's been making a habit of it. Us having to hide behind bushes is not exactly fun, but with – things like him lurking about it's enough to make anyone sick!'

Goofy was looking distinctly uneasy. 'I was only joking.' The words all but tumbled out of his mouth. 'I'm sorry I did what I did. It won't happen again.'

'You can bet your sweet life it won't,' Ginnie told him, her voice crystal clear. 'You haven't heard the last of this, Harvey.'

'Don't tell on me, Land Army. I didn't mean no harm.' Goofy was out of his league and he knew it. 'I was sent here by Mr Endercot. I'm to tell you that when you've finished here you can go home for the day.'

'Really?' Ginnie was neither pleased nor amused. 'And because you brought along a message, you thought you'd enjoy a picture-show as payment in kind – is that it? I'll tell you this here and now, Goofy Harvey, we will have respect from you and your lot before we're through, I swear it. Now get out of my sight.'

'I'm giving you the message,' Goofy said, and now he looked mean and ready to fight back. 'Mr Endercot says as how it was Mr St John's orders. He reckons that as you've all been up and about since early this morning, you could do with a rest.' Goofy took another step backwards, but continued defiantly, 'And I wanna know why! We don't get given no rest.'

'Perhaps because you don't offer to work overtime to get a job finished like we do,' Hannah told him nastily. 'Or perhaps because we don't spend two-thirds of the day hanging about smoking Woodbines and talking football. Also perhaps because we don't mosey off every two minutes to grab a pint the moment the Rookwood opens its doors. All of which I know you do, Goofy my old China – and don't push it because I still want to black your beady little eye. So what do you say to that?'

Goofy threw caution to the winds. 'Same's I'm going to tell 'em all, Land Army. Yes – my dad, my uncle and all their mates – just what a rum do it was, coming up on you just when you was showing a fair old arse to the wind.'

'And won't that be hysterical?' she bluffed, cheeks flaming again. 'They'll all be doubled up, just thinking about my bum. Oh come off it, Goofy!'

'If you don't leave,' Ginnie ordered, 'I shall go to Mr St John here and now. Then you'll be out of a job, as will your father and your uncle and all your mates. Yes, when Mr St John learns about this, you'll all go, believe me.'

'Oh, make him buzz off and let's forget it,' Hannah said suddenly. 'He's as thick as two planks and wouldn't understand sensitive feelings if he had to eat them for breakfast. He's simply not worth making a scene over. Get him out of my sight.'

She turned on her heels and made her way back to collect her gloves and pick, praying that James never got to hear of this latest unladylike happening. And then Hannah was thanking God that it had only been Goofy behind the holly bush and not James St John. Perish the thought! She went hot and cold; her mouth felt dry.

Suddenly, the need to cringe evaporated. Her chagrin turned to anger. To the devil with what James thought! Why should his attitude towards her matter? It didn't, not at all. But he was indeed bombastic, and round here his word was law. Well, she needed to change the law – or at least one small part of it – for Frank's sake.

She heard Raven and Ginnie walking behind her. They were tactfully leaving her alone until she felt better. She heard them making plans for a lazy afternoon, and an evening at the Rookwood.

'You're coming, naturally,' Ginnie called out. 'Orders!'

'Of course.' She slowed down and waited for them to catch up. 'After all, I have a very famous backside now. I reckon they'll all be there just to see if I have the . . . er . . . *bottom* to go in and play darts as usual.'

'They'll be there in their hundreds,' Ginnie giggled. 'Queuing up behind James! After all, young Hannah York being caught with her knickers down is world-shattering news. It will quite wipe out the war.'

'Oh Hannah, dear,' Raven put in, 'stop looking so tragic! By tomorrow you'll see the funny side and we will all have a good laugh.'

'Ha ha!' Hannah said and smiled dutifully, but her mind was racing. Would James be in the Rookwood tonight? He seemed to turn up whenever he had the chance. She suspected that he liked to be near Raven. What man wouldn't? Raven was so lovely, sweet, and so nice.

It might be a good idea if she, Hannah, did not leave trying to see him until tonight in the Rookwood, where everyone and anyone could overhear. It would be much better to strike while the iron was hot. Yes – she would walk over to Knollys later on, and try to catch His Highness there. After all, she and he had a bone to pick . . .

Chapter Thirty-One

It was still light, though Hannah had her torch for later on. She could have ridden to Knollys on her bone-shaker, the Min-Ag black bike loathed by all three girls, but as ever she she preferred to walk.

Again she was conscious of the countryside. The world was filled with the smell of grass and earth and rain-wet fallen leaves. The hedges, far more sheltered here, were berry-filled. Birds flew among thorny branches, flicking their wings, heads moving jerkily from side to side. They were surveying the scene with suspicious bead-bright eyes, ready at all times to pick and peck and fly.

The air was frosty; Hannah's cheeks held the colour of hipsy-haws. Her hobnailed working boots splashed along the lane that soon petered out as it neared Knollys – and James.

The house that Raven admitted she had come to love, stood there, old and mellowed. It did not have the imposing air of Hawksley, but rather a shabby dignity, a sense perhaps of – *home*. It was a nice place.

When Hannah and her friends had spoken about it, only a few nights previously, both she and Ginnie had admitted that they liked Hawksley best, for it had a sort of timelessness about it, a graciousness. It was secure. They couldn't quite understand Raven's preference for Knollys, and secretly wondered whether it was because James chose the place. When they had said as much, Raven laughed in her calm, unhurried way.

'Yes, to answer your question yet again, I *do* like James. He is a strong and hypnotic person. And yet I am not quite so comfortable with James as I am with you two. I think I understand Sophia rather more.'

'I agree,' Hannah said surprisingly. 'She's looked after us all right. What's more, I really like the pictures she paints. She took me up to her attic studio once, just to show me round. There's a huge skylight and about three different sized easels, thousands of brushes by the looks of things, paints – and everything. It was really interesting. But the old girl bites your head off and is as prickly as nettles most of the time.'

'I wonder who she reminds me of?' Raven had teased, and ducked as a pillow flew towards her head.

As Hannah neared Knollys' lopsided nameplate, she tried to look at the ivy-clad house through Raven's eyes. There was one thing she *did* know – it knocked Walker Street into a cocked hat, all right.

Hannah's thoughts turned me to the reasons for her visit. Like the very first time she had been there, she could hear piano music. It wasn't a bit like Glenn Miller, or the Andrews Sisters, but it was nice all the same. James certainly had a gentle touch. She grinned to herself, wondering just what kind of fist James would make of playing a rousing *Knees up, Muvver Brown*. Stiff and starchy old thing. She tried to picture him belting out a song of any kind. Her eyes began to dance at the thought.

She drew in a deep breath, marched up to the door and knocked hard with the kind of self-important bang that the rent man used on Walker Street front doors. Then James was standing there, like the Rock of Gibraltar, and she was tossing her head at him, undismayed by his reciprocal glare.

'Well, well,' he drawled. 'If it isn't little Miss York.'

'Mr St John,' she said in the like tone, 'may I have a few words?'

'Forgive me,' he replied, 'but only a *few* words? That sounds uncharacteristic.'

There he was, getting under her skin again. But she tried very hard not to react. The words all but stuck in her throat.

'Mr St John,' she began sweetly, 'I have come to ask you a very special favour.'

'Oh?' Wintry amusement gleamed in his eyes. 'Not to blow my head off? That was the impression I got in the Rookwood.'

She took a step nearer to him, chin uptilted. 'Am I so low that I don't warrant courtesy? Aren't you even going to ask me in?'

He immediately stepped aside, leaving the way open. She walked past him, conscious of his height, his overpowering personality. Stick a load of fur all over him, she thought, and he'd make a wonderful Beast for Beauty. But a prince underneath? Nah – never!

She marched straight on and into the room where she and her friends had first come across him. The piano was open and there was music on the stand. But piled up on a large desk that had not been there before were masses of ledgers, piles of forms, writing materials, labels, all kinds of things. The desk-top was all but groaning under the

262

weight. So! He brought some of his workload home. Now Hannah understood how it was that he was able to get back more often. Probably in order to ride with Raven. Her friend and Blue Rinse were a regular pair these days.

Hannah nodded towards the desk. 'Looks quite a heap,' she said. 'Poor old you.'

'It's a job.' He brushed her comment away.

'Raven likes all that sort of thing,' she persisted, hoping to get in his good books. 'Writing and brainy stuff like that. I was a real dunce at school.'

'I can't and won't believe that,' he replied firmly. 'Please sit down, Miss York.'

'Why Miss York all of a sudden?'

'Why the pointed Mr St James?'

'Because you act like a boss – not a friend.'

'Ah! Yet I believed that people who tried to help others could be listed as friends.'

'But you don't actually ease situations, do you?' She ignored his offer of a chair, and cast caution to the four winds. She folded her arms and began pacing up and down in front of him. And in spite of trying not to, becoming more agitated by the minute. 'I suppose you think like Raven?'

'How does she think?'

'That I'm ungracious to be angry about what you did. But it doesn't alter the fact that I wanted to die, does it? Yes, wanted the ground to open up. I didn't want that awful old man Harvey and his crowd to know my business. And how do you think Frank felt, being made to stand centre-stage like that?'

'I was trying to scotch rumours, that's all.'

'And on top of making him into a kind of exhibition,' she rushed on, 'you're after breaking his heart as well.'

'How?'

'How?' She ceased her pacing and stood directly in front of him, dark curls flying, amber eyes glowing with golden lights. 'You don't know? By taking him away from Snow Queen, of course!'

'So that's it – my brother's horse. Oh, for Lord's sake, Hannah, sit down!'

'I don't want to. I can't. I'm too worked up and—'

'Sit!' He pushed the chair forwards and then his hands were on her shoulders, pressing her onto it. 'Now calm down, and explain yourself rationally. Stop spitting fire, Hannah. It doesn't work with me, you know.' He allowed himself a wide grin. 'In fact, if necessary, I could eat young ladies like you for breakfast.'

263

She stared up at him, taken back by that grin. It made him human – approachable even. She might even be able to get him on her side.

'If I've got to sit, you must sit too,' she ordered. 'I'm getting a crick in my neck trying to look up at you.'

'And you're like a pain in my neck,' he told her, but sat down all the same. 'Now tell me just what it is that makes you fight the world so hard. Because that's what you do, you know. You're like a young boxer listening for the bell that starts the next round, and I wonder why. Tell me about yourself.'

'That's my business.'

'I'm making it mine.'

His expression was such that she found herself obeying him.

Cheeks flaming, she told him all about Walker Street, her life there, and how Frank had once been a milkman and rather nice. How he had changed after the death of her mother, then of his fury and grief when they had put down the beloved Firelord. How he'd lost the job that had been his for years because he had threatened to do for the man who had had Firelord put down. She finished up saying:

'Then to cap it all, he got into Val Marner's clutches. Val's a woman who – who likes men more than somewhat. In fact, she lives and sleeps and dreams about men, but she actually fell for Frank! Val's big brother is the local bully. There are rumours that he literally cuts up people who cross him.' She shuddered.

'Val found something in Frank that she liked,' Hannah went on painfully, avoiding James's eyes. 'She used to goad him into hitting her quite deliberately. Then . . . one night, she went too far. Even worse, so did Frank.' She bit her lip, blushing furiously. 'That's about it. A tawdry and disgusting story. I'm sure you don't want to hear more.'

'Actually, I do,' he replied calmly.

'Why?' she asked brightly, although there were tears in her eyes. 'I'm getting fed up with talking about my own humble self. And I'll tell you something else. I'm not ashamed of anything. The past, and what we sprang form, is nothing much to worry about. Anyway, worry is a killer. No, it's how we set out to change things for the better that really matters. That's what Miss Pitt says.'

She couldn't tell from his expression what he was really thinking. He was staring at her hard, then he suddenly announced. 'I like the sound of your Miss Pitt. She must be a decent sort.'

'And not the kind you'd think to find in or near Walker Street?' she flared up immediately. 'You were born with a silver spoon in your mouth, so naturally listening about how the other half lives must bore you to bits.'

'Ye gods,' he sighed, 'what a mixed-up creature you are. Don't give me much credit, do you? Hannah York, you've got to stop to take breath. You've got to grow up.'

'That's what Matt told me,' she sparked up. 'I could take it from him. He's a good mate!'

'And I'm merely the upstart James St John?'

'If you like.'

'I see.' He straightened in his chair, 'Well, perhaps you'll get down to telling me the real reason for this visit.'

'You mean you don't know?' She laughed disbelievingly. 'You're going to send Frank off to the workhorse stables at Cobbitt Way and I want you to change your mind.'

'I'm sorry. He'll have his own cottage there, next to Clancy Mac-Craig, so he'll have a good chap to talk to and be pals with. Clancy's a nice old fellow and he knows how to laugh. Life will be easier for Frank all round from now on. Is that so bad?'

'He'll lose Snow Queen.'

'He has permission to see her any time.'

'Only as a kind of outsider, once he moves. Before he can get to see that darned old horse, he'll have to run the gauntlet of Trixie Drew and her toadies, not forgetting her father. Thank you very much!'

He leaned back in his chair, folded his arms and grinned again, which quite took the wind out of her sails. She knew deep down that here was someone she didn't know how to handle. She could jump and scream and gibber for all he'd react. She hated him.

'There really is no pleasing you, is there?' he asked companionably. 'You need looking after, or at least someone to tighten your reins. Above all, you really should learn to relax. I play music to calm me down. You ought to try it.'

'I don't play anything,' she admitted. Then hoping against hope that he would change his mind about sending Frank away: 'I've never had a gramophone. I like the wireless though.'

'Music is special,' he told her. 'Different kinds of music mean different things to people.'

'I know,' she replied politely, thinking that he was about to lecture her all over again. To make it clear that she understood what he was getting at, she enlarged. 'Raven told me that her father, a doctor, was kind and sweet and gentle. People adored him. He liked to play golf and to listen to the sort of music that you play. Ginnie's dad is different. He loves everything military, and is mad about big brass bands. I like Jeanette MacDonald and Nelson Eddy, Vera Lynn, Gracie Fields, George Formby, Alan Breeze, all kinds.' In full spate, she couldn't help adding sarcastically, 'Some of them not up to your high standards, of course.'

265

He looked thunderous. 'You little brat,' he told her. 'You just can't help yourself, can you? You are always trying to cut me down to size. Know something? I am rather flattered that you find it matters so much. Now, since you have said all that you came to say, please go.' Then he added, as she jumped to her feet furious, 'I take it you came by bike?'

'I walked.'

'Then I shall take you back, and after that . . .'

'No!' she replied haughtily. 'I prefer to go as I came – alone!' Without waiting a second longer, she turned and began marching towards the door.

'Stop right there,' the order cracked out. She froze, then slowly turned. He was standing by his chair, arms folded, tall and fierce and with a face like stone. 'Come here!'

She refused to move.

'*Now!*'

She took one small tentative step towards him.

'Nearer.' He seemed to be standing even taller.

She could not look away from his eyes.

'Nearer still.'

Hannah took the few steps necessary, her heart racing. Perhaps she could get round him even at this late stage. For Frank. Yes, this was for Frank! She was directly in front of him now and it was like facing a brick wall. Then unbelievably she was being held against him. His face came down, then his lips covered hers. She gasped, for a wild sensation was rushing through her; she felt she was tingling from head to toe. She tried to pull away, but instead remained transfixed, then wanted to melt. This was wild and wonderful and . . .

He pushed her away and just stood there watching her. She swung round and once more made for the door, opened it – and he let her go . . .

The wind whipped the colour into her cheeks as she followed the crazily bouncing circle of light from her torch. She was shaken to the core and not too sure about anything any more. In the far distance she heard the thin wail of Moaning Minnie, but did not care. The whole world was a rotten bad egg and James St John was the worst of them all. She loathed and detested him, and she would get her own back one bright fine day.

The worst thing of all, he had insulted her twice in the last hour. He had called her a brat, which meant he wouldn't change his mind about moving Frank. No, he wouldn't change his mind at all, arrogant pig! And then to prove how small and helpless she was, he had kissed her. Yes, he had done it just to exert his influence and power. And that kiss

266

had made her feel things. She had wanted to – faint? No! Wanted to kill the man stone dead.

A siren, nearer this time, growled its warning then sprang high, only to go on, looping the loop in great swathes of sound. The rotters are after Matching again, Hannah thought feverishly, trying to dismiss the memory of that kiss. The Spits will be after them. Good old Spits, Lancasters too. I wonder how our bombers are. The Stirlings, Blenheims, Wellingtons and the like.

In spite of everything, her mind went back to Knollys. She wanted to laugh and to cry, to loathe herself, to be scared. Please dear God, she thought, don't let him think I'm like Val. Then – why should I care what he thinks? He's a bloody awful man! He shouldn't have kissed me. It was like eating fire! It wasn't all sweet and sort of dizzy fun like with Matt.

Impatient with herself and with the world in general, she fiercely brushed away unshed tears. High up, unseen, she heard the sound of planes and found herself asking, I wonder how Matt is? Dear Matt. I hope he's warm and safe somewhere . . .

The going was getting tougher in the mountains, Matt thought, and wished he was back in Madame's cupboard again. Not for himself, for Jacques, who refused to leave him behind. Miguelito, the guide from Andorra, was a giant of a man with eyes like twin sloes, black hair, a skin tanned like old leather, and a mean attitude. He was dressed in gaiters, spiked boots, green corduroy trousers and a woolly hat. He carried a stout staff. Miguelito was a devil from hell, and from the outset had not let up at all.

He had told the group that he was paid by the head for those he got through. So he intended to get them to España by hook or crook. He then added that anyone dropping out would be shot. No one must be captured by the Boches. For under duress, prisoners might give the rest of them away. He had brandished his gun to show that he meant business. He had finished by saying coldly, 'I promise you, you will not miss me when I die.' Then, *'Vamos!'*

'If he finds out your weakness,' Jacques had whispered under his breath, 'it will be the finish, eh? You understand?'

'Why have they allowed me to try?' Matt whispered back.

'Because we are not in the position to get you proper treatment, my friend. We think you deserve a chance. You have suffered a great deal and been very brave. We honour the RAF.'

'If I fall behind, don't wait. I want your word.'

Jacques shrugged. 'You are a challenge. Besides, I gave Madame my word.'

267

It had been no follow-my-leader after that. Fit men were running, leaping, scrambling after the guide. Others were stumbling, falling, swearing, limping. And always there was Miguelito barking orders at them.

Cold and drenched through, Matt pressed on. Again and again he pulled himself upwards until every muscle creaked and groaned. His legs and back seemed to be screaming at him to give himself up. There was one certain fact: he could not hurry. In the end he sat down and swore that he would not move another step unless Jacques went on without him. He meant it. Finally, with a bad grace, Jacques did as he was asked. Matt did not pull himself to his feet until the Frenchman was well out of sight . . .

Conditions in the mountains had worsened. Freezing and inhospitable, the craggy pathways became more hazardous. However, Matt was getting a little stronger, more able to cope, and although far behind the others, he was making progress. The rocky trail that went up and down and round, and often disappeared altogether, now led steeply upwards. Although he could not see the rest of the party, Matt knew by the occasional falling stones that he must be directly underneath them. Heartened by this knowledge, he tried to catch up.

Suddenly he heard a rumbling. An avalanche of boulders came bouncing downwards and he was right in its path! Matt turned blindly and clung on to a stunted tree. He swore as chunks of rock fell around and on him. Then yelled as a jagged piece smashed against his leg. He jerked away and felt fresh agony, then stayed still until the pain was replaced by the monotonous throbbing that he had tried so hard to ignore before. After a while he calmed and began a trembling ascent on all fours. Above him came the sound of purposeful movement. Miguelito was coming down the treacherously steep path like an antelope.

God! Matt thought. The bastard's going to shoot me.

Then the guide had reached him and, giving a deep-throated roar, lifted his staff and struck Matt furiously across the back and shoulders. The blows rained down and the guide was incessantly bawling at him to get up and be on his way!

Matt became consumed with rage and wanted to kill the guide. Instead he crawled and scrabbled, and as the blows and accompanying shouts forced him ever upwards, his anger made him strong and he forged ahead, mouthing every swearword he could call up.

After an eternity the blows ceased to fall and the going was easier. He struggled to his feet and although his leg was dragging badly, he made better time. Finally he reached the others. They were resting. Jacques and one of the Americans was not with them. Trembling, and weak with spent passion, Matt sank down. The guide went further on, now totally ignoring him. Matt gasped out, 'Jacques?'

'He's gone,' came the reply. 'He and Starky fell. They're both dead.'

Matt turned away so that they couldn't see him cry . . .

Chapter Thirty-Two

Now it was autumn already and at work with her friends, hoeing, Hannah amused herself by thinking back.

From December 1941, the previous year, when the unwarranted attack by the Japanese on Pearl Harbor had happened, Americans were now looked at in a different light. The people in the Rookwood who had previously not been too keen on the Yanks because they were 'over sexed, overpaid and over here,' presently looked upon the GIs, as chums.

The Americans were one hundred per cent in the war, and baying for enemy blood. They were absolutely stiff with national pride and energy, their armed forces tough and brave and top-class. It was comforting to know that! They were splendid chaps all round. And what was more, they held dances and parties on their base. Marvellous do's where food and drink were plentiful. Cigarettes were on offer, and bottles of Coke, and even the odd pair of nylons – which the village girls would kill for.

By common consent it was believed that every American had a posh house in New York, or were ex-cowboys from ranches as big as England. On the other hand, some owned oil-wells. Others lived among the stars in Hollywood and personally knew such people as Greer Garson, Ronald Colman, Gary Cooper, Carole Lombard and the rest.

To charm the Yanks, village girls now sported the 'Vingle' hairstyle. This special short-cut incorporated partings forming four V's, hence 'V-ingle'. It had been conceived in order to keep hair tidy and out of machines, but the style caught on.

During the festive season, the Americans had been as generous as ever with their hosting. A whole party of folk from Lindell were invited over to celebrate. Hannah had not joined them. She still felt embarrassed at the memory of Spence. This even though she understood he had been stationed elsewhere long since.

Those who stayed behind had been as determinedly Christmassy as possible. The Church now relaxed one of its rules. Women no longer had to wear hats. However, tradition continued in Lindell and the church had been filled. Tears fells, prayers rose, and hearts were full. And Hannah remembered Richard, and Matt. She thought of Ma Carpenter, and the old man and his dog Meg, still up there in The Smoke facing it all. She found herself grateful that Frank was here, in the country, near her. And she thought of James who, even though he worked like ten tigers, sometimes up to about eighteen hours a day, seemed to be everywhere she looked.

He was a man of mystery really, she thought. He held a bitter secret of some kind which he kept close to his heart. Whatever had happened, she could not even begin to guess. But a woman was at the bottom of it, she knew it as sure as eggs were eggs. Had he loved that woman? Had the woman loved him? James St John was capable of deep and abiding passion. That had come across the moment his lips had claimed hers. Something deep inside of herself had wanted to respond to that kiss. It had not been fresh and bracing, like Matt's. No, it had seemed that James could quite possible eat her alive. Consume her in fire ... She blushed and pushed the thought away.

'Hannah, darling,' Raven said, 'what are you thinking about? You have been quiet for such a long time. Are you worrying about something?'

'No. I was remembering last Christmas, that's all.'

'It was a headache buying presents,' Ginnie observed. 'It'll be even worse this year. "The Country" needed everything.'

'Even old records,' Hannah quipped, 'for their shellac!'

'The wrought-iron railings in front of my father's house are long gone,' Raven observed. 'Spare saucepans went ages ago.'

'My greatest headache,' Hannah admitted, 'was finding that trainset for the twins. It cost four shillings and sixpence, and a fortune in shoe-leather and time. Now we're heading for Christmas again.'

They fell silent once more, each busy with their memories. Hannah was remembering how it was during last Christmas that she and Frank had at last been able to turn back the clock.

It had been a time of cheer after all, Hannah remembered. Frank's new home, Cobbitt Cottage B, was quite dinky in a basic way. There was an old black kitchen range, table and chairs, a dresser with drawers and cupboards underneath. There was cutlery, crockery, a kettle, teapot and cleaning things – indeed, everything necessary for civilised living. There was a tiny front room barely large enough to hold the floral-covered cottage-style suite. Upstairs, a decently

271

furnished bedroom was next to a boxroom which held a single bed and a chest of drawers with a mirror on top. This, Frank had told Hannah off handedly, was for her, if she ever wanted to stay. Outside, a huge mound of chopped wood ensured heat for cooking and warmth.

Clancy MacCraig's place was adjoining and equally diminutive. Hannah suspected that at one stage, the two buildings had been one. There was a shared toilet outside and no fence to divide the yard in which grew a scraggy-looking cherry tree, and a William pear in rather better shape, and most impressive of all, an elderberry tree.

Clancy was a jolly old man with loosely flowing iron-grey hair, a big ready grin and periwinkle-blue eyes. His hobby, wine-making, was well known, for his sweet white elderflower wine had won many prizes at the village horticultural show. He and Hannah got on at the moment of meeting, and already he and Frank had become mates. This was pretty wonderful, Hannah thought, because for as long as she remembered, Frank had never had a friend. Clancy had altered that! And there was one other regular visitor to Cobbitt Cottages A and B; none other than Peggy Powell. She and Clancy had become friends. Clancy actually knew how to make the lady smile.

The stables at Cobbitt were large and warm and were never short of clean straw. The horses were huge, and magnificent. They were called Shah, Rourke, Kelly, Raff, Chap, Nicky and Nosh. It was Clancy and Frank's job to care for these, and to do general farming chores. Some of the fields to be worked were three miles away from Knolly's, and that excluded the orchard land.

Hannah had come to like visiting Cobbitt. She learned a great deal. There was so much work for the gentle giants to do. Harrowing, ralling, preparing for spring rowing . . . and so it went on. Their power was immense.

There were lots of different chores to be managed on this part of the Estate. Shorthorn cows needed to be fed. Stacked hay was to be cut into flaps with a hay-knife – hard work when there was lots to do. Then there was turnip-cutting for sheep in the fold. Turnips were set out in large heaps. Clancy would pull the cutter from heap to heap, then pitch-fork the turnips into it. Whistling shrilly or else roaring out, 'Bless 'em All!', he'd then turn the handle like a maniac. The turnips came flying out like chips to fall into the scuttle. When the scuttle was filled the turnip chips were put into troughs so that the sheep could help themselves.

Where animals were concerned there were no days off. Hannah was glad that she was a fieldworker, and although she loved being with

Frank and Clancy, and even dour old Peg, she was happiest with her friends.

Christmas had been a parting of the ways for The Three Musketeers, and they had lots to talk about once they were reunited. Raven had chosen to stay with Lily and the boys in Rose Cottage. Ginnie had gone home, and Hannah, who with the best will in the world had determined to make a nice Christmas for Frank, found that he and she were guests in Clancys' place. One way and another, a good time was had by all. If only they could have heard from Matt!

Very unwillingly, during that time, Hannah had come to admit to herself that James had been right all along. Frank was growing stronger and happier by the day. He had horses to look after, and even though admitting to missing Snow Queen, he was now leading a full and contented life. Hannah had said to him once, 'Well, Skipper, you've fallen on your feet. Funny, in a way just like me.'

'How come?'

'I've got Ginnie and Raven. You've got Clancy and Peg. Lucky, aren't we?'

'You need a man, gel.' He had grinned a gap-toothed grin. 'Your own fella. Somebody what'll be ter you what your ma was to me. Ain't there no one? No one at all?'

'I took a fancy to someone once,' she admitted hesitantly. 'At least, I think I did. But perhaps he was just a friend. Anyway, it's all of no account now. He was shot down and I think he's somewhere in France. Perhaps he's a prisoner of war, I don't know. He kissed me once.'

'Bloody hell,' Frank hooted, 'that ain't much to go on. Proper little innocent, ain't you? D'yer mean ter say as how he was the only bloke what's give yer a smacker?'

She went pink. 'Our boss did – once.'

'What?' Frank was scowling now, suspicious.

'Just to give me a lesson,' she said tightly. 'Mean rotten pig. That was his way of shutting me up. He told me I had to grow up, Frank. And – and he still didn't let you stay with Snow Queen. That's all I went after him for.'

'You bearded that old devil for me, Han?' Frank whistled, then shook his head. 'Jesus Christ, gel, I don't deserve you.'

'Oh, you're not so bad – taken in small doses,' she had lipped him. But the memory of her humiliation had risen to the fore again, and for perhaps the millionth time she found herself wishing that she could kill James St John stone dead . . .

All of that was in the past now. Even the wonderful Harvest Festival had come and gone. There were still sunny days, like last spring in fact

273

when there had been baby animals, and primroses had thickly starred the shade. Then, high above swallows had been cleaving the air with metallic blue wings. And fluting against the sky, a cuckoo called. Nature was as always indomitably continuing to follow its own pattern, taking heed of neither man nor war.

Now robin redbreasts were hopping about. Squirrels gathered the last of the nuts. In the Rookwood, interest was growing in the darts team. It was really believed that they could and would give Norseby a leathering. But for the moment it was decided Lindell would be waving the white flag. They were going *en masse* to the enemy camp, to the Village Hall, to hear one of their own sons. It was going to be young Lenny Madeira's big day, to commemorate him passing a very special musical exam. In fact, he had passed it with Honours. Everyone believed that the young man would go far.

Walter had given the go-ahead for his nephew to have special tuition. He and Betty and the whole of Lindell were as pleased as Punch. Not a single soul remembered referring to the musical genius as that thickhead, half-baked slow-wit, the Madeira Muddle-bonce. Now everyone remembered knowing right from the start that the young 'un was a genius in the making.

Busily hoeing, Hannah smiled wryly. The Harvey gang were the greatest hypocrites of all! Still, the recital was to be held at the weekend. But first things first. This evening, Hannah had taken on Ellery in a game of darts. The last time they had played together, she faltered and missed double top by a whisker – because James had turned up. She had gone to pieces after that. Especially as he was leaning against the bar, watching her, with that faint amusement glinting in the back of his eyes.

'A penny for them,' Ginnie called.

'Not even worth a farthing, I'm afraid.'

'You were looking terribly serious just then,' Raven observed. 'Darling, you have a very expressive face.'

'I was thinking about darts.'

'Well, you're the champion. Don't forget that we're all banking on you.'

'Pull the other one, Raven,' Hannah retorted and began working furiously down the line.

At that moment she was full of worries and woes. It was too much of a responsibility. This village lark was a bit much, what with winning cricket matches, and horticultural gatherings, WI shows, and now darts competitions. And the rotten thing was, the Rookwood regulars all thought she was a star and they all looked to her – and that included His Nibs. He expected her to get doubles every time – and when he was watching her she found that she could not. Every time she faced the board and played, he expected the scorer to bawl out, 'One Hundred and Eight-ty!'

No, she told herself firmly, now I'm exaggerating. And tonight Ellery's there, not James. It's just practice, after all.

Overhead the bombers droned onwards like giant buzzer-bees. She hoped that they would all return safely. And that if there was a raid, that the enemy would not head for home and dump their bombs on the way. One of the jobs farmworkers had to do these days was to fill in bomb craters which were a hazard for man and beast.

According to the wireless the war effort was not going so well abroad. Worse, convoys at sea were still taking a terrible pounding by German subs. It was all too depressing if one sat down and really and truly thought about it all. But one had to get on, do one's best, though sometimes it was hard. Still, it would be marvellous to listen to Lenny playing his violin, Hannah thought, wanting to hug herself at the thought. Apparently the Norseby orchestra was going to accompany him. But whatever he played, Hannah knew that it would not sound better than the boy's own music that she and Matt had heard that night.

Hannah wondered whether Lenny had ever received any news of Matt. The boy hero-worshipped him and rightly so. Matt! Hannah blinked hard and tried to picture him as she had seen him last. Clean-shaven, blue eyes, a fine stockily-built man with a great ready laugh. A joker. A great all-rounder. A thoroughly nice chap who liked kids and dogs – and her! But memory played tricks and slipped easily away from one's mind when faced with reality. And reality was this life, this here, and this now.

Suddenly Hannah felt rather lost and very confused, so she pulled herself together and worked like a maniac for the rest of the day, Not interested in Raven and Ginnie's chatter at all. Ginnie with her ever-lasting cookery and home-making stuff, and conversations about how mapped out and perfect her life would be after the war as Aiden's wife. And Raven, polite as ever, going along with all the housey housey business, but really into her own obsession, horse-riding, and being mates with Sophia. She was even talking about cars! Raven really admired James's red Jag. Her doctor father had owned a car, and Raven herself could drive. In Hannah's world, the only people with cars were toffs.

After work that evening, having washed and changed into civvies, they enjoyed liver and bacon. It was a hot-pot, à la Marguerite Patten, and cooked by Peg. This dish was served with dumplings accompanied by a monologue from Peg about how long it had taken to queue up at the butchers to get the liver, which was as yet unrationed.

'And there I was,' Peg said, 'just standing in line like a bit of cold cod, waiting and praying as how the supply would last until it was my turn to be served.' She smiled dourly at Hannah, a friend in the camp seeing they often met in Cobbitt. 'But I got a lift back, in Mr St John's çar. Talk about feeling like Lady Muck! Enjoyed the ride no end I did.'

'He's home?' Hannah asked. 'I thought he'd gone back.'

'Well, it weren't no ghost what give me a ride. So yes, I reckon he's home.'

'Damn!'

Raven smiled and Ginnie raised her brows. They were waiting for Hannah to explode, but she did not. Just put on a brave face, deciding that the fault was hers. Just because the man was her boss was no reason to fall to pieces. Bosses had never scared her in the past. But then no other boss had witnessed her writhing on the ground, in the mud, everything on display, with a Yank on top of her, and her kicking and screeching like a banshee. Bloody hell, she thought for the millionth time. Trust him to there. Just my luck!

Then she had to thank the powers that be that James *had* been there. She finished up feeling more confused than before.

Hannah was just tightening the belt round her waist and straightening her skirt, when a message came that Sophia wanted to see her.

'You go on,' Hannah told Raven and Ginnie. 'I'll catch up.'

They wanted to wait, but she was adamant, secretly grateful for an excuse to put off the moment of coming face to face with James. When they had left, she drew in a deep breath and made her way to Sophia's private apartment. She was not in her sitting room, but up the short flight of wooden stairs, in her studio.

'Sit!' Sophia commanded and she watched satisfied, as Hannah obediently placed herself on the edge of a wooden chair.

'You wished to see me, Sophia?'

'I hate it when the light's gone,' Sophia snapped, the moment Hannah settled. 'I have been trying to get a certain effect up here, but electric light is a mere imitation and simply will not do!'

Hannah looked away from the woman to stare at the big beautiful canvas. Sophia was as dramatic an artist as she was a person. Not for her the chocolate-box anodyne picture of a scene. She believed in transferring what she felt rather than what she saw. Hannah found herself remembering a past conversation.

'There's a strength out there,' Sophia had said to Hannah once. 'Strength and savagery. I can feel the sheer indomitability of nature. I

276

can sense the timeless power of the hills and mountains! Have you ever been to the mountains, the Alps?'

'No. But I've seen them – at the cinema.'

'You've missed something, girl. One can sense the monstrous upheaval that in the beginning caused it all. The Alps are a wrinkling of the earth's crust – which can mean everything, or nothing, whichever way you look at it. One can get the idea of the beginning of things in Wales and Scotland, but Switzerland's best. Even here, in Essex, there are signs – hills and giant mounds of earth, not forgetting cliffs, leading down either to estuary or sea. One sinks into it all, just to let the senses take over!'

Maybe she was feeling lonely again, Hannah thought. Something must be worrying her. Probably she hates her painting. Heaven only knows why. It's terrific so far as I can tell. But something *is* wrong. When she's upset she always goes off like this.

Hannah knew, from previous conversations, that Sophia had studied every effect of sunlight on horizons. She was determined to explore its change of colour over hills and peaks. The canvas she was currently working on, of distant hills rising up from a rolling landscape, showed ethereal peaks suspended in mist like maids-in-waiting.

'I can't get the effect I need,' Sophia snapped. 'There are times when I feel I shall go mad!'

'Like that bloke what chopped off his own ear?'

Green eyes screwed up in an icy stare. 'Are you being facetious, Hannah?'

'Could be,' Hannah replied cheerfully, 'if I knew what that meant.'

'Don't play that "Poor Ignorant Me" game. And don't be such a little snob. You are not the only one on God's earth to have had a tough upbringing. My father was an artist and yes, in the early days we *did* have it hard. So I can probably tell you just how far two pounds of scrag end of mutton can go.'

'I get it.' Hannah smiled mischievously. 'You want to pick a fight. Why don't you ever pick fights with Raven – or Ginnie, come to that?'

'Because it's more fun with you.'

'Thank you very much! But I think it's going to rain, and as I'm going out, please will you tell me why am I here?'

'Have you spoken with James yet? Has he mentioned anything to you?'

'What about?'

'My son's horse.'

'Horse? His horse? You mean Pegasus?'

'Snow Queen.'

277

Hannah was frowning now, and suddenly wary. 'What's the matter with Snow Queen? Is she ill?'

'Oh, this is as useless as hell!' Sophia said fiercely and threw her paint-soaked brush down with such force that it bounced and splattered twice on the wooden floor. She glared at Hannah who was sitting there looking younger than her years in her black skirt and white blouse. She had put her Land Army coat over the back of the chair. 'You must know damned well that he will never admit to being wrong. Never!'

'I thought Snow Queen was a she.' Hannah was being deliberately dense because she did not like what she thought was going to happen. Bloody St Johns, she was thinking. They're going to ask Frank to leave that cottage. They want him back at Drews to look after Snow Queen. That wasn't fair!

'Hannah,' Sophia gritted, 'I'm not speaking about my boy's mare, but about James, and well you know it.'

'Isn't James your boy too?' Hannah asked flatly and glared right back at the older woman with the over-carmined lips. Oh yes, trust Sophia to have a secret hoard of cosmetics. Many young women were now reduced to using beetroot juice to colour their lips.

'How dare you!' Sophia's look held poison.

Hannah stood up and began donning her coat. 'I'm sorry, Sophia, but my name's not Raven; she tends to say nothing just to maintain a quiet life. To my mind you're not making sense. If Mr St John, your son, has anything to say to me, I'm sure he will say it all in his own good time. And now I really must go.'

'But I want you to stay.'

'So you can enjoy a jolly good row and vent your feelings? Sorry! The others will be wondering where I've got to.' She stood up, then added, 'Oh and something else. It wouldn't kill you to openly admit to caring, would it? I mean, you seem quite frantic about old Snow Queen because she belonged to Miles. That's all very well, but I don't think you should decry James in front of outsiders. Whether he ever admits to being wrong or not is between you and him, and nothing whatever to do with me.'

Before the woman could argue, Hannah about faced and all but ran out of the studio and down the stairs.

She was halfway to the Rookwood when James came striding towards her. She knew it was him before she could actually see his features. No one else had quite that stance nor stood so tall.

'Ah!' he said upon reaching her, his stern face etched in shadows. 'I wondered where you were.'

'You came looking – for me?'

'Of course.'

'Why?' she asked silkily. 'Is something wrong?'

'I'm not too happy about you coming and going on your own.'

'Is that all?'

'Isn't that enough?'

'Nice try,' she told him, 'but isn't there also something to do with Snow Queen?'

'She does seem unsettled,' he told her, 'but that's not why I'm here now. And about the old girl, yes – if it didn't seem so unusual, I'd say she's showing off because she's missing Frank.'

'Why unusual? I mean, isn't Frank good enough?'

'Tell me,' he drawled, 'are you needing to pick a fight?'

'Yes,' she replied tightly, 'just like your mother was about twenty minutes ago. Now please explain about Snow Queen.'

'It's unusual for an animal to take such an instant liking to a stranger. There are people there she has known for years, who have cared for and spoiled her. But she and Frank seem to have an affinity and now we think she is actually missing him. She is getting to be quite cussed and this is worrying Mother.'

'Particularly because she is Miles's horse?'

'Yes.'

'Where do I come in?'

'You don't.'

'Then why did Sophia send for me to speak about it?'

'I don't know,' he told her loftily, 'And frankly, I will never know. She is an enigma to me. All women are.'

'And you neither like nor trust us, do you?'

'No.'

'Why?'

'That's my business.' he told her. 'Now come along, let's hurry. Great things are expected of you, and it must be practice, practice, practice.'

'Before I take a single step further,' she told him dogmatically, 'you must tell me one thing. Are you going to make Frank go back to that room at Drews?'

'Lord no!' He sounded genuinely surprised. 'I intend to go over there tomorrow and make arrangements for Snow Queen to be stabled at Cobbitt with Shah, Rourke, Kelly and co. We'll see how things work out. If the old girl's happy and settled there I'll be indebted to your stepfather. Snow Queen is – special.'

'More so than Pegasus?'

'I sometimes think,' he told her evenly, 'that Pegasus is my greatest friend.'

'Nonsense,' she said, shocked, because right out of the blue she thought he seemed lonely. Then something came over her and before she realised what she was about, she stood up on tiptoe and kissed him. 'And that's for letting Frank stay in his lovely little cottage. Come on, let's hurry. I need to get my eye in if I'm to be a whizz at getting double tops.'

She grabbed hold of his arm and walked jauntily alongside him as though it was the most natural thing in the world.

Chapter Thirty-Three

It was really wonderful, Hannah thought blissfully, how great an ovation young Lenny received on his big night. Oh, so far as national events went, the concert at Norseby Village hall was no big deal, but to Lenny and his audience, it was the highlight of the year. He looked so young! So fervent, and so nice in his dark suit, white shirt, and black bow tie. And the Norseby Youth Orchestra, composed of young and immensely dedicated musicians, backed him to the hilt. Not unnaturally, Walter was puffed up with pride.

After the recital, when Lenny was free of well-wishers, he came over to where Hannah stood with the twins. He was smiling and flushed, his eyes bright with excitement.

'I had a letter today,' he said, the words tumbling out, 'and it's great news! Matt is safe!'

'What?' Hannah felt a surge of great joy. Chris and Chook yelled 'Hooray!' in unison and began a war-dance of delight. 'Oh Lenny!' Hannah was fighting back tears. 'You're not having me on? You really mean it – it's definitely true?'

'He has been very ill, and was injured which is rotten, but he reached Spain safely. Once there, he was put in hospital for a long time. For a while he couldn't remember who he was apparently, but as soon as he is well enough he says he will have sick leave. He has been told that his room is waiting for him in Mr Endercot's house. I expect he'll be writing to us when he can. The Red Cross bloke said that if he receives letters from us it will help him to get better. I'm going to write to him lots and lots!' He held out a slip of exercise paper. 'I've copied out his address. Hannah, I reckon this is the happiest day of my life!'

'Thank you, Lenny,' Hannah whispered shakily. 'Mine too.'

Button-bright, the lad went off to talk to Walter and Betty and his very nice foster-parents. Watching him, Hannah thanked God that the frightened youngster she had first met, was long gone. Lenny Madeira had found his feet and was downtrodden no more. And better still, he had brought such wonderful news! Matt was safe.

Soon after dawn on Saturday Hannah arrived at Cobbitt. She saw that James had beaten her to it. He was already preparing to exercise Snow Queen – he liked to do that himself when he could, leaving Pegasus happily wandering free in the field, nibbling fresh grass.

'Back again?' Hannah enquired, rosy-cheeked and beaming. 'Raven will be along soon. Ginnie's off and away seeing that this is one of our very rare full weekends.'

'You don't do so badly as Land Girls go,' he replied carefully, 'Especially you, young Hannah. You get away with murder, the way you lip the boss.'

'I wouldn't dare – sir!' she twinkled up at him.

'And I think I know why you are looking so pleased with yourself,' he told her.

'Have you heard already? That Matt's safe!'

James smiled his brooding smile. 'I think the whole village knows. The chap has been through hell, by all accounts. It'll be good to have him back.'

'I expect Ellery told you?'

'Yes.'

'Then – I don't suppose he has an idea when . . .'

'He's not certain, but seems to think it won't be for at least another month. Mind you, messages coming from abroad these days can get crossed and uncrossed. Uncertain times, eh?' He turned as there came the sound of hoofbeats. 'Ah! Here she is at last.'

Raven, on Blue Rinse, came galloping up. When they stopped, Hannah chuckled, 'Blow me, Raven. Long time no see!'

'Really, was breakfast *that* long ago?' Raven went on to make her usual threat. 'One of these bright fine days, darling, I'm going to get you on the back of a horse.'

'Kicking and screaming, luv,' Hannah quipped and stood watching them as they left. They made a lovely couple. They sat tall. They were, in her opinion, perfectly matched.

Hannah had come to accept James these days. And at times like this, when he seemed prepared to meet her halfway, she even, rather begrudgingly, saw what it was about him that Raven liked. However, he always kept one part of himself at stand-off as it were. He was impossible to really get to know or fully understand. But at least you knew where you were with him. Above all, it was very comforting to know that he was on one's side. These days she never felt quite so on edge when he came to Cobbitt, which was at least once during the weekends he had off from his work.

282

Perhaps it was not so strange after Snow Queen's installation in Cobbitt Stables, that James should turn up so regularly, Hannah thought. He had always made it quite clear that he was fond of his brother's pet, so there was no change there.

She loved it when he forgot himself sufficiently to laugh out loud at one of Clancy's jokes. Apparently he had known Clancy all of his life. The old man and James's father had been friends. But James still maintained a kind of reserve where she, Hannah, and all women were concerned. Except Trixie of course, and Raven. Then it was horses, horses, all the way.

'Gawd 'elp us!' Frank said as he joined her. 'What are yer mooning about watching them for?'

'I was thinking that they make a lovely couple, that's all.'

'Nah! That gel ain't for him. She's too refined. Too ladylike.'

She raised her brows, surprised. 'He's in her class, so I would have thought . . .'

'Ain't nothing to do with class, mate. He's a bloke what needs someone to take him down a peg. Young Raven's a bit above that sort of thing.'

'She's got me on her side, Skipper,' Hannah told him stoutly, then beamed. 'You really like Raven, don't you?'

'Yers. An' also young Gin. You've got yerself some good mates there.'

'And you'll like Matt too. He's so . . .'

'Now look 'ere, Han,' Frank's tone was quite serious now. 'From all I hear, he made that journey against some bloody 'orrible odds. I got the gist of it first thing. Walt stopped by to speak to Clance about that fallow top field. Walt said he'd got a phone call from young Lenny's foster-dad, and went on about some of the things what was put in that letter. I understand your airman lost a couple of mates along the way. One what fell over a cliff, and another when some Krauts took pot-shots at them. The poor devil's injuries finally made it impossible for him to walk. There was a guide what finished up carrying him for the last part of the journey. That guide deserves a medal in my book.'

'Yes, oh yes, he does!'

'But what strikes me,' Frank told her carefully, 'is that this Matt might not be like what you remembered. Savvy?'

'Skip!' Hannah was smiling through her tears. 'Of course I understand that, and thanks.'

'What for, mate?'

'For not wanting me to be upset. I will be, of course, but I'll drop dead myself before ever letting him know. Now, the reason I'm here. I

283

came to tell you that you're invited over to Lily's for tea. No, don't pull a face. I'd love you to really get to know the boys.'

'Thanks for asking, mate,' Frank said hastily, 'but me and Clancy have made other plans.' He ruffled her hair jokily. 'Besides, I might just get to the point of swearing blue murder at them young perishers.'

'Frank! Sam's home on leave and you like him a lot. As for the twins, they're angels,' she laughed. 'I adore them.'

'And Sam and Lily do too I've no doubt, but they're little sods, and well you know it. Strike me! I reckon I've heard enough bleeding elephant jokes to last me a lifetime. And as for questions! They only know one word – Why? And since they automatically ask Why? after every word I say, I just might flip my lid. Drive a bloke to drink they do.'

'Which you don't do any more, do you? You and Clancy never go to the Rookwood.'

'No need. It's toasting our toes, listening to the wireless, and sometimes taking a sip of elderflower wine. Only a sip mind, just to be sociable.'

'That's a real victory, Frank,' Hannah replied, believing him implicitly. 'As for Chris and Chook, you should have known them when they had to stay and have school dinners.' She was chuckling richly now. 'They were a million times worse. They loathed and detested the headmistress, who they still call Dragon Drawers.'

'I 'ated school meself,' Frank observed. 'I'm with them there.'

'The battles they had with that woman used to make poor Lily want to tear out her hair. Now they go home midday, and everyone's happy. Ol' Mo's ecstatic, of course. He waits for them outside the school gates as regular as clockwork. It's so sweet! Betty and Peg coming to Hawksley has made a world of difference for Lily.' She gave Frank a mischievous look. 'You like Peg, don't you?'

'She ain't a bad old stick. Me and Clance reckon as how she fits in fine. When yer get to our ages it's nice to have people round what make yer feel comfy like.' He gave her a quick look. 'But women – as far as women go, if yer know what I mean – are dead out. And, Han, I ain't never going back to The Smoke again. Is that all right with you?'

'Truly!' she told him earnestly and felt as affectionate as she had when she was little, and he'd held her hand in such a nice rough and ready, protective way, and taken her with him to pick hops.

I must remember all the good things, she told herself, and forget the bad. The man with me now is the real Frank. The terrible drunken ogre was Frank gone mad.

'You going ter stay today?' Frank asked.

She shook her head. 'No. I'm going back. I have a date.'

284

'Who with?'

'Who'd you think? Two young men and a really soppy dog. We're going for one of our long walks. Probably get as far as Marsh Flats, though the Lord only knows where we'll actually finish up. It certainly won't be anywhere near Matching Airfield.'

'What you going out all that time for?'

'Don't worry, we won't starve. We're taking a large flask of vegetable soup, and wedges of dry bread. Something for Ol' Mo of course, since he'll carry on rotten else. We love walking, Frank.'

'But for miles, mate? Yer need yer head examined.'

'Not really. It will give Lily and Sam a chance to be on their own for a while, you see. And it promises to be another nice day. But we have been ordered back in time for tea.'

'All right, gel. Have a good time.'

'I will. Give my love to Clancy.'

'Sauce-box!' He stood there, hunched up, hands in pockets, watching as she walked away.

She reached the village and was met just by Duck Pond Corner by Chris and Chook. Mr Mo was rakishly sporting a sprig of hawthorn in his collar.

'Thought you weren't going to be long,' Chris challenged. 'We told Mum we'd wait for breakfast till you came back. Honestly Hannah, you've taken hours.'

'No, I haven't.'

'Let's hurry up,' Chook said urgently. 'I'm starving.'

Laughing they began to run back to Rose Cottage and all but fell inside only to pull up short. A man was standing there, in the kitchen doorway. A man with his very stiff back to the light. Even so it was plain to see that he was thin and gaunt and dressed in Airforce uniform, and held a walking stick.

'Matt!' Hannah breathed his name, and walked towards him, arms opened wide. 'Oh Matt!'

Then Mr Moses bayed joyously, ran past her and jumped up at his old friend. Matt clung on to the doorpost and would have fallen if Sam had not been directly behind him to hold him up.

'Down boy!' Sam yelled so fiercely that a madly wagging russet tail immediately drooped between back legs. Two boys, happy grins banished, faltered. Hannah froze.

They all finished up in the kitchen, of course. Mr Moses was banished to his basket outside. The boys sat, wide-eyed and wondering, obediently spooning porridge into their mouths.

'Off you both go,' Lily said brightly to Hannah and Matt, 'into the front room. The fire's alight. I'll bring in tea.'

Hannah took hold of Matt's hand and walked with him into the front room. It was small and cosy, white-washed and black-beamed. Matt sat stiffly in a small armchair covered, as was the rest of the small suite, in dark red velveteen. Impulsively Hannah kissed him on the lips. He smiled into her tear-filled eyes.

'Don't,' he told her. 'Please don't! You don't want to see me blub, do you? It's so jolly decent to be back – so normal, Hannah.'

She plonked herself down on the chair opposite him and trying to stem her surge of emotion, chuckled, saying, 'Normal, Matt? If you listen to my mates you'd think the opposite was the case. But what is very wonderful indeed, is the fact that young Lenny's at music school and doing very well.'

Hannah was in the middle of telling Matt all the news when Lily came in with cups of tea.

Hannah sipped at the tea, grateful for the excuse to stop her jolly-dee act. It had cost her, to be the life and soul of the party when deep down she wanted to weep. Matt had suffered, was in great discomfort now, and it showed. But his whole character had changed, she could sense it – and it had been caused by something other than his own injuries, that was clear.

He had witnessed people being shot, seen them dying. . . watched as planes fell like burning darts, crashing and splintering onto the ground. And he had lost Mrs Gibson, his room in her home, and more than a few of his closest mates. Silently watching him Hannah thought that perhaps a part of Matt himself had died. It was heartbreaking. She turned, tear-blinded, to stare into the glowing embers of the fire. She would make it up to him, devote the rest of her life to him, try to comfort him as best she could.

She continued to stare silently into the heart of the fire.

'I say,' Matt's eyes were beginning to twinkle, though the lines on his face showed weariness and strain. 'It's not like you to be so quiet, Hannah. I'm sorry if I've put a damper on things.'

'Oh, you didn't,' she said quickly. 'You couldn't have. We – we just didn't know! We didn't expect you yet. They said you'd not be back for at least a month. We . . . we should have come in like normal human beings and not a tribe of banshees. I'm – I'm so sorry, Matt.'

'I should have let you know I was home. I've been in Warden Air-base Hospital.' He smiled. 'Didn't know much about it for a while. Then, when I got the hang of things, and knew I had a few days before. . . I couldn't wait to come back here. It's so good of the Ender-cots and all of you, and to see you, old girl. They have granted me a week's leave.'

'Oh, we're so glad!' Hannah was watching him. He looked so lined.

286

Probably it was a corset of some kind that was supporting his back, making him look so upright and stiff. Whatever it was he was wearing, it was killing him, she could tell. His legs must be bad too. He had been holding one walking stick to support himself just now, but beside his chair she saw the second one. Mute evidence of how difficult he was finding it just to move about.

She felt a fierce need to protect him, to see him all right. To let him know that he need never be alone while she was around. She would devote the rest of her life to him – willingly.

'It's hard cheese about Mrs Gibson,' Matt said gruffly, his smile dying almost before it had been born. 'She was a bit special, and always good to me. Stiff and starchy, but with a heart of gold.'

'I know, Matt,' Hannah almost crooned her agreement. 'But you have us now, and Eloise . . .'

'I'm sorry?' he frowned.

'Mrs Endercot! You have a room in her house. She's a darling and she's fond of you. So's Ellery and Walter of course, and all of us here.'

'That could be a problem for them.' His voice sounded grey, dusty, sad. 'I reckon I must be a jinx. All my friends seem to get blown away. But I had to come here – to you and to where everything seems so sane.'

'A few days before what, Matt?' Hannah asked suddenly. 'You still haven't said.'

'I'm sorry?'

'A few minutes ago you said you had a few days before . . . then you stopped. What is going to happen then?'

'My leg – it's ulcerated, and an old wound went wrong. Oh, and when it was broken it didn't set properly, so it splays out rather. It got worse when a boulder fell on it, and. . .' The ghost of his old grin flashed out. 'Bit of a mess, eh? I'm playing for sympathy for all I'm worth, and putting on a wizard show by the look of things. You ought to see your face, old thing.'

'Matt!'

'I'm fine, and damned lucky to be alive,' he told her firmly. 'There's nothing much to be bothered about. I'll be as good as new inside two shakes. Have to wait for further treatment, that's all. They wanted to build me up, they said. I told them I'd be like ten men after spending just a few minutes down here. It paid off and I've wangled these few days. Now I can't wait to come back again.'

'I'll look after you,' she told him urgently. 'Matt, I'll be at Eloise's place at every opportunity I get. When you come back after your operations, I'll make things up to you. Oh Matt! Matt darling, just having you home safe has answered all my prayers.'

She left her chair and knelt on the hearthrug, looking up into his blue eyes that had so many crinkly lines round them now. She took his hand in hers and kissed it; she was quivering with emotion and again needing to burst into tears. He sat there, stiff, still, looking down sadly at her tangle of curls.

'Oh matey,' he told her, 'you're so special to have around. Don't carry on about things, and by the way, it's me that should be looking after you.'

And then Lily came bustling in, bright and beaming, her apron covered with full-blown marigolds. 'More tea, anyone? No? Matt dear, you must be getting back soon. You've been travelling through the night, and hanging about on the station, and now here. Dear boy, you must be pretty-well done in. Eloise will be along in two shakes to fetch you. She has borrowed Ellery's runabout, remember?'

'I'll come too,' Hannah said at once.

'No,' Matt told her. 'I want you to go on your walk with the boys. And remember, it won't be all that long before I'll be able to join you three – not forgetting Ol' Mo – for a far longer time. No arguments, my girl. Please?'

Because he looked so worn and strained Hannah did not try to force the issue. She stood on the step with the others, waving goodbye and chunky, businesslike Eloise Endercot drove him away.

During the time Matt was home Hannah spent every available minute with him. When he fell into one of his silences she would chat away nineteen to the dozen, trying everything she could to rekindle the old sparkle in him that she remembered so well. She gained most success when she was speaking of the twins and of Lenny, who had already come from Norseby twice to see him.

'Little Norseby, isn't that strange?' Hannah asked Matt one evening. 'It might still be called village, but I'd say it's more like a small country town. It has just about everything.'

'Everything?' Matt repeated, smiling a little. It was difficult not to be swept along by Hannah.

'Well, it has a little flea-pit of a cinema, a Cottage Hospital, the music school as well as two others, primary and general. Properly set out tennis courts, a football pitch, things like that. On the other hand, we have one main road, with extra houses and things placed hugamug here and there. And we use The Green for everything. Oh, and another thing. Little Norseby has a fish and chip shop. Yum yum! Not forgetting the Hall.' She chuckled. 'I'll never forget how surprised I was at our first show here. I mean, overnight, there sprang up this massive tent and there was room for long benches and tables and chairs, and lots and lots of people. I couldn't believe my eyes.' She paused for breath then added, 'But when I come to think about it, I like our tent. It has character!'

She had cracked it. For the first time since returning, Matt laughed. It was a little rusty, a little feeble, but it was a laugh.

'Oh I do love you!' she told him.

'And I love you, matey.'

'Truly?'

'Of course.'

She eyed him tragically. 'But you love the twins and Lily and Ginnie, and Raven of course. You like it when she massages your neck, don't you?'

'Bliss!' he told her, smiling. 'And she reminds me of a painting I saw once. In fact, when she came in with you the other day I was quite struck by her calm face and her velvety brown eyes. Quite took my breath away.'

'So that's it! I saw you look at her, and you seemed sort of shocked and I thought . . .'

'That I was dumbstruck?' He ruffled her hair, something he often did these days. 'Perhaps I was, in a way. I was wondering where I had seen her before. She has the face of a particularly lovely icon that I prayed to once. I'm sorry for going on, old girl. I still get mixed up, you see.'

'Well, I'm glad that you like her, and that she can massage some of your aches and pains away. She trained as a nurse, you know. She – she nursed her husband until he died. My beloved Raven is one of the gentle carers of this world.'

'And Ginnie's the clear-cut dependable kind.'

'And me?'

'You're the greatest cheerer-upper I know,' he told her, 'God bless you, matey. You have the biggest and most generous heart, and you've brought the sunshine back into my life.'

'Then that will do for starters,' she told him and gave him one of her enthusiastic kisses, which bent his head back too far and made him wince, and there she was, apologising all over again.

Hannah cried when she left for work on the day Matt had to leave. It was Raven who drove Matt to the station, in the Endercot car. James had given his permission, since there was no one else available. Apple-picking was still the order of the day, and now the Land Girls were roped in for that chore.

There was a golden haze over everything and a pale purple skyline looked mysterious and wonderful. The road to the station, now very familiar, wound round before them. Matt looked at Raven's profile and said quietly, 'It was you I saw. *You!*'

Raven looked away from the road for an instant, her eyes large and luminous.

He laughed in a dry, self-conscious way. 'Damn, I'm making a mess of this. I told Hannah how it was. It seemed that you were there, Raven. I saw you!'

She stopped the car in a break in the verge and faced him. 'The mind can play strange tricks, Matt. When I first visited you, when you were sitting in Eloise's parlour, I thought of something Hannah said once. I did not know her very well at the time, but it was so apt. She looked at a photograph of someone I loved and said that. . . Matt, just for an instant, you looked silvery!'

'Thank you,' he said quietly. 'I'm glad.'

She started the motor again. They did not speak until they reached the station. They sat side by side on a bench and waited and Matt spoke again.

'We had a guide. He was called Miguelito. He reckoned he'd shoot laggards. I knew I'd be the one he'd do for in the end. Funny, he was the one that finished up literally carrying me. I owe him my life; we all do. I wasn't to know that at the time. And when I was really out on the limb, on the day I found that for all his shouting and prodding, I just couldn't move, I prayed. And my prayers were answered. I had Miguelito to carry my body, and you, my icon, to give me faith. Does that sound mad?'

She turned to look up at him and very gently he cupped her face in his hands and kissed her. It was a benediction.

The train came roaring into the station and he boarded it with her help. They smiled at each other and the whistle blew.

Raven just stood there, alone on the platform, watching the train disappear. She continued to stand, listening until she could no longer hear the racing of its huge iron wheels. She should be going back, but for once, Raven wanted to play truant.

The weather was still holding, which was wonderful. The countryside echoed with the sound of tractors cutting grass for silage. It was the season of mists and mellow fruitfulness. Now the last of the apples were being gathered in. Apple mountains were being built.

Villagers and friends from far afield would be getting together quite soon for the annual cider-making. For a number of years enthusiasts had gathered to participate. Here old Walt came into his own yet again. As well as his thresher, he also had a mobile cider press. But all that was still to come. For now it was fruit-picking time.

As agile as a monkey, Hannah perched on the topmost rung of the ladder. She had tirelessly filled basket after basket. She worked hard,

290

laughing with the others, many of whom she knew. She was happy, for Matt had gone back for fresh treatment; he would return as soon as he could. He had explained that he would be allowed sick leave, and then be grounded for a while. They would find him duties he could cope with until he was back to full health and could fly again. Dear Matt. How much better he looked now! Raven's massages had something to do with it, she felt sure. Her friend must have healing hands.

James was beneath her, lifting the filled baskets, looking relaxed and sporty in casual clothes – unusual for him. Big and strong, he was a man among men. She pictured Matt as she had seen him last and sighed. The poor darling had lost several stones in weight, she was sure, but the smile was already coming back into his eyes.

She breathed in the apple smell, and saw how the autumn sunlight dappled the leaves. It was like being in a private world of whispering foliage, and the breeze was the fruit-perfumed breath of God. How different all this was from Walker Street.

Walker Street. Thank heaven she need never go there again. Just remembering the evil look on Ram's face made her break out in a cold sweat. Thank goodness Sophia had come up with such a brilliant idea. The Marner mob would be no trouble, knowing what a bombshell Sophia's bank safe held. Then why was it that when at noon, Raven had still not come back, and Trixie arrived, leaping from Tan-Tivvy's back, the fear suddenly rising in Hannah was almost a physical pain?

She stood at the top of the ladder, poised like a statue among the concealing leaves, and heard Trixie's voice below.

'Darling,' she was saying to James, 'what on earth made you leave us last night? After all, the Rising Sun is hardly the Rookwood. The evening was so interesting. I met a rather nasty bald-headed man who said he was looking for a Land Girl who, by the description he gave, sounded just like one of your lot. He was looking for a Londoner.'

The words went on. Light, bright, terrifying words. It seemed that Trixie had made it her business to get to know the bald-headed man – who must surely be Ram. She had answered his questions and in turn questioned him.

'And of course, darling,' Trixie went on, 'I did not go into details. I mean, I did not disclose the fact that we have not one but *two* people of that ilk in our employ. But I did say that you had several Land Girls. He was just gasping to meet you. You can't imagine how disappointing it all was when I found that you had sneaked out on me.'

'Sneaked out, nonsense!' James was saying crisply. 'There was paperwork waiting to be done. Now if you don't mind – we're busy people round here.'

291

She laughed, but her annoyance was obvious. Then she spurred Tan-Tivvy, and streaked off like a messenger from hell.

'Oh shit!' Hannah breathed. 'Our plan's gone wrong.' Then hope filled her. If Ma had passed on that message, Biff and Co would not be searching for her at all. It must be a queer kind of mistake. There were millions of bald-headed men about, and not all of them could be Ram. In any case, the Rising Sun was in Norseby and not in Lindell. Suddenly, very desperately, Hannah wished she could stay where she was, half-hidden among the leafy branches of the apple tree. But time seemed to fly.

Now the pickers were leaving off and shouting to each other not to be late. They moved away in groups, sharing transport where they could, or walked, went on horseback or rode bikes. Walter came up, grinning at James who was waiting with the three girls.

'Don't forget we've got the fight of our lives on tonight, Mr St John. That there Norseby lot have sworn to give us a run for our money. They're laying bets, and the odds are agin us.'

'Then they're on a losing streak, Walter,' James replied calmly. 'They know nothing of our team, but I do. I also know quite a bit about their play. Since I am the captain, I have made it my business to watch them at their game over the past few months.' He smiled his stiff smile. 'It will be quite safe for you to put money on Lindell.'

Walter chuckled and nodded his head, before walking off with the eagerness of a young man, to join Bet.

Chapter Thirty-Four

'*Too tired*?' James looked both disbelieving and furious. 'Nonsense!'

'I am. I am!' Hannah told him frantically. 'It's cost me all my strength to come plodding up here to Knollys. All I wanted to do was go home to bed.'

'But we need you to help us win.'

She put her hand nervously to her brow and pleaded the beginnings of a headache as well. Somehow, she went on, she hadn't felt right since Matt's return and now he had gone back it was a kind of let-down. And also it was such a worrying time, the state of his spine and legs. She enlarged on this theme, despising herself, for using Matt's name in vain. Could James tell what a hypocrite she was?

Hannah kept her face hidden in the shadows of the room he used as an office. James was sitting at his desk; his face under the desk-light looked stern, hawk-like and – contemptuous.

She felt as though her heart was bleeding, it hurt so much to let him and her friends down. But how could she go with them to the Rising Sun tonight – or any other night, if it came to that? Above all else, she must lie low. She would have to hide until Ram went away again – or until he found her. It was vital that he never discovered the where-abouts of Frank. Did any of them in fact know that Frank had sur-vived their near-fatal beating? They would soon want to alter that!

Hannah racked her brains, trying to remember what Ma Carpenter might have said. Had she, Hannah, pointed out quite clearly that the letter was meant just to involve herself, to safeguard herself, unless it became necessary to say otherwise? Frank was in no condition to stand up to anyone, let alone a murdering swine. She drew in a deep shaky breath and looked at James pleadingly.

'I honestly don't feel well enough.'

He leaned back in his chair, not taking his eyes away from her face for a moment, then he very slowly and deliberately folded his arms.

293

The silence was unbearable. She longed to cut and run – make a dash for it. But where could she go? All she had was Walker Street and a pile of rubble, and Hawksley, and here. Yes, Knollys – where it felt safe in spite of the presence of this insufferable man.

She was half out of her chair when his voice cracked out. 'Sit down!'

She obeyed automatically, hating herself for doing so.

'Bloody hell!' she exploded. 'D'you want to give me a heart attack?'

He smiled bleakly. 'That's better,' he told her. 'Now you're the Hannah I know.'

'Because I swore?' She was glaring, needing to hurt someone. 'Thank you very much. If you must know, I try hard *not* to be me. I try simply because I don't want to let Ginnie or Raven down. I thought I was doing quite well, but you have a really rotten effect on me. You look down your nose, and act like the god your mum's always calling on, and sometimes – sometimes I just can't stand the sight of you!'

'Feeling's mutual,' he told her crisply. 'Now tell me the truth.'

'I told you. I'm tired and depressed, and I have a headache.'

'I see. So you can't be yourself and give the occasional cuss in case you let your friends down, but you can let the whole of Lindell down because of a pseudo-headache.'

Her cheeks were flaming. He was hateful, hateful! He could see right through her. She fancied that he always could, right from the start. Old devil! She wanted very much to take him down a peg, but she couldn't. He held all the aces, and in the final analysis, he was the big cheese around here. There was absolutely nothing she could do about that.

He had her floundering. She could tell by his expression that he knew it. Now he pressed home his point.

'You are happy to let us all down? Even my mother, who is now, amazingly, quite interested in our match. Oh, she won't grace us with her presence – that's not her style, but she wants us to win. *I* want us to win. My dear good girl, are you really so determined?'

Momentarily Hannah was unable to reply. He went on, his voice grave-cold: 'And since you brought my mother into it, shall I tell you something else? Sometimes you are too damned like her to be true. But she can and has opted out of things that didn't suit her. She has, without hesitation, always put herself first – something I never thought you'd do. Are you quite determined to emulate her?'

'Yes. No. I don't know. Oh, shut up!' She felt so trapped that she had to let fly – and James St John was the only one near. 'And don't be so sarcastic,' she flared. 'You'd try the patience of a saint with your overbearing ways. You're not being fair. You take a mean advantage because you're the boss. Well, let me tell you this, I reckon—'

'Stop posturing,' he cut in ruthlessly. 'And tell me what's really the matter. What's going on?'

Posturing, so that's what he called it. He had recognised her act for what it was worth. Worse, he must suspect that deep inside she was nothing but a quivering wreck.

Suddenly, humiliatingly, she could not keep up her façade. Hot angry tears began to flow. She hated crying; it left her without dignity. Fancy blubbing like a two-year-old. That was bad at the best of times, but in front of him!

She hid her face in her hands, and did not hear him approach. Then she felt his arm round her shoulders. 'Come on, girl. Let's have the truth now, eh? Is it because your airman's gone back?'

She shook her head. 'No.'

'Then what is it exactly? Trust me – two heads are better than one.'

'It's – it's what Trixie said,' she replied tragically. 'I'm scared stiff that she might have been talking to Ram Rawlins. You know, the man who—'

'If it was, it was,' he told her blandly. 'But unless we go to the Rising Sun, we won't find out, will we? I need you there, if only to tell me if it really is him. If your suspicions are correct, just leave things to me.'

She smiled a wobbly smile and asked shakily, 'You mean you'll clock him one?'

'If necessary. But it would be better in this particular instance, if we roped in PC Dalton. Keep things official, you understand?'

'James,' she said quietly, 'you make things sound so plain sailing, so – easy. I was a quivering jelly a minute ago and now you . . .' She looked searchingly into his eyes. 'Cunning old devil, aren't you?' she laughed, and gave a sob at the same time. 'You know all the right things to say. And I reckon you've never been scared in your life.'

'Well, there you are wrong,' he told her. 'I have been very afraid and felt so betrayed that it has scarred me for life.'

'If I said that to you,' she told him carefully, 'you would tell me, no, *command* me to explain.'

'Am I that bad?'

'Like a devil from hell.'

'Then I stand corrected.' His tone was such that she felt irritated again.

'Now you're treating me like a child. Well, I'm not. And I don't like the way you talk about your mum either.' She jutted out her chin. 'I bet you'd have given me short shrift if *I'd* said she was selfish, and accused her of things. You'd hate anyone who tried to put her down. And she would be the same regarding you. I don't understand you

295

people, but I'm old enough to know that blood's thicker than water any time.'

'Atta girl,' he said, and suddenly there was laughter in his eyes. 'I really do stand corrected.'

'There you go again! When will you accept that I'm not the age of Lily's twins?' She bit her lip, suddenly realising the real truth of it. 'No!' she exclaimed. 'You don't think I'm a kid and that's the problem, isn't it? You know I'm adult! And that's why you so carefully keep me in my place. I reckon – yes, I really believe that if I was as young as the boys, you'd accept me as a mate! As it is, you wouldn't trust me no further than you could throw Cobbitt's prize bull.'

Unbelievably his arm tightened round her and he was looking down at her in a searching way.

'Strangely,' he told her, 'I do trust you. Out of them all, I trust you! You are too open and above board for me to believe anything else.'

'More even than Raven?' she asked, taken back.

'And your beloved straightforward Ginnie,' He was faintly teasing now, which made her feel mad as hell, because at times like this she quite liked him.

'I can't imagine you ever being scared,' she told him again. 'And as for being betrayed, well – I think that most folk round here would be too terrified to even try to do you down.'

'Hannah,' he asked her, dismissing the last remark, 'are you or are you not going to play for the village tonight?'

'Yes,' she told him firmly. 'I *am* going to play for the village. After all, how could I possibly defy you?'

Then she jumped up, refusing his offer of a lift back in his snazzy red Jaguar, and rushed outside to her bike. She had to pedal like crazy because time was getting on and she knew her friends would be getting fidgety. Perhaps even beginning to despair. Hannah never was a one for being too punctual, or tidy, or patient, or . . .

'I might as well admit it,' she said out loud. 'I'm really a lost cause. Thank goodness I've got so many nice people on my side!'

The Rising Sun was larger than the Rookwood, more brightly lit, more up-to-date, and crowded with Yanks since it was nearer to Matching. There were many English airmen too, but none that the girls recognised. Full of dread, Hannah searched the crowds for Ram's huge bald head. Then James was there, speaking easily, making it seem that it was by sheer accident that he was at Hannah's side. She breathed in shakily. Against all the odds, she had a champion. It was absurd how dearly she would have liked to throw herself at his feet to

296

thank him. Stupid, in fact. Instead, she looked up rather a long way, and smiled warmly and wonderfully into his eyes.

The game progressed. It was a glorious evening. And Hannah became a heroine.

'You'll be going down in village history for that winning throw,' Ellery told her. 'Never has there been such a swift and effective double top.'

Flushed with pleasure, Hannah found herself caught up in the joy of the evening. Every so often she looked across at James. He was sitting with Raven on one side of him and Trixie on the other.

Bloody hell, Hannah thought. That Trixie would like to kill Raven stone dead – and I swear that James looks positively smug.

After the celebratory drinks, and arranging of a return match, Hannah piled into the back of Ellery's lorry and joined in with half the village in a sing-song. They roared their way through *Roll out the Barrel, She'll Be Coming Round the Mountain, The Old Bull and Bush, Lambeth Walk* and other well-knowns. For a while all was forgotten except the joy of victory.

Raven and Ginnie were asleep long before Hannah. She lay in her bed, tossing and turning, until she finally closed her eyes.

Her dreams were peopled with men whose eyes narrowed menacingly. And too, there were tarty, hostile women with blood round their mouths. They were all whispering together, and Hannah knew they sensed she was in mortal danger and waiting, giggling maliciously behind their hands.

The dream went on, like it did on the screen of Norseby picturehouse. And Hannah knew that she had to run. Yes, run like mad for her life. But something terrible had happened to her legs. She looked down and saw that they were encased in blue, Air-Force blue, where they should have been covered by breeches coloured donkey-brown. But it did not matter; what *did* was that her treacherous legs were refusing to move.

And Ram was there, his head floating in air, like an obscene balloon. His disembodied hand was floating too, towards her, and it was clenching a sharp and glittering knife. Then a shrivelled-up Frank appeared, standing between them both. Poor old Frank, who was now too weak to take the skin off a rice pudding, was trying to defend her. She yelled with all her might, trying to warn him, and pushed him away. The knife was still coming for her – it was touching her chest. She felt pain.

Even in her dream Hannah heard the scream and recognised it as her own. Her heart was beating, her mouth had gone dry, and for all her terror, her airman's legs still refused to move. Then Raven was

297

there, cradling her in her arms, and Ginnie was scolding her in a gentle way and telling her not to be a chump. There was nothing to be scared of – it was only a dream. They were there and always would be. She was not to worry. She was with her mates.

Then it was Raven's turn, speaking sweet, cool sentences that held all the calm certainty in the world. And as the soft assurances continued, Hannah nestled against the security of Raven's bosom, wept a little, and finally fell dreamlessly to sleep.

Alone in Knollys James sat pensively before the fire. It was the early hours, but sleep refused to come. He kept thinking about Hannah, remembering how he had spotted her once when she had been alone on one of her walks. She was laughing and feeding ducks and also some wild geese. The weather was worsening and the creatures had been crowding round her feet, quacking and honking, and making such a noise that she hadn't heard James's approach. He had reined in Pegasus, content to watch her.

She was slender, boyishly so in her working dungarees and too-large white sweater, one that he recognised as Raven's, for Hannah herself seemed to have very few clothes. Her brown hair was windswept, and as she laughed aloud James noticed again her strong, white even teeth.

Suddenly, she noticed that she was not alone. If anything, her smile widened.

'I hope you've brought some scraps with you,' she called. 'These birds have such appetites they'd eat old Pegasus, given half the chance.'

He had smiled cynically. 'Don't encourage them,' he called. 'Especially the geese. There are those around here who just love them with apple sauce.'

She had raised her brows and he had felt the scrutiny of her eyes. It was the merest flick of a glance, yet it had given him the uncomfortable sensation of having been weighed up and found wanting.

'Do they like squirrel pie too?' she asked, her voice unamused. 'There are lots of them in the trees round Knollys. I like to feed them too. Don't tell me they're actually safe? You don't seem to like anything very much, do you, Mr St John?'

There it was again, her capacity for putting him in his place.

The irritation she always managed to make him feel rose to the fore again. She was lively and sometimes seemed too damned sure of herself. She obviously got a kick out of lipping him, and even standing toe to toe with him at times. Darn it, there wasn't a ha'pporth of her; her head barely reached his chest. Even so, in spite of everything, even when she was angry, she was astonishingly attractive. There was a

298

richness in her colouring; her face was small and mischievous; her mouth generous and good-humoured, and there were little laughter lines at the corners of her eyes.

Suddenly James wanted to have her there before him so that he could take her by the shoulders and shake her. Shake her and tell her that she might know a hell of a lot about lipping a chap and laughing at him too, but she didn't know a single damned thing about men. Then he wanted to tell her to stay near to hand simply because he missed her when she was not around. God! Now who was the fool?

Had she really been unaware of how desirable she was, the evening before, when they had been here in Knollys alone? She had been so determined not to go to the Rising Sun. He had worn her down and learned that it had nothing to do with darts. He just wanted her to be there, the Lord only knew why. Fiery young devil, always ready to spar up. But even when she glared, there was something in him that made him want to hold out a helping hand. And then she had finally let go and cried! Dammit! She got right under his skin. And there was something else. Something foreign to his belief about women.

Somehow he knew that *she* would never ever let anyone down. How different things would have been, had he known Hannah then! He found himself wishing that he had known her, and she him, in his hour of need. Yes. They should have known each other long ago. How different it might have turned out if he had seen her sitting there, on his side, that day in court.

James began remembering . . .

Chapter Thirty-Five

It was early still, before noon, and autumn gold dusted the day. Hannah stayed alone, in the sitting room that had a window facing the grounds at the front of the house. Her mind was on James. Why was it that women angered him so? She remembered the raggedness of his voice when he was upset. It gave away the fact that he had feelings, but that he was used to holding them down. This was so sad, she thought, but then the whole world was sad and worrying; uncertainty was everywhere – even for animals, who were innocent enough. Why, just a week ago a stray bomb had descended on one of the fields outside Matching. It had managed to kill three poor old milch cows that hadn't done anyone harm. Life simply wasn't fair.

Just consider what had happened to Matt! She would work and slave for the rest of her life, to try and make things better for him. . . *if* fate and Ram Rawlins let her survive, of course.

Then the breath caught in her throat, for she saw James, on Pegasus, approaching the house. She remembered all over again how she had lost face and admitted to him how afraid she was – she'd even blubbed! It was awful! Where he was concerned, she really needed to hold on to her dignity. It mattered more than anything else.

She watched as he dismounted agilely; he really was a fine magnificent figure of a man. She could understand why he hated the fact that he had been turned down for active service, and could well imagine the snide remarks he might have received because of it. Some people weren't all that far removed from those types who'd handed out white feathers during the First World War. Poor old James. No wonder he was bitter and twisted most of the time.

Yet his was a great responsibility, making sure that there was as much produce as possible to each acre of the land. Striving so that Britishers had a little sugar for their famous cups of tea. And the paperwork! Lord Almighty, there were mountains of it on his desk. It took a determined man to even dare try to tackle it. There were many kinds of bravery and she knew that James St John *was* brave. For starters, he had knocked tough, supremely fit Spence for six.

She heard his footsteps outside. Something made her move away from the window, and quickly sit down on one of the easy chairs beside the fire. The door opened and he came in, arrogant and by the look on his face, daring her to disobey.

'Pack your things,' he commanded. 'I'm getting you out of here.'

Shocked, not believing her ears, she snapped back, 'Not on your nellie!'

'Do as I say, or I'll have you sent away,' he told her in a matter-of-fact tone. 'There's a hostel at Takely. Or I could get you back in Colchester's Lexton Road. There are also plenty of other options.' He gave her a frosty smile. 'And the more you argue, the further away you'll go.'

'Do you wanna bet?' she challenged him, 'I told you. I'm staying here.'

He folded his arms and looked down his nose. 'My girl, you will do as you're told.'

She laughed, incredulous. Was he really going to send her away from her friends, The Musketeers? From all the lovely people she knew? She had to stop this.

'I won't go,' she told him flatly. 'I'll ask Sophia to help me fight you on this one. Believe me, I will.'

'She has no authority. This is a Ministry matter, and I shall see to it that my word goes. Scat!'

'I will not!'

'All right, my girl, here it is. I wanted to hide the fact from you, but – unfortunately, I believe it is your unsavoury London friend who approached Trixie. He has taken a room in Little Norseby, and has been making enquiries about someone whose description fits you. The person he seeks is a Land Girl who is stationed near or around Matching Airfield. The reason he needs to find her is that he has a message from her stepfather. Need I go on?'

'Oh!' Her face went white with misery. 'And I suppose darling Trixie couldn't wait to tell him all about Frank!'

'Actually, she did not. All right?'

'I don't even know why you like that woman,' she grumbled. 'Raven is the one you should look at. Raven's—'

'Perfection all round,' he finished. 'Stop wasting time.'

'Where do you think you're going to take me?'

'Knollys.'

'Ha!' Her tone now became as sarcastic as his. 'Trixie would go over to Norseby and deliberately seek out Ram if that happened.' She shrugged and shook her head. 'You don't know anything about women, do you?'

'No – and I don't want to.'

'Why?' she flung at him. 'Be honest for a change, and tell me why!'

'No. That's beside the point and to do with my private life.'

'Ha! And the decision you're making for me, is *not* about my private life, I suppose. Have a heart, James. Come on, fair do's!'

He gave her a long stony look, then turned and deliberately shut the door. After that he strode across the room and sat on the chair opposite her.

'Last night,' he told her, 'you let your hair down to me. Now I shall do the same to you. All right?'

'I'm sorry about last night. I shouldn't have . . .'

'Be quiet, Hannah. It's my turn. You should know that my brother and I had a best friend His name was Deacon. His father was a kind of priest in a rather dotty religion. He was considered to be something of a nut, but his followers had an almost fanatical faith. Non-believers also gave him a grudging respect, especially the women. Even quite a few of them here – usually those with well-filled purses. But they believed him to be the soul of love and kindness. In fact, so spiritual and wonderful that he could all but sprout wings.'

'Was that really so bad?' Hannah asked, wondering where all of this was leading to. 'At least they had faith in him. Miss Pitt told me that if you take away someone's faith you damn them for life. She meant any kind of belief – in God, or Jesus, Buddha, even the Red Indians' spirit gods. She told me once . . .'

'We are not speaking about faith, but rather of Reverend Stiles,' James corrected her. 'Because of him, and only him, nervous, ineffectual but pretty little Mrs Stiles was accepted into all sorts of exclusive societies, and invited to all kinds of social affairs. She became one of the most popular ladies in the community. She revelled in all that! It gave her a sense of importance that she never had at home.'

'I don't see much harm in that, and where's all this leading to?'

'Would it kill you,' he asked, 'to just hold your tongue for a few minutes and let me get on? I don't think Mrs Stiles was all that happy with her husband, but she truly loved Deacon. Also, she was wonderfully welcoming to us St Johns, simply because we were his best chums. On our side, we thought she was just the sort that Miles and I would have loved to call Mother. She was very feminine, loving and kind. Occasionally she seemed a bit nervous and fluffy, but she always had time for us boys. My brother and I adored her. When Miles and Deacon suddenly decided to leave home, Deacon made a point of asking me to keep an eye on her. I promised gladly.' He stopped and looked down.

'And then what happened?' Hannah prompted him quietly.

'One evening, when out riding, Pegasus slipped a shoe, so I stabled him at the Stiles's place, and went up to the house that Miles and I had come to look on as a second home. Reverend Stiles was drunk and in the process of savagely beating his wife. He looked incredibly evil. I pulled him off her and when he tried to have a go at me, I punched him – hard. He fell, hit his head and died instantly.'

'Strike me pink!' He had all of her attention now. 'That must have been sticky, James!'

'It was a nightmare after that. The inquest was awful. Innuendo after innuendo. I was accused of having had a passion for the woman, and of killing her husband in a jealous rage. The police took it seriously and I finished up in court.' James's expression was now grave-grey, bleak. 'And that pretty woman, whom I had looked upon as sweet and angelic, stood there and kept her mouth shut. She did not attempt to deny the rumour of my adoration. Even seemed to go along with my so-called lover's jealous rage. Worst of all, she stood there and denied the fact that Stiles had ever laid a hand on her. When she did open her mouth, it was to say that her husband was a saint who wouldn't harm a fly.'

'If I'd been her I would have spilt a bibful about the mean old swine,' Hannah said stoutly. 'And I would have dropped dead before I'd defend him at your expense.' Her tone was indignant. 'What a rotten thing to do. I can't understand women like that.'

'That's because you are as straight as a die and besides . . . You wouldn't have allowed the man to illtreat you in the first place.'

She gave him a wicked grin. 'Course I wouldn't. Bloody hell, he'd have to sleep sometime and then – wham! Right on top of the noddle with the biggest saucepan I could find. He wouldn't come to for weeks.'

'Clearly Mrs Stiles did not want it known that her husband was a sadist, and a cruel father to boot – a slimy hypocrite she had kow-towed to all of her married life. It did not go with the public image, you see. She was used to basking in his reflected glory, and did not want to lose what popularity she had. She was playing to all her old cronies – who incidentally, were lapping everything up. Especially the lies about me. They wanted to believe in their saintly Reverend, and his martyrdom. I was out in the cold, I can tell you.'

'But where was Sophia in all of this?'

'It was not her fault, not really. I did not let her know the full extent of my troubles. She has always been so dedicated to her art – always

303

put it first, you see. So, since at the time she was staying in the city, trying to get an exhibition together, I played it down. The upshot being that she telephoned to say that she would be back as soon as she could. She did not know that I was a dead duck, at least that's how I felt.'

Hannah's eyes were wide with distress for him. She could imagine how awful it had been, and knew first-hand all about having to face troubles alone.

'James,' she said quietly, 'I'm so sorry.'

'Oh, it wasn't so bad, not in the end. Deacon was contacted, guessed what had happened, and got compassionate leave. He flew home and arrived – in the nick of time. He didn't give a tuppenny cuss about any illusions his father's devotees had. He told the court, and the world, the real truth. Nailed Stiles for the brute he was. He went on to explain why he had joined the Navy as soon as he could, just to escape. He even went so far as to tell the court that there were medical records of the many injuries he himself had received. Sometimes even broken bones. All listed as accidents, of course. To think, Deacon had never breathed a word to us!'

'What happened after that?'

'He took his mother away to live with relatives in New Zealand. I never hear from him now – too embarrassed, I suppose, and of course there's the war. Anyway, for quite a while the old hags in this area had a beanfeast. It's a wonder their tongues never dropped off. I swear that some of the really old girls around here still half-believe I'm a murderer.'

'And it has all left a very nasty taste in your mouth, hasn't it, James?' she asked, her heart going out to him. She could imagine how it had been. Him standing there, mutely defiant, haughty and proud. He had not run away like Deacon, or like Miles, come to that. He had faced them all. She went on, 'I suppose it has made you suspicious of – of female friends since?'

He thought about what she said and nodded briefly. 'I suppose so, Hannah. Yes, you could say that.'

'Well,' she informed him firmly, 'I just wish that I had been here for you then. I would have told them a thing or two!'

'I know.' His smile blazed out and it so transformed him that it took her breath away. 'Hannah,' he went on, 'you can have no idea just how great a weight I've just pushed off my chest. Just as you did by telling me your troubles last night. It must have brought you some kind of relief – if only to know that you're not alone. So – will you now let me help?'

'It would kill me, to leave Ginnie and Raven. And—'

304

'If you won't come with me to Knollys, how about going to Cobbitt with Frank?'

'I might just as well stay here.'

'A registered Land Army keep?'

'Oh!'

'We can at least hope that if he gets this far, he'll see that you're not in residence and so try hostels elsewhere. And in the meantime, Clancy has a phone, and I'll be in contact every day. I promise to leave no stone unturned to keep you safe. So what do you say?'

It did not make sense; she did not want to go. But willy-nilly she found herself packing her cardboard suitcase, and writing swift little explanatory notes to the two remaining Musketeers . . .

It was strange, how everything fell into shape after that. And how everyone in turn came to see Snow Queen – never mentioning Hannah, of course. No questions were asked, not to Hannah at least, and because it was such a busy time, Hannah herself tried not to mind. Frank and Clancy made a great fuss of her, and dear old Peg was like a hen with one chick.

Now villagers and friends came specially to assist in the cider-making. Walt drove up with the necessary equipment in the back of his rusty old lorry. Everyone around waited, ready for action in their woollies and wellies. Rubber boots were very necessary since all too soon the ground would become like glue, as slippery as an ice rink by the end of the day. And the smell of crushed apples would rise above all.

The work began. It was Hannah's job to fill up buckets from the apple mountains. Buckets were put in place, bung ready, and the hopper machine began grinding whole apples into soggy mash. The pulp was collected in a large bucket, then shovelled onto cloth that fitted onto a wooden frame. Another cloth was placed over the fruit, then more apple, more cloths, and so on.

A cheer went up when the first layered pile was pulled under the press, which was operated by Walter armed with a jack. The apple cloth frames were carefully kept level and the free-flowing juice raced through a tube and into a waiting pail. After that, the juice was poured into oak barrels – lovely old things waiting and ready to receive such bountiful good cheer.

The work went on all day, and would continue until the last apple mountain had gone. In the end it was all a glorious lark as the helpers became covered in juice and flying fruit debris. Breathing in the tangy odour, looking around at all her country friends, Hannah's heart was full to overflowing.

And then, amazingly, leaning on his crutches and looking the hand-somest young devil there, she saw Matt.

She ran to him, messy and beaming, arms open wide.

'Matt, Matt, what are you doing here?'

'They're not ready for me yet, old girl,' he told her happily. 'I have been given a further break.' He pulled a face. 'I didn't realise that you'd moved. I'm not going to get over here to see you as much as I'd like. The old back and legs are still being a bit of a nuisance, I'm afraid. Maybe if I can get a lift now and then? Mrs Endercot brought me just now.'

'There'll be millions of people just aching to help,' she told him. 'You wait and see.' At that moment a group of locals were taking their leave and waved their hands in a friendly way to Matt. He responded by grinning widely and calling, 'Wizard to be back. Pip-pip!'

Hannah cringed, but heard herself continuing breezily, 'And when you can't make it, I'm sure that Raven or Ginnie will see to it that you don't get bored.'

'Or you could cycle over to meet me, eh?'

'Of course,' she replied stoutly, knowing deep down that James would never allow that – at least for her to attempt it alone. She looked over to where he was standing, talking to Walter, determinedly not looking her way. It's my own fault, she told herself. I never miss a chance to jump down his throat. Still, she comforted herself, perhaps everything would work out – eventually.

She came back to the present because Matt was continuing his silly ass act. What was wrong with the man?

'Why are you continually speaking like that?' she blurted out before she could stop herself. 'I thought you'd stopped, but you've been putting on that old toffee ever since you came back. What with your pip-pip and stuff, you sound daft! What's got into you?'

He shrugged, all pretence leaving him now. 'Can we be alone for a minute or two, Hannah?'

'Of course,' she told him. 'Can you make it to just behind those trees?' She laughed saucily. 'They'll think we're off to have a kiss and cuddle, of course. Do you mind?'

'Not if you don't.'

She was very aware that James was watching them as they walked slowly away from the main group. Matt found the going tough, but she helped him as best she could. They gained privacy of sorts and with great difficulty Matt lowered himself; she sat next to him on the ground that was thickly carpeted with leaves.

'Hannah, I'm not the bloke you knew,' he told her raggedly. 'God help me, I don't think I'll ever be the same again. I've been acting up, trying to fool myself more than anyone else.'

'Why?' she asked quietly. 'There's no need.'

He shrugged, all pretence leaving him now. 'I think there is. It's nothing to do with what happened to me, rather what a vicious fate has slung at so many others I cared for. I can't seem to get them out of my mind. Any of them! I – dammit, I feel that I can't truly laugh ever again. Only as you saw – act it out, pretend none of it matters. I think Raven understands.'

'Tell me about it,' she told him tearfully because now she saw how bereft he was. 'Explain it to me, Matt.'

'Oh God! You don't need to know.'

'Perhaps . . . perhaps I do!'

'I have lost friends, Hannah,' he told her painfully. 'Chaps who were so alive, so full of plans for the future. Then there was Titch. He was like a younger brother to me. All gone, yes all of them, and for what? There was another youngster too. A Frenchman, a baker's son. He risked his life for me, as did all of his family and friends. Each and every one determined to get people at risk away to safety.'

'Surely that should make you proud and grateful, Matt. Not sad?'

'I reached Spain, and had to wait a while for the formalities – you know, to verify we were who we said, official debriefing, that sort of thing. In the meantime another group of escapees came to join us. They were a week or so later than us. I – I learned that the Gestapo had caught up with my French family and shot them all. I understand too, that they tortured the baker's son, but he never gave them the names of other members of the Resistance. That's how the last batch got safely away.'

'Oh Matt! I'm so sorry.' Hannah was weeping because of the terrible tale, and the deep grief in Matt's voice. 'I never dreamed . . .'

'Of course you didn't,' he told her. 'How could you? But I have come to the conclusion that I'm far from being alone. It seems to me that the whole of this damned world is full of desperate people. I believe that Raven understands something of how I feel.'

'Yes. Yes! She has suffered terribly, over losing Francis.'

'Being here has helped her,' he continued, 'just as I knew, while up there in the mountains, that being here would help me. I had to get back. I thought of you, and the boys, and just about everyone. And,' he looked self-conscious, 'when things were really tough I thought I saw Raven's face. She appeared to me as a Madonna. She – she is very, very special, Hannah, and seems like an angel to me. She is immensely lovable.'

'Matt,' she told him unsteadily, 'what makes you think I didn't know?'

At that moment James came stalking towards them, his expression bleak.

'Time to get back,' he told them both. 'And the ground's too damp to be sitting there.' He bent over Matt. 'Come on, friend, let me help you up.'

Two evenings later Hannah sat with Clancy and Frank. Peg was there too, and knitting like mad – lots of woolly squares that would eventually be joined together to make a blanket for someone in need. It was, she told them happily, 'A good and satisfying thing to do.'

The weather had changed and grown very cold. Now morning light glinted on frost-laden ground. Frank fussed and fretted about Snow Queen, even though the magnificent mare was safe and content in the stable block. This was situated near the two cottages, and directly before the paddock.

'Snow Queen ain't so tough as your big old boys,' Frank kept saying dogmatically. ''P'raps it'd be best if I stayed wiv her for a while. What d'yer say, Clance?'

'That a townie like you ought to know better.'

'How come?'

'Mists! We've got no pavements here, cocker. We've got no yellow fog, but we've got the mists and the dew. And our damp air don't have masses of brick walls and streets of houses to warm it all up. Now, thinking about your state of health, I'd say you'd be better off staying inside where it's warm. We don't have no hearths in the stables, nor braziers, and things of that sort.'

'It strikes me you ain't got sod-all,' Frank observed. 'Gawd 'elp us, Clance, you ought to walk them city streets what you think are so warm. Enough to freeze the balls off a brass monkey, they are. Still, that ain't the point. D'yer reckon Snow Queen's got enough straw? D'yer reckon a horse blanket might make things easier for her? When I first came here she'd been sick, yer know. I wonder if the ol' girl's really all right?'

'Bet your life she is,' Clance said comfortingly. 'Come on, Frank, have a drop of the old elderflower wine. I don't know what's got into you.'

'Dunno myself,' Frank admitted. 'I just get the feeling that some-think's up, that's all.'

'Don't worry, Frank,' Peggy soothed, and put her knitting down. 'It's because of the change in the weather. We all know now that winter's here. Tell you what, I'll make us some cocoa before I go.'

'That'd be nice,' Clancy told her. 'I'd like some too. Then after that I'll walk you back home.'

Hannah, curled up in an armchair in Clancy's cottage, watched and listened to all three of them in turn. She felt a cosy glow because Frank was really at home here, and comfortable with his friends.

When Peggy had to leave, Frank and Hannah said good night and went next door. Tired now, because 'beet-bashing' was once again the order of the day, Hannah went upstairs and prepared for bed. She lay there for a while, trying to imagine what Matt was doing. Had he gone to the Rookwood for a while? Were her two mates making a great fuss of him? She hoped so, especially Raven who had once trained as a nurse. Raven would be at home caring for a sick person. She had cared for Francis too.

Oh yes, Matt was in good hands with Raven there to care. Looking after Matt might give Raven a bit of a purpose in life – and it would perhaps make James a bit jealous too. The man took his power over ladies for granted. What with Raven and Trixie always there, riding beside him at Drews, trying to impress. Still, he was a film-star sort. Big and strong and very, very male.

Suddenly she felt guilty for not thinking of Matt's feelings in all this, but only of James. She kept remembering what he had told her. How awful it must have been.

She could picture him then, when he had stood in court. What torture. And where was bloody Sophia at that crucial moment? Stone the crows! Couldn't the woman have guessed what was happening, or at least taken the trouble to find out?

She was still thinking of James when she went to sleep. How long she slept, she did not know, but when she woke, she had the feeling that the cottage was empty. It occurred to her that Frank had decided to spend some time in the stable with Snow Queen after all. Silly man! He would die of cold out there. He was far from strong these days. She decided she would go after him and rake him back inside here where he belonged . . .

Chapter Thirty-Six

Ram Rawlins was skulking in the stables and swearing because the animals were large and their snorting and snuffling got on his nerves. He was glad they were separated from him by their stalls; even so, the damned things looked as if they could kill. God, how he hated the country.

He had not wanted to leave Jamaica Street, only Biff's orders had made him turn his back on The Smoke. First it had been to Colchester, filled with uniformed kids. Cocky little sods. Biff smiled in his catfish way. When the Forces needed older blokes, he told himself, he'd join up like a shot. As it was, he'd been in Barrack City long enough to wish himself back with the bombs. Watching them young bread-snappers, all done up like dog's dinners, pouncing about had made him wonder how they'd face up to the Blitz. Plonkers! Give him London every time. London was his place. He was at home there. London was life!

Shah, suddenly ill at ease, snorted, then whinneyed high and shrill. Unnerved, Ram jumped, and without noticing, let the lighted cigarette drop from his fingers. All he cared about at the moment was that he had to get away from these bloody awful creatures. They stank! He darted outside, stopped abruptly, then froze.

Hannah York was hurrying towards the stable-block. Ram slunk behind an adjacent tree, keeping within its shadow. So, he was thinking, that snotty bitch what spoke with a plum in her mouth was right: Frank Neilson's kid *was* here!

He'd have to shut the posh woman's gob once he'd done for the York girl. She'd put the finger on him otherwise. Yes, it would be a piece of cake. Then he could get back to Val, who'd promised he could do what he wanted with her every single night. He was her willing slave.

·His mind tried to grapple with what Biff had said. On their way to a

310

fortune they were, provided Neilson and York were shut up for good and all. Carried on, had Biff, about buying and selling and profits and stuff. But it was Val who would explain it all to him, add up the pounds, shilling and pence. Gawd, he was a lucky bloke to have her. And ol' bruvver Biff to look after him too.

Hannah was hurrying past him now. He would wait till he could grab her from behind. One twist of the neck should do the trick.

The night wind gusted in through the open stable door, and played with the cigarette end until its feeble glow became bright orange. It smouldered then leaped into a small flame that quickly sprang along the straw. A whiff of smoke spiralled upwards. Then other flames, tiny still, were dancing like diminutive devils with electric eyes. They were spitting and sparking, greedily eating the dry straw, growing all the time.

Shah tossed his head and his nostrils flared and twitched as they smelled danger. He whinneyed uneasily and in the next stall Kelly neighed high and wild. No one could mistake the terror in that sound.

Shocked, stopping dead in her tracks, Hannah half-turned and saw a large figure coming at her from behind. Ram Rawlins! The ice of her terror made her mouth dry and a pulse beat frantically in her throat. But then smoke eddying from the stable door, a high-pitched neigh and hoofs beating against walls penetrated her senses. The sound scared the man too. He hesitated, then as a fresh pounding of hoofs sounded as though the stables would be knocked down like matches, he turned tail and bolted.

Dismissing him, realising there was no time to worry about Ram now, Hannah's only thoughts were for the missing Frank and the poor old horses.

She was near the paddock and had in an instant, turned the padlock key and opened the gate. Then without stopping, conscious only that Shah and Kelly were trapped, she ran. As she did so she tore off her woolly, pausing only to plunge it into the water barrel that stood under the guttering at the end of the wall. Then she was pushing against the heat-blistering door.

The smoke stung her eyes and irritated her lungs. Greedy orange tongues were even now leaping across the intervening space between the outer stable walls that held the plunging animals prisoner.

'Frank!' she was screaming. 'Where are you? Get out, Frank!'

Hannah unbolted the half-door that was holding Shah, her fingers trembling, and already scorched. Shah backed away, eyes rolling. He seemed the size of a house to Hannah, but the situation was too desperate for her to give in to fear. The animal was trembling and she knew she had to calm him. But how? Dear God in Heaven, how?

311

'Shah,' she croaked, eyes streaming because of the smoke. 'It's all right. Come here, Shah. Come on, old boy.'

All the time she was speaking she was edging nearer until with a single wild throw she enveloped his head in the soaking woolly. He snorted and tried to throw off the clinging wool. He plunged as Hannah desperately caught hold of his mane. Still talking to him, she began trying to pull him towards the door.

He hesitated and she tugged harder; coughing and gasping, she was herself sick with fear of the fire. The flames were racing nearer and Kelly was plunging and screaming next door. Suddenly Shah was moving in the right direction, his hoofs trotting over the burning straw as Hannah guided him out from the stall. Now he caught the scent of fresh air and was moving fast towards the door. As he reached it Hannah snatched off the woolly, sobbing with relief as she saw him pass the flames in safety, and gallop off.

Now for Kelly, she thought dazedly. I must save him. I must save them all! She plunged once more into the inferno. The bolt of Kelly's stall seared her fingers. Flames were already eating into the stall itself. She could hear the other animals shrieking high and wild. In desperation she began beating out the flames with her bare hands, inching her way forwards.

She tried to soothe Kelly, but the huge animal was beyond comforting. He was showing the whites of his eyes, and he reared and reared again. Hannah tried to catch him, to hold on to his mane as she had Shah's, but it only increased his terror, and his flailing hoofs caught her a glancing blow. She had the impression of a tremendous Catherine wheel spinning before her eyes, the great orange disc growing large, then larger still.

She screamed, but the sound came from her mind, not her tortured throat.

'James! James! You promised to keep me safe. Where are you? Please, James . . .'

But there was no help for her, nothing but this scarlet curtain of death. Then looming out of the swirling fumes came the figure of a large man. He seemed to tower over her. Oh God, it was Ram! He had come back. He was going to finish her for good and all. She screamed and tried to pull away. She tried to fight, but she was in pain, exhausted . . . and then, suddenly, she was just too tired.

She was swung up into a pair of strong arms, and as she waited for the final blow, weak tears poured down her blackened face. And then, miraculously, she was in smoke-free air and looking up at stars. The night breeze was clean, but cold, cold cold.

Hannah was shivering, her teeth chattering. Her limbs hurt like hell,

312

and her lungs were on fire. In shock after the trauma, there was nothing she could do but lie still and wheeze, drawing in the precious air. The world held nothing but agony; and she felt nauseous from the acrid smell on and all around her. If Ram Rawlins was going to kill her, let him get on with it. She closed her eyes.

As if from a million miles away she heard someone groan – a heart-wrenching sound. She came back to the here and now, unsteady, hopeful. Was she dreaming? Could it be James? Suddenly the arms holding her felt like his. But everything was so confusing, and she couldn't see properly. Could not focus. Her eyes were still streaming, so terribly sore. She blinked and blinked again.

For an unknown reason she was looking behind the man who was so anxiously leaning over her. She found herself staring at the tree. There was nothing left of it, nothing living except a bare ash-white shape. In the half-light it looked just like a huge coral branch. A ghost of a tree already? It must have gone up like tinder, just as the stable walls had. Even the far end walls were blazing away. It had all happened so quickly. How very strange . . .

'The tree,' she whispered, wondering why it hurt her to speak.

'Tree?' James, beside himself, turned and looked at the tree, glowing in the milky moonlight. 'It will live,' he told her unsteadily. 'Just as the horses will, specially Shah and Kelly – all thanks to you.'

'Frank?' It was agony to move her lips – but she must pull herself together! Must press on. Miss Pitt would say . . .

'Frank and Clancy got the others out,' James was telling her in a dry, harsh way. 'But none of that matters.' His voice grew deeper with the emotion he was trying to hold at bay, then, 'Oh Hannah, to the devil with horses and trees. Hannah!'

She became aware of those arms again, holding her gently, as though fearful she would break. His arms made her feel safe – so safe. She closed her eyes. Then she felt James' cheek against her hair. He was rocking her backwards and forwards as he might a baby. And his tone, though little more than a whisper, held fear and a kind of desperation. What was he saying? She could barely distinguish his words.

'Darling, don't leave me!' he was pleading. 'Never, ever leave me. Darling, please answer! It will cut out my heart if I lose you now. Hannah, my love . . .'

Love, she thought dazedly. James was saying that he loved her? He was asking her not to leave him? She could never do that. Would never do that in a million years . . . because she loved him too. Why hadn't she thought of it before? How odd. She loved James with all her heart and soul. Perhaps she would tell him so, when she wasn't so very, very weary.

What was that sound? It hurt her. She couldn't think straight any more. Everything kept sliding away and there seemed to be lots of black wings flapping round her head. The whole world was spinning and whirling. Everything was so strange . . .

High and clear in the night there came the strident clanging of a fire engine. Then Frank was shouting over the space as he moved nearer.

'It's all right, Mr St John. They've got 'im! I saw Rawlins cut and run when I left ol' Snow Queen. Dalton's got the big bugger. He's carting him off to the clink now. I swear I'm gonna talk my 'ead off to the cops. I'll see the whole lot of them bastards rot for life for what they tried to do.' His voice held a sob of distress for his beloved horses.

He stopped running and bent double, gasping, to catch his breath. When he looked up, his voice was charged with shock as he rasped: 'What's this? My Han? What's she doing here? My God, Mr St John, just look at the pore kid's hands! Is she – is she alive?'

Fresh tears squeezed under Hannah's fluttering eyelids. She was not listening to Frank. It was sufficient that he was here, alive, and as ever, mouthing on.

Then the black wings could be held back no longer. With a sigh Hannah slipped into unconsciousness.

When Hannah returned to the world sufficiently to take in what was going on, she found that she was in a small side room in Norseby Cottage Hospital. She lay very still and quiet, gradually focusing. Then she saw that Raven was there, and Matt. They were speaking quietly, unaware that she was awake. Then, as if it was the most natural thing in the world, they leaned towards each other and kissed.

'Charming!' Hannah whispered. 'What about me?'

Then they were both beaming at her, Raven's eyes brighter than Hannah had ever seen them before.

'Darling,' Raven said, 'you're awake at last. How do you feel?'

'Like nothing on this earth.'

'But you're with us,' Matt told her, 'and it's happened during our turn. They're queuing up for visits outside. We had to all but fight our way in.'

'Don't be daft.' Hannah went pink and looked self-conscious.

'Matt's telling the truth,' Raven told her. 'Ginnie gave in to us in very bad grace, but she was here through the night, so had to give way. Even Sophia wants to see you. Hannah, you are a very popular girl.'

'Not so popular as you – so far as Matt's concerned,' Hannah joked.

She looked at Matt, warmly and lovingly, the faint twinkle of old making little imps in her eyes. 'I thought you were *my* airman,' she told him. '*I* found you first!'

They both looked taken back, Raven horrified.

'Darling,' she began, 'I couldn't – We wouldn't . . .'

'Of course you wouldn't.' Hannah gave the ghost of her usual hearty chuckle. 'You're much too nice, both of you, and you have my blessing. We're all mates together, eh?'

'For life, old dear,' Matt told her.

'Musketeers for ever,' Raven nodded.

When they had gone Hannah lay very still, glad that the visitors' bell had clanged before anyone else could come in. She wondered how long she had been in hospital and marvelled at how huge her hands were, the bandages making them giant-sized. Her right leg was heavily bandaged too. How odd! She hadn't felt a thing at the time.

She became aware of flowers. Beautiful flowers – lots of them, home-grown in people's private lean-tos. Florists were mostly out of business because of the war. But hang on a mo' – there were some red roses! Those tall, magnificent red blooms had been placed separately from the rest. Professionally grown, Hannah felt sure.

It occurred to her that she had never received flowers in her life before. These all had cards on them, but she could not reach them, nor feel them through the bandages. Perhaps the nurse would read the cards and she would find out who loved her enough to send flowers. And who loved her enough to send red roses.

She remembered Frank, the tone of his voice when he had queried, '*My* Han?' He loved her in his funny old way. Yes, that had plainly shown. Matt loved her in his own special manner, too. Just as did her two dearest friends. And frosty old Sophia? She could afford red roses – masses, in fact. It was rather nice of her to actually come to the hospital to visit. Hannah wanted to chuckle at the thought of a stone-hearted Sister turning away someone as awesome as Sophia St John.

Hannah looked from the roses to the other offerings, mostly chrys-anthemums and Michaelmas Daisies, then especially at a vase holding sprays of green leaves and a few red berries. By the ink smudges on the card she could tell that these had been painstakingly gathered by the boys. Tears spurted against her eyelids. The twins, how she adored them! All of the flowers made her feel very special.

Again she found herself looking at the red roses and then unexpect-edly, she wanted to cry for real. Break her heart, in fact. She was unsettled and insecure, and her hands hurt, her leg too. Over and above all she couldn't be sure of exactly what had happened. Of exact-ly what had been said!

Had she dreamed that last, crazy, impossible thing? Why wasn't

315

James here? Had she imagined him cradling her in his arms and whispering those wonderful words?

Visiting was over long since. No one else would be allowed in until the evening-time, hours away. She felt lost and lonely, couldn't bear the uncertainty. And above all, she was frightened in case she had imagined the whole thing. Had suffered hallucinations from shock.

Depressed, Hannah turned her face to the wall.

She heard the door open, but did not look round. She did not wish to speak to the nurses even though she felt sure that they were all very nice.

'Well, well,' James said gently from behind her. 'After I've bearded a dragon-like Sister in her den, and practically begged her to let me in, no smile?'

'Oh!' Hannah breathed and turned to him, wide-eyed and tremulous. 'James!'

'Who else?' he teased, and before she could reply he was holding her in his arms and his lips were on hers. His kiss was masterful, passionate and took her breath away. And in spite of her hands, she was clinging to him, kissing him in return, smiling against his mouth, and there was a shining glory in her eyes.

'You sent the roses,' she whispered and felt very shy. 'Oh James!'

'You'll carry a whole basketful of the things on the day we get wed,' he told her. 'We will live in Knollys and—'

'And – and live in the country for ever?' she cut in, her heart going crazy, she was so wild with joy. 'I'm a Londoner, James. A Londoner born and bred. Live here for ever? I don't know about that!'

'Ye gods,' he groaned and looked up at the ceiling for inspiration. 'Will the day ever come when this young woman won't want to back-answer me?'

'And will the time ever arrive,' Hannah asked the ceiling plaintively, 'when this man forgets to command, and actually asks?'

'Some people have town houses and they also have country houses,' he told her firmly. 'There, will that do?'

'I suppose it will have to,' she responded haughtily, blissfully remembering how beautifully the trees grew round Knollys. How spacious the kitchen was, and the polished surface on the piano that James played so sensitively and well. 'But . . .'

'But nothing,' he said decisively. 'Come here!'

Then his passionate kisses made it impossible for her to argue – for a moment at least.